THE MASKED
CHARLATAN
A MOUNTING UNREST

PART 2

ALAN KEITH

AuthorHouse™ UK
1663 Liberty Drive
Bloomington, IN 47403 USA
www.authorhouse.co.uk
Phone: 0800.197.4150

Published by AuthorHouse 02/26/2015

ISBN: 978-1-5049-3835-8 (sc)
ISBN: 978-1-5049-3836-5 (e)

Print information available on the last page.

Any people depicted in stock imagery provided by Thinkstock are models,
and such images are being used for illustrative purposes only.
Certain stock imagery © Thinkstock.

This book is printed on acid-free paper.

Contents

CHAPTER ONE 1

CHAPTER TWO 53

CHAPTER THREE 105

CHAPTER FOUR 159

CHAPTER FIVE 211

CHAPTER SIX 263

CHAPTER SEVEN 315

PROLOGUE

The mounting class division between the prosperous and the poor continues to rise throughout England which simply leads to growing hostility and mass protests. The high rise in the cost of food, drink and clothes forces more people out of their homes, men, women and children together. Throughout the country there is absolutely no sign at all that there will be any end to such a terrible and mundane atmosphere.

With Parliament having no fixed place to meet and the authority at the very highest level being so poorly run with nobody properly understanding how the penniless families were suffering it seems as though England, a once powerful country and revered all across the world is only going to continue its decline. Just as Guy Fawkes, Sir Robert Catesby and the other Gunpowder plotters had been hoping for it appears as though there will be a mass uprising that shall take place as a Civil War and a new monarch will be the result, Queen Elizabeth, a young queen who can be manipulated by themselves who they believe will be the eventual victors. To the plotters, their carefully organise gunpowder plot will have paid off completely.

CHAPTER ONE

Even after George had carefully taken all the luggage from the farmhouse and tied it to the hired packhorse he was still unsure if he and Elizabeth were at all sensible to begin their trek to York on the very same day when his wife had been told she was going very soon to give birth. He had gone very briefly with his father to the local inn for a glass of ale before leaving and explained their decision to begin a new life in York. 'All the local farmers will think nothing of you for leaving farming and beginning a new career completely.' George did appear a little reluctant about the decision yet at the same time he was unwilling to yield in his position; 'I haven't told you the wonderful news yet father,' Peter had a drink of ale and was already smiling at his son's comment which George found a little irritating. 'You know what the doctor said do you father?'

'That Elizabeth is going to have a baby.' George looked disappointed that his father already knew what Doctor Baker had explained. 'How did you know that father?'

'For the simple reason that you and she were trying hard enough for a very long time.' He raised his half empty glass and said in a loud and raucous voice; 'WELL DONE BOTH OF YOU!' More quietly George had a drink and looked sternly at his father; 'We feel we need to have a new beginning with our lives, living somewhere quieter where we know we can bring up our new child safely and away from farming. Remember the trouble there was the previous summer and the fierce jealousy that has been shown towards our successful business by all those men who had their rented land retaken, including James and

John Harper. Father my wife and I need to make a new start in our lives.' Peter however did not look at all taken by his son's explanation. 'It is only Lord Montagu and Lord Whitby who are still keeping their retaken land and using Jamaican slaves and that has been overruled as unlawful. Very soon early next year I believe they shall be arrested and the farmers shall have their rented land returned so there will once more be peace here.'

'I am sorry father, it is too late to change our minds, we both want a new beginning in our lives.' George finished his glass of ale and went to the bar to buy himself another as his father watched him feeling particularly disappointed and let down.

George on returning to the farmhouse had expected Elizabeth to be in the sitting room dressed and already waiting for his return yet he found the farmhouse silent when he came back and entered the bedchamber to discover Elizabeth only half dressed. 'Our luggage is on the packhorse if you still wish to begin the journey today.......' George paused half-hoping his wife would decide to remain at home for one more night yet looking pasty faced as she was putting on her petticoat she remained encouraging with her decision; 'The moment I am dressed and have had a wash then we must go. It is going to be a long and difficult journey so let us delay no longer.' They started out only twenty minutes later with Elizabeth looking a little uncomfortable as she rode her light domesticated horse sidesaddle and her face remained pale and tired. Peter and Francesca had willed them both to changed their minds and remain at High Hill Farm and local children from many surrounding villages and hamlets had come out to see their departure. 'I never realised we were so popular.' Elizabeth commented as she listened to the children's cheery voices calling to her words that were too much out of earshot to understand. As they left High Hill Farm for their last time and began to make their way slowly towards the small village of Nuneaton Elizabeth smiled a little asking; 'Why is your family farm called High Hill when all the surrounding land is completely flat?'

'That is something I have never understood.' George had replied and shrugged with apologies. Elizabeth had dressed in her warmest clothes and was covered with a very heavy long cloak to keep out the strong cold wind that was increasingly getting up. 'This journey going at this gentle pace is going to be an extremely long one.'

'No matter;' Elizabeth had responded in her usual authoritative way. 'I suggest we should stay overnight at a small inn during our journey for a little rest before continuing the following morning.' George looked up at the dull dreary sky that had formed in only the last few minutes since their journey had begun. 'I have a feeling that there won't be much more light to help us today. Nuneaton or perhaps Leicester will be our first stop for tonight.' In Nuneaton as George and Elizabeth made their slow passage through the doors of every house as they came into view opened and men and women appeared watching them with curiosity and pointing fingers at them discussing where they might suddenly be making for. 'Are you going to travel back to Whitby in time and tell your father about the great changes that have most recently occurred in our married life?' Elizabeth looked up sadly to George and pursed her lips tightly.

'I am no longer speaking with father, not since he shot and killed two of my close friends and he has now also made many enemies by refusing to return any of his land which he violently took from all the local farmers.'

'Father tells me that Lord Whitby shall be arrested in January for breaking court orders and continuing to use Jamaican slaves which has now been made unlawful.'

'That is the way my father has always acted, he does what he always believes is right whether he is breaking the law or not. If he goes to prison then it shall serve him right!'

The first day on the road was long and tiring when they finally arrived on the outskirts of Leicester. George had decided after riding beside Elizabeth for a long period that she was in desperate need of a good night's sleep and rest. Their accommodation was just a small, unsophisticated and grubby inn yet at the same time the food was good and it was at least somewhere to sleep for a little while. The following day as they travelled further north the air seemingly continued getting colder and the land more barren and unproductive. 'I believe one more night of rest here outside Huddersfield and then tomorrow we can complete our journey.' George sounded extremely grateful as they came insight of yet another small inn which they were intending to stay at for the night. 'I believe looking in the distance straight on I can see the top of the North Yorkshire Moors with snow on the top.'

'Now that I can believe!' George had muttered as they entered the grounds of the small unattractive building. He helped Elizabeth from her horse and inside the building asked for their three horses to be looked after. 'We would like to sleep here just for the one night.' The local man with his West Yorkshire accent had asked for the details of George and his sweet partner and without any problems had found them a room for the night. 'At this time of the year we never have many people travelling through Huddersfield sir.' George and Elizabeth looked around the double room at the rough and ready layout of the furniture and other items and nodded at each other. 'We would like a meal prepared for us in about half an hour when we have had a chance to unpack a few things.' They were left alone and George having another look around the room frowned; 'At least our stay is only one night.'

As they unpacked George took an outline of York city from a pocket of his case and sat looking closely at it. 'Our home is at the north end of York not too far from the cathedral.' Already Elizabeth's eyes lit up with excitement. 'And then this time tomorrow we can say our new start in life has begun.'

'I wish we had an idea just when you were to give birth, that was something the doctor did not explain.' George looked with some deep concern at his wife's unusually pale face and asked her to sit down for a while before they went for their prepared meal.

Their overnight stay was not memorable for the friendship or the standard of food they had eaten, at least however there was a comfortable bed on which to sleep. The next morning to their disappointment when their bags were packed and they came to have a light breakfast they could see through the window that rain was falling steadily. 'Is that rain only recent?' George asked the waiter when their breakfast was brought over to them. 'Unfortunately that began in the early hours of the morning and some roads are already flooded.'

'It won't make the last part of our journey easy, 'specially with a very heavy packhorse carrying all our heavy possessions.' Elizabeth looked at her plate of fresh bacon and eggs that made her wince;

'I don't feel at all hungry this morning.' George looked at her pale face and sick expression.

'The sooner we get this final part of our journey over and get ourselves settled in to our new home the better. I'll pay the bill and I suggest we go.'

'What about your breakfast?'

'I suddenly don't feel hungry either.' George carefully helped Elizabeth onto her feet and asked the manager for their luggage to be taken and their horses to be prepared for leaving. 'Is it sensible sir to be travelling in such awful conditions?' George had ignored the question completely and was already sorting the finances out.

Immediately as they left the inn's grounds and the horses were gaiting very slowly the mud had reached their knees and the rain was falling heavily. 'At least we are approaching the moors so I would hope there in the short distance is the small city of York.' Elizabeth followed the direction of George's pointing finger with rainwater dripping from it and nodding. 'That indeed is the magnificent city of York what I remember of it from my last visit.' George watched the air from his horse's mouth spiralling up into the air blown by the bitter cold wind and shook his head as the rain became drops of ice being blown hard into his face. As they continued to get closer travellers began to pass them approaching the city from all directions following the Rivers Ouse and Foss. 'So, this is what York looks like.' he commented leaning his head forward and squinting his eyes to try and see ahead through the clouds of sweeping rain. 'Have you never been to York George?' Elizabeth asked and laughed a little as though teasing.

'Father never brought me to York not even to the regular cattle market that is held here.' They followed the line of the river Ouse until reaching a bridge going across and towards the city centre. 'It is this way we need to continue towards the large market place.' George was surprised by the sudden ringing of so many bells together. 'Why are the church bells all ringing at the same time?' They rode side by side over the bridge and travelled northwards listening to the sounds of church bells ringing and rainfall sweeping the city grounds. 'Some bells have been telling the hour, it is now just on two o'clock, some are calling people to church meetings, and some of them will be for a service, perhaps a wedding or sadly a funeral.' George looked completely bemused. 'That just shows you Elizabeth, my father kept me out of ordinary everyday life like this and made it clear to me that my life was only about farming.'

'Your father underneath must be extremely disappointed that you left High Hill Farm.'

'Of course father is disappointed I left the farm. He is hoping still that one day there will be a knock on the farmhouse door and I will have returned with the little baby as well.' Elizabeth joked;

'And then your father knows that in several years time when you retire from farming there will be a young man in the family to continue on the farm.'

'Of course! It is only that damn farm my father thinks about.' They passed a number of inns, alehouses and the city's only small hospital, before approaching Stonegate before George pointed ahead towards the abbey. 'Our house is right beside it. I have the front door key and then tomorrow we can think about going to the Mall and buying some new furniture to place inside.'

'Isn't the air so fresh don't you think?' Elizabeth raised her head and inhaled long and hard through her nostrils the refreshing cold air. 'And the beauty not only of the pleasant little villages around but also of the countryside surrounding every part of York.' Elizabeth could feel her excitement inside her growing as they could see their new small house right ahead. 'This is where our new life begins.' she said excitedly. They pulled their horses up right outside the front door and waited for the large packhorse to catch them up before George found his front door key and a little nervously unlocked the door and went inside. 'I believe for you and me this house will be ample.'

'And the baby whenever he arrives in our lives.' Elizabeth gasped slightly and found a chair on which to sit down. 'We have no stables in which to keep the horses but we can keep them in the large fields just opposite the house.'

'And tomorrow I must ride the large slow packhorse back to the stables in Leamington village and pay Mr Keating for the loan.' George's smile dropped as he looked at Elizabeth's increasingly pale face.

'I would suggest I put the two heavy cases in our bedchamber and you change into some fresh and dry clothes and then we can go out and treat ourselves to a meal.'

'It looks as though there is a farm somewhere here on the north side of the house.' Elizabeth commented from the bedchamber. George went in and watched out of the window to see a single shepherd passing along a lane close by muddy and almost knee deep in water trying to guide his sheep a lengthy distance ahead towards some kennels. 'Perhaps he is a rival to my father.' George chuckled.

'We shall very soon be able to meet all the local folks when the festive season arrives and we can go often to the local church of England building on the other side of the house.' George as he watched his wife getting some fresh dry clothes out of the case and begin to change gently took hold of her naked body whispering in her ear; 'Are you really glad you married me rather than continuing to lead a life inside a rich family and with a wealthy father?' Elizabeth kissed George passionately on his cheek whispering back;

'I have never regretted my decision. Now I am excited about our child who shall be arriving soon and then all together we have a new challenge and adventure to look forward to!'

Towards the end of the year all through England the fine summer weather had not completely ended until the middle of October and then the autumn had altered in early December from being very dry and mild to extremely wet and cold. In Chelsea Lord Egerton had gone into the small garden at his large home and plucked a sweet smelling red rose that was still growing in the warmer air of west London and taken it to the nearby cottage hospital where his wife Elizabeth was even now lying unconscious and in spite of all her excellent care and treatment suffering from a severe infection that had struck her down a number of weeks before. He had ridden to the hospital with the red rose in hand and given it to her on the bed as she lay with her eyes tightly closed. 'This is a beautiful red rose I have chosen for you. Get better soon I beseech of you.' He leaned down and kissed her hot brow before returning outside to his horse, tied to a tree to try and shelter her from the rain which was continuing to fall heavily. Seeing Elizabeth still suffering severely from a fever and blemished with two bad rashes, one down her neck and the other down one side of her face he knew then he would be spending most of his Christmas with Elizabeth and Anne, for the most part challenging Elizabeth on the chess board, horse riding with Anne and attending dance concerts with her as well.

At the same time Anne, Elizabeth and Lord Egerton were undeniably enjoying an exceptional festive season together they like the small minority of rich titled gentlemen and nobility remained oblivious to the atmosphere of scepticism and mistrust that was hanging everywhere.

The distribution of pamphlets everywhere still informed the ordinary individuals of the unsettled atmosphere around the country that ended peoples' bright outlook they once had towards their difficult situations when the Cross Cabinet was still working and bringing new answers slowly and cautiously to fixing some of the peoples' most terrifying worries. There had been for a short time at least a hope after the motion opposing Jamaican slaves and enclosures had been successfully passed that Parliament was at long last going to start and find solutions to the many difficult concerns England's large majority of ordinary people was having to cope with yet once more such hopes towards the politicians had slowly dwindled as even with a new Speaker Parliament showed only disorganisation, a lack of leadership and very few and imprecise sittings. The fact that the new schemes of Hackney Carriages, the beginning of a new sewage system for London, the increased building of new homes throughout England's towns and cities and the prison reform had all immediately been ended when Parliament had voted to close the Cross Cabinet still made many of the country's ordinary citizens very fractious. Even during the festive season many young men penniless and seeking work and a little money could be seen walking long distances to towns and in particular the growing cities where work was most likely to be discovered. Still skirmishes were occurring between young men who had no work and those who were living with jobs and in comfortable homes, skirmishes caused most of all by resentment, suspicion and distrust. Streets skirmishes were an ongoing problem especially throughout London.

While Lord Egerton and the majority of his well-heeled friends were enjoying Christmas and the new year and partying and feasting almost every day the majority of people living in such a situation of disharmony and glumness as the year changed saw no reason to celebrate the start of a newborn year.

Lord Egerton and Elizabeth had seen in the new year at home playing a new round of chess matches and listening to the magnificent sound of piano music wafting downstairs from Anne's private music-room. The following morning they were all pleased when they woke and having dressed being informed by the less able butler that breakfast was ready in the dining room that the sun was shining brightly and the light snow that had been falling the previous evening had stopped. As Anne poured the coffee she commented cheerfully to Lord Egerton, 'We shall be able to go riding a little later.' Lord Egerton helped himself to a piece of toast and some fresh cooked bacon. 'That shall depend on my work. I have to arrange for the arrests of Lord Montagu and Lord Whitby later this month and I expect while I am in Westminster Hall to meet Sir Edward Coke who when not officially working in court and often as you have seen twice sentencing people to death likes to talk almost non-stop sometimes.'

'Well do remember Thomas, this evening we are going to the dance. It has been rather a quiet Christmas for once and I believe we deserve a night out. Do you wish to come as well dear?' Elizabeth hung her head at an angle as she considered her mother's question. 'I think you know mama

I am too young for that sort of an evening out. When I am old enough then I shall come along.'

'Are you sure such rules actually have the same meaning for a Princess?' Lord Egerton had asked ridiculing such a directive to a member of the monarchy a little. 'I am going to the theatre this evening to see a young drama group performing a play which I believe was written by Phillip Massinger.'

'Then you must tell us about it when we see you again later.' Lord Egerton finished his breakfast and three cups of strong rich coffee before carefully preparing himself to go out even going as far as combing his long moustache and thick dark beard to look his best. 'Sir Edward Coke is always critical of other people and their appearance, just as he was critical of Guy Fawkes and Sir Robert Catesby when he was sentencing them to death. I am sure if we do meet and I do not look as tidy as I possibly could then he shall be critical direct to my face. I shall see you this afternoon and immediately I return I shall dress for this evening on the Strand.' He found Sally once again had been looked after carefully in the stable overnight and brought outside by the senior stable boy the moment he arrived outside the door. 'Happy new year!' Lord Egerton had called out into the stable as the tall young man was lying half asleep on a bundle of soft dry hay. He hurried outside seeing a gold sovereign tinted by the bright sunlight. 'Thanky' kindly sir!' he called excitedly and immediately he had taken the coin it had been pushed deep into a pocket of his marked and thinning breeches. As usual Lord Egerton took the reins and jumped onto Sally before guiding her slowly out of the grounds of Anne's large house and then kicking his heels into her and feeling the chill wind blowing against his face as his wonderful sturdy horse galloped down towards the Thames river and onwards in the direction of the Palace of Westminster and beside it Westminster Hall.

Lord Egerton arrived in Westminster Hall in his dependability as Lord Keeper. He looked at the far office of the ground floor and looking at the closed door hoped that the room was completely empty and even approached it a little anxiously. When he went in there was no sign of anyone else being inside and so he went to his own side of the desk feeling a lot more assured and remote than he had before coming in. Just as he was looking in his bottom drawer at some papers which had especially been placed there for him he heard a voice come from around the corner where Sir Edward had been examining some documents and papers. 'Good afternoon Thomas, happy new year.' Lord Egerton's heart sank.

'Good afternoon Sir Edward, a very happy new year to you too.' Finding the papers that he was looking for almost immediately made Lord Egerton feel a little better. 'I shall not be here very long I have to complete these forms for the arrest of Lord Montagu and Lord Whitby and then go home and change for a dance with my lady friend this evening.' Sir Edward looked most impressed. A box that he had begun to sort out was left momentarily as he looked up at Lord Egerton impressed by the dress sense his colleague had. The wired collar with lace trim and slashed doublet and sleeves most astounded him. 'Would your lady friend you speak of mean Anne of Denmark?'

'Indeed it would.'

'Anne of Denmark I have to say is a most remarkable and stunning lady friend to have along with her pretty daughter of course, Princess Elizabeth Stuart.'

'It is a pleasure spending so much of my time with them except I have to say Elizabeth has become over fond of chess.'

'You should be proud of being a good chess player Thomas you need a great deal of intelligence to be able to play chess well.'

'The trouble is now that Elizabeth is always beating me.' Lord Egerton sighed. 'Tell me Sir Edward, are you or any of your colleagues here making any further progress into finding out just who else was involved in that damned gunpowder plot?' To Lord Egerton's surprise Sir Edward passed across the table two pieces of paper with lots of information scribbled down with a full quill pen. 'How did you come across the names Sir Everard Digby, Robert Keyes and John Grant?'

'Don't ask me Thomas ask the people below me who investigate on my behalf. When these men are arrested and come to court with no evidence to defend them then I just sentence them to death.' Lord Egerton passed the papers back and laughed as he did; 'Being the Attorney General cannot really be a difficult job can it Sir Edward, simply reading out the sentences and smiling as you do?' Sir Edward scowled across his rugged face, 'It is not as simple as that Thomas being Attorney General. Just like your jobs as Lord Keeper and Lord Chancellor, I do not believe they are as simple as merely pushing pieces of paper around.' Sir Edward coughed with a little tickle in his throat, 'I should have realised already that your two lady friends were Anne of Denmark and Princess Elizabeth Stuart, when I was reading the sentences of Guy Fawkes and Sir Robert Catesby I saw you altogether in the front row of the gallery.' Lord Egerton looked at his watch and began to make relevant notes and signings with his quill ordering the arrests of the two Lords. As he was painstakingly examining the two papers he heard Sir Edward comment in his deep thoughtful voice; 'Syllables govern the world.' Lord Egerton lifted an eyebrow and with one eye examined his friend more casually dressed than he in hose, breeches, plain white linen shirt and a blue doublet. 'Pardon?' Lord Egerton responded still examining the papers in front of his face. 'Oh nothing, I was just talking to myself.' Lord Egerton mused quietly to himself and nodded his approval. They chatted quietly to themselves at opposite ends of the long desk as they progressed with their work until Sir Edward put down some papers speaking more audibly as he did; 'Magna Charta is such a fellow that he will have no sovereign.' Lord Egerton sighed heavily and this time raised his complete head and wearily repeated; 'Magna Charta..........will have no sovereign.......That is something I have never really considered Sir Edward I must say.' Sir Edward appeared a little surprised by Lord Egerton's response. He looked at Lord Egerton until deciding that he would get no further response before returning fully to his own papers. Finally finishing all the sections he had been expected to sign Lord Egerton commented under his breath some satisfaction; "I suppose Lord Whitby and Lord Montagu have been living fine lives in their magnificent mansions but such fine lives shall be brought to an end in just a few weeks time." He put his quill pen down and left the papers exactly where they were. 'My secretary shall come and collect these a little bit later this afternoon Sir Edward. At least this means no longer shall any young Jamaican men be used as slaves to work the land in England. Later this month Lord's Montagu and Whitby shall be arrested at their homes and put in prison until a date is set for their court hearing.' Sir Edward this time raised an eyelid to Lord Egerton's remark and replied slowly and again thoughtfully; 'For a man a house is his castle.' As Lord Egerton was putting his brown doublet back on and preparing to leave he responded; 'I believe that is a perfectly sensible comment to make. I am very surprised that nobody has ever moved into St James's Palace since Anne of Denmark moved out. Now Sir Edward if you will excuse me I must return to Anne and Elizabeth.' He excused himself politely and returned to Sally who was once more waiting patiently opposite the door.

Anne was already dressed for the evening ahead with Lord Egerton and was being taught the game of chess by her daughter. When Lord Egerton arrived they both turned to the door as the butler was showing him inside and seemed to gasp a sigh of great relief. 'We have both been waiting impatiently for your arrival.'

'The reason I was delayed was because Sir Edward Coke just as I expected to be was in the office when I arrived and spent a lot of time talking. He said one or two things that took me a little by surprise.'

'What kind of things did Sir Edward say that took you by surprise?' Elizabeth commented already setting the chess board up for the start of a new game. 'He told me that *"Syllables govern the world"* and that *"Magna Charta is such a fellow that he will have no sovereign."* Once more Lord Egerton looked extremely baffled when he repeated Sir Edward's comments. 'I never realised Sir Edward Coke was so philosophical.' Anne responded.

'Maybe that is because you only see Sir Edward Coke in his brightly coloured robes and white wig doing his duty as Attorney General and mostly sentencing people to their deaths as he did with Guy Fawkes and Sir Robert Catesby mama.' Anne turned to the butler who was about to leave the room,

'Butler, while Thomas is changing and preparing himself for an evening at the dancing we would be very pleased if you were to pour three drinks, a pineapple juice for my daughter, a glass of whisky for Thomas and a glass of port and lemon for myself.' Anne with bodily movements urged Lord Egerton to go upstairs and change, Lord Egerton immediately followed his given orders.

'Your drink is here on the table, Anne ordered your horse and trap to take you both to the Strand at seven thirty. We have time for one game of chess if you are ready.' Elizabeth's mind was already made up. Lord Egerton swiftly moved to the table and made the first move on the chess board. The game went on for sometime before Elizabeth pushed her knight to one side that made Lord Egerton for once while playing Elizabeth at chess smile. He made his precise move and smiled. 'Checkmate!' As Anne was entering the room and explaining that the horse and trap had arrived Elizabeth glowered at the board and moved in a frustrated manner from the table. 'Congratulations!' she murmured to Lord Egerton and straightaway disappeared up the stairs to get changed for the evening at the theatre.

'You look very attractive tonight Thomas.' Anne remarked as she and Lord Egerton sat watching the first dance. Lord Egerton briefly turned his attention away from the pretty young girls he had been watching on the dance floor and looked a little puzzled at Anne. 'I thought I always looked attractive during our dance nights.'

'There are many young ladies here in the dance hall tonight who would dearly like to dance with you.' Lord Egerton looked around the tables at some of the young ladies who were not yet dancing and grinned, 'You are talking as though I was still just a young man. I am sixty-six years old and in recent weeks I have started very much to feel it.' He turned his attention to Anne and her slender figure; 'I believe you are more of a dancer than myself.' Anne thanked Lord Egerton for his gentile remark.

'I do have two dances prepared with friends later on.' Anne gave a smile of pleasure at such a thought to herself before going and getting two drinks from the far table.

'I am still trying to work out what Sir Edward was talking about earlier this afternoon. Sometimes he really does come out with the most unusual remarks.' There was a sprinkling of applause as the first dance of the evening ended and the couples came off the dance floor. 'I shall remain seated and watch you dance next.' Lord Egerton commented as a slight tease. 'I shall take you up on your remark.' Anne very quickly introduced Lord Egerton to her dance partner Lord Westerman before they took to the floor. 'I have never seen Anne of Denmark dance before.' Lord Egerton looked up from his chair to see his occasional friend Sir Peter Cartwright standing beside him. 'When did you return to England? The last I heard of you I was told you were still working in Sweden.'

'I only returned early this afternoon and the moment I met my wife again she told me she had tickets for tonight's dance night.' Lord Egerton watched Anne dancing extremely impressed by her poise and flamboyance. She put in three additional steps at every half turn and Lord Egerton was extremely amused and particularly complimentary. For once she had dressed in a simple white gown and shoes which were casual and perfect for an evening of dancing. 'Jemima tells me you and Anne have treated yourselves to a new dog.'

'That was more Anne's idea than my own and Elizabeth is not at all amused by the little animal.'

'I believe Anne of Denmark has changed a great deal since the death of her husband James.'

'She has but she keeps telling me that I have helped her through these difficult times.' Lord Egerton looked more closely at Sir Peter's olive complexion and hummed a little resentment to himself. 'I believe the fresh air of north Europe has done your wellbeing a great deal of good.'

'I believe so.' Sir Peter responded simply.

'Strangely;' Lord Egerton said slowly. '........all the times I have come with Anne to one of these evenings I have not until now seen her dance before.' He leaned his head on one side and focussed his golden gaze on the wild figure until the dance ended to a light applause. 'Sir Peter, it has been quite a long time since we last talked.' Sir Peter gave Anne a pleasant smile and very quickly left she and Lord Egerton alone.

'Has Sir Peter said something to upset you?'

'Not me personally but he and my late husband had a series of arguments over official business which were never properly reconciled.' Anne finished drinking her wine and went over to get herself another glass of white before returning to Lord Egerton with a very tall young lady beside her. 'Thomas, Lady Bennett would like to dance with you.' Lord Egerton put his glass down and with a little reluctance got up off the chair and took the hand already waiting in front of him. 'You look gay tonight.' Lady Bennett remarked in a very excited voice. 'I have heard another lady who once invited me onto the dance floor make exactly the same remark. Is there anything wrong with my looking gay?' Lady Bennett smiled with her two dazzlingly bright green eyes into Lord Egerton's more weary expression and gently shook her head to his question; 'Nothing wrong at all, it was just a mere remark. Anne tells me you are now her new gentleman friend now that her husband is no longer with her and being King of England.'

'I have never heard Anne directly call me her gentleman friend but if that is how she wants to put it then I shall accept the term.'

'You dance very well.' Lord Egerton believed he was becoming slow on the dance floor, even more so when dancing with someone like Lady Bennett with a tall lean figure and very long legs. 'I hope that is not just a little bit of irony.' he commented already becoming increasingly breathless. 'Anne tells me she has a dance partner for me a little later in the evening but unfortunately I am going to have to tell her that the one dance is enough for me, chess and horse riding I believe are now my limit for pastimes.' By the time the dance finished Lord Egerton was only just able to make it to the chair beside Anne before falling heavily down and asking for another drink to be brought across. 'I believe Thomas it is fair to say that time inflicts many changes.' Anne looked at Lord Egerton's deep red cheeks burning with the heat in the hall and particularly after dancing. 'That maybe is one of Sir Edward's comments.' Earl Haversham brought Lord Egerton the glass of wine and smiled a little mockingly at him as he passed over the glass; 'I believe the sentence and execution of Sir Robert Catesby has aged you Thomas.' he remarked which made Lord Egerton's heart feel pain as he considered Earl Haversham's opinion. 'I believe you may well be right by your observation. We were very good friends and I admired him for his hard work in Parliament and in court.' Lord Egerton had a drink and turned his sad expression away from Anne's curious gaze.

'You never told me that you admired Sir Robert Catesby so much Thomas.' Lord Egerton suddenly got up and was looking for another dance partner before the next dance began. 'I'd leave him alone now if I were you.'

Earl Haversham laid a hand on Anne's shoulder and turned her round to look at his unusually large round head and bulging black eyes. As they watched the next dance begin they saw Lord Egerton dancing with a more middle-aged lady smaller and more round in her appearance with her face covered in cream and ointment and long earrings which seemed to make her very small face look a little more attractive. 'I believe Thomas has aged a great deal over the last three or four weeks.' Earl Haversham remarked as they watched Lord Egerton dancing a great deal more slowly and tenderly than he had ever danced before. 'I never realised he and Sir Robert Catesby were so close.'

'I think you should just ignore my remark, perhaps really I did not know what I was saying.' Anne had a drink of wine and sniffed her disapproval towards him. 'You can sometimes be a very arrogant and disrespectful young man.' She glowered at him briefly and turned and walked away.

'Are you enjoying the evening Thomas?' Anne asked quietly as she and Lord Egerton found themselves dancing slowly together. 'Absolutely, I always do.'

'The dark blue of your slashed doublet and breeches I believe goes with the colour of your complexion more than anything else you ever wear.' Lord Egerton was most surprised by Anne's observation.

'I suppose that has a meaning though I'm not exactly sure what.' he laughed as they went around the dance floor. 'I have some news which I did not give you earlier.' Anne lowered her eyes and frowned slightly;

'Is it official news?'

'It was given to me in the office by Sir Edward and it is referring to the continuing investigations into the gunpowder conspiracy.' Anne's scowl got increasingly angry.

'Is this the time to start telling me about the investigations into the gunpowder conspiracy Thomas, when we are on the dance floor?' Lord Egerton remarked quickly;

'His group of investigators have discovered two more people who were involved -'

'Very well Thomas,' Anne interrupted, '.....you can give me all the details when we are ridden home later!'

The dance ended just after midnight and amazingly to Lord Egerton there were still a great many young couples seated around the hall whose fresh youthful faces made them look as though they were ready to continue dancing for many more hours to come. 'I suggest we return home now and find out how your daughter enjoyed her night at the theatre.' Anne went to her table and finished her fourth glass of the very best white wine before after another first-rate evening on the Strand had ended she and Lord Egerton went to the young butler on official duty and asked him to fetch their garments without any delay.

Throughout January there were few indications that a bitter winter was approaching. Across England only a fine light snow had fallen and already the air was beginning to feel a little warmer and there were some signs that possibly spring was not too far away. Lord Montagu and Lord Whitby had been arrested at their fine mansions on

January 20th and were being held in relevant prisons until a date had been arranged in Westminster Hall for their court hearings. Already the land they had retaken from ordinary tenant farmers without giving them any statement of intent was being shared out between the tenant farmers once more which was making many men throughout Yorkshire and the Midlands extremely satisfied. The two ships transporting young Jamaican men to England having docked in Newcastle had been turned back to the Bahamas by representatives of the English military. George and Elizabeth Bertram had very quickly settled into their new home in York. Already their house was well furnished and during Christmas they had spent much of their time attending festive church services regarding them as their opportunity to get to meet and properly know the local folks. George rode into the city centre on only the third day in the new year and began to make arrangements for setting up his new business as a knife grinder which eventually he opened beside the cattle market. He woke up exceptionally early every morning and after dressing and washing he would have a light breakfast before taking his mount from the field and riding to work. Elizabeth was increasingly feeling uncomfortable and believing that very soon she would be giving birth to their baby. It was at the very end of January that Elizabeth at long last went into labour one particularly perishing winter day. Elizabeth even though she had felt extremely unwell and uncomfortable at home the closer the delivery time had come had not been taken into hospital but had remained in the confined bedchamber with only the occasional support of her husband when he was still at home. That day however George when waking up and preparing himself for work suspected there was something not right with his wife that morning and being unable to concentrate on anything else had ridden swiftly to St Leonard's Hospital and pleaded with Dr Franks to come back with him and watch over his wife as the childbirth got closer. A very young village nurse had gone into the bedchamber to tend to Elizabeth. It was no use anyone informing George that childbirth was a natural process which many women experienced every single day. Pacing up and down the small hallway and hearing Elizabeth wailing he wished he could take her pain himself and began to blame himself for making her pregnant in the first place. Seeing Dr Franks standing at the end of the passageway waiting to be given some instructions George invited him into the front room and poured him a large cup of whisky. 'I hope all this trouble doesn't make Elizabeth now feel she wishes she had never married me.' Dr Franks unblinking and always looking on the brighter side chuckled loud enough for George to be able to hear above the screams that were coming rapidly from the bedchamber. 'You must surely have decided on having a baby together!' George was not amused by the doctor's comment.

'Perhaps I would be feeling better if this had not been my wife's first baby and everything had gone well the first time. The fact that it is makes things more difficult to tolerate.'

'There is no need to concern yourself Mr Bertram, I am sure very soon your wife will be absolutely fine.' George looked longingly at the whisky Dr Franks was drinking and got up to pour himself a cup. 'You probably regard me as a weak minded buffoon.'

'Not at all but instead I regard you as a normal concerned husband worrying about your wife and your future child.'

'I believe now we should have stayed at High Hill Farm until this baby had been born, my mother could have sat with her...........I wish I could be in the bedchamber with her until this birth is over.' George had not intended the words to come out but could not stop himself from saying it. The doctor put a hand on George's chin as his head was now looking down at the wooden floor and commented gently; 'Now George, that sort of thing simply would never do. One nurse is all your wife needs not family in with her.' George looked piteously at Dr Franks and nodded his agreement wearily. 'I at least hope all my employees are getting on at work without me.' Dr Franks attempted to distract George's thoughts and worries away from the ongoing childbirth of Elizabeth. 'Oh yes, and what business is that you are thinking about?'

'I have just begun my own business as a knife grinder.'

'Oh...........how.......very interesting.' the doctor murmured slightly.

'Shouldn't Elizabeth be in hospital now doctor rather than lying in bed in the small and rather dark bedchamber?'

'I would like to see how she is feeling when the baby has been born and after that I shall decide what exactly her position is.' George had a drink of whisky and listened to the continued screaming though by now the calls were becoming a little more subdued. 'Your wife would not be happy after the birth has happened if you were to say that you had been in the bedchamber and watching all this going on, it is simply not dignified.' George glowered at the doctor and got up from the chair prowling up and down the hallway made him feel slightly less worried. The doctor eventually came out of the front room and stood by the front door watching George as he paced up and down in the near pitch dark until completely unexpected there came the sound of a baby's crying which stung George's heart and made tears come into his eyes as the loud shrill crying continued. *"Oh thank God the baby has been born safe and well…..thank God…."* Yet he still did not feel secure as the bedchamber door showed no signs of opening. 'Will my wife be safe do you think doctor?'

'Do not continue to worry yourself Mr Bertram, I am sure that everything will be absolutely fine.' After several minutes of baby cries silence fell over the small house and once more George felt his legs go weak and begin to shake. He could not stop himself from collapsing to the hard wooden floor with his tired heavy eyes closed. The doctor quickly came over to him and helped him back to his feet. 'This is not right doctor, but for a single nurse my wife needs someone more senior in the room with her helping her give birth…..the baby's crying has stopped…..what is wrong doctor?' Dr Franks refused to answer the question but led George back into the front room and after carefully sitting him back down refilled his cup with whisky and with his own handkerchief gingerly wiped the tears away from George's eyes. They sat quietly for another twenty minutes before Dr Franks seeing George was almost asleep took it on himself to go into the bedchamber and with the young nurse have a look at Elizabeth's present state. When he returned to the front room he found George completely asleep and woke him rather cautiously. 'Your wife has given birth to a beautiful dark haired little boy. Unfortunately she has lost a fair amount of blood. I would suggest that your long journey to York during such difficult conditions made things uncomfortable for your wife when she was already close to child labour.'

'That was something I pointed out to Elizabeth before we left High Hill Farm but she took absolutely no notice of me at all.'

'There is no need to concern yourself too much as it does happen occasionally during childbirth. What I suggest is that I shall ride into the centre of York and hire a horse and trap to drive Elizabeth and your child to the hospital where they both will get the very best looking after and she will be well fed to make her feel strong again and become the wonderful wife that you were telling me about just after entering the hospital. Afterwards when your wife is well again she can come home and together you can bring up your child with care and love.' George at last was able to smile at least a little cautiously.

'You do sometimes say some polite things doctor.' Dr Franks finished his cup of whisky and went out into the teaming rain to get his horse and ride her into town. 'I should not be too long and you can ride to the hospital with her.' Though George knew Dr Franks would not approve he slowly went into the bedchamber where he found

Elizabeth and the baby boy lying sound asleep, Elizabeth looked completely fatigued. The young nurse he had been considering in the bedchamber with Elizabeth was now asleep herself on a chair opposite the bed. A little nervous not to disturb either Elizabeth or the nurse after her long afternoon of sweat and toil George entered the bedchamber gently and as silently as he possibly could. He sat beside Elizabeth and stroked his hand loosely through her hair whispering; 'You are magnificent…….I hope you will forgive me for everything you have gone through over the last number of weeks……..' To his relief Dr Franks was not away very long before returning driving the horse and trap himself. 'We should put a cloak over your wife to protect her from the bitter wind and cold and help her outside with the baby boy into the trap then we can get her to the hospital quickly.' George peered at the young nurse still sound asleep after her afternoon's work before snatching Elizabeth's nearest cloak and then with Dr Franks raising her and the baby from the bed and after putting the cloak safely and tightly around her assisting them both outside into the trap. The doctor personally took it on himself to drive the horse towards the city and aside to St Leonard's Hospital. Very soon when they entered the hospital a nurse directed them to a bed which had already been made warm for the patient's arrival and Elizabeth and her lovely baby boy were helped gently inside until once more they had fallen fast asleep holding each other with great gentleness and love in their eyes.

George left the hospital the moment Elizabeth's thin weak body had lay down and hurried through the falling rain to his knife grinding factory which already employed five local men. He went inside and found every one of his employees doing his job properly and there was nothing untoward happening to give him any concern. 'How di' go then?' His youngest employee who was examining a knife which he had only just finished completing looked up at his employer and asked the question extremely simply. 'My wife has given birth to a baby boy.' To those words George received a great amount of applause before quickly adding; 'She is in hospital now although I can't remember what the doctor told me was exactly wrong with her.'

'Have you thought of a name yet for your little boy?' George looked across the grimy and darkened factory to see Tim working with some cutlery and tools and lifting an eyelid as he asked George the question. 'We have not thought of a name yet we just wanted to make sure first of all that the baby was born without any concerns and as yet that is not so.' He had a look around to check on all the work until very soon he felt he had to leave and return to the hospital and revisit Elizabeth. 'I will see you all tomorrow morning.' he remarked very simply and returned back outside to the cold and dark conditions.

Only a short time after Elizabeth had returned home from hospital she was resting early one morning when George had just left home for work and was disturbed by an unusually loud long banging on the front door of the house. Elizabeth's frail figure was puffing with exhaustion as she opened the door holding a small bundle carefully in her hands. She was extremely confused when seeing the tall gentleman outside scratching his head firmly and grimacing apparently to himself on and off. The tall gentleman recoiled as though nervously when the door opened. Before looking at the lady of the house he set his eyes on the little face looking eagerly back at him and gave a hazy smile; 'What a beautiful little boy.' Elizabeth was not at all amused by what the stranger had said; 'Please can you just tell me what you wish to speak to me about.'

'Is your name Elizabeth Penfield please could you tell me lady?'

'It is, I take it there is a reason why you have asked me such a question.'

'Your father Lord Whitby would like to speak with you immediately, it is something very important he has to speak to you about.' Elizabeth laughed her disgust quietly so as not wanting to disturb the little boy.

'I no longer wish to speak with my father and tell me, who are you and how did you find me at my new home?'

'My name is Job and I am a business agent for your father. I have been asking around for your new place of residence so as you might gather this searching has taken me quite some time.'

'And is this visit simply to tell me that my father at his nice comfortable home wishes to speak with me? I have known that for a long time but after he shot two of my good friends dead then I cannot forgive him. Good day.' Elizabeth's firm attempt to close the door woke the baby boy and his sudden and unexpected crying spell made Elizabeth feel extremely angry. 'I believe we have nothing else to talk about so if you would please just leave me and my baby boy alone.' Before Elizabeth could attempt to close the door again the stranger explained as simply as he could. 'Your father Miss Penfield is no longer at his large home in Whitby but he was arrested by the army in the middle of January and has been taken to Leeds Prison where he is being held. He wishes frantically that you would go and visit him to speak before he believes the other jealous prisoners who are not as high up in society as he is turn on him and together end his life.' Elizabeth considered the gentleman's comment at the same time she was trying to calm her baby boy down and quell the flowing tears. 'If I am to go and visit father I shall need my husband here to look after our small child. I want you to ride immediately to the new knife grinding factory beside the market and bring him home to look after the baby while I am away otherwise I simply shall be in no fit position to visit father. Go and fetch my husband back for me and I shall be waiting and ready to leave.' Without staying to discuss the matter any more the gentleman lifted the brim of his black hat and returned to his black horse before quickly riding back towards the city.

George looked equally as angry as Elizabeth had earlier when he was brought back home in the early afternoon. 'You told me that from now on you were having nothing more to do with your father!' Elizabeth took hold of the baby and waited until her husband had taken off his cloak and sat down before handing him over. 'I am sorry George but this is different. I cannot leave father alone in a filthy prison cell when he tells me that he believes his life is in danger.'

'But what about your state of health? The nurse told both of us after releasing you from hospital care that you are still weak and have not yet fully recovered from all the blood you lost giving birth to our beautiful baby boy.' The tall stranger still standing at the door quickly excused himself and returning to his tall black horse rode away before being involved any further in the ongoing heated disagreement. 'Leeds Prison is not a long ride from here and I do not believe I shall be having much of a conversation with father except to say his imprisonment is his own fault. I shall probably be back before nightfall.' George looked at the baby's round eyes wide open and staring at him in complete silence. Feeling the little bundle in his arms made him want to weep. 'Are you going to ever believe marrying me was the right thing you did, just a simple farmer unlike the rich and high-flying background there was in your own family?' Elizabeth again was taken very much by surprise at George's question. 'I shall never regret marrying someone as kind and as handsome as yourself and taking me away from such a formal and arrogant life as I used to live. And now on top of everything else we have a beautiful baby boy to look after and bring up. Now please, I must go.' Elizabeth bent down and kissed both her husband and son softly and then going outside into the fresh chill air of the small city she went into the field where grass was beginning to appear from the soil once more and mounting her horse the usual way began the horse ride westward towards west Yorkshire and the growing city of Leeds.

It was not too long into her ride across Yorkshire that Elizabeth could see the outskirts of Leeds city where many rows of wooden huts had seemingly quickly been built along which a large almshouse looked as though from the brightness of the bricks and the larger windows that had been fitted it had only just been completed and opened. Through control of the reins her young and very healthy horse reduced its gallop to a gentle trot as she went deeper into the unknown city looking in every direction to try and find out where the large prison was. The city centre was extremely busy with a street market continuing and travellers and vagabonds walking backwards and forwards looking by the puzzled expressions covering their faces rather lost. She had been riding for a considerable length of time trying to find out where Leeds prison was until reluctantly asking one of the many young travellers roaming the high street. She was directed well onward through the city before she was to find the grey brick building and as she began to approach she increasingly felt nervous of what she would find when meeting her father after years of living a high-life now surviving in a dirty unhygienic building along with many people who were jealous of him and his wealthy background and all his money. On seeing the building she almost felt as though she was going to faint and her legs were going to collapse beneath her frail light body. After standing outside the large front iron door she took some time to get her breath before dismounting and tying her horse to a post not too far away.

For a long time Elizabeth stood outside the large door unsure how to enter the building until she was approached by a gentleman who introduced himself as Sir John Lenthal the prison marshal. He was able to have the door unlocked and invited Elizabeth to follow him inside. The stench and sounds of shrill screeching coming from all quarters made her eyes and mouth close tightly and her whole body fall backwards with the horrifying surprise and terrible shock. 'Can I help you dear lady?' she was greeted by a raw and hollow voice soon after she had started to recover from her entrance. 'I wish to speak to my dear father Lord Whitby.' The guard Elizabeth could only just see through the miserable gloom sniffed strongly just in front of her eyes and commented as he was releasing a long gasp of air. 'Many prisoners in this building do not agree with your word *dear*. There is a great deal of jealousy and resentment towards the wealth and power your father once had and the class difference is perfectly obvious. For his own safety we keep him locked in a cell on his own. Follow me young lady.' She was led through several long dark tunnels through the continued foul stench and the increasing ear-splitting noises of squeaking and squawking as they got deeper into the building. Prisoners could be seen almost naked, their skin filthy black and on some their arms and legs in particular bloodied by lashings and beatings. 'How far are we going into this building?' Elizabeth asked very anxiously.

'Your father's cell is right down the other end.' The prisoners together were crying wildly and exclaiming remarks of regret and begging anyone who went past their cell for forgiveness. 'Do these people ever get fed?' she asked again horrified this time by the ghostly figures who were holding onto the bars as she looked back at them, their bodies were almost all bones and nothing more. 'They are fed a little when we can afford the food but it is only occasional.' Eventually after an extremely long walk which had exhausted Elizabeth in her delicate state she saw her father through a slight beam of light lying in one corner of his small cell surrounded by animals of one sort or another. 'What are all those little animals running around the cell floor?' Elizabeth was almost certain she knew what the answer would be but was hoping that she would be proved to be wrong. 'They are vermin rats and mice carrying disease which is in this building all the time and kills a lot of people or if not then makes them extremely ill.' Seeing that her father seemed fully asleep and was surrounded by rodents made her think about turning around and walking back out however she asked the guard to open the cell gate and let her inside. As the gate was unlocked the air from the cell seemed even more disgusting than it was outside however she told the guard she would call him when she wanted to be let out and asked him to lock the gate and leave them alone to talk.

'Father,' she almost whispered at last down at the little bundle curled up on the floor and surrounded by vermin all running up and down his body as if to try and feed or find somewhere to hide for a while. 'Father......you wanted to see me.......at least that was what one of your gentleman allies told me.' After a few minutes the bundle that was curled up on the floor slowly began to move and Lord Whitby lifted his head out of his arms for a time confused by the voice that had called to him. 'Who are you?' he croaked at last and lifted his head upwards wailing harshly with pain as he did. He like the other prisoners was almost completely naked. His body was black and dirty and he too had got deep red cuts and scars from where seemingly whips had been used to strike him. 'Elizabeth;' he croaked again, '……is that you?'

'Yes father, it is Elizabeth as you asked me to come. I am assuming you have some news to give me yet I do not understand why as we have so little in common with each other any more.' Lord Whitby got up off the floor so quickly and jumped at her with hollow eyes gazing that it made her once more recoil with horror. 'Won't you kiss me my beautiful young daughter?' Lord Whitby almost cried.

'I shall not kiss you father, not until you are released from this disgusting place and you apologise to me properly for all the sins you have inflicted on not just my life but the life of my innocent and harmless husband too. Do you remember father, your wickedness began all that time ago when I told you I was going to marry George and then when he came to see you you intended shooting my husband to be dead you wicked….evil man!!' Lord Whitby's hollow dark ringed eyes began streaming with tears as he looked to her daughter for an immediate act of forgiveness. 'I am very sorry for that and for shooting your two friends during their intended break in…..I wish I had never done it my beautiful daughter…….please Lizzie…..will you now forgive me?' Elizabeth again from a distance stared up and down her father's pathetic and bony figure. 'My God father, to think what a powerful, plump and wealthy man you used to be boastful of your position in life and willing to condemn anybody at all you believed were beneath you in class or the amount of money they had.' Elizabeth creased her face tightly and chewed on her lips as she rasped, 'You used to think yourself so high and mighty father now look at you, father you are absolutely pathetic!' Hearing his young daughter speak with such hatred towards him made Lord Whitby collapse back to the hard brick floor back amongst the screaming rats and other filthy vermin. 'Before I leave you father I have some news.' Lord Whitby remained sitting on the hard floor curled up and no longer interested in her daughter's news after the way she had condemned him for his past behaviour however amongst the whistling of the rats he whistled through his teeth; 'Please my child, let me hear your news.' Elizabeth found it a little difficult speaking to a small skinny bundle on the floor after her childhood of speaking to a powerful and authoritative father however she stood over him and began; 'I along with my wonderful husband George am no longer living at High Hill Farm but have moved to the lovely little city of York where George has opened up a brand new career as a knife grinder.' Lord Whitby raised his head slowly unsure if he had heard the news correctly. 'Your husband is no longer a farmer?'

'No father, George is no longer a farmer and I am no longer a farmer's wife doing the boring repetitive jobs a farmer's wife has to do every day of her life. And in addition I have given birth to a baby boy. We have not thought of a name to call him yet however you said for a long time you wanted me to have a baby and I have.' At that news Lord Whitby from out of nowhere jumped up onto his cut up feet bare and blooded and put his arms firmly around Elizabeth crying out with tears coming from his blackened eyes and running down his yellow hollow cheeks, 'I am so delighted for you my beautiful child I am so happy. When can I see the baby?' Although Elizabeth was still a little weak after the large loss of blood she had suffered during the childbirth she was still strong enough to pull her father's hold off herself and force herself away from him and his feeble figure. 'Father I told you the news merely because I thought as your daughter it was my responsibility to tell you however once I have left this prison with your pathetic figure trapped inside I have no intention to see you again. Do you understand father? This place gives me the creeps, as a young woman in here I feel frightened of all the men who are peering at me as I walk past their cells. You embarrass me father, as you did when you were using Jamaican slaves on the land you had taken from the ordinary farmers because of your simple greed for money. Now the land has been given back to the ordinary hard working farmers and in time you shall be appearing in court for your sins, that is of course if you come out of here alive.' Elizabeth could feel tears beginning to swell in her eyes too and very quickly turned round and cried out along the narrow passageway for the guard to come and release her. 'This is it father, here my new life is beginning completely without you.' The guard came swiftly and unlocked the heavy iron gate and Elizabeth left before any further words could be spoken. Lord Whitby's poor pathetic figure once more fell back onto the hard floor with the shrill and loud sounds of rats and other infected rodents continuing all around him.

Though intending to keep her visit inside Leeds prison short Elizabeth had spent over three hours speaking with her father and by the time she had come out of the eerie building it was beginning to turn dark after what had been for the most part a fine and pleasantly warm day. She mounted her horse and immediately kicked her heels into the horse's sides and began to gallop through the city centre which was still extremely busy with the market continuing and with travellers still hurrying into Leeds and then once out of the city she turned her horse left and across country back towards the North Yorkshire Moors and York city itself. It was not until after ten that night when she returned to their small house and there was a star filled sky and very wintry bitter cold air. 'I have missed you.' she commented anxiously as she pushed open the front door. 'We have missed you too, haven't we.' George and the baby still were seated in exactly the same position as they had been when Elizabeth had first left them alone earlier. 'And what then did your father have to say to you?' George's tone had lowered and his voice sounded most unusual.

'My father said nothing that I wanted to listen to all I did was tell him of our new position with our lives. I told him that we have a baby and that we have moved away from the farm and into York.'

'So now I hope you will have no further desire to see him.'

'None at all, I shall not even attend his funeral which I do not think will be very long now. There is some disease which is going around the prison and prisoners in almost every cell were coughing extremely badly. From now on our life means only us and our beautiful baby. I would suggest now we have something to eat as I am feeling extremely hungry after the long horse ride home and then after that I believe we both need a good night's rest before you are up again early in the morning for work.' Elizabeth went over to George and the baby kissing them both with all the passion she could bring forth.

It had not been easy trying to find John Harper when he had been thrown out of his farmhouse by Lord Montagu and had found another village close by and a small abandoned house in which he could rest and lay his head. He had hoped that one day Lord Montagu would be thrown off the farmland that he had retaken and Harper Farm would be returned to him. Yet when he had been offered the farmland and farmhouse back by a number of his friends he had rejected their offer and decided to find employment somewhere else. Early in February he had packed his bag with the few possessions he had carefully placed inside and had begun to walk southwards with the thought of beginning a new life in London. It had been a very cold night when he had set off on his long trek down England yet he had no intention of being prevented in any way at all of beginning his new life alone. He had absolutely no money when he set off and so knew that at some time he might need to rely on simple theft to help him get a little food when necessary. The clothes he wore were now threadbare and unclean and the shoes that he walked on were almost totally wrecked after years of wearing them without ever being changed. At least under a starlit sky and bright moon he was pleased to see the farmland he and his father used to run and work no longer full of young Jamaican men being used as slaves by Lord Montagu which had sickened him to his very stomach. As he walked steadily across the flat land and southwards he found it increasingly difficult to believe what his life had come to after years of arguing with his father about the farm and its future. He could not now believe that his mother was dead and his father had simply disappeared almost as soon as he had been to the hospital and learned the terrible news of his beautiful wife's tragic death. He believed for a long time that one day he would become the new manager of Harper Farm but not that he would be walking towards London searching for a brand new career. He walked through two small hamlets and one small village before approaching the larger town of Bedford and finding a tavern on the edge of the town he decided to go inside and ask for a room just for one night and find out in the morning just what the consequences of his having no money may be. John's pale thin figure as he slowly pushed open the door was received with silence around the bar which was extremely busy and a look of scepticism from the manager John recognised yet had only spoken to when his father had been by his side. There was a period when nobody spoke at all until Mr Bowes the manager with his sceptical voice asked John what he wanted. 'A room for the night would be very welcome sir.' John replied trying to smile a little too in such uncomfortable circumstances. Mr

Bowes pushed out his lips and continued to stare at John with a sceptic expression. 'I have never seen you before without your father by your side, it is James who always deals with the financial aspect of business.'

'My father has disappeared very suddenly.' John's head fell and at the same time he dropped his cases on the hard floor as they were beginning to feel extremely heavy. 'I would expect John that you have absolutely no money on you at all. Am I right in my assumption?' Somewhat shamefaced John looked up at Mr Bowes and with his cheeks flushed red he said very quietly; 'Yes Mr Bowes, you are right.' Just as Mr Bowes was considering his response to John's feeble reply he heard the elegant voice of his daughter call out from the staircase as she was slowly coming down. 'John Harper, I haven't seen you for many years now, not since we were small children who used to play together in the field just outside the hamlet of Wellingborough if you cast your memory back far enough.' Mr Bowes felt suddenly irritated by his daughter's intervention in the earlier conversation however John was already regarding Mr Bowes's daughter more carefully now that her pretty small figure was standing right in front of him. 'Deborah if I am not mistaken……' he ruminated slowly. 'Please forgive me if I am wrong with the name.' Deborah beamed one of her most charming smiles at him which he definitely remembered from when he was just a little boy and they would play outside together as his father was working hard with his hands on Harper Farm and Mr Bowes and his wife Margaret were running a small inn beside the small hamlet. As her father was becoming tired of listening to their continued reminiscing he eventually walked over and was preparing to turn John away until Deborah spoke to him a little sharply; 'Don't turn John away father, prepare him a meal and a room for however long he wishes to stay. After that he and I have our own personal decisions to discuss privately, don't we John?' John was completely thrown by Deborah's remark however he responded;

'Yes of course…….we have much to discuss.' Deborah smiled scornfully as her father began to make the arrangements his daughter had quietly demanded. 'You sit down John, I shall get the head butler to take your cases and I shall return and join you when father has prepared your meal. If I may say so, you look as though you have barely eaten for weeks.'

John was taken to a small dining room at the back of the tavern and given a plate of cold chicken, bread and butter and a glass of ale which Deborah seemed a little embarrassed about as she sat opposite and watched John eat. 'I thought father might have prepared you something a little more appetising than cold meat and bread and butter.'

'This is absolutely fine.' he replied with his mouth full of food.

'What has brought you here to our small tavern in the first place?'

'Things went badly wrong at Harper Farm and father vanished after his lovely wife was taken into hospital with a fever and then died very soon after sadly. I don't know if I shall ever see father again.'

'And so what are your intentions now that you have lost the farm?' John had a mouth of ale and shrugged slightly.

'When I left the small house in the nearby village late last night I did intend walking on towards London and beginning a new life on my own, now that I have sat back down again I am not sure I am capable of walking the rest of the long distance.' After having another mouthful of the chicken he peered closely again at Deborah's face and nodded; 'Strangely after all these years since we last met and played together your face and complete figure have hardly changed at all, you are still slim, elegant and with a wonderful smile.'

'Thank you for such sweet talk.' She responded laughing gently at him. 'If you would like me to be absolutely honest with you John I believe working hard on a farm with your bullying father has aged you slightly.'

'There is nothing wrong with what you have said, my father was for a long time a bully and I have been thinking for many years about leaving Harper Farm and beginning a new career in another part of the country. The thought of becoming a fisherman in Bristol, Plymouth or possibly Southampton had appealed to me but father just laughed in my face when I suggested it.'

'Then I have an offer which you may like to take me up on.' John was taken aback by Deborah's remark;

'I am sure whatever your offer is I shall be extremely taken by.'

'You may have gathered when you saw myself and father speaking for a short time in the corridor that we do not get on at all well, that has been how we have lived together ever since he and mother separated over two years ago.' Deborah hesitated and looked across the table at John who had almost finished his meal and was looking a great deal happier for it. She licked her lips and rubbed her eyes which were stinging with tiredness. 'I decided several weeks ago;' she continued thoughtfully. '.....that what I would do one day would be to pack all my belongings and go and buy myself a horse with the small sum of money I have and ride away from here to begin a new life far away from my father and this tavern that he is so proud of.

Tomorrow if you would like you can come with me to the stables nearby and with my money we can buy two horses which are not the most expensive I admit. If you wait for me to pack my things then we shall leave here together, probably tomorrow night and ride down to London where we can begin a completely new life.'

'That would be absolutely magnificent!' he answered without any thought whatsoever. John had never experienced a coup of such fortune before and with his circumstances being so desperate and unforgiving the time for a coup could not have been transcended. 'Tomorrow then we shall go and buy the horses and we can take things from there.' Deborah saw the head butler passing by, in a more manly act she snapped her fingers loudly to attract his attention and ordered two glasses of ale and told him to hurry. 'I would never be so forceful as that.' John scoffed. The butler returned quickly with the two glasses and disappeared with equal haste. 'I hope your father will not hold your sudden disappearance from his tavern against me.' Deborah shrugged; 'It will not matter if he does. Once we are beginning a new life in the capital then I shall never see father again, life will just be for you and me.'

The room John had been afforded by Mr Bowes was by no means comfortable or welcoming yet perfection was not what he had expected when first walking through the door with absolutely no money. At least however it was a somewhere for him to be able to rest his weary head and then his life would begin a new and exciting venture. He had slept lightly the one and went down to breakfast with Deborah just after seven o'clock. 'You look a great deal better for the night's sleep. The bacon and egg boiled over the spit is fresh and bought from a farm just the opposite side of the field.' John had a piece of the bacon and his face smiled widely with delight at the taste. 'That bacon is absolutely excellent.'

'The stables where people buy and sell their horses are just a short walk away from the tavern. When we have chosen our horses we shall return here and immediately I shall collect my belongings and we can go. Father will be surprised.' Deborah went into the kitchen and returned with a pot of coffee and two cups which she filled up the moment the tray was placed on the table. 'I hope you know just what to look for when choosing a horse to ride.' John sighed and looked a little anxiously at Deborah as he made the comment. 'Most of all I want two horses that are light, domesticated and have their front and cheek teeth undamaged in any way.'

'As you say, you may realise that father when it came to selecting horses only made the choices himself.' Deborah had a drink of the strong coffee and mused, 'Do you think you will ever want to go and start looking for your father again?'

'No, not now we are planning a new beginning together, you are the only person from now on who will matter in my life.' John had a drink of coffee and hummed his admiration. 'This is something we can do one day together, begin a new coffee shop in central London.'

'That to me sounds an excellent idea.' As they were gently discussing their possible future direction Deborah's father came across and asked about their private conversation. 'We are going shortly father to buy two horses and then when I have returned and packed all my belongings I am leaving for London with John Harper here.'

'So what about us Deborah and the future of the tavern when I retire in several years time?'

'That father is something you must think about yourself, our future will be in the bright lights of the capital where fortunes are to be made.' Mr Bowes let out an ungenlemanly scoff at his daughter's comment.

'That is what people say but it is completely untrue, London is a place people go to try and make a fortune and end up on the streets with the politicians who are supposed to be running the country and putting things right now they have got rid of the successful Cross Cabinet only looking after themselves. I would advise you Deborah to stay here and take up the running of my successful tavern instead.' Suddenly Deborah's pretty creaseless face became an expression of fury and without asking John if he wanted to leave his breakfast she took a hand and almost dragged him outside the tavern and onwards in the direction of the stables. 'As I have already explained, I no longer get on at all well with father. The stables are just ahead, when

I have chosen and bought the horses we shall ride back here I will put my belongings into a suitcase and we shall immediately leave. The stables were short of horses which were for sale. Deborah handed over the only money she had, a gold sovereign and a shilling piece to the horse trader and on the two large and more elderly horses that had been bought they rode back to the tavern where they prepared their belongings for leaving. 'You never were very good at trading in horses were you Deborah!' Mr Bowes once more scoffed as he examined the horses they would be riding to London on. Deborah and John ignored Mr Bowes completely until all their luggage was divided between their mounts and they were ready to leave. 'I'm sorry our relationship has had to end this way father but after the way you separated with mother I have never really forgiven you. Maybe one day I shall come looking for you again but overall my future is with John.' She urged John to jump up onto his horse and with more of a struggle Deborah climbed up the taller of the two. 'As there is nothing more to speak to my father about John I suggest we begin our journey and our new beginning too. Come on.' Though not yet an experienced horse rider Deborah kicked her heels into the horse's side and looking a little weary already the two horses began their trek towards London.

CHAPTER TWO

Lord Egerton returned home to Chelsea one day in June still feeling in deep shock and disbelief after the news he had been told at the local cottage hospital. As the horse gently trotted into the yard he leapt down almost unable to control his emotions as he came into confrontation with his young stable boy and gave him the reins. 'Tend her, feed her and wash her I will be going out again later this morning.'

'I always do your lordship if you don't mind my saying so.' Lord Egerton glowered at the boy who had already turned his back and was leading Sally slowly into the stables. *"Maybe,"* Lord Egerton thought, *"I wouldn't feel so terrible if the rain was not so heavy."* Throughout the night and still at half past six that same morning the rain was almost washing his face and clothes falling like a monsoon. Now more than anything else he needed to change his clothes, dry himself fully and get himself a nice hot drink. His slashed doublet, hose and breeches were all dripping with water even though he had been wearing a long thick cloak over the top, a large black hat and knee length riding boots. He hurried upstairs to his large bedchamber and without any hesitation began to strip himself naked with some fresh dry clothes there beside him on his bed. As he stood opposite the mirror almost fully naked he glanced at his reflected face slowly turning it one way and then the other starting to realise just how ashen and sick his own face was looking. He had not eaten anything since early the previous evening yet did not feel at all hungry only a cup of strong black coffee in such difficult circumstances would suffice. Turning his attention away from his own reflection Lord Egerton began to feel the wonderful effects of being dry again and began to dress himself in his breeches, shirt and short-waisted doublet before carefully brushing his bedraggled hair and painstakingly combing his ragged beard and moustache. After some considerable time preparing himself to appear respectable again he began to look around the house and think about one day soon stripping the place totally and moving to somewhere smaller nearer the centre of London. After several minutes gazing all around the house Lord Egerton returned to the kitchen and prepared himself a large cup of hot dark coffee and buttered himself two pieces of bread before then preparing to go out again and have a few words with the stable boy which he believed may prove to be slightly awkward. The news of his wife's fever totally out of the blue getting a great deal worse before making her heartbeat stop entirely when nobody was tending her in the space of only two or three minutes had come as a complete shock and had struck his heart almost as savagely as a spear being thrust right through. The fact that he and Elizabeth had spent a great deal of their married time quarrelling had merely made the news of her death a great deal worse. He ate his bread and butter slowly and without any great taste inside him, instead the cup of hot dark coffee and the rich aroma it was letting off in its film was unequalled.

Lord Egerton peered out of the large window before leaving the house once more just to see if the heavy rain from the very early hours of the morning had yet stopped. The sky was still black and the ground was completely saturated yet at the same time there were some indications the heavy rain had at long last relented. He decided that whatever the weather was doing now if he wanted to go and speak with Mr Miller, one of the best funeral directors London had ever seen then he would have to go out now as Mr Miller always left his office at ten o'clock for some reason which Lord Egerton could not understand. Before going out he dressed finally in his finest black shoes and a fresh cape and as he stepped out of the door he put on his best tall black hat. The stable boy appeared from the stable the moment Lord Egerton came outside and proudly led Sally out behind. 'Your horse has been washed, fed and her shoes have all been fully checked your lordship.' Lord Egerton got his purse from a pocket of his cape and produced two large gold sovereigns to pass across. 'Why thank y' y'r lordship.' the stable boy said proudly. 'Are you feelin' generous this morning y'r lordship?'

'It's not that I am feeling generous this morning... ....I wanted to tell you now.....I have to go and make arrangements for my wife's funeral and then once the funeral is over I shall be making preparations for my leaving this large house. As I am sure you will understand, a house this size is too big for one person.' The stable boy at first looked rather puzzled by his lordship's announcement and was unsure how to reply until eventually he asked; 'Has something awful happened your lordship?' Lord Egerton knew that although the young man was an excellent stable boy he was not at all well educated. 'I found out at the local hospital early this morning that my dear wife Elizabeth died in the very early hours. Now I must go and speak with Mr Miller and make her funeral arrangements. As I told you, once my dear wife's funeral is over I am going to find myself somewhere smaller to live and have this house cleared as soon as I possibly can and leave.' This time the young man understood exactly what his lordship had said and cried; 'But what 'bout me your lordship and my work here?'

'You will very soon be able to find yourself work somewhere else I'm sure as you are such a fine hard-working and reliable young man. Now, I must go and see Mr Miller.' There were light spots of rain gently beginning to fall again making Lord Egerton leap onto his horse and ignore the boy's tears slowly rolling down his face. Taking the reins firmly he led Sally outside into the muddied flat open land and then kicking his heels in led his mount in a gallop to the centre of London to go and see the funeral director.

It was twenty minutes to ten o'clock when Lord Egerton arrived at Mr Miller's office and he knocked on the office door gently before hearing Mr Miller's usual sturdy voice asking him to come inside and take a seat. 'Lord Egerton how lovely to see you. I do not believe we have spoken since arranging the funeral of the late King James I. The country is still in quite a state even though those in authority have had a fair amount of time to at least try and make England strong again.' Lord Egerton sat down at the desk as requested and looked extremely irritated by Mr Miller's observations of the country's present state of affairs. 'Mr Miller I do find your observations very interesting I have to say but that was not actually the reason why I have come here to see you this morning. I believe you always leave your office at ten o'clock every morning though I do not know why, however I wish to discuss another funeral and I do not have a lot of time.'

'Lord Egerton there is no need for you to worry about time, I would always make you an exception with my business arrangements. I always go and see my staff on a morning in their separate office in Whitechapel and give them their orders for the work that has been prepared every day of the week. That is where I go, now tell me Lord Egerton, who is the funeral for?'

'It is a funeral sadly for my wife who died in the local hospital during the very early hours of this morning.'

'My dear Lord Egerton, I am so terribly sorry!' Suddenly Mr Miller was no longer sounding so calm but anxiously gazing at Lord Egerton whose face in particular he had only just noticed looked extremely pale and his cheeks hollow. 'I never realised Elizabeth was unwell.'

'Why should you have known?' Lord Egerton remarked. 'I had not seen you for such a long time and the last time I did see you Elizabeth was absolutely fine except that she had an ongoing bee in her bonnet about myself and the way I spent the family finances. I shall never be able to find out now just what on earth she was really unhappy about.' Seeing Lord Egerton's very pasty face and listening to his voice shaking Mr Miller passed over a box to him and asked him to open it. 'Take one out and I think I will smoke one as well.' Lord Egerton looked at the item of paper rounded carefully and with a slight unusual smell when pushed right up to the nose. 'What is it?' he asked with a more collected besides ever more suspicious voice as he continued to examine the object from end to end. 'It is called a cigarette, they just arrived in England from Mauritius three days ago. You hold one between two fingers and light it with a match. You put the dark end in your mouth and inhale. I don't know exactly what is inside them as nobody has yet told me however they are very good and certainly help you relax.' Mr Miller took a cigarette from the box too and lit a match asking Lord Egerton to pass over one end of his cigarette and then try it. 'They are good don't you think?' Lord Egerton inhaled a little deeper the second time and almost choked as he did so. 'You put the ashes from the opposite end in this tray and enjoy the smoke.' Lord Egerton tried inhaling the blue smoke one more time before putting the remnants into the tray and watching Mr Miller continuing to inhale and enjoying every moment as he did so. Lord Egerton eventually believed he was going to start and sob. 'Mr Miller, I have had to make funeral arrangements before but obviously until now never funeral arrangements for my own wife.........it just feels so awful.' Mr Miller took in another deep breath with the rolled up cigarette spilling out blue smoke from his lips which was now almost shrouding the office before finally becoming more attentive of his client's request. 'As it is Friday today your wife's funeral cannot take place until the Monday. Have you yet decided where you would like it to take place?'

'Not really,' Lord Egerton answered candidly. 'But I would suggest St Mary's church in Chelsea not too far from where we lived together. Elizabeth was a very religious person and she used to attend many services there. I believe those people who work in St Mary's church will be delighted to hold it.' With his quill pen Mr Miller began making some positive notes and taking down particular details. 'Do you wish for your dear wife's funeral just to be a quiet family occasion?'

'Of course except I shall have to invite my lady friend Anne of Denmark too.'

'Just as she invited you to her late husband's funeral service I presume?'

'Exactly.'

'Very well Lord Egerton, I shall ask my staff in Whitechapel when I go and see them shortly to make all the arrangements and I can tell you now the funeral service shall take place at St Mary's church at half past two on Monday afternoon.'

'I shall sort out all the financial matters later once the event is over and I have had a chance to recover from such an awful incident as this. Now I must go.' By this time as he stood up Lord Egerton was trying to hold his breath as the strong smell of cigarette smoke was almost choking him totally. The office was now completely blue with thick smog from the rolled up object and Lord Egerton had to wave some of the cloud from his eyes to be able to see the door handle. 'Thank you again Mr Miller, you really are a blessing sometimes.' He left the office quickly and although it was raining again steadily outside and mist was beginning to fall onto the city Lord Egerton was merely pleased to get outside and into the almost *fresh* air.

Anne and Elizabeth did not realise there was anything disturbing Lord Egerton even when he arrived at their house so early on the Friday morning. 'Are we going riding this morning?' he had asked Anne almost the very moment the butler had let him inside the hallway. Anne looked at him a little oddly and led him into the living room. 'The butler can pour you a glass of whisky and we shall see by the time you have drunk it if the heavy rain has stopped.' The butler without being asked by Anne personally filled up a glass of whisky and put it down on the table by Lord Egerton's side. 'I notice the chess board for once is not prepared for a new game.' Anne scratched her head and looked a little thoughtfully at Lord Egerton,

'Elizabeth is touring England with the drama group she went to see last Christmas. She told me she has been made the company's personal Patron.' Lord Egerton leaned his head to one side appearing a little amused by the thought. 'Isn't your daughter a little young to be Patron?' Anne returned Lord Egerton's bemused expression and went to pour herself a glass of port. 'The violent rainstorm we suffered for much of the night is at last showing signs of easing and I do believe there is a little patch of blue sky beginning to appear.' Though not intending yet to break the news Lord Egerton after having another drink of whisky could not stop himself remarking; 'Elizabeth my wife....' he found himself stammering a moment, '........not your daughter.......my wife died during the night!' The sudden silence that filled the room after Lord Egerton's short and open remark was broken by the white little dog that hastily ran into the room with its tongue hanging out and its large green eyes gazing at both Anne and Lord Egerton for some attention. 'I thought your silly little dog spent most of its time with the young maid who was having some problems of her own to cope with.' Anne put her drink down and to Lord Egerton's further irritation came over and picked her little dog up, holding it like a baby which made Lord Egerton's face knit tightly glaring at the animal. 'I have things I wish to discuss with you, damn it we shall have to wait until our ride!' The puppy was breathing heavily and glaring at Lord Egerton with some amusement in its eyes.

'This damn rain just refuses to stop.' Lord Egerton commented as they were mounting their horses and the dark rain clouds were still being blown across London on a strong chilly wind. The horses were trotting across fields deep in mud and rainwater. 'I suggest we stop at the White Swan for a little lunch, as it is not too far from here and then you can tell me the rest of your news.'

'The news that was earlier interrupted by that irritating little dog of yours!' Anne looked at Lord Egerton appearing somewhat disturbed by his angry voice. 'I thought you liked the little dog you brought me.' Lord Egerton's shoulders dropped and he apologised for his irritated voice. 'It's only just after midday yet being up and at the hospital at four o'clock in the morning makes today already seem extremely long.' Very quickly they arrived at the tavern which was quiet and devoid of any customers at all. They tied their horses up and went inside for a drink and some light refreshment. 'What would you like?' Lord Egerton asked simply as they arrived at the bar. They chose quickly and selected a table in readiness for the waiter's arrival. 'Now Thomas please tell me, what was it that finally killed Elizabeth?' Lord Egerton shrugged.

'At the hospital unfortunately they were not at all clear except my wife's severe temperature rose sharply during the early hours of the morning and the very high temperature caused her heart to stop. That very simply was what I was told.'

'I am extremely sorry Thomas. Have you had any time yet to arrange your wife's funeral?'

'That I have already spoken to Mr Miller about, it is to take place on Monday afternoon at St Mary's church in Chelsea.' The young waiter arrived with their drinks and lunch and was given a large tip by Lord Egerton for his extreme act of graciousness shown as he attended them. 'This weekend I must ride round and inform all Elizabeth's friends and family of her sad death and then of the funeral arrangements and I must find someone to organise a little light food and drink at my house for later in the afternoon. I am hoping Anne that you will come too.'

'Is that really necessary?' Anne's very sudden response took Lord Egerton by surprise and upset him a little. 'I did not expect that kind of hostile reply from you I must say. I do hope you will at least show your face just as I supported you during the service for your late husband.' Anne nodded her head and accepted Lord Egerton's remark. 'As you wish.' Very quickly Anne changed the subject and her facial expression became more severe. 'Have you collected a copy of the most recent pamphlet which is available?' Lord Egerton sighed heavily, street pamphlets he was occasionally finding very irritating. 'I have not collected a copy yet Anne no!'

'It says on the front page there is to be a special sitting in the House of Commons on June 30 to debate a motion which has been proposed by the Deputy Speaker which suggests sharing out more power with local parish governments.' Lord Egerton looked enraged by Anne's information.

'Just where do these journalists get all this news and information!? That is something I as a politician have heard absolutely nothing about!' As they ate in such awkward circumstances the tavern began slowly to fill up which helped take Lord Egerton's mind off his many frustrations that had occurred already that day. 'I at least hope on Monday afternoon the weather is a great deal better than it has been today. I am wondering Anne if you have need for another stable boy.' Lord Egerton made the remark a little cautiously.

'What makes you ask such a strange question?' Anne mused.

'I told my very good and reliable stable boy that after my wife's funeral on Monday I am going to begin gathering things up around the house and very soon once all my possessions have been properly sorted out and Elizabeth's have been completely discarded then I am going to find myself somewhere smaller to live, probably a small flat near the centre of London. The young man was more concerned about his own future employment than about the death of my lovely wife.'

'I can speak with him after the funeral has ended.'

'The young man will be absolutely overjoyed.' Lord Egerton's thoughts were for once as they ate attracted to the dress Anne was wearing. The dress, petticoat and linen jacket were all decorated with delicate floral embroidery and Lord Egerton had never seen her wear it before. 'That dress is absolutely delightful, is it new?'

'Elizabeth bought it for me the day before she left London with the drama company. She told me I needed a new dress as my wardrobe was looking a little unfilled.' Lord Egerton could not prevent himself from laughing. 'Was that really what she said, *"unfilled"*?'

'That was exactly what Elizabeth told me.'

Very quickly when they were coming to the end of their meals Lord Egerton's eyes narrowed and he looked at his watch. 'I am glad you told me about the special sitting there is going to be in Parliament, that is something I must prepare for. After a little work which I must complete in Westminster Hall then I will have to return home and begin writing some invitation cards for Elizabeth's funeral and take them round as swiftly as I possibly can.' They finished their glasses of wine and in a more leisurely manner began to make arrangements for their ride back to Covent Garden.

There had not been a large congregation at St Mary's church that hot Monday afternoon and afterwards as the congregants had gathered at Lord Egerton's house for refreshments Lord Egerton was still concerned over his own notification of the funeral service. Everybody had clearly prepared themselves carefully for the sombre occasion. All had dressed in black suits and many had brushed and tidied their hair, eyebrows, beards and moustaches to perfection also. In the house he personally thanked everyone for attending the service before he ushered Anne outside into the pleasant little garden where they sat together on a wooden bench and drinking a cup of coffee each they talked quietly. The sun was extremely hot and there were several large bees toiling amongst the nearby red roses. 'I can't thank you enough for coming.' Lord Egerton remarked softly. Anne's heart at that moment rolled over with devotion and sympathy for Lord Egerton. Lord Egerton looking back at Anne could not understand just how ever since King James's funeral all those months ago under such apprehension Anne had hardly aged at all in her appearance. 'There are now two free bedchambers in my house.' Anne commented softly so that no-one else could hear. Lord Egerton smiled as he considered Anne's enticing remark. 'I need somewhere for myself, just so I can rest on my own whenever I need to.'

'Is that going to be your simple reply Thomas?' Lord Egerton was a little confused by Anne's question.

'For the time being at least until our relationship becomes more……..' his voice faded and as his cheeks flushed dark red with embarrassment Anne finished his remark. 'More intimate you mean.'

'Yes, that was what I meant.' As the remaining congregants began slowly to depart the formal occasion Lord Egerton suggested Anne went with him to the stable to speak with his stable boy about possible future employment. From a distance Lord Egerton watched them talking and the boy's rapidly changing expressions as he listened. 'I have at least made your stable boy happy.' Anne remarked smiling at Lord Egerton. 'David is hard-working and trustworthy, I admit he is not at all educated but horses he can tend to exactness.' Lord Egerton moved away from Anne briefly to see the final two guests from the house before looking anxiously downward biting his lip and commenting, 'I do hope I did not forget anyone for this funeral.' Anne gently took a hand of Lord Egerton and whispered;

'Don't worry yourself silly Thomas, you have done your best in such difficult circumstances and nobody could do any more.'

'If only they had not been so inefficient at the hospital……I told you about Elizabeth's quarrelsome side but at the same time there was a feeling of love between us though you may well not believe that now…..if only the hospital had not neglected her…' Anne took Lord Egerton back outside to the bright hot sunshine and the roses still surrounded by continuously buzzing bees. 'I believe you and your late wife loved each other Thomas and I shall never think otherwise.' Lord Egerton held Anne's hand firmly as he sighed and remembered Anne's anguish at the time of James's funeral. 'Just as I told you after your husband had died, now we must start and look ahead.'

Lord Egerton had almost completed his move to the small flat in Westminster when Parliament was recalled to debate the Deputy Speaker's motion. Many politicians had arrived very early in the morning at the Houses of Parliament even though the debate did not begin until half past two. Lord Egerton and a number of other MPs sat in the library until after having had lunch in the bar going outside and enjoying the dazzling sunlight as they walked slowly and thoughtfully around the rose garden. Throughout the summer so far the weather had been divided between periods of heavy monsoon rain and spells of exceptionally hot arid periods. This day of the House's sitting the hot dazzling sunlight was shining and politicians were taking advantage before their being subjected to another long sitting in the Lower Chamber. 'I don't even know who the Deputy Speaker is.' Lord Egerton was somewhat discomfited by the remark he made yet he was not alone. 'I believe his name is Hugh Glaser MP for Chester.' came a reply from behind him.

'What many of us want to know is how do the writers for the street pamphlet find out such private and confidential information.' Tom Harrod's comment raised a lot of eyebrows.

'Have you decided if you are going to vote for or against this blessed motion on giving more power to Parish governments?' Richard Silverwood spent a large part of his time complaining and his question was ignored by the large gathering of politicians now wandering round the garden much to his further annoyance. There was a fair amount of ruminating over the afternoon's debate before the ten minute bell sounded and the politicians began to make their way towards the Chamber.

To the surprise of many MPs it looked as though the House was going to be completely full for once. There was for a change an air of quietude by the time the Deputy

Speaker arrived looking a little sheepish standing fully clad in his red and white robes. As the new Deputy Speaker Hugh Glaser believed it was his responsibility having proposed the day's motion to help get it pushed through by whatever means necessary. The Deputy Speaker like many politicians sitting in front of him realised just how important government funding for Parish councils was especially when the Parish councils could spend the money themselves.

'*Order Order!*' he began a little nervously. '*The motion placed on the table before us today is the handing over of most Parliamentary power to local Parish councils.*' Edward Bowes MP who had seconded the motion began the debate and sounded enormously favourable towards such a meaningful proposal.

The motion that was being considered in the Chamber was bizarrely debated with civility and not even one politician was in no doubt which way the motion would go. Lord Egerton and a number of his close political allies left the debate early for a drink and met in the Lower Chamber wine bar. 'Have you decided which way you are going to vote yet Thomas?' Lord Egerton held his glass of wine in the air for several minutes as he considered his friend's question. 'I think though I have to add here I am not absolutely certain I favour presenting most of the political power Parliament at this time possesses to local Parishes, especially when we have sittings which are so infrequent and so it seems to me are only made known through those damned street pamphlets.'

'But what about Westminster where most of the political power is supposed to lie, handing power to local parishes almost means as politicians we shall have nothing to do.' Tony Banks MP gazed at Lord Egerton with his dark ringed eyes and coughed gently before having a drink of whisky. 'That I believe Tony is not a level-headed way of considering the issue. We do always have overall power to vote to reverse the division of political power. I hope unlike happened with the Cross Cabinet if this motion is passed then we give Parish councils a chance to show if they can work successfully alone. Perhaps I'd believe Parliament should have most of the country's political power if we had more regular sittings and were able to debate Parliamentary Bills and make them law with immediate effect for the benefit of England's population. Unfortunately that of course is not how things are at the moment.'

'I believe the new Speaker of the House, Anthony Turpin is going to call a general election some time early next year and afterwards he is going to start and reform Parliament completely.' Lord Egerton asked a more irate question; 'How did you find that out Tony, was it through reading one of the street pamphlets or some other more reasonable means?'

'I was actually told by the Speaker himself one afternoon when we were bird watching in Speaker's Green.'

'In that case keep the news just between the politicians and don't pass it on to anybody else otherwise before we know it the whole country will be talking about the next general election and there will be anger between the voters and non-voters if there wasn't enough rivalry in the country already!' For a time politics remained a strongly divided subject until the members rejoined the remainder of the debate which was already coming to its conclusion. There was a pleasant hushed silence that filled the Chamber air until the final words that were uttered. As the division bell rang the line of politicians entering the opposite lobbies appeared to be evenly balanced making the anticipation in the Chamber as MPs returned extremely high and the atmosphere almost a hushed silence. The Deputy Speaker looked extremely grave and in his rather timid voice asked the House for silence. As the small timid figure stood before the House there were rumours seeping around the Chamber of Mr Glaser's feeble chances of remaining Deputy Speaker with such an irresolute appearance and unexceptional characteristic. The piece of paper with the final result on it was passed over to the clerk sitting at the front of the table who read out in a voluble and commanding voice;

'The "ayes" to the right 285 votes, the "noes" to the left 240 votes. The "ayes" have it with a majority of 45 votes!"

There was a great chorus of approval towards the result and an uncharacteristic beaming grin of accomplishment on the Deputy Speaker's face as the Chamber began to clear. 'Should we go to the bar and celebrate the result Thomas?' Lord Egerton recognised the voice as that of James Truman MP for Warwickshire. As they were leaving the Chamber side by side Lord Egerton temporarily considered the question but then looked at his watched and thought about the time and his remaining devices for the late evening. 'I'd better not James, I'm completing my move to my new flat in Westminster where I intend being by midnight or hopefully before.'

'Why are you leaving your lovely house in Chelsea after living there with your lovely wife for so many years?' Lord Egerton turned his head round and looked upward towards the tall gentleman's large round face. 'Sadly Elizabeth died in hospital after suffering some awful infection which I believe was sweeping London when she was first struck down by it.'

'Thomas that is extremely sad to hear. Please....I am assuming the funeral has been completed....'

"I knew it!" Lord Egerton remarked to himself, 'I knew I would forget to ask somebody to Elizabeth's funeral, you James were always very close with Elizabeth weren't you -' Seeing the solemn expression on Lord Egerton's face he quickly cut in; 'Never mind Thomas, I always have your late wife's thoughts and opinions in my mind and I shall never forget her. Now please Thomas for me let me take you upstairs to the bar and buy you a drink before you go home and do whatever business you were telling me you have to do.' James with his youthful face gave Lord Egerton one of his most insistent expressions. Lord Egerton's shoulders fell and suddenly he deemed too tired and faint-hearted to argue the matter any further. 'Come on then James, a glass of strong Scotch is what I would like as you are asking!'

Robert Keyes, Sir Everard Digby and John Grant were sitting together inside John Grant's large house in Norbrook waiting for Edmund Campion the Jesuit Priest to arrive and host a further hitherto successful secret Catholic prayer evening. Together their regular prayer evenings in Warwickshire and all across the Midlands were proving to be an enormous spectacle with the number of people present every Sunday rising all the time. The three gentlemen sat together in the drawing room waiting patiently for the usual faces and some unusual faces to start and arrive at the door drinking wine and ale and for once becoming slightly ill at ease as the early evening had arrived yet intriguingly nobody had yet appeared on the doorstep. John Grant's less collected temperament had made him particularly fidgety and he was pacing up and down the room waiting with some annoyance for people to arrive. 'It does not help that fellow conspirators have already been executed and that such overwhelming news is made known across England in those street pamphlets.' Sir Everard frowned annoyance at his companion and raising both hands calmly in the air told John to quieten down. 'You have never changed John have you, you always were totally unreasonable and unable to think in a level-headed manner.'

'I wish I had never been persuaded by Sir Robert Catesby to get involved in the gunpowder conspiracy. The ridiculous vision of a Catholic uprising in England not surprisingly never materialized only the snaring and executing of our allies Sir Robert and Guy Fawkes...........' John's voice faded away a little as there was a knocking at the front door and a group of their regular worshippers arrived. 'Please Sir Everard will you pour the drinks, I'm sure Edmund won't be long now.' The four people who had just arrived were all led into the drawing room and glasses of white wine were poured. Between the guests there already was a great deal of gossiping and excitement as they looked ahead to the evening. 'Perhaps this terrible weather is keeping your large gathering away.' Sir Everard nodded his agreement with the local young farmer.

'I can take it from what you have said sir that the rain is still falling?'

'It is raining very heavily indeed and some of the fields and paths round and about are already flooded.' John suddenly appeared to relax significantly, 'That would explain a great deal then. If Edmund Campion does not arrive in the next half an hour I can lead the prayer evening myself.' Robert Keyes smirked at his suggestion. 'If that is what you believe though I must say John I would have my misgivings about such an idea!'

'I nearly forgot to ask you Sir Everard, what has happened to your brother who until this very evening always came to our Sunday congregations?' Sir Everard shrugged.

'He told me simply he had decided no longer to take part in the Catholic prayer evenings yet never told me exactly why.'

'It may be the street pamphlets that are responsible, they keep on referring to these weekly prayer evenings which King James condemned when he found out about them.'

'And that the Catholics Sir Robert Catesby and Guy Fawkes were arrested and executed for their part in the King's murder. I believe that has put a lot of people off coming to these prayer evenings.' The suggestion which had been put forward by the young local farmer got a noise of agreement from the other three followers and three fierce glares by the conspirators. 'I am beginning to believe nobody else is intending to come for the evening if the weather is so bad not even our usual host Edmund Campion. I shall lead the evening myself.' There seemed to be a nod of approval from everybody inside the drawing room at Sir Everard's suggestion who many people regarded as a more authoritative as well as exceptionally clever man. He suggested everybody followed him up the staircase into the largest of the bedchambers which was fully prepared with the chandelier unlit and the room under the light only of candles. In the shadows of the four regular guests came John Grant and Robert Keyes and for the first time that evening an atmosphere of calm and tranquillity filled the air. 'Now that we are all in and the door has been closed and locked the prayers can begin immediately.' Sir Everard took the prayer book and opened it at the very first page before they all heard a heavy knocking on the front door. 'Is the front door locked John? Generally if it was Edmund arriving he would have let himself in.'

'The door is still unlocked. By our usual standards I should go and find out who the mystery caller is if you wouldn't disapprove of delaying the evening a moment or two.' Everybody in the bedchamber with their faces silhouetted on the walls looked indignant to the idea of a latecomer being able to disturb their private evening however there was a reluctant pause as John went downstairs to answer the door. 'Who on earth are you?' John was taken greatly by surprise when pulling the door open gently he was greeted with a matchlock pointed straight at his chest. 'Would you be good enough to give me your name?' The caller's voice was deep and intimidating; 'John Grant.' John uttered with his voice shaking all of a sudden. Richard Walsh's deep black cloak, wide rimmed black hat and knee length black boots made his powerful large figure appear even more threatening than he already was in his personality. 'Then John my name is Richard Walsh, I am the Sheriff of Worcester and this is my small band of men behind me. I have a warrant signed by Sir Edward Coke for your arrest. Can you tell me if there are two of your friends hiding in this house, their names are Sir Everard Digby and Mr Robert Keyes?'

'NO!' he replied quickly. 'I have no knowledge of those two gentlemen you are referring to.' Before he was able to stop the men Richard Walsh with his large imposing figure had simply propelled John Grant aside and out of the way and had already been seized by another of Richard Walsh's lesser men. 'I suggest we go this way men.' Richard without any uncertainty in his mind strode dauntingly up the staircase as John Grant watched on gasping for them to leave his house without delay but to no avail.

The prayers were already being recited by Sir Everard who along with his guests had no further time of their own simply to overlook. The heavy knocking on the bedchamber door broke the prayer reading and Sir Everard closed the prayer book hard before answering the door angrily himself. 'If you are coming to one of our prayer evenings I suggest young man you try and get yourself here a little earlier!' Richard Walsh lifted his matchlock and pointed it at Sir Everard's throat. 'I have explained the situation to your friend downstairs. My name is Richard Walsh and I am the Sheriff of Worcester, I have a signed arrest warrant for Sir Everard Digby and Mr Robert Keyes. I suggest your little gathering ends this minute and you all follow me downstairs then I can arrest the right people before having them driven to London and taken for questioning inside the Tower of London.' Richard stood by the side of the door as the six men inside came out nervously in a line before going inside the bedchamber and carefully blowing the candles out. 'Sir Everard Digby and Mr Robert Keyes, you two,' Richard took the two suspects aside and motioned for all the innocent guests to leave. 'On this arrest warrant that has been signed by Sir Edward Coke it suggests that you were all involved in the gunpowder conspiracy to kill the late King James I. Whether that is true or not personally I don't know however that is not for me to work out. I am having guards take you to London without delay and the questioning will begin very soon after you are in the Tower. Bring them outside, the horse and carriage is waiting.' Sir Everard Digby, John Grant and Robert Keyes were marched outside and led firmly to the waiting carriage and in his usual calm and relaxed manner Richard Walsh quietly pulled the large front door of the impressive mansion closed and went outside also into the monsoon rain.

From the very moment Parish councils were provided with many more powers and not inconsiderable finances by the Lower House their representatives took full advantage setting up new schemes to help each local town, village and city recover from decades of simple neglect by the Houses of Parliament. The Parish councillors began to meet more often than they used to holding official meetings once a month instead of what had been considered the standard once yearly. Schemes regarding more public transport with more regular horse and trap services through the different neighbourhoods, new sewage systems to be built under every river and every house in the country to help with water supplies and the cleaning up of rivers, lakes and streams and the building of more homes swiftly had already begun. Just as there had been when the Cross Cabinet had begun similar schemes before the Cabinet's quick eradication there once more was a growing air of optimism that was being assisted by the ongoing dissemination of pamphlets now in almost every street, alleyway and lane throughout England. There were many more businesses being set up in the majority of towns and cities across the whole country and less people were wandering the streets friendless and malnourished unable to find any labour and change at all.

The unsettled summer climate merging very rainy weather with exceptionally hot and dry conditions appeared to be ending in an extremely damp climate. Although the air remained sultry and sometimes almost choking rain continue to fall through late August and onwards into and through September. Despite new farming techniques such as advanced harrowing, improved soil maintenance and enhanced crop rotation farmers were still suffering severely damaged harvests, the consequences of much extraordinarily terrible weather. Going into November as local Parish councils continued to develop new schemes to enhance public services of many kinds England was undergoing a period of transition from an atmosphere of resentment and despair to an air of optimism and eagerness.

By the middle of November Nicholas and Arabella who used to live together in West Yorkshire while Nicholas was running the family furniture making business had not long ago moved to London where they had been on the day of the State Opening of Parliament. Their experience of watching the Sovereign Entrance to the Houses of Parliament being blown apart by Guy Fawkes's barrel of gunpowder as well as inhaling clouds of the capital's blue reeking smog which that day in particular had shrouded the city had not put them off wishing to move to London once Arabella had given birth to a child she had been expecting for a great many months. Once more due to her poor health Arabella had had to ride sidesaddle as Nicholas had driven the horse and trap with the two babies, one a little boy the other a tiny girl on board. After thinking about names a short time they had eventually decided to call the boy Adrian and the girl Mary. Arabella had arrived with Nicholas and the children at their large house in Bond Street feeling extremely weak after having lost a great deal of blood when giving birth yet she was absolutely delighted to see the magnificent two floor house they were moving into. The house had very quickly been completely furnished and decorated and in advance of their leaving West Yorkshire for their very last time together Nicholas had already set up his new business as a hatter in Oxford Street with his wife to work with him as salesman. The very first morning they had been preparing to leave for work together, a small business only two long streets away they were also waiting for the arrival of a young woman who for a generous salary had agreed to act as their nursery maid. Together both had been woken especially early that morning by their two children's piercing crying and Nicholas and Arabella had embraced them softly and after a lengthy time being rocked and hummed to they had both quickly gone back to sleep. Nicholas and Arabella had chosen their very best clothes to wear for work that day, Arabella had dressed in her favourite embroidered blue dress and tinted linen jacket and Nicholas in his much preferred wired collar lace trim, slashed doublet and sleeves. As they had sat in the kitchen with the two little children beside them having breakfast they had once more looked ahead excitedly to their forthcoming day at the hat shop as Nicholas and his five employees were working at the back of the shop producing further hats to sell. 'When we were living for all those years in West Yorkshire and I was simply acting as your hard working wife looking after the ordinary tedious jobs in the house I would never have believed anyone if then they had told me that one day I would be working in Bond Street with my husband in a hat shop.'

'And at the same time being the wonderful mother to a beautiful daughter and wonderful son.'

'I would never have believed after experiencing the huge explosion occur inside Parliament I would ever be brave enough to come back to London.'

'The furniture business we used to own in Leeds sold extremely well to buy us this large house and get our own nursery maid to look after the two children while we are out.' Nicholas buttered himself some bread and put a little jam on top. 'The jam they sell at the north London farm is excellent.' he commented smiling. Yet at the same time Nicholas was happy he and all his family had moved down to London lastingly he was besides disappointed none of his devoted friends residing in Leeds had moved to London with him. He poured himself a cup of fresh coffee and remarked; 'I was hoping Mark and Peter especially might have come with us to London and begun a new life like we have.'

'We have the money my love, Mark and Peter do not. We made several thousand pounds for the sale of your furniture business remember.' Nicholas reluctantly nodded his head in agreement.

'I would suggest when we return home from work this evening and paid the nursery maid we take the children with us and go out and have a meal as we will be hungry not having eaten properly for much of the day.'

'I have looked around the corner from our hat shop and there is a good little coffee house newly opened in Regent Street, we can try there if you like, we can close the hat shop for an hour as a kind of lunch break.' Nicholas had a drink of coffee and smiled his approval. 'You really do have some good ideas some times.' 'What time is the young nursery maid supposed to be coming?' Nicholas looked at his watch.

'In about ten minutes time if she is on time that is.' Nicholas had another piece of bread and butter and suddenly feeling slightly anxious he got up and had a look out of the front door. 'There are no signs of her coming at the moment.' Arabella since she had given birth and become a mother of two children had become a more self-confident and authoritative young woman than she ever used to be. She looked at her husband's thinner figure and told him to sit back down and not worry so much. Arabella had a drink of tea which had only just arrived in London and hummed her contentment for its taste. 'Tea is a most lovely new drink, I must have it more often.'

'I have heard of something else that has just arrived in England,'

'Oh yes, and what might that be called?'

'They are called cigarettes and are almost like rolled up pieces of paper which you set light to and then put in your mouth and smoke.'

'How extraordinary dear, have you tried smoking one?'

'No I haven't but I have seen someone else smoking a cigarette and smelled the blue smoke that comes from it.'

'What is its smell like? Is it as disgusting as the horrible blue fog that comes off the river Thames?' Nicholas laughed at Arabella's suggestion that at the same time made Adrian and Mary wake up with a chuckle too. 'I don't think anything could smell as disgusting as the smog from the river Thames and all the pollution and disease that it causes -'

'Yes dear,' Arabella interrupted, 'I was not being serious.'

'I believe that young nursery maid is late this morning.' Just as Nicholas had once more eyed his watch with much anxiety there was a forceful knocking on the front door.

'There you are dear, don't be so anxious so much of the time.' Nicholas almost bowed his head with apologies as he got up and left the table.

'I believe the name is Nicholas Holmes.' the plump broad-shouldered young woman commented with a loud throaty voice. 'Yes it is, you must be....' Nicholas hesitated with a little uncertainty.

'Angela Grant.'

'Yes, of course. Please do come in Angela and I shall introduce you to my wife and two wonderful little children.' Angela followed Nicholas inside the house in her most authoritative and forceful manner and into the kitchen where she turned her large round head to Arabella and looked at her cup of tea. 'Tea is something I am just beginning to enjoy as well as cigarettes. Have either of you tried them?' Nicholas looked nervously at Arabella who stood up and decided there and then to take control of the situation. 'That is something we might discuss at some other time. For now however we should introduce you to the little children Adrian and Mary and show you where the relevant bits and pieces can be found when you need them. My name by the way is Arabella and it is very delightful to make your acquaintance. I must also add at this moment, as I have never had such a thing as a cigarette before and I have no idea about their taste or smell I must say right now I do not wish you to smoke any of those things in my house.' After Arabella had spoken with much more firmness than her husband had at that moment Angela became somewhat inarticulate. 'Yes.....of course as you so wish.......your ladyship.' Arabella showed

Angela all around the kitchen, bathroom and living room before eventually she and Nicholas prepared to leave for their very first day of work as hatters. They picked up their two hats to wear and left the house trusting their nursery maid to have the ability to cope with the somewhat thorny circumstances.

'It is only two streets away to our shop and factory and I hope that our first day at our new job is a satisfactory one.' In Regent's Street Nicholas picked up a copy of the latest pamphlet that was being distributed and began reading some of the more positive news printed to Arabella. 'It seems as though the new councils are succeeding with all the power and money Parliament has given them. It says that all over the country councils are spending their separate allocations of money in the same way with work on new medicines, regular horse and trap services and increased house building all prospering.' Arabella stared at Nicholas with her eyes widening and almost bulging from the extent to which she was widening them. 'Well let's just hope those foolish politicians in London don't decide to do away with the new councils as they did with the brilliant Cross Cabinet.'

'Of course, as usual dear you are absolutely right.' He folded the pamphlet up and putting it away decided to change the subject. 'I saw when I first came to London alone and set up this new shop and factory there is a sword craftor's shop beside us called Nickleby's.' Again Arabella teased a little,

'Are they really the sort of things people buy, crafted swords? Why on earth does somebody buy a crafted sword?'

'I did go inside the shop and asked Michael that very same question.'

'And, what answer did he give you?'

'According to Michael he has been running the family business for over thirty years and it always makes a profit, every year.'

'How most unusual. At least if ever we want a sword then we only have to go next door.' They were glad to get to their new shop as the rain once more was beginning to fall steadily. It was not very long as they were looking around at the hats already on display for the shop's opening that the five young men Nicholas had interviewed the two days he was alone in London came in and introduced themselves. 'It is almost nine o'clock Arabella, you can open the shop and we shall go through the back to begin our hat making. I shall see you at twelve for a little lunch and a break. Good luck!'

For a number of weeks Nicholas and Arabella were not regarded as particularly outstanding or unique but merely as a good hat shop in the eventful and fashionable Oxford Street however their business redoubled from mid-November onwards when by some twist of fate Sir Edward Coke was striding by on his way to work in court. He paused for a short time to look at the large variety of hats in the window before soon after his original hesitation he went inside to take a closer look. Arabella was sitting quietly at her desk when Sir Edward arrived and for a time she sat looking at the burly customer smartly dressed in breeches and a doublet of brown and silver and a dark cloak all trimmed with silver lace and with a silver cane in one hand. Eventually after watching the customer with some fascination and curiosity Arabella went over to him and a little anxiously asked if she could help. Sir Edward lifted one side of his wide blue hat and replied pleasantly. 'I am just looking at the grand selection of hats that are on sale my good lady.' Arabella was thinking about showing the customer all the hats and conscientiously explaining them and their different styles as there was no-one else in the shop to watch over until the back door opened suddenly and Nicholas came in to speak to his wife until his eyes nearly burst out of their sockets when he saw who the customer was. 'Sir Edward Coke, how lovely to see you in our little hat shop!' Sir Edward was taken by surprise at the wonderful welcome he received as Nicholas put out a hand for him to shake. 'How lovely it is to make your acquaintance.'

'I knew I recognised that face,' Arabella commented smiling at her husband. 'Are you on your way to work Sir Edward or is today a day off for you?' Sir Edward was a little bemused by the continued friendliness he was receiving. 'I am just on my way to the courts and I am in a little bit of a hurry at the moment. However I shall call back when I have a little more time and a chance to look around your lovely little shop when I do indeed have a day off work.' He raised the rim of his hat and in his fine attire and with his most eloquent tongue he commented; 'I shall see you both soon when we have more time to talk. Good morning.' Once he had left the shop and closed the door carefully behind Nicholas smiled broadly at Arabella and commented in a very satisfied voice; 'I believe having Sir Edward Coke in our shop might prove to be just the kind of fortune this shop has really needed if we are to compete with some of the other large businesses in this highly fashionable street.'

To Arabella and Nicholas as time went by it seemed as though Sir Edward had been spreading the word around with all his top colleagues and courtiers. After Sir Edward's first arrival in their hat shop they began to see a great many more customers coming through their door and often gentlemen clad in similar expensive style of dress to that of Sir Edward Coke. It was as though it had very quickly become a genuinely fashionable hat shop and it was always thronging with customers of all classes. Not only did people merely arrive inside to look at the latest fashion of hats on sale but they began to regard the shop moreover as a place to meet on their way to work and socialise. On the last day of the month as snow began falling heavily Lord Egerton on his way to his office in Piccadilly and Sir Edward Coke who was strolling towards Westminster crossed paths at Arabella and Nicholas's hat shop and to Arabella's slight irritation they took their interest away from the hats and began to discuss the future of the three men most recently arrested on suspicion of being involved with the gunpowder plot. Lord Egerton lifted his hat towards Arabella and quietly urged Sir Edward to come over to one corner of the shop and speak privately with him. 'What is the situation with the three most recently arrested gentlemen, Sir Everard Digby, Robert Keyes and John Grant? It is almost eleven months since you passed me a slip of paper when we were in the office saying that they were going to be arrested.'

'They were arrested Lord Egerton in the summer. They have been questioned about the gunpowder conspiracy and have admitted they were involved.'

'And have they given you any more names of those involved with the conspiracy?'

'No they have not. They have been tortured several times but have still given no further information. They are going to be hanged in private at the Tower on new year's day.'

'What a strange time to hang the men, on new year's day.'

'That was not my decision but the decision of one of my colleagues, Lord Wordsmith. Sometimes he has these strange ideas but nobody disputes them as he can have a wild and almost uncontrollable temper.'

'I take it this means they are not going to be given a proper trial in court before their execution?'

'No, why would we waste the court's time when the three men have already admitted their involvement in the gunpowder plot?' Lord Egerton shrugged.

'I suppose it would be meaningless, rather like those of Guy Fawkes and Sir Robert Catesby. Would it be alright if I was to attend the hanging with Anne of Denmark? She has made it perfectly clear to me a number of times she wants personally to see all those gentlemen involved with her husband's murder executed.'

'If she would like to come to the Tower and watch the event in person then she will be perfectly welcome. The execution shall take place at twelve o'clock.' As their deep conversation continued Arabella was becoming increasingly irritated by them both and eventually she decided to intrude upon their conversation. 'Excuse me gentlemen, I do not like to break into your conversation but are you simply going to remain there for most of the day or are you going to buy a hat and hold your private conversation elsewhere please?' Lord Egerton and Sir Edward Coke looked suddenly humbled after their important discussion and automatically together selected the most expensive hats in the shop they could find. They each bought a fashionable capotain and Sir Edward bought in addition two coifs for friends. Arabella took the large number of gold sovereigns they handed her with great delight. As Lord Egerton and Sir Edward were about to part company outside Sir Edward as the snowfall began to come down more heavily dropped his tone to a sombre sounding voice; 'I do not believe I have yet after all this time given my message of sympathy to you since the death of your wife.'

'It does not matter Sir Edward I know you cared a great deal about her.'

'Is Anne of Denmark supporting you as you supported she after the terrible loss of her husband James?'

'Of course, Anne is being most supportive........' Lord Egerton's voice petered out as the large snowflakes were beginning to pierce his head and neck as they fell and he felt he had to leave immediately. 'If I don't see you at work for a while then I do sincerely believe at some point our paths will cross again at this wonderful little hat shop.' They separated quickly from outside the busy hat shop as Arabella and Nicholas watched on through the window. Nicholas commented quickly before returning back to the factory, 'I believe those two gentlemen are very soon to become our two most reliable and wealthy customers.'

Towards Christmas York city like so many cities, towns and villages was prospering from its new powers and the large share of Parliamentary funds it had been given to spend. An increase in the building of small houses covering the outskirts of the city, a new horse and trap service for the local people and the building of a new sewage system were just some of the schemes that were flourishing. There was an air of optimism in the city and new businesses were frequently beginning throughout the neighbourhoods and the much favoured market place. The cattle market was suddenly a bigger occasion for farmers all around Yorkshire and just before Christmas as heavy snow lay on the ground by twist of fate one Sunday morning George and his father Peter met there as the market was just opening. 'Father, this is a surprise isn't it. I didn't think you ever came to York cattle market. You never brought me anyway.' For once Peter looked a little sheepish.

'I admit I never did bring you……..I only came to York today because I wanted to see if I could find you.'

George's father turned his eyes away from his son and blushed. 'Father, what a nice thing to say……you have changed a great deal since we last saw each other at High Hill Farm. There you used to almost bully me on the farm and hardly ever listened to me about the farm itself.' Peter frowned.

'I have some news for you about the farm, it might be best if we were to go and talk somewhere quietly away from all these noisy chattering farmers and the many sounds of whining cattle.'

'Very well father, there is a newly opened coffee house just a street away from here. Why don't we go and have a coffee and something to eat if you wish to talk quietly.'

'You must be doing well with your little business, coffee houses are expensive places.'

'My knife grinding business is doing well and making quite a nice little profit thank you father.'

'Two cappuccinos and two chocolate biscuits please.' George asked quietly at the counter. He and the young assistant eyed each other smiling in their usual agreeable manner and exchanging pleasantries in their usual almost silent friendly way.

'I take it you two know each other well.' Peter remarked when George came over with the tray.

'It is mostly in a business way, this new coffee house bought a large amount of cutlery from my establishment just before it opened.' Peter examined his knife and spoon before he began stirring his cappuccino. 'Magnificent,' he muttered under his breath and grinning to himself. 'Have you missed farming since you left High Hill and began your new knife grinding business?'

'NOT AT ALL!' George retorted fiercely without any thought. 'I told you a number of times I was sick and tired of farming, especially when you frequently made it clear to me you were in charge of High Hill Farm and I had no say at all in its running. For a long time father I was sick and tired of farming. Now that my wonderful wife and me are living in this pretty quiet little city and we have a beautiful young child to bring up and look after life to both of us has never been better.'

'This drink is absolutely delicious.' Peter remarked after having another mouthful.

'It is called *cappuccino* father, a drink that I believe originated in Italy. Now, tell me father. You said when we met at the cattle market you had some news to give me.'

'Your mother and I have sold High Hill Farm and have moved to Derby.'

'FATHER……..NEVER!…….I don't believe it!' George almost shrieked his disbelief gasping as he spoke.

'Tell me father, whose decision was it to leave the farm, was it yours or that of mother?' Peter inhaled and his deep red cheeks widened as he blew out and narrowed his eye as he considered his son's question. 'I would say overall the decision to leave High Hill was a joint one between your mother and myself.'

'And some of your friends at the local alehouse who used to advise you on many subjects is that not so father?' Again Peter's usual forceful figure changed and he answered sheepishly and looking extremely red faced; 'That is so, John, David and Andrew all suggested I sold High Hill Farm when I told them I was seriously considering the matter.'

'And you listened to them and took more notice than you listened to mother.'

'George I don't know why I try and tell small fibs to you, you can read my mind and way of thinking easily,' Peter had a piece of his chocolate biscuit and nodded. 'These biscuits are just like the cap…..capu… -'

'Cappuccino father.' George teased.

'Yes…cappu……ccino. I decided after discussing the matter with my friends at the alehouse to sell the farm and divide it up between a number of small farmers around the west Midlands. When I told Francesca I was intending to sell the farm she was not at all happy.'

'The way mother enjoyed running the dairy alone and ordering all her female friends around I would say father my dear mother would probably be outraged at your decision.'

'Yes George that word would best describe your mother's temper when she heard the farm was to be sold.'

'I hope you have at least sold it for a reasonable profit.'

'£5000. I know you will criticise me but it was the best I could do.'

'Damn it father, Lord Whitby offered all of us a lot more money than that small sum. Why on earth didn't you do as I suggested and accept Lord Whitby's offer? Lord Whitby now has no money left and his property and land have all been taken from him as you may already know.'

'I have read about it in the pamphlet. At least his arrest has meant that there are no longer Jamaican slaves being worked on the land and there are no more angry demonstrations continuing.' George had another mouth of his cappuccino and sighed. 'Tell me father, after what happened with High Hill Farm, what is your present relationship like with my mother?'

'We are at least still living together, with the money we have made from the sale of the farm we have bought a reasonable house in Derby but although we are living in the same house we barely talk.'

'And is this what you do now father, spend most of your time outside and away from mother's angry glare and fierce temper?'

'Again George, you are right.'

'And was that why you decided to spend a little time here in York at the growing cattle market?'

'I was also hoping that I would meet you here and you may invite me to come and see your lovely little boy.' George clicked his tongue and rolled his head to one side as he considered his father's request.

'I hope this is not going to become a more regular wish of yours father. Elizabeth and I have just started our new life together away from our families and that is how we want things to remain.' Peter appeared rather distressed by his son's angry comment yet as he closed his eyes slowly he nodded his head commenting; 'I understand George, after this I will not return any more.' They finished their cappuccinos quietly listening instead to the increasing sounds of gossip as the coffee house began to fill up. 'Most of the customers have come over from the cattle market the way they are talking about prices and sales.' They finished their drinks and chocolate biscuits and went outside into the chilly wind that was just beginning to pick up. 'Have you and mother made any arrangements for Christmas?' George inquired. Peter gazed at his son sombrely.

'I have had no chance to discuss the Christmas season with Francesca, not since what happened with High Hill Farm. I have no idea exactly what I will be doing over Christmas.' They briefly looked impassively at each other before hurrying over the roadside in front of the latest horse and trap as it was arriving with its two customers at the market. George led his father through the city centre and towards the edge of York and into the small house where Elizabeth was sitting quietly alone from the baby for a short time at least. 'Somebody has come to see you.' George remarked trying to sound enthusiastic as he made the observation. Elizabeth turned her weary head round and upwards and peered at Peter's weathered face and thin dishevelled figure. 'Oh Peter, how nice to see you....please take a seat and I'll get you a drink. Would a cup of whisky be all right for you?' Peter took off his cap and nodded. Elizabeth yawned heavily as she got up and out of Peter's view she gazed with an angry expression at her husband. 'What is your father doing here?' she asked in a hushed voice.

'I'm sorry but what else could I do?' George raised his shoulders high and took Elizabeth's near hand and kissed it in a telling way. 'He won't be here long I promise.' Elizabeth's nostrils let out a frustrated breath and she disappeared into the front room to get Peter his drink.

'Do you have a lot to tell us Peter as you have come all this way to York to see us?'

'We have sold High Hill Farm.'

'You should have sold High Hill Farm when my father offered you such a large amount of money for it.' Peter could only agree with Elizabeth's fierce observation. 'As usual Elizabeth, you are right. May I ask how is your father now? Have you heard anything more about him since his arrest?'

'I have been once to see father in Leeds prison but since then I have made it clear that father is no longer a part of my life.'

'Can my father see our baby now?' This time it was George who looked appealingly at Elizabeth.

'I have only just got the baby off to sleep and now he is in his cot I am not going to wake him up again till he is hungry. Can't you tell George, I am feeling absolutely exhausted,' While Peter's tired eyes were closed Elizabeth mouthed to George, '*I really am damned exhausted!*' George went and sat back down beside his father and said to him simply, 'I am sorry father but you cannot see our baby boy now……unfortunately we have very little else to talk about so I suggest -'

'You suggest that I leave,' Peter interrupted. 'I think I have made a mistake coming in the first place. I will give your love to Francesca and hopefully sometime we may meet again in Derby.' Peter finished his cup and pulling his thinning cloak down fully to protect himself from the cold wind and putting on his cap he wished Elizabeth and George a good day and left before either of them could reply. As George was about to close the front door he could see a very tall gentleman in a black suit and sitting on a very tall horse riding towards the house. 'Tell me Elizabeth, do you recognise this gentlemen and the jet black horse he is riding?'

'Yes, I recognise him, he spoke to me about my damn father when he came and told me he was being held in Leeds prison. If it is news about my father I am not interested!' The tall gentleman did not dismount his horse only doffed his hat and lowered his head as a mark of respect. 'It is about your father ma'am. I have some news which you may find of some interest if you will be kind enough to let me finish and then I shall be on my way.' Elizabeth scowled and folded her arms tightly as she waited for the visitor to explain himself. 'Two minutes is all you have.'

'I am sorry to say that Lord Whitby was found dead in his cell four days ago and his body has been ravaged by rats. The prison guards have taken your father's body to an empty room at the front of the prison and have said if nobody from Lord Whitby's family comes in the next forty-eight hours to take his body away and organise a private funeral for him then they will simply dig a grave behind the prison where the ordinary prisoners are buried if they die in their cell when they are being held. Do you want to return to the prison and take your father's dead corpse and give him a respectable funeral?'

'No damn it man I do not! Now I wish to talk with you no longer. Good Day!' Before the visitor could say any more Elizabeth had slammed the door in his face and woken the baby too. 'Was that really necessary Elizabeth being so rough with the man?' Elizabeth laughed at that.

'After the latest events with both our fathers I believe now we can say our lives are free from our irritating families for good!' She gave her husband one of her more redoubtable expressions and hurried past him to take care of their child.

When the festive season filled England the ever-increasing atmosphere of hopefulness and self-belief among nearly every individual continued to grow. Ever since the passing of the Deputy Speaker's motion there had been no further sittings in the Lower Chamber and with that no further opportunities for the politicians to vote the Deputy Speaker's passed motion down. Yet through December and into the new year the air of optimism that filled every street, lane and thoroughfare could not keep the towns, cities and villages active with the people nor keep businesses of many kinds working. Deep snow which was falling heavily every day was at night freezing hard making travelling of all kinds extremely dangerous. Such dangerous and terrifying conditions meant that outside from north to south and east to west places were eerily desolate and nearly silent but for the occasional sound of bird or animal life. For once even Rose the flower girl could not be seen in her usual position in the Strand selling her flowers. Arabella and her husband Nicholas had had no choice but to stay at home and keep their hat shop closed until the better weather arrived and in York George reluctantly kept his knife grinding business shut until there were signs that at last the heavy snow was beginning to ease at least slightly. On the 1st day of January Anne of Denmark was looking ahead to the hanging of Sir Everard Digby, Robert Keyes and John Grant, three more men she desperately wished to see hanged by their throats for their involvement in the gunpowder plot yet just this once she knew she would simply have to miss the occasion. Lord Egerton had come to see Anne in ever more dangerous snowy conditions and after his arrival he had not been able to leave and return to his small flat in Westminster.

As Anne was unable to leave home at all she spent much time in the music-room playing the piano for her own self-satisfaction and to the delight of Lord Egerton and all of her loyal staff. 'How did you find out about something so secretive as the hidden executions of the three plotters?' Anne asked as she sat beside Lord Egerton in the living room having a drink and watching the snow still falling heavily from the grey leaden sky. 'I met Sir Edward in the newly opened hat shop in Oxford Street before it like most shops and businesses was forced to close because of the terrible conditions.'

'I have never been to the hat shop in Oxford Street yet I have still heard people say that it is already extremely popular.'

'It is becoming increasingly popular every day it is open and is extremely fashionable. There are so I have heard and found out for myself many people of London who do not simply regard the hat shop as a place to buy hats but also as a place to meet and gossip. When I called in one morning I met Sir Edward browsing the many lines of hats of different kinds and styles and I could not prevent myself from going over to speak with him and enquire about the three men. We were not very popular with Arabella the lady who owns and manages the hat shop with her husband as we blocked part of the shop with our gossiping however Sir Edward did then tell me that the execution of the three me was to take place on new year's day and that was without any trial at all.'

'I have heard however Thomas that like Mr Fawkes and Sir Robert Catesby they had already admitted they were all involved in the gunpowder conspiracy and so a trial would once more have been a complete waste of peoples' time.'

'As usual Anne with your rational way of looking at an argument you are right.'

'Thank you Thomas!' Anne smiled her complete satisfaction with Lord Egerton's remark.

'Have you heard anything at all about your daughter during the Christmas period?' Pursing her lips in a more thoughtful and slightly nervous way Anne then looked blankly at Lord Egerton. 'Unfortunately Thomas I have not heard anything about Elizabeth since the moment her case was fully packed and she got in the carriage that had arrived for her and was taken away by one magnificent chocolate coloured steed.'

'At least Elizabeth's disappearance this time is nothing to do with a kidnap.' Anne's head dropped as she gave a heavy sigh of relief; 'Thankfully not this time.' She emptied her glass of white wine and asked the butler to refill it. 'Where is your little puppy? I haven't heard it or seen it since I arrived.'

'I have absolutely no idea. I am sure if it has not appeared when my daughter next comes in then she will not be at all sorry.'

'Your daughter never really has got on with that dog has she.'

'Absolutely not, Elizabeth and the little dog simply do not get on well at all.' The butler arrived with a fresh full glass of wine and commented that the puppy was last seen hiding under the large bed in the spare bedchamber. 'It must be frightened of all this heavy snow.' Lord Egerton remarked with a slight mocking chuckle. 'When my glass of wine is empty I shall go upstairs to my music-room and play a while on the piano as there is obviously no way we can get to any dance night tonight.'

'I do not believe anything can surpass listening to you playing the piano with such grace and elegance.' Anne smiled warmly at Lord Egerton and commented with a noticeably more demonstrative face than usual; 'Sometimes Thomas you can say the kindest things.' Before the butler was about to leave them Anne once more called him back; 'Tell me, with the weather being so terrible has any member of my staff been able to leave this house and buy any fresh food for a meal tonight?' Lord Egerton even frowned at such a question.

'Alfred your gardener shall be going out shortly to buy something for tonight.' The butler retorted with an underhand expression. 'Providing any of the shops are open in these conditions.' Lord Egerton pointed out.

'I am sure sir Alfred will find somewhere in London that is open, he is that kind of man, a man who will not be beaten whatever the circumstances are.' As the butler disappeared from the room Anne took the remainder of her glass of wine upstairs to her music-room and before very long the piano had started being played with its usual elegance and self-assurance and quickly the complete house was filled with magnificent music. Lord Egerton as he listened increasingly believed Anne was playing a piece of music written originally by John Barbour. For some considerable time well on into the evening the music was unbroken and its sweeping the house made Lord Egerton sit back and for a little while at least forget about his different worries. Later when the skies had completely darkened and the chandelier's bright sparkle lit up the complete living room in brilliance the relaxing atmosphere was lightly broken as the sound of pleasant conversation from the back entrance could clearly be heard. Lord Egerton sat up and began to pay more attention to the tête-à-tête than the refined sound of piano music. The sight of Elizabeth coming excitedly into the living room came as a great delight to Lord Egerton who could not help widening his arms for her to run into and calling out to the delicate and elegant figure; 'Please Lizzie come here to me!' Elizabeth immediately was more firm with Lord Egerton putting the palms of her hands up in front of her body and saying decisively; 'Lord Egerton you are a good friend of mama's but you are not my father!' Lord Egerton closed his arms immediately and was full of apologies. 'Please Elizabeth I am sorry it was just my not having seen you for such a long time……' He paused for a brief second as his mouth became parched until finally he was able to complete, '…….we were worried about you after your kidnapping that fateful afternoon.'

'All right…….Thomas, that's enough with the apologies. Butler can you get me a glass of pineapple juice at once.'

'Of course your ladyship.' Lord Egerton lowered his head and laughed a little at the graceful wording the butler used for someone so young, still in her youthful appearance only a child. 'Please do tell me Elizabeth how did your tour go?'

'The tour was a great success for the company and as it went on the audiences around the country kept on rising as people seem to be getting more money in their pockets now that the politicians have given almost all their power and money to local councils. I think the theatre really will be for me.'

'Is that as a future star on stage?'

'Perhaps,' she mused. '..One day.'

'Your mother is upstairs in her music-room.' Elizabeth glared at Lord Egerton.

'I guessed as much as I listened to the piano being played the moment I came in the house. However Thomas what I have missed most of all is the chess board set up with you and myself on opposite sides of the table competing with such great poise and brainpower. I am going upstairs to unpack my small case and then the moment I appear again a fresh game can begin.' Lord Egerton lay back in his chair and closed his eyes to rest them before the next extreme game of chess began once more.

CHAPTER THREE

By two o'clock that warm mid-February morning there were rumbles of thunder getting closer towards Birmingham quickly. The thought of a thunderstorm hanging over the city almost certainly for the rest of the night once more filled Jack Parker with complete terror. He lay in bed praying the storm would blow over and shook frenziedly every time the thunder rolled. If circumstances had not been horrifying enough for Jack already, since November 5th 1605 when he had been attending the State Opening of Parliament in his role as one of King James's security advisors the explosion inside Sovereign's Entrance which he had seen from the opposite side of Whitehall and heard nearly as though the barrel of gunpowder had been ignited by his side haunted him severely every time he closed his eyes.

Jack's original quiet life when his father had wished him to work on the nearest farm as an ordinary labourer like most of the family had changed seven years ago when he had left home and strolled purposely down to London trying to find work and had arrived in the city on his twenty-first birthday. Instead of trying to find work with just anybody of no significance Jack had strode to St James's Palace feeling self-confident and persuasive. He spoke just inside the front entrance to once of Queen Elizabeth's clerks and after the clerk had discussed Jack Parker's capabilities and decisiveness with more senior officials in the Palace as well as having a short conversation with the Queen herself Jack had a drink at the near alehouse with the same clerk he had spoken to originally and was offered a position as a simple gardener living with other members of Elizabeth's servants. From that first day employed as a member of the monarchy's team Jack's life at work and during his spare time merging with ordinary Londoners had slowly continued to thrive and expand. He had worked inside the Palace garden under the supervision of one of the Queen's most experienced gardeners before staff had closely followed his temperament and viewpoints and he had eventually after a period when he was asked in the Palace for his more serious opinions about security for the Queen he had ended up on a board of security advisors preparing in advance of any of Queen Elizabeth's official duties. When he had first arrived outside St James's Palace Jack would never have believed that one day he would have been selected to work on such an influential committee for the reigning monarch. Jack's self-confidence and decisive character had become increasingly well known and admired at work and in social circles as he spent much time mingling with the more common clique of men drinking at simple small inns and taverns near his flat which he later bought just east of the capital where houses were slowly being built and flat bare land was being developed. As a member later of King James's security advisors Jack personally had always blamed himself for not checking on the Houses of Parliament before the State Opening had taken place and had accepted the death of King James I completely.

Since the very moment the barrel of gunpowder had exploded and the King had been killed Jack's life had utterly shattered. As the onlookers of the explosion had been pushed away from around Whitehall and the Mall

Jack had stumbled back to his flat shaking completely with the sound of the explosion still echoing round and round in his mind and the massive explosion he had viewed clearly with the other onlookers had forever remained as detailed in his eyes whenever he closed them as the very moment it had happened. From his return to the east London flat he bought not too long before Jack had remained fearful of almost anything involving too much sound and even feared ordinary people when they approached him. Although friends and officials had all told him he could not blame himself for failing to prevent the devastating gunpowder explosion Jack had taken not the slightest notice and having packed his case at the flat he had begun his long walk back to Birmingham. He no longer ate the lavish food he used to eat when his life in London with so many people was prospering and faltered back an increasingly bony, hollow cheeked and pale faced figure. His original slight, powerful, broad shouldered and muscular stature faded completely and he unsteadily walked up through Hertfordshire and Buckinghamshire feeling completely overcome by exhaustion and starvation. He feared the many travellers and vagabonds he crossed paths with, many who were walking the opposite way towards London hoping to find some work and make their fortunes as the heedless rumour which had spread England suggested. When living and enjoying his short life in London Jack had spent a lot of money buying himself flamboyant clothes and even his very own rapier from Nickleby's in Oxford Street which he had carried everywhere he walked in London to direct many more eager eyes to observe his every move. As the eyes turned to him seeking his attention Jack had taken full gains and partied privately at his flat with many young female followers during evening and night time and basked in every moment of his personal wining and dining too. His sudden walk away from London was hurried giving nobody any time to take him calmly to one side and persuade him not to be foolish and blame himself for the gunpowder explosion.

Returning to the Midlands was sometimes pleasingly a lonely, private and almost silent affair and on other occasions it was an unwelcome period of socialising when he had stayed each night at a local inn, alehouse or tavern which had come into his line of vision just as there were signs of dusk beginning to arrive. At least he had kept a great amount of his earnings with him when he was walking away from London, shaking with fear at every faint sound he heard and any figure of whatever height, age and appearance who came into his path. At every night lodging he had stopped at for night time accommodation staff had always welcomed him strangely as they had looked admiringly at his brightly fashionable clothes, his buff leather jerkin, shorter waisted bright blue doublet, brown leather gloves and knee length boots yet immediately they looked at him they felt concerned and a little suspicious seeing he had a silver rapier by his side and all ready for use. His appearance everywhere he stopped had received diverse feelings, concern and some disquiet for his thin ghostlike figure, admiration towards his majestic and expensive dress yet also fear of his ready weapon. The large amount of money he had offered for a single night's stay nevertheless in such challenging economic circumstances had always persuaded the landowner at length to accept him.

Now he had been back in Birmingham a number of months his feeble and meaningless life had not changed at all. He still feared most noises, still became haunted by the morning of November 5th when the Houses of Parliament had been infiltrated every single time he closed his eyes and still felt uneasy and distrustful when any stranger approached him. Now as he lay in bed with his dark and bloodshot eyes widely open he was shaking with great fear every time there was any sound of thunder or flash of lightning which made him jump with the greatest anxiety inside himself. As the thunder got closer and Jack began increasingly to feel sweat on his face and down his back he knew he could not sleep at all until the thunderstorm that was getting closer all the time passed over and so put on his expensive clothes and barefooted went downstairs with his rapier at one side to ask someone for a simple drink so at least when the storm was at its climax he would not have to face its harshness and severity alone.

Mary and Colin were not in the bar but to Jack's relief the light was still shining brightly and when he went inside he immediately knocked on the table for some attention. 'Jack what are you doing in the bar so early in the morning?' The young man's voice made him shake fleetingly with a little dread before he answered the question as usual with honesty; 'I can't sleep, the horrible increasingly loud sound of rumbling thunder and increasingly bright flashes of lightning which are lighting up my room and making shadows on the walls are terrifying me.'

'Very well Jack sit down at your favourite table in the centre of the room and I will get you a drink. What would you like, is it to be the usual, a tall glass of ale?' Jack gave a simple nod.

'Thank you Jack, a tall glass of ale is coming up.' At least sitting alone in the centre of the lounge meant the sounds of thunder and the dazzling flashes of lightning could not fill him with dread as easily as the storm could when he lay on his bed wakeful in his room. 'Those clothes must have been expensive and your sword.' The young man put Jack's tall glass down on the table in front of him and he stood back once more admiring his customer's clothes sense yet at the same time becoming increasingly concerned at his emaciated figure, his face shrivelled and hollow cheeked and his complete ghostlike outline. 'Please Jack, can't I tempt you to eat something?' Jack put his arms on the table and rested his chin on them. He murmured his frustrated reply; 'No thanks, the ale is all I want.' When he was left alone he drank his ale slowly and rested his eyes still picturing only his time standing in Whitehall and watching the massive explosion that had killed King James I. The thunderstorm slowly arrived right over the top of the tavern with the loud booming rumbles of thunder making the tavern floor shake slightly and making Jack's sweating even worse. 'Jack, do you take that silver rapier everywhere you go?' Jack lifted his head and as his eyes rolled upwards he saw Edward who like himself was one of the tavern's more long-term customers. 'What are you doing downstairs at about quarter past two in the morning Edward?'

'I could ask you the same question Jack. Perhaps you like me couldn't sleep and needed a drink for a dry mouth. The stuffiness in my room has made my mouth completely parched I don't know about you although I would guess by the large glass of ale you are drinking you feel the same way.' Jack gave a loud yawn as another loud rumble of thunder shook the complete building. 'I'll be glad when this storm passes over.' Jack almost groaned and had another drink. The young barman brought Edward a glass of ale and a ham sandwich and automatically Edward handed the plate over to Jack urging him to eat something. 'Please Jack take one half otherwise you're going to just fade away.' Edward grinned all over his face yet Jack since walking away from London had lost his entire sense of fun and laughter. 'No thanks Edward, I'm just not hungry.' Edward pointed a finger again at Jack's rapier.

'Is your rapier always by your side for a reason? Do you think eventually somebody is going to seriously attack you or perhaps it is by your side as a lucky charm.' Just the thought of replying to Edward's question made Jack feel increasingly weary. 'It is something I keep with me merely as a reminder of the days I worked in London as a security advisor for the Queen and King, that is all....' his tired slow answer was broken again by a deep rumble of thunder and several flashes of bright lightning which made Jack's dark sore eyes blink speedily a number of times. 'I'll be glad when this damn storm has passed over.' he murmured once more.

'Have you seen your father since your return to Birmingham?'

"What a strange and annoying question to ask." Jack thought as he closed his eyes again to rest them. 'No I haven't seen father ever since I returned here but Edward I have no reason to see my father unless some day I need to share the large amount of money that he has been left from his own father's will.'

'Well if it's of interest to you I spoke with him yesterday on Home Farm when I was there buying some butter and cream. Our conversation was only short before Mark had to return to his sowing but I told him again you were almost living here and he was very interested in your health.'

'Oh yes, so what did you tell father about my *health* which was a personal matter?'

'I didn't have time to answer his question before Farmer Westerman shouted over to him to stop talking and go and clean the yard and stables.'

'Good! My present state of health or mind is no concern of father's.'

'Your father did say however -' Still Jack was unable to contain himself any more from the irritating sound of Edward's dull one tone voice. 'Excuse me Edward I must go back to my room and try and get a little sleep.' He left his half full glass of ale on the table and got up as another bright flash of lightning blazed and thunder rolled. 'At least the storm seems to be passing over.' A voice called from behind the bar Jack did not recognise. He totally ignored the remark and went back outside and up the small flight of stairs to his room which was seemingly quiet and still again.

There came the sound of birds singing and a bright sunlight shining through Jack's big room window as his alarm began sounding just after eight o'clock. He dressed again in some of the expensive gear he had bought during his years in London. The shirtwaisted leather buff jerkin and breeches trimmed with ribbon bows had turned many eyes to look at him when he had been striding through the ordinary London streets and across London Bridge on many occasions passing out coins to the penniless vagabonds begging for a little money. As usual he put on his high heel boots and finished by placing his rapier under the belt. He went back downstairs with few definite plans for the day. After having a cup of coffee amongst some more calmer faces in the tavern he went outside into the fresh cooler air and recoiled at the echoing sound of horses hooves striding in front of him. The regular young man who acted as a pamphleteer on the nearby street corner Jack believed looked just as dishevelled as he did. Normally he walked in front of the pamphleteer ignoring his long arm that always held out the pamphlet as he was passing but for once there was an article that caught his attention on the front page. Automatically picking up the pamphlet from the tousled young man his concentration was caught on the front page corroborating what many people in Birmingham already seemed to know by the gossip going round that Birmingham's present politician Martin Grainger MP had died of a heart attack in the previous twenty-four hours and the constituency was now available for anyone whose background and present living conditions were respectable enough if requested to stand in the city's by-election. Although the city streets were quiet as already many people were at work the regular horse and traps that were going by him in both directions made him shake with fear as the loud continuing clip clop clip clop of horse's hooves until they had gone completely out of sight was echoing wildly inside his head. He walked shakily to the nearest park and sat down on a bench that was still sodden after last night's heavy thundery rain and his emaciated hollow figure fell down just glad to be alone and in a place of peace and some tranquillity. Thinking about standing at the by-election Jack believed he would have a real chance of winning over people's hearts and minds when he made his position clear during campaigning. Although he could see every time he went outside the tavern where he was now living permanently that the city every single day was growing and benefiting from the increasing local businesses it was also true that such growth was nothing to do with Parliament and to stand as someone who would fight to reform Parliament as well as argue for a new monarch sitting on the throne he knew he would have terrific support even though he also knew his tall bony figure would put some people off voting for him. He sat out of the sun's dazzling light for a time under a willow tree which was still in the middle of its fresh growth until with a great deal of reluctance he decided the time had finally come to go and see his mother and father who had a large amount of money stored away somewhere in their house received from his grandfather's will soon after he had died. It was a house his father had told Edward about a number of times and Edward had forwarded the message on to him so he knew where the house he was looking for was situated, almost beside the Cathedral.

Outside the front door he paused as he had been about to knock and did momentarily think about twisting around and walking away however he sighed heavily as he could see his mother's unchanged figure through the glass looking back in his direction. Not giving him any more time to consider his decision Jack's mother Nicole had opened the door and was gazing down with disbelief at her son's sudden and unexpected presence again after such a long time away. 'Good God, Jack……..what are you suddenly doing back here on the doorstep? It's such a long time since I last saw you.' She gasped after exploding as she had made all her personal emotional feelings evident now she stepped aside and asked for Jack to come inside and talk to her. 'Please Jack come into the living room, make yourself at home and I will get you a mug of gin.' Jack went inside the living room to see a cot with a little baby sound asleep and beside a black and white dog which was in just as deep a sleep as the baby. 'Mother, when did you have your baby?' Nicole handed her son the mug and sat down carefully on the sofa. 'I had the baby only seven months ago. We have named him Simon.'

'And how long have you had your dog? I don't ever remember it resting itself like it is now when I was still living with you.' Nicole rolled her eyes round at him, a most peculiar expression she had always had that continually made him wince whenever she had rolled her wide blue eyes round her sockets directly in his face. 'What's the matter Jack? I can see already you are trembling with nerves.' That was a long story to explain Jack knew. 'I am assuming father is still working on the local farm is he like he has for most of his life?'

'His farm has changed recently to Bright Water Farm. Now tell me, before I say anything more about Mark and his work on the farm what has happened to you since you left home all those years ago that made you shake with nerves so easily and why are you looking so thin and pale faced? When you left home not quite twenty-one years old you were strong, self-willed, strong-minded and had a fine olive complexion. At that time if you remember many of the young girls round here and back in Warwick where we used to live admired you.' Jack closed his eyes and at that time just wanted to drop off to sleep, more especially after having his previous night's sleep severely broken by the thunderstorm. 'Mother I left home about seven years ago believing I would be able to find a job in London with the monarchy if I went directly to St James's Palace and told whoever answered my hard knocking on the door that I deeply admired the Queen and I was desperate to work for her whatever my job might be.' To begin with Nicole blew out her cheeks before exhaling her non-belief at such a story yet she was surprised when her son continued with his assured story. 'After several weeks when I was renting a small flat near the Palace the official who I had originally spoken with came to see me and over a drink at the nearest alehouse I was told I had been given a job as the senior gardener's assistant.' Again Nicole chuckled a little at her son's story.

'But Jack, you know absolutely nothing about gardening.' Jack's nostrils blew out his complete agreement. 'I know that mother just like you do, I told the royal official I know nothing about gardening and yet I was told I would make no decisions but simply do what I was told when the senior and experienced gardener ordered me.' Jack had a drink before jumping almost off the chair. 'That stupid damn dog of yours mother!' The dog's large green eyes had rolled open and seeing a new indistinguishable face in the room it had barked either with fear or shock, which Jack did not know yet very quickly, having not moved at all it had simply closed its eyes once more and gone back to sleep. 'These stupid dogs!' Jack whispered.

'Carry on with your story son. Was that your final position, working as a gardener's assistant inside the Palace's garden?'

'No mother not at all. The way that I used to speak to the senior gardener, not about gardening but about my many continual comments concerning the Palace's security over months must have been picked up by other staff officials when they asked me to leave the garden and go into one of the private rooms and speak with them about my true beliefs concerning the Queen, the Palace and all the security. From that moment onwards my work was changed from gardening to being at first one of the minor figures on the security board. From there I began simply listening to others and doing what they told me to until eventually other people on the board wanted me to say more. My position grew as did my large salary and I was increasingly respected in London both as an official and as an ordinary member of the public.' There Jack had to hesitate once more as the baby began very suddenly to cry with increasing strength yet again making Jack recoil from the ear-splitting noise, very quickly putting his hands over his ears to protect himself. 'Please mother can you do something to keep my little brother silent……..or almost silent please?' Nicole got up quickly seeing just how severely Jack was suffering and carefully picked the child up out of the cot and began holding him in her arms rocking him and singing softly in his ears. 'Now carry on Jack just what you were telling me, about your position as one of the security team.' Jack looked at the baby's little bundle wrapped in white cloth and a slight smiled crossed his lips, 'Isn't he lovely.' Hearing that the crying had almost petered out he took his hands from his ears and continued with his story. 'I took full advantage of my powerful position in my social life and hosted many cocktail parties and wine and cheese parties and invited many pretty young girls to my little flat to come and see me in the evenings when I was away from work and after having a few drinks and a talk I asked if they wanted to stay with me overnight too.'

'And I suppose there were some who said yes.' Nicole's dropped eyebrows and screwed up little round face expressed her displeasure, especially as Jack had been brought up as a deeply religious person. 'I know you won't be happy mother but I did sleep with a number of pretty young girls.' As Simon had very soon after his waking up fallen back into a deep sleep Nicole got up and very gently placed the bundle back in the cot. 'Strangely when seeing you on my doorstep I never noticed your rapier and yet now as I stand in front of you the silver is glinting off the sun's rays. I hope you never use it.'

'Of course I never use it mother, I bought it to get more people to turn their gaze to me in addition to the expensive dress I bought at some of London's most fashionable clothes shops in Oxford and Bond Streets, the rapier I bought from a shop named Nickleby's in Oxford Street. Ever since I left London it became my providential keepsake.'

'So tell me, what has happened to change you and make you look so hollow cheeked and thin?' Jack looked somewhat hurt my his mother's honest opinion. 'I am sorry Jack but after what you have told me about your earlier good times in London something has obviously happened to change you, your appearance and your nervousness especially. Already the short time you have been here the simple barking of my dog and the baby's crying have made you almost hide for cover.' Jack had another sip of his drink and lowered his head. His pale cheeks briefly became deep red as they flushed with his slight discomfiture. 'Mother it was simply the terrible events in London on November 5th 1605 outside the Houses of Parliament. That morning changed my complete life.'

'I would suppose you were in Whitehall watching the State Opening of Parliament when Guy Fawkes lit his barrel of gunpowder.'

'Not only was I opposite Sovereign's Entrance watching the explosion that killed the King but also I was blaming myself for its happening.'

'Pardon! Jack, that is simply a preposterous thought.'

'I am beginning to look back on my behaviour when the incident happened and how I behaved afterwards and I think now maybe I was over-reacting but that did not change how I behaved and felt at the time. I returned to my small flat and ignoring all the kind London people who were asking me where I was going……..' Jack's throat became dry and he had another swig of his drink before continuing. '…..I packed my case and all my nice new clothes and brought with me all my money as well as my rapier and I walked away quickly from London and all its people, the whole city in such a short space of time that I used to love and all its people I admired suddenly filled me only with fear. Everybody I saw coming anywhere near me and every noise of any kind I heard made me shake with fear. I walked all the way back from London hardly eating and fearing every stranger I used to see walking the opposite way to London if ever they turned their head to me just simply to say *"hello."* As you have said mother, my life has changed a great deal.' There was a moment of silence until simply to change the subject and make them both feel a little more comfortable Nicole looked straight ahead through the window commenting, 'It is lovely to see the sun shining again. Your father believed when we were kept awake throughout the night by both the thunder and heavy rain battering on the roof and window that there would be no work at the farm today yet he went back to the farm this morning and has never returned home.'

'Have you got any other news to tell me mother apart from having this little baby and moving from your previous house in Warwick?' Nicole shook her head gently.

'Very little. As you can obviously see your father continues working most of each day on the farm and my position has always been as a simple housewife doing a housewife's job to look after her husband. Only in recent months Simon has made my usually tedious job increasingly delightful.'

'And are you still as passionate about religion as you were when I was always a young boy and still living at home with you and father?'

'It is the local church that most of the time gives me the only chance I have to get outside and enjoy a little bit of fresh air and some social life.' Jack began to examine his mother's own slightly gaunt and thin figure.

'I would like to ask something of you and give you a chance to properly use your intelligence that I would believe after what you have told me about your almost unchanging life has hardly been worked at all.' His mother's lips tightened and eyes narrowed as Jack was about to continue although he too became a little tongue-tied as he had a feeling his mother would probably make fun of him. Finally he felt courageous enough to explain a little guardedly; 'I was reading of the Birmingham MP's recent heart attack.' Jack passed over the pamphlet he had collected a little earlier in the day. Nicole's face looked completely blank. 'I certainly don't recognise his name, I don't believe he has ever done anything of any significance for the local Birmingham people.'

'That is because Parliament has handed all its powers now to the Parish councils and all the money and they are working as many small governments together.' Once more Jack was interrupted as the dog got up off the floor and this time rather than barking loudly at the stranger it went over to Jack wagging its tail and obviously seeking some attention from the thin visitor. 'What kind of a dog is this mother? I must admit, I never was at all keen on dogs.'

'Can't you tell by its shape and colour Jack, it is a sheep dog.'

'Of course.' Jack mused as he looked at it and felt its long hot tongue licking the palm of one of his hands up and down as though with some kind of deep affection. 'Was this type of dog father's idea to buy as a farm labourer?'

'It was Mark's decision to buy a sheep dog. Sometimes Lassie goes onto the farm with your father instead of staying here with me and Simon at home. Tell me Jack, where are you living now as you've not yet decided to move back in with us?'

'Just at one of the local taverns. Tell me mother, if I say I am going to stand as one of the local candidates at the by-election here in just three weeks time with all the money that I believe father must still have from his own father's will can you do all the official business for me with the necessary money and have my name put forward as a contestant?' As he stroked Lassie with one hand and tolerated the sheep dog's continued licking of the palm of his other, breathing its mildewed hot breath into his face Jack expected his mother's face to eventually burst out into a bright laugh and say to him under her breath, *"Oh Jack, don't be so silly!"* yet she had not done that and had taken his comment seriously. 'I can do all the official paperwork for you if you tell all the local people of your intended sensible policies.'

'I have two policies which I believe will be taken extremely sensibly. I want to see all the Parish councils lose all their great powers and that returns to Parliament where all the political powers should lie if the parliamentary system is organised properly and a reforming of the shambles of a political system that is unorganised is required to have a political system that once more is run and organised with efficiency to make the Houses of Parliament strong again.' Jack hesitated at that moment slightly red faced and breathless. 'When I speak to the local people then I will have to explain a little more clearly than that of course.'

'That will win you a lot of votes. There are many people of the small number who are allowed to vote throughout England who are angry with the way all local Parish councils keep on putting taxes up particularly the land tax which has become so high there are a number of people who have had to move out of their original houses and into small flats to keep the high taxes down.'

'The only point that could counter that mother is what the council is doing with the money it is raising from these high taxes and the money it is receiving from Parliament. Like many councils here in Birmingham much is being done with the money, more homes are being built, enormous sewage systems are being prepared and there are more horse and traps going backwards and forwards every day which the noise made by those horseshoes makes me fill with dread.'

'Then what you must do apart from anything else with campaigning is come here every day and I will give you a good meal with meat roasted on the spit and potatoes to build you up otherwise people will not vote for your frightened skeletal character no matter what they think of your policies. Now tell me, have you any other policies or is that your only one?'

'I have one other policy mother which I believe not just in Birmingham but all over England people are becoming increasingly in favour of. I believe that once more the majority of people in England would like to see this country have a monarch who can lead the country and its people from the throne rather than having politicians try and lead themselves but only with incompetence and inefficiency.'

'Now there too I would agree with you. There are many people who have spoken to me saying how they would like to see us having Princess Elizabeth on the throne as Queen Elizabeth II although for the next few years helped on the throne as Queen Elizabeth II of England by yet more officials.'

'Well even if I had to do it myself in Parliament then I would although I admit fighting for it alone may not be at all easy.' Jack looked up towards the cot now Lassie had gone to lie back down between the far chair and the cot as there were signs that Simon's very large round eyes were opening again and he was going to start crying in his ear-piercing manner. 'Please tell me mother, what is your child going to start doing very loudly then I can prepare.'

'You had better close your ears. About this time every day, about late afternoon time Simon becomes hungry and begins to either cry or scream for something to eat……..' Nicole hesitated as the first cries were beginning and the baby's quivering was beginning to shake the cot. 'Block your ears and I shall take Simon into the kitchen and give him something to eat. If you wish to wait until your father comes home from work then you can both go out for a drink at the tavern where you are staying then I shall get you something more substantial to eat than you tell me you have been eating for a number of months.' As the baby's original cries were becoming slight screams and Simon's mouth was getting wider Jack quickly responded, 'I would be delighted to wait mother.' and then he covered his ears completely.

'This meal is excellent mother, father was right, I should have come home a long time ago.'

'The clothes you bought in London were obviously expensive and a little gaudy. I have not seen that kind of jerkin before or such tall boots, certainly nowhere here in Birmingham.'

'I believe styles of clothing like this are only sold in the capital. At least the clothes and rapier were some things I was able to remember London with although if people do elect me as their new MP it will feel strange after the way I hastily departed the city after the tragic event that killed the King. I believe the country has never fully recovered from the King's death and England would pick up with its true morals led from the very top if we had a monarch again.'

'There are increasing numbers of people in Birmingham that talk like you do and increasingly too there are more and more items written for the street pamphlet saying the same thing.' Jack was halfway through his meal when his father came in through the door. As if simply habitual Lassie leapt up from the floor and went trotting outside to the front door to meet him. 'This food really is excellent mother.' Unknowingly before he had had the plate put in front of him at the table his mother had roasted some chicken on the stove and prepared fresh potatoes in boiling water on the log fire. After two hours preparing them all the food was regarded as excellent and filling. 'This is the sort of thing I used to eat when I was living at my very best in London and inviting young women to come and stay overnight with me.'

'That is something Jack neither your father nor myself wish to hear you speak about any more.'

'Where's the baby?' Mark asked without any words pleasantries about his return home.

'Simon as usual is in the small bedchamber in his cot and sound asleep now he has been fed.'

'Thank goodness for that!' he snapped quickly. 'Is there any food prepared like you've done for Jack?'

'Your father is always like this when he comes in. I believe it is just part of the Parker family the way his father could go on sometimes.' Looking exhausted Mark sat down on the one empty chair and Lassie fell down on all fours on the carpet beside him. 'Is this as I have asked your friend Edward many times, are you here to stay with us permanently now or is this just a quick visit?'

'For now it is just a single visit but as your mother and myself were talking earlier I have changed my mind now for the first time since my return from London I have made some definite plans with mother. I am intending to stand as a candidate during Birmingham's by-election as I believe I will have a chance to win the seat and begin a new career as a politician.' Mark smiled with a little amusement at the thought.

'You need to put on a great deal of weight and not look so hollow faced if you are to have any chance of winning the by-election. I'm sorry to say it son but people will not vote for a ghost.' To quickly change the subject after being ridiculed a little Jack suggested to his father they went out for a drink at his residency the nearby tavern later. 'I just need to have a wash in the horse trough after I have eaten and then I will come with you.'

'Pardon father……are you being serious when you say *"wash in the horse trough,"* People don't do that now like they used to.'

'I have always washed myself in a horse trough as I always used to when I worked as a farmer's assistant when I was just a youth and should have been at school but wasn't. Ever since those days I have been perfectly happy washing in a horse trough.' Jack looked still open mouthed at his father's revelation.

'Very well,' he replied finally. '……….when you have eaten and had a wash in the horse trough we can go to the tavern and have a drink and talk.' Nicole was not long before bringing in another plate of boiled potatoes, hot chicken and two pieces of bread and butter and then Mark's sweating, filthy figure came over to the table to eat with Lassie awake once more and following by his side.

'Father perhaps not surprisingly I believe Lassie wants to come with you. If you look down you'll see she is coming out the front door with us.' Mark's gristly weathered face and dark ringed watery eyes peered down at the dog and its long dark nose and whispered some words that made her stay back and wait until the door was closed. 'The tavern where I am sleeping is not far from here.'

'That's why I've been surprised you've never simply collected all your things together and returned to us and save yourself a large amount of money.'

'I still have a large amount of money I made when I was working with the security officials for the Queen and then King James I.'

'If you were one of the security officials working for King James what happened when the explosion occurred caused by Guy Fawkes and his helpers?' Jack looked through the darkness but for a street light with a faint brightness and almost began to weep. 'That is a question I have been asking myself ever since King James was killed in the explosion. I don't know what we were doing before the State Opening of Parliament took place. Perhaps we all simply assumed as the Houses of Parliament had apparently been checked the night before the explosion took place everything was safe and there was nothing to discuss. I heard after leaving London that Guy Fawkes and Sir Robert Catesby were given some inside information from one of the King's close advisors because of his deep Catholic faith which he kept just to himself. The explosion almost killed me afterwards and I nearly destroyed myself starving myself and walking all the way back to Birmingham from London.'

'Here we are Jack. If you are going to stand as a candidate at the by-election we may as well see now how many of all the people here this evening would vote for you. I'll buy the drinks. What do you want?'

'As usual just a large glass of ale. That's all I ever ask for in here. I'll get my usual centre table.' Jack to his satisfaction discovered the centre table was available though the noise level as the lounge was very busy was particularly high which still made him shiver with fear. 'Thank you father.' he commented merely under his breath more as a whisper when Mark returned with two large glasses of ale. 'The landlord says he would vote for you and that was even before I told him what your main campaign policies were. That is something I don't know yet.' Jack raised his glass for his father's good health before having a drink and explaining his two main policies simply. 'To reform Parliament and have a new monarch instated.'

'They sound extremely sensible policies. The high taxes the Birmingham council keeps on raising has angered many people.'

'Mother told me.' Jack had another drink and briefly changed the subject. 'You took me by surprise telling me that you wash yourself in a horse trough father although looking at you after your wash earlier you are a great deal cleaner than when you came into the house after your day of farming.' Mark raised his head and widened his eyes as much as he possibly could as though staring at his son with pride. 'When I began working with my father as a nine year old every day Farmer Crickson said after a day of work on the farm he would allow me to have a wash before leaving work in the trough with rainwater and a bar of greasy soap. So that was what I did about six o'clock every night before going home to bed. That is something I have done every day of my life. I bought a trough when we were living in Warwick and then when we moved here to Birmingham I brought my trough with me.' Mark before having a drink of ale raised his glass to his son's good health and returned the subject to the forthcoming by-election. 'If you wish to campaign all around Birmingham Jack which I suggest you do then I can hire two horses from the farm. I shall ride around Birmingham with you calling out your name and asking people to vote for you. You Jack will have to ride sidesaddle unless you learned to ride a horse when you were living in London.'

'No father, I never had time to learn to ride in London I was always either too busy with official business or else socialising either at home with the girl friends I used to have or else I was drinking at the nearby alehouse, tavern or wine bar and drinking with just ordinary people. However father I always thought having seen somebody like yourself being capable of riding a horse that anybody could do it and riding sidesaddle was just for women who were wearing rather large underwear and were not able to sit on their horses properly.'

'No Jack, that is why some women may have to ride sidesaddle but before becoming a professional horse rider then you will also have to ride sidesaddle. Before you have time to begin riding a horse properly you will have to follow me riding sidesaddle and afterwards I can teach you to become a professional horse rider.' Jack's neck lowered and his ears tightened as the noise in the lounge began to get louder and once more it was echoing inside his mind. 'I have never got over that father, the loud piercing sound when Guy Fawkes set fire to the barrel of gunpowder and it exploded right in front of where I was standing. The fact that I blamed myself for the complete event has never helped.' Mark shrugged and had another drink.

'Don't you think that was simply nonsense to blame yourself for the incident?' Jack nodded his head and his creased face frowned at the question. 'Yes father, I do believe now that I was not being at all sensible when I blamed myself for not preventing Guy Fawkes from putting a barrel of gunpowder under the Houses of Parliament but of course now father it is too late to stop myself from the way I behaved after the explosion had occurred and ever since the morning of November 5th 1605 went by I have always been haunted by that morning in London. If I do win the campaign it will seem strange going back to the capital once more as an official in the building where the explosion occurred.' Jack gave a brooding laugh and smile before having another drink and complimenting the staff at the tavern. 'They have been extremely supportive towards me ever since I returned to Birmingham looking three quarters starved and almost ghostlike.'

'Weren't they a little concerned when you arrived with that long curved rapier by your side believing you may be preparing to use it?' Jack laughed thoughtfully as he mused about the night when he did first arrive inside. 'I was looked at in different ways by staff and customers. There were many customers seeing me in finely designed clothes which after wearing them continuously had almost become rags who felt only sympathy for me especially too when I arrived looking extremely thin and almost white. Yet there were others who believed I was going to use the rapier to attack them.' Jack sighed and laughed with almost great relief. 'Eventually the majority believed I was safe and I should be allowed to stay. They saw I had a grand amount of money with me and that perhaps made their minds up about my trustworthiness. I only keep this rapier by my side to remind me of my time in London when I was at my strongest mentally and physically before the violent death of King James went and changed my whole life for me. I believe my being elected as Birmingham's next MP will help to turn a page on my present wrecked life.'

'In that case your mother and myself will do our best to help you win this seat and then you can begin a new life.' Starting to look extremely weary with his eyelids almost falling completely Mark finished his glass of ale and turned to his attention fully to his son. 'I must return home and get some sleep. I believe when I was sowing seeds and sweeping the yard clean the fresh air after last night's extremely severe thunderstorm has effected me.'

'You also have to help mother look after the little baby don't forget.' Mark hissed something not particularly pleasant before patting Jack on one shoulder, wishing him a goodnight and turning round to leave. As the loud sounds of a cacophony of voices all nattering together continued to get increasingly louder Jack watched his father disappear out the door and very quickly finished his own drink and waving goodnight to everybody went upstairs to his room for a little peace, some much needed rest and a little solitude too.

Jack became increasingly excited about the possible outcome of Birmingham's by-election. As he and his father rode steadily around the city asking for votes more people kept on following behind them and cheering their support for Jack Parker. 'The fact that you've put on a great deal of weight in the last two weeks and made yourself look more human helps.' Jack bought two glasses of ale at the Blue Boar inn near the far south district of the city and led his father to the far table. 'Possibly when the result is announced this will be the start of a new life back in London again and still with my silver rapier beside me.'

'I hope so after how you left home when you were young and already then looking ahead to a new life in the city. I hardly recognised you the day you eventually returned home.'

'It doesn't help my image when I am having to ride around the city sidesaddle which is not how men are expected to ride horseback is it father.' Jack had a mouthful of his ale and frowned slightly towards his father. 'If you do win the by-election then before returning to London I shall take time aside from my farming and show you how to become a proper horseman.'

'I believe the result of this by-election will be closer than the way you both are already talking.' Jack raised his head looking over his father's shoulder to find out who had made the comment. 'Edward, what are you doing following us?'

'I'm giving you a little bit of moral support. It will be the day of the vote in just two days time and I believed my moral support may be welcome.' Jack whispered a few words to himself before going to the bar and buying Edward a glass of ale. 'I'm not in any position to argue now am I, at least not until after the vote has been held.'

'More than anything else since Lord Montagu was arrested people throughout the Midlands are pleased to see all the farming fields worked by English farmhands and not Jamaican slaves.' Mark looked particularly pleased at Edward's comment. 'When all but a few of the farms were re-taken by the landowners and those who are already wealthy enough to buy large amounts of land most tenant farmers lost their farms for many months, it is something many people hold against the politicians in Parliament and their incompetence for not stopping the introduction of enclosures sooner.' Jack had a drink for his dry throat and nodded his definite agreement. 'That is something I want to stop although I know it won't be easy, there are many people who do already regard the politicians as incompetent.'

'Have you heard anything from your farmer Mark since beginning to take time off work to instead go round with your son supporting him during the campaign?' Edward had a long drink of ale and grinned widely at Mark. 'I have found out at least twice when we have stopped on the farm to speak just how threatening and loud mouthed your employer can be.' Mark's head suddenly dropped and his shoulders sagged.

'I haven't seen the farmer since I took the two horses away from the field and told him without his permission I was going to take time off work to support Jack during the by-election campaign. My employer said nothing but gave me one of his fiercest stares. I am sure once the by-election is over and the result has been announced then he will be able to tell me exactly how he felt towards my decision.' Jack laughed.

'It's about time you retired from farming father as you began when only a child and you have kept the farming tradition of washing in a horse trough.' Hearing Jack's comment Edward looked at Mark and smiled an unusual almost half-wicked smile towards Mark. 'Is Jack being serious Mark or was that meant to be some kind of humorous comment?'

'Jack was being open about what had been until now a more private matter.' As if to end the small conference quickly Mark commented to Jack they had to move on and leave the remainder of their drinks behind. He had another lengthy drink of ale and urged his son to hurry up and follow.

'At least you appear to be coping with the many loud sounds around you more than you had been for a long time after returning home from London.' Mark commented gently as they remounted their hired horses and Jack ungainly made himself as comfortable as he could in a riding position. 'Thankfully father that concern I suffered until only very recently after returning home from London has almost gone. I certainly couldn't return to the mighty capital if I still had that as an ongoing problem.' As they began to ride gently on through the city's increasing house-building, the new shops and small businesses that were just preparing to open and the arrangements continuing for the start of the building of Birmingham's own sewage system Jack commented in a more complimentary manner towards the council's work. 'At least this is more than was ever done for Birmingham when all the political power was held by Parliament.' Mark knew at that comment he could only agree yet he was continually made fractious by the subject of the increasingly high council taxes. 'That now is how the council makes most of its money by continuing to increase the taxes something that many people who live here cannot afford to pay.'

'In that case let's hope that for one reason or another the voters of Birmingham decide after a long or short think about it to give me a chance and vote for me in a very short time father.'

Edward had been right with his prediction when meeting Jack and Mark at the Blue Boar inn suggesting the Birmingham by-election would be close. With Jack's three other constituency candidates it produced the result, Jack Parker, 758 votes, Peter West 670 votes; Timothy Durrell 705 votes, Martin Longpole 725 votes. Now the thought of returning to London in his capacity once more as a senior official really began to have an emotional impact upon him. He had a drink at the nearby alehouse with Lassie beside them and began wholly to look ahead to his strange and unexpected future in the capital. Mark looked at the fashionable clothes his son was wearing once again and the rapier by his side as usual. 'Perhaps your rapier has brought you your good luck.'

'I will have to return to Nickleby's sword shop in Oxford Street the very moment I ride back into London and thank the manager if he still runs the shop.' Jack had a drink of celebratory wine thinking ahead towards his approaching return to London; 'It will seem strange father, walking through Sovereign's Entrance where King James was struck down and I believe the entrance still has not yet fully been repaired.'

'At least you are now looking human again. All I have to do now the weather is becoming like late spring and early summer is teach you to ride a horse and you can prepare yourself to ride down to London rather than walk. When is Parliament's next sitting.' Jack had another small drink of wine and shrugged.

'Father that is something that needs properly organising with Parliament an appropriate timetable so all politicians know when they are supposed to attend. When I was working in London and Queen Elizabeth was head of state and then for a short time King James became the new head of state for England the politicians had someone to look up to and respect who would lead them properly and with a definite timetable of events that were to take place in the Houses of Parliament. Without any monarch

England has been without any organised Parliament which has completely fallen apart and there is not one politician who can take things upon himself to lead Parliament. I have no idea yet how on earth I will do it or how long it will take but I am going to investigate how to reform Parliament and persuade the politicians to vote for a new monarch for this country's people to respect and admire and for other nation's leaders to admire as well.'

'It sounds very good Jack but I believe you will have a real task on your hands when you return to London and for the next sitting of Parliament don't forget to prepare your maiden speech.' Jack looked up at the barman and smiled. 'That is going to be my next job when this glass of wine is empty!'

That early March morning Lord Egerton and Anne had dismounted their horses and Lord Egerton had promised for the first time to take Anne into Oxford Street to have a look at Nicholas and Arabella's hat shop. 'It is possible we may bump into Sir Edward while we are in the shop, apparently many people have said he has become one of their best and most regular customers.' Anne smiled as they turned into Regent Street past some of the other fashionable clothes, jewellery and food shops. 'Elizabeth has been telling me ever since she was found in Spain and returned home that bitter cold day I have needed a new hat.' This time it was Lord Egerton who grinned. 'You have plenty of hats to wear just as you have at least one wardrobe full of the finest clothes.' Just as Lord Egerton had already commented to Anne the hat shop was busy inside and outside there appeared a large crowd of people talking business and family matters rather than looking around the shop itself. 'It is Mr Nickleby the sword crafter I feel slightly sorry for. Until the hat shop opened next door he was always doing a very good trade yet now every time I look through the window there seems to be not one customer inside and Mr Nickleby has a rather worried expression on his face.' As Anne made her way through the large crowd outside the hat shop Lord Egerton decided to try and make himself supportive of Mr Nickleby. 'I would like one of your finest silver swords and a more expensive golden hilt.' Mr Nickleby for a very short moment raised a relieved smile before getting down to his extremely swift business. 'Unfortunately if business continues to decline the way it has done since Nicholas and Arabella opened up their hat shop next door then this business will have to close.' Mr Nickleby short and plump and dressed in the finest fashionable doublet and breeches looked out through the window with some envy in his eyes at the large gathering crowds gossiping for long periods before moving on and appeared a little angry also at the way the hat shop had suddenly taken Nickleby's many regular customers from him. Mr Nickleby began work on Lord Egerton's desired sword. 'It shan't take long if you have time to wait.' Lord Egerton watched Mr Nickleby begin his work in earnest. 'It says in the latest pamphlet which is being handed out in Oxford Street that Jack Parker has just won the by-election that was held in the Birmingham constituency.'

'I believe I recognise that name.....' Lord Egerton's voice tailed off as he began to consider the name.

'At least if I do have to close my shop I can say that a politician now sitting in the Lower House has been to my sword crafter's shop and bought a rapier here some years ago.'

'I believe Jack Parker was a security official although I don't believe I ever spoke with him, I did hear several people say he had been seriously effected in his mind by the explosion that killed King James. Obviously he has been able to recover and fight for a place at the next sitting.'

'If you know when the next sitting is of course.' Lord Egerton shrugged.

'I have absolutely no idea at all.' For a time Lord Egerton watched Mr Nickleby work until more quickly than he had expected Mr Nickleby said that he had completed his work. 'It is all finished if you would like to examine both ends.' Lord Egerton had a quick glance at the hilt and nodded his approval of the work. 'Excellent!' he commented in a convincing deep voice. They sorted out all the financial dealings before taking the fine silver sword with him Lord Egerton went into the hat shop to look around for Anne.

'You missed Sir Edward Coke by about one hour I'm afraid.' Lord Egerton turned around to see Arabella's shorter figure beside him. 'I wasn't looking for Sir Edward I was looking for Anne of Denmark who is just ahead of me.' Arabella looked a little surprised by Lord Egerton's response and pardoned herself for the interruption. Anne was gazing at several ladies hats to choose from. 'What on earth have you bought yourself a sword for?!' she asked in a loud and very disruptive voice. All of the customers inside the shop turned to look by Lord Egerton's side and gasped when they saw the long sword hanging there. 'It was simply to try and help Mr Nickleby to try and prevent him from going out of business.' Anne, continuing to examine the different coloured hats and different styles tutted her discern. 'Who on earth would believe they could continue doing business by selling swords?' Eventually Anne made her mind up to select the least expensive of the three she had been examining the linen coif with a decorative lace trim. 'Is that all you are going to treat yourself to?' Lord Egerton smiled.

'For now that will do. Then when this is paid for we should quickly return to our horses and I would suggest a ride up northwards towards Finsbury Fields before turning back and having some lunch in Lincolns Inn.' As they approached their horses tied up expertly to trees Lord Egerton looked sadly at Sally. 'Unfortunately my lovely horse that has been most loyal and reliable to me is now past her healthiest and needs to rest. Before we go and have lunch I must go to the north London stables and choose myself a younger and healthier one again.' Lord Egerton stroked his horse somewhat thoughtfully probably for the final time. 'She has been an extremely good and reliable horse for me ever since I bought her at exactly the same stables.'

'I know she has been a good and reliable horse as I have seen her in action so many times and in all kinds of conditions as well.' They mounted their horses at a grassy patch of ground at the end of Regent Street and rode gently northwards towards Moorfields to give their horses a good run before going once more to the north London stables to choose the replacement for Sally. Approaching the stables Lord Egerton looked to Anne as there was such a large number of horses waiting to be bought. 'How on earth am I supposed to choose a new horse from such a large bunch?' Anne tilted her head to an angle as she considered the horses of different colours, heights and ages and selected one that she preferred. 'If you would like me to help you choose a new horse then I do have one in mind.'

'Then please, the moment we get down from our horses tell me which one you prefer.'

Greeting them outside the stables Jack recognised one of the most regular horse dealers who had been working at the north London horse stables for over forty-five years. 'Mr Hitching you're still working here after all these years.'

'As you can see Thomas, I just love doing my work. I take it clearly you believe Sally needs retiring?'

'I believe that is about it yes.'

'Of all the horses you can see in front of you in the field have you any one in mind that you prefer or do you wish just to have a look for now?' Lord Egerton pointed to Anne who was already stroking one particular reddish brown horse on its white muzzle. 'My friend here has more idea about selecting one of all your wonderful horses than I do.' They strolled over to Anne who was talking to the horse and the way it was looking directly at her Lord Egerton and Mr Hitching believed the horse must be listening to her and understanding every word Anne was saying. 'Anne I take it this is the horse you have already chosen for me.'

'If you would like my opinion about your next horse then I would definitely go for this beautiful horse with its long fine white mane, larger head, physically heavier jaws than any other horses here have and its tall strong back. I believe this horse would be perfect to last you a number of years reliably.'

'I will go along with your advice Anne. Please tell me Mr Hitching, has your lovely horse here a name?'

'I believe so.' Mr Hitching went to his small wooden office and brought back a piece of paper which he examined before looking back at the large group of horses in the field. 'This steed is called Pegasus.' Lord Egerton and Anne turned to each other seemingly a little curious at the name before Lord Egerton asked about the cost. 'For you Thomas 30 sovereigns.' Lord Egerton checked through his purse selecting the relevant amount of money before passing it over to Mr Hitching and being given the reins. 'I had better say my final farewell to Sally before we go.' Anne watched Lord Egerton walk over slowly to Sally standing alone and talking to her for a while before returning. 'I'm sure I can see a tear in his eye Mr Hitching.' She turned to Lord Egerton and urged him to hurry up and mount his new horse. 'I suggest we go, I'm feeling a little hungry.' Lord Egerton did as he was instructed and after riding steadily away from the stables they galloped the rest of the way towards Lincolns Inn.

'That's quite a spend this morning Thomas, a new sword and a new horse as well. You are an excellent horse rider will you learn to become an excellent swordsman too?' Lord Egerton sniffed his rejection of the idea. 'Becoming a swordsman is something I would never do.' Outside Lincolns Inn there was a pamphleteer who by the expression on his face as he was wiping his mouth and face clear had just called in to have something to eat. As Lord Egerton was tying up his horse for once he motioned to the young man for a copy to be handed across to him. 'I thought you were a severe critic of the pamphlets, especially the way you tell me they get inside information into the ongoing events in Parliament.'

'Just this once, I would like to see if there is any more information which refers to the newly elected MP Jack Parker. His name is mentioned on the inside page and there is a great amount of information about him and his plans for a better Houses of Parliament.' As they entered the inn Anne could not prevent herself laughing out loud. 'If that is what Birmingham's new MP wants then he has got quite a job on his hands whenever Parliament does sit again. Have you any idea of the date of the next sitting Thomas?' Thomas shrugged and again became red faced; 'At the moment I have no idea. I would guess there will be a next meeting sometime in July or August but what Parliament will discuss I have no idea as it is the Parish councils that have all the power there is and they are all successfully spending the money to help the country go forward.' After Lord Egerton had finished his small rant they went to the bar to have a look at the offers. 'What can I get you to eat and to drink Anne?' As they stood looking at the choices in front of them Lord Egerton was given a long suspicious stare by the manager when he came forward personally to serve them. 'Roast chicken with currants, sugar and dates, potatoes and two slices of bread and butter and of course a glass of white wine would finish the meal off perfectly.'

Lord Egerton nodded his head in complete agreement. 'To make it simple just prepare two dishes exactly the same way.' He paid what he regarded as a reasonable sum of money and joined Anne at the back table to wait. 'It says lower down on the pamphlet that the next sitting in the Lower Chamber is on the 15th June though it also suggests the main reason for that is so that Jack Parker MP can make his maiden speech.'

'And will it be worth going into Parliament just to hear a new MP make his maiden speech?'

'That's a very good question. I believe it shall be interesting just to hear what he has to say but I will guess now that an awful lot of politicians will simply remain at work and not even try and arrive.' The young waitress came swiftly to their table and served their plates and drinks and was given a good tip by Lord Egerton to which she almost fully curtsied to; 'Perhaps she would have curtsied to you if she wasn't wearing such a large petticoat.' Anne joked watching the young lady trying to bow extremely low.

'If what it states in this article about Jack Parker MP is absolutely correct and it probably is the way their reporters so far have got every detail of every article written absolutely perfect then it states here Jack not only wants Parliament to be reformed but also he wants the politicians to elect a new monarch for the English people to be able to respect once more just as they respected Queen Elizabeth I and King James I before his wicked murder.'

'In which case Parliament's new politician has got some very sensible ideas.'

'Unfortunately an awful lot of our present politicians are perfectly satisfied with the way the country is being run at the moment, by lots of Parish councils all around the country and without any monarch on the throne at all.'

'In other words you believe poor Jack Parker has got a long exhausting challenge ahead of him if this is what he is going to fight for?'

'I would say that sums the situation up perfectly.' Lord Egerton took a piece of meat carefully on his fork and placed it gently in his mouth; 'This meat is absolutely delicious.'

'Do you want a game of chess when we return home with Elizabeth?' Lord Egerton was slightly surprised by Anne's unexpected question and considered it only briefly; 'I will not be able to stay too long this evening, there are some documents I need to examine and sign for the Westminster courts before three trials take place over the next month.'

'Whatever happened to Lord Whitby and Lord Montagu who after being arrested and kept in prison have so far not been officially charged with anything yet?' Lord Egerton's head was lowered to the table and his cheeks blushed with some further official embarrassment. 'I believe England's legal system needs greatly reforming as well as the parliamentary system. Both Lords have never been charged with any crime or were ever sent to court to face trial.'

'You seem to be suggesting Thomas that both Lords have died while being kept in prison. That is certainly not the right way to treat people who have never been officially charged. I hope if nothing else then they were at least given decent funerals by their families.' Lord Egerton had some more food and shook his head slowly. 'There are two separate stories to that question. Lord Whitby died in his prison cell and nobody in his family came to the prison to take the remains of his dead corpse home so he was buried in the prison graveyard with other dead prisoners. On the other hand Lord Montagu's brother came to Manchester prison where he had been transferred and finally died in and took his dead body back to his large mansion in Northampton on a horse and cart. There he was buried in the family plot alongside the grave of his father.' As she was cutting up her chicken Anne's face tightened and momentarily she felt a little sick as she thought about Lord Egerton's reply. 'At least one of the two got a decent burial.'

'If you're realistic about the situation now Anne you must admit most people simply do not care about what happened to the two Lords. I would say about 90% of people in England forgot all about their existence altogether when they were arrested and put in prison. They angered most people for their continued use of Jamaican slaves and the horrible way they took farmland of innocent farm workers simply working hard and trying to make some kind of a living so they could buy food and pay the high taxes to keep and look after their families. There is no more violence now on any of the farms, instead all farmers are working together on smaller and equally divided fields.' Anne had a drink of wine and grinned her approval to Lord Egerton. 'I believe you explained the current situation perfectly.' They had the rest of their meal quietly simply watching the other customers arriving and smiling and chuckling to each other about different matters. 'It is nice to see people looking so happy for a change.' Anne commented.

'Whatever Jack Parker MP may think about reforming Parliament and at some time having power returned to the House of Commons Parish councils with all their money and power and more regular sittings are being extremely successful in developing England into having a stronger economy as well as having many happy people once more.'

'The meal really was excellent and the glass of wine just finished it perfectly. I would suggest if you want to go and speak with Elizabeth for any particular reason you should go immediately as she will more than likely be preparing herself for the opera right now.'

'That sounds interesting, whereabouts in London is the opera?'

'I believe Elizabeth told me it is in Fleet Street and has only recently opened.' Lord Egerton got up from the table. 'In that case I suggest we should go.'

As Anne had expected Elizabeth was in her room and preparing herself for a night at the opera. The butler immediately having seen Anne and Lord Egerton into the house watched Anne go upstairs to speak with her daughter and prepared Lord Egerton a glass of whisky as he waited for some attention. Eventually after a lengthy wait Elizabeth came slowly downstairs dressed in her flame coloured satin dress and kerchief and high heeled black shoes and had her long black hair brushed neatly down to her shoulders. 'You look absolutely magnificent dressed like that.' Lord Egerton commented looking form the sofa across to the staircase. 'Will you have any time for a game of chess before you go out later?' Elizabeth murmured to herself before for once setting the chess pieces up but with her mind and thoughts somewhere else. 'Your move.' she commented quietly as Lord Egerton was just sitting down at the table. 'That damn dog.' she grumbled as the growing puppy came into the living room and breathing heavily sat down beside Elizabeth to watch the contestants. Briefly Anne sat near the table watching the game before going upstairs to her music-room for a period of piano playing. The chess match went on for over an hour until eventually Elizabeth's tolerance finally snapped. She looked at her watch and down at the large bulging eyes of the little dog and getting up quickly from the table commented; 'We must call this a draw it is time I was going out.' Just as she had finished speaking and walking a little clumsily over the dog the butler came in to tell her that her horse and trap to take her to Fleet Street had arrived. She excused herself to Lord Egerton and very swiftly left. A little while longer Lord Egerton sat with the puppy sitting on the floor beside him and listening to the usual magnificent piano playing until deciding he had work to do. He finished his whisky and handing the empty glass to the butler excused himself and left the house on his brand new horse which had been carefully groomed and fed by his old stable boy he recognised easily from his large house in Chelsea.

On the very early morning of June 15th as the sun was just beginning to rise Jack Parker MP was preparing his young jet black horse his father Mark had bought him only in early May and not long after his riding lessons had finished for his ride back down to London and the first parliamentary sitting since his election as the new Birmingham MP. This was a day strangely Jack had been both excited about and worried towards both at the same time. He was wearing some of the most expensive fashionable clothes he had bought when he was earlier living in London and had dressed in his slashed doublet, wide reticella lace collar and cuffs and his broad rimmed hat. His fine silk breeches were laced with bows and his knee length black riding boots were some of the most expensive riding boots in all of England. He was preparing his horse at his mother and father's house and after having a good fried breakfast he was at last ready to mount his new horse and begin his journey. 'At least this way of travelling is definitely better than walking.' Nicole checked the horse before Jack mounted; 'Have you your rapier with you as your lucky charm?'

'Of course mother round the other side. I take my rapier everywhere I go.' Before he mounted his horse he was given a lengthy handshake of good luck by his father and an affectionate kiss on the cheek by his mother. 'Remember all I have tought you about riding a horse.' Mark commented with a cautionary finger pointing towards the horse's present jumpiness as it waited for its rider to get on. 'Yes father, I promise, I will not forget one word of what you have told me about riding a horse. I also have a copy of my maiden speech carefully tucked away in the back pocket here. It is more than likely most of my speech will be picked up and re-written in the next copy of the street pamphlet.' He mounted his tall high backed horse perfectly and after saying goodbye several times took the reins and guided his horse out of the gravelly pathway and towards the flat open land before gently kicking his heels in to the horse's sides and galloping southwards towards to London.

His return journey to London by horse not by foot and under clear blue sky and across hard dry land brought back memories by which he had always been haunted as he had walked slowly for many long hours and days passing through the counties of Warwickshire, Buckinghamshire and Oxfordshire. He could even remember some of the inns, taverns and public houses where he had stayed overnight on his long walk back after the ghastly explosion that had killed King James I and he had walked back home almost looking like a ghost, half starved and extremely white feeling complete shame for the attack on the King that he and his fellow security staff had completely failed to check and stop. There were a number of travellers and vagrants he hurried by as he galloped southwards looking just as exhausted and blank faced as he had when he had walked the two long journeys to London and back to the Midlands. Eventually after only a short space of time he reached Hertfordshire and became closer to the capital which had grown he could see already from quite a distance since he was last there. Just the first appearance of some of London's buildings and the twisting murky water of the river Thames began to bring back memories both good and bad recollections and as he got deeper into Hertfordshire his horse's gallop very rapidly became a more gentle trot as he could feel his stomach tighten and heartbeat become increasingly louder and eventually as he entered the outskirts of the city he pulled on the horse's reins just as his father had taught him to slow his horse down to a very gentle canter as he heaved a deep sigh and peered carefully at the many tall buildings, the winding river and its many bridges that with the sun shining brightly over the complete city made a magnificent picturesque backdrop.

He rode his splendid jet black horse slowly into north London carefully examining the outstanding development that had taken place since his time of leaving as he rode through the many lanes and streets with many new shops being built and opened and increasing numbers of houses already rising around Finsbury Fields, Moorfields and the flat open land of Tottenham. He rode on gently towards Clerkenwell and Hobsborn before deciding to guide his horse towards Westminster and return to Oxford Street to find out if Nickleby's where he had bought his fine rapier was still open. He was impressed by the great increase in horse and traps which were travelling frequently to and from the centre of the city and the number of people who were walking the streets in different directions probably he believed looking at his new watch just on their way to work. He dismounted his horse not too far from St Pauls where a great deal of business appeared to be going on with the sound of much rapid conversation and the frequent comment referring to cost. Already Jack knew that a great deal of work still needed to be done on improving the appearance of the river as he towed his horse to the river's edge curling his nose up as tightly as he could to try and prevent himself inhaling the strong foul stench arising with the blue smog from the filthy brown water. For a time he looked at some of the small dinghies and other vessels making their slow ways across the water until deciding to walk the short distance into Oxford Street to see if again he could find the sword crafter's shop.

He tied his horse up to a tree right outside the door of Nickleby's and was pleased to see it was still open though surprised to see there was no-one inside being served. 'It's been a long time since I last came in here to buy my rapier.' The shop assistant was taken aback to see Jack Parker returning to the shop again. 'Jack, I haven't seen you for years………I believe the manager did tell me you have just been elected as the new MP for Birmingham.'

'That is right, I would guess that information was read in one of the latest copies of the now countrywide street pamphlets.'

'That was what Mr Nickleby told me. It is good to see you have always kept the fine rapier that we made for you. It's just very unfortunate that Mr Nickleby told me that very soon his shop will have to be closed permanently as all our business now has been taken by the new hat shop that opened several months ago next to us.' Jack looked extremely shocked by news he had received.

'As a new member of Parliament I shall see if there is anything I may be able to do to help keep you open.' He looked once more at his watch and after hearing the news decided as he was a little confused he had to move onwards towards Parliament. He mumbled; 'As I'm to give my maiden speech at half past two this afternoon I should go and get some lunch in the Lower Chamber bar.' Before any further words could be spoken Jack had left the small shop with his rapier by his side and untying his horse made the rest of the way to the Houses of Parliament without stopping again.

Riding his horse slowly into Whitehall once more brought shocking memories to his mind of the terrifying morning when he had been standing opposite Sovereign's Entrance, just like the enormous crowd that had surrounded him excitedly watching the King stepping out of the royal carriage and marching inside Parliament and then watching the enormous explosion that had occurred. The same question remained in his mind and a question he still could not answer; *"Why did we not know in advance this barrel of gunpowder inside Sovereign's Entrance had been placed and readied to explode?"* Dismounting his magnificent new horse Jack tied her to a tree standing in exactly the same position he had stood on November 5th before walking across the road and inside Sovereign's Entrance showing the newly established security guard his parliamentary membership card and pass before being fully allowed inside. He followed a series of long passageways and corridors before finding the Lower Chamber and the bar and treating himself to a glass of wine and cold ham sandwich and a little ice cream. 'You must be the newly elected MP for Birmingham.' Jack was surrounded by a small group of politicians who looked at him a little curiously. 'I remember your face when you were in London several years ago and the rapier you always carried by your side.' Jack nodded his head and responded wearily, 'I was a member of the monarch's security staff who did nothing to check Parliament the day before the State Opening of

Parliament took place. If that is what you are intending to state then you are right, unfortunately I have had to live with that bad mistake ever since the King's violent death. Now will you leave me alone to have this little lunch and then very shortly I shall have to stand up in the Chamber and make my maiden speech which I am extremely worried about already.' The MPs who had sat down and surrounded Jack to his great relief got up and left him alone to have his little lunch before the Lower Chamber bell sounded and he got up and with the others made his way cautiously to the Lower House.

The Chamber when the last MP of the session came in was only half full as the new Speaker of the House Christopher Hopson MP who had only just been elected stood up and commented with a loud, broad accent;

"For all the MPs who have actually taken the time to come in to Parliament today, before any other business is done I would like to invite the newly elected MP for Birmingham Mr Jack Parker to stand up before us and make his maiden speech thank you!"

The Speaker's slightly uncertain statement announced in the Chamber was greeted with a few humorous remarks and some comments of derision until eventually Jack Parker's tall and slightly nervous figure stood up at the back of the Chamber and began his speech nervously;

"I must begin by saying.......it's very nice to be with you all........I have definite intentions I want to enforce during the time I remain as Birmingham's MP. First of all I wish to have Parliament reformed and looking like a proper and respectable organisation again. Secondly after failing seriously

as a security advisor to both Queen Elizabeth I and King James I I want to get this House to elect a new monarch to sit on the throne to be respected and admired and represent England with authority and dignity. They are two proposals I am going to fight for while I am still working here. After failing badly in my position as a security advisor this time I am determined I shall not fail in my clear-cut intentions!"

Although there was much more to read out to the Lower House Jack's legs began to shake badly and he became breathless however as there was much muttering and a great many whispers going round Jack knew at that moment as he sat back down he had made his real intentions as the newest of all MPs perfectly clear to all the politicians who were seated around him and what his real dispute was to be.

CHAPTER FOUR

The night of partying at the Black Bull inn had not been difficult for Martin to organise and tempt his fellow farmers to attend. To many people living in the smallest villages and hamlets around the east Midlands this night had merely been regarded as a further opportunity to escape the great number of daily stresses and strains simple agricultural life provided. Martin Walters used to own a large farm in Leicester before the landowners and noble gentlemen had decided sometimes in the most troublesome ways to retake their land and from that moment work on the large and small farms alike had become ghastly. This evening as he was drinking his second large glass of ale he had watched his pretty daughter Elaine dancing and smiling broadly on her round face almost incessantly. The occasion was an enormous celebration for Martin's daughter, first of all it was a chance to celebrate her twenty-first birthday and in addition a celebration in advance of her marriage with Christopher to take place at Tugby village church the following Wednesday. For all the guests a special supper had been laid out at the inn and the night so far was proving to be a great success. Throughout the many east Midland villages the smaller Parish councils had done very little with their share of money they had been given to help develop the region. No village had seen any signs of re-building or the installing of any new public services and there was a great deal of anger and concern towards the councils' neglect. As the latest in the long line of dances came to an end and most of the young men and women found a new partner to dance with Martin's lengthy spell of solitude at the bar was broken when one of his many fellow farmers patted him on the back and passed him a fresh glass of ale. 'It's a magnificent night. You must be so proud of your daughter, celebrating her twenty-first birthday and then very soon she will be getting married to another young man just one year older and extremely fine looking.' Martin had to wait before he could grumble his reply as the next dance began. He watched Christopher and Elaine for once dancing in each other's arms and grumbled to himself as he finished his second glass of ale. 'I wish I knew more about my daughter's fiance Christopher……..' Martin hesitated and lifted his eyebrows high as he felt once more frustrated by the young man. 'You see how much I know about Christopher and his background, I don't even know his second name. I don't believe I have even spoken to him one single time.' Abram was regarded by many local farmers as a good and understanding man yet there were times when Martin could find him more of an irritation with some of his more personal observations. 'The fact that my daughter's case is all ready packed and she and Christopher will be travelling down to London in their hired gold stagecoach almost the very moment they step out of Tugby church I find particularly upsetting not giving me or my wife Rosemary one single opportunity to speak to him.'

'My son Robert has become very good friends with Christopher and he has told me Christopher is a very pleasant and at times shy young man who simply doesn't like talking about farming which he finds completely boring. Don't take his rejction of you personally Martin but I believe Christopher only speaks with the younger generation who are all dancing on stage tonight.' As the next dance came to an end Martin wiped his brow and gave a yawn. 'I wish I could dance like they all can, the party has been going on about four hours now and they've all been dancing wildly ever since they came into the lounge.' In particular as the younger generation prepared for yet another Martin watched Christopher's moves and eyed him suspiciously; 'If I was my daughter I would just not trust Christopher.' Abram looked at Martin a little surprised by his comment. 'What makes you say something like that Martin?'

'I believe tonight Christopher has danced closely with every young female who has come here and have you seen just how he and all his dance partner look so warmly into each other's eyes when they are dancing round the stage? Christopher and his good looks and charming personality is loved by every young woman who is inside the Black Bull tonight.' Abram threw Martin a more knowing gaze.

'Robert tells me when he and Christopher have been out drinking alone together Christopher has been open and honest with him when they have spoken saying he does like many young women but Elaine is the young woman he loves and respects more than any other and it is your daughter he wishes to spend the rest of his married life with.' Martin shook his head and scoffed slightly at Abram's remark.

'If my daughter comes hurrying back up from London 'cause her husband has left her then I will have no sympathy for her.' As the next dance progressed Abram finished his glass of ale and went across to buy himself another before returning and seeing Farmer Blackwood now keeping Martin company. Farmer Blackwood was regarded by many farmers throughout the Midlands as one of the more extravagant and he had dressed for the evening in some of his more extravagant clothes. The wired collar with lace trim, and dark slashed doublet were clothes few of the farmers could afford along with the knee length black leather boots and dark velvet breeches. He put his full glass of wine down and chuckled in his deep telling tone at Martin; 'I thought you would be drinking something a little more than simple ale for tonight's celebartions.' Martin pointed at his wrinkled and weathered face. 'A few glasses of ale will do me nowadays not the more telling wine. Anyway Paul I haven't seen your daughter here at Elaine's birthday party celebrating too.' Farmer Blackwood raised his head and looked over at Christopher and Elaine holding each other and preparing to dance together again. 'Christine unfortunately can't be here this evening as there is a very large amount of wool that has to be spun by ten o'clock tomorrow morning when the agent shall be calling to collect the yarn and pay her, the amount of wool that has collected over the last number of months has filled most of the attic there is so much.' Martin pursed his lips and looked at Farmer Blackwood a little sadly.

'Elaine has very much missed her this evening. I do hope Christine shan't miss the wedding too.' Farmer

Blackwood very quickly replied putting an immediate end to Martin's concerns. 'Elizabeth will be at your daughter's wedding I can assure you of that for certain.' To Martin's surprise in particular when the latest dance finished Elaine and Christopher came hurrying off stage together and up to the bar for a drink. Christopher bought two glasses of wine and after they had spoken a few more loving words Christopher turned his attention fully to Martin. 'I don't believe we have met before. I'm Christopher Tanner and am very soon going to marry your beautiful daughter.' Christopher's height standing so close took Martin by surprise as he had to crane his neck fully to look at the tall elegant gentleman. 'At least we can speak briefly before you steal my daughter away with you to London.' Martin grumbled. 'Elaine has told me a little about you but I'm sure there is much she has never once mentioned. Why do you want to go and live in London so soon after the wedding anyway?'

'Christopher all ready has a good job lined up for when we arrive.' Elaine answered excitedly much to her father's annoyance. 'Tell me Christopher please; what is your new job and where abouts in London are you going to live with my wonderful daughter?' Christopher had a drink of wine and spoke a few words in Elaine's ear which for some reason made her giggle gently before in a conceited manner deciding to return his attention to Martin. 'I am going to be a cooper with my own business and shop set up in Fulham where we are going to live.'

'The pleasant little house that we have bought is all ready furnished;' Elaine again took over her fiance's explanation with much eagerness, '...........and Christopher has all ready interviewed all his staff who are going to work with him. Isn't that so my lovely?' Elaine went over to Christopher and hugged him which brought a pleasant grin to his subtle olive skinned face. 'You two look so fit and dainty on the dance floor.' Abram commented with another fresh glass of ale in one hand. Martin returned to the subject of Christopher's new career. 'You could if you wished set up your own business as a cooper here in the Midlands, coopers are very much required in every village in both the east and the west Midlands.'

'That is not completely the point father,' Martin sighed heavily and beckoned for Christopher to reply alone. 'We wish to begin a new life away from the Midlands and in the mighty capital where there is life and excitement all the time, sadly I do not like saying it Martin but now as more young people are moving away from these small villages there is hardly any life at all but for a little farming and all the alehouses, inns and taverns being full of activity on a night. We are hoping that one day we shall have a baby and we want to bring that baby up in a place of life and activity.'

'Do you see father?' Elaine added with one of her furtive expressions covering her face. Elaine and Christopher had another drink before there were sounds of music once more. 'The music is starting again, we must go and take our places.' Christopher's wide green eyes seemed to sparkle as he took Elaine's small hand and lead her gently to the dance floor. 'At least now Martin you know something about your future son- in-law.' Abram bought himself a fourth glass of ale and was beginning to look slightly overcome by the large amount of ale he had been drinking on that single night. 'Does your wife ever plague the life out of you Martin?' Abram asked with his voice raised above the sound of the music.

'What a strange question to ask Abram. Not at all. Now tell me, what makes you ask?'

'Mary has been going on at me ever since the size of my farm was severely reduced to buy her several more cows and sheep to tend alone and without my help........ she believes now in her unusual way that I am no longer the man who is in charge with the business back home........' Abram had another drink and looked angrily at Martin and Farmer Blackwood. 'Ever since my farmland was reduced to just two lines of crops she has merely teased me about it............' He began to look increasingly red faced and putting his glass down his legs began shaking and he collapsed to the floor. Farmer Blackwood with his long and muscular arms and big strong hands picked the heavy body of Abram up and he commented to Martin. 'You look after my drink and I'll take Abram home. I'll be back shortly.' Farmer Blackwood was able to carry Abram outside and very quickly he had gone. At the end of the next dance Martin was approached by Farmer Carr who looked enviously at Martin as he was watching his daughter and Christopher take hands and prepare once more to dance. 'Your daughter I believe must be the fittest person on stage tonight the way she has been dancing non-stop from the very beginning of this marvellous evening.' Martin shrugged and looked down at Farmer Carr's shorter figure and fixed outlandish face. 'How my daughter looks and where she goes or who she speaks with will very soon be absolutely nothing to do with me any more.' Farmer Carr went up to Martin and commented in a whispered breath; 'You're talking as though once your daughter has left for London then she will see you absolutely no more, I don't believe Elaine would treat you with such disrespect as you seem to be suggesting.' Martin wheezed with tiredness and cursed quietly as the music was playing and he could not be heard. 'It will not be my daughter's decision whether or not she comes back up from London when she is married but that damned husband's.' Martin moaned when the dancing once more had come to an end for a short time. Very soon before Farmer Blackwood could return and once more begin his conversation Martin finished his drink of ale and made his excuses to Farmer Carr and everyone else anywhere nearby and decided there and then to go back home and have a good night's sleep. As he left the inn's pleasant unadorned lounge there were no signs at all with the loud sound of music and the excited screams and yells of joy and elation arising from inside the four walls that the partying was yet coming to its conclusion.

For Christopher and Elaine the evening at the Black Bull had been absolutely spectacular and a wonderful, energetic preparation for their wedding day. On the dance floor Elaine regarded her fiance as brilliant-eyed, swift and stable and having speedy jumpy hands. Away from the dancing she considered Christopher as being quick-witted, self-assured, extremely gifted and open-handed. 'I believe you have danced with every young woman who was invited to this party.' Elaine commented as the latest dance came to an end and a gentle ripple of applause rang out. 'Are you making any insinuation with that remark?' Christopher retorted with a slight curiosity. Elaine looked up at Christopher's thin grinning face and sparkling eyes and shook her head. 'I think we should have another glass of wine before the next dance and then we should think about going home. It has been a magnificent night and when we are alone in London this is something we shall be able to do more often.' Holding each other closely they returned to the bar and Christopher bought two further glasses of wine before once more they returned to the dance floor and taking hands and gazing devotedly into each other's eyes not for the last time that night they began dancing again.

Martin and Rosemary were up early the following morning and having their usual plain breakfast of a bowl of pottage and cup of ale. Martin and Rosemary had taken completely different approaches towards their daughter's young fiance and their approaching wedding. 'I spoke to Christopher for the briefest time last night and he told me the smallest amount about himself.' Martin had a spoon of pottage and expected his wife to respond however she just stared at her husband and waited for him to continue. 'They will be marrying very soon and then disappearing from us and yet I still know very little about my future son-in-law except for the fact he has already set up his own business as a cooper and they will be living in a reasonable house in Fulham.'

'Isn't that enough to know dear? After all when they have moved to London then their married life will be nothing to do with us at all will it.' Again Martin could not prevent himself from grumbling.

'London is where the trouble is brewing once more, this time the increasing public resentment is towards the politicians and their refusal to have a new monarch re-elected. London is not a secure city to be living in if you ask my opinion.' Rosemary had some pottage and merely remarked;

'I always want your opinion dear however our daughter and her future husband I don't believe together have ever asked for your opinion on anything so that simply doesn't matter.' Once more feeling frustrated Martin finished his pottage and took his drink outside into the small garden to go and have an inspection of the two long strips of land he was provided with where the crops were growing steadily. 'I believe the farming has started aging you dear.' Martin was a little surprised that Rosemary had come outside with him.

'It was the demonstrations against Lord Montagu that aged me Rose not the farming, farming has never aged me. Now look at what I have after my big farm I used to manage, I feel my life has been completely turned on its head since that Lord gentleman came and threw me off my land damn him.' Rosemary put one of her large hands on his shoulder and turned him round to face her. 'I'm sorry Martin, I wish I could say more but at least on the green we have our small flock of sheep and two cattle which make us a little money and we are managing financially, that's what matters more than anything else.'

'It does not help that the Leicester Parish council keep on increasing the land tax every month and around in these little villages we are seeing no benefits for that increased tax.' Martin felt like making more of a protest on the present situation but felt simply too exhausted. 'Tell me Rose, what does Christopher like doing with his free time?' Rosemary tilted her head to one side as she considered her husband's question.

'Most of his life apparently Christopher's father brought him up to be an excellent horse rider and bought him a pony when he was only five years old and then from the age of thirteen he began to go out with his father often hunting. Otherwise he and Elaine like to go out occasionally drinking and socialising with people of their own age and socialising is what they are planning on doing when not at work.' By the scowl on her husband's face Rosemary could tell Martin was obviously not impressed. 'Elaine is telling me often that they are planning on having a baby in the next few years.' Martin turned back round and continued his walk to the end of the two arable lines of crops deep in thought and emotions. 'I must go back inside now and prepare a meat pie for Elaine's visit later and then after that I have a large amount of wool to weave as our personal agent will be coming to collect it about this time tomorrow and we will be making a little more money.'

'Did Elaine tell you why she will be coming later? I believe it will be for no other reason than to be given something free to eat.' Rosemary looked at her husband's moody face and shook her head.

'You really are miserable with everything and everyone today aren't you. She told me she wanted to check on our preparations for the wedding day, things such as the readiness of her wedding dress and the invitation card being sent out, those sorts of things.'

'What is the point in keeping all this?' Martin asked as he looked in the stone barn at the end of one line of crops and discovered a large collection of farming tools which had remained inside the barn for a number of months unused. 'At least you do still have your own fine horse and so you can still go out riding if indeed you do ever decide to.' Martin for the first time that morning actually managed to force a smile across his face; 'That at least is true.' On seeing her husband's face fleetingly light up Rosemary turned round and went back in to the farmhouse to begin her day of work. Martin closed the barn door and quickly finishing his inspection of the two fields he followed his wife back inside.

All the farmers who had been attending Elaine's successful birthday party the previous night were hard at work on their much reduced farmland. Throughout the many east Midland villages and hamlets it was the cider making season and already though it was still very warm August weather harvesting was just beginning on some land and a number of the young people who had been dancing wildly at the party the previous night were now in a number of fields gathering in the harvests. Farmer Blackwood was extremely surprised when he rode up to his bigger field outside Broughton to find amongst the many young women who were helping that morning Elaine Walters was also at hand working. 'I thought you had other things to think about rather than helping to bring in the harvest.' Kneeling on all fours for a short time Elaine pulled herself up to talk and found her eyes began to feel sore. 'I think it's all the horrible little insects amongst the hay that have got into my eyes.' she almost screamed at Farmer Blackwood as she rubbed at her eyes hard to try and clear them. 'I can help for a short time, that is what Christopher tells me at least and this is something I have done since being just a very little girl of only two or three years of age, that was when father had a much lager farm.'

'So are you fully packed and ready for your journey to London and new beginning?'

'I believe so. Christopher has the coachmen hired from Worcester to drive us right down to our Fulham home and I guess that is about everything prepared.' With his tall and wide rimmed hat on Farmer Blackwood was fully protected from the strong heat of the bright sunshine but Elaine was beginning to perspire badly. 'I must get on Farmer Blackwood and then I am going to ride over to see mother and father and find out about the progress of their own wedding arrangements for the big day.' Farmer Blackwood watched Elaine getting back down and continuing with her work before riding slowly round the field and following all the gatherers before going a little further up a high hill and looking one at a time at the large herd of sheep that had evidently only recently been sheared. Eventually after riding around thoughtfully and examining all of the farmland and the wild stock that he did still look after

Farmer Blackwood returned home to the farmhouse to get himself another cup of cold ale for his increasingly dry and very sore throat.

'Mark has sheared the sheep brilliantly don't you think dear?' Rosemary commented as she and Martin were standing on the village green and looking at Rosemary's small flock. 'The raw wool is now in the house and waiting for you to sit down and weave.' Martin grumbled once more. 'When are you expecting our little daughter to arrive?'

'That will probably depend on the length of time she keeps harvesting with the others if I read her mind correctly.' To their surprise although there was a clear blue sky and baking sunshine above them there were rumbles of thunder in the far distance. 'I would suggest any storm that might be on the horizon will be coming across from the west the way that muggy breeze is blowing against our faces.'

'In that case before we go back in the house I must put my wonderful horse back into the little stable and make sure she is fully protected from any rain we may have.' Briefly he went over the other side of the field where his tall chestnut horse was standing and took her gently into the stable before following Rosemary into the farmhouse. 'I must go and have a look on the stove and check how my meat pie is coming on.' Martin sniffed the air hard with his nostrils. 'From here in the hallway your meat pie as usual smells absolutely wonderful.'

'I hope Elaine gets here before the storm does,' Rosemary bent down to take a clearer look out of the large front window and turned to Martin looking rather concerned. 'The very dark clouds are approaching increasingly quickly.' Martin shrugged and gave an indifferent and uncaring response;

'At least that will make my little work on my few crops complete today. They are looking very parched at the moment.' Rosemary snorted.

'You seem to think nothing about your little daughter any more since she first met Christopher do you?' Martin shrugged slightly; 'Not as much as I used to I admit.' At least to Rosemary's relief the front door opened and Elaine's slim pale figure arrived and automatically she stood up on tiptoe and kissed her father before embracing more warmly with her mother. 'I've put my horse into the stable with yours father as I believe the rain will soon be upon us and my horse I believe is afraid of thunder and lightning.'

'I'm not very fond of it myself.' Rosemary remarked anxiously as there was a flicker of lightning suddenly illuminating the kitchen. 'What have you been doing with yourself today dear?' Rosemary inquired as Elaine went into the living room to sit down. 'I thought it may be rather nice to give Farmer Blackwood and his assistants a little help with the harvesting. He was grateful at least father.' Martin's grizzly expression on his already dry and gnarled face suggested his utter contempt of the matter. 'You used to help as a gatherer for your old father with his harvesting when I had a respectable farm for people to admire rather than just two small strips of land.' Elaine's reply was halted by a louder rumble of thunder.

'I'm sorry for what happened to your farm father but there is nothing I can do about the nasty takeover there was not all that long ago.' As she was laying the table Rosemary was forced to recoil by a bright long flash of lightning directly in front of her eyes. Elaine got up and took the cutlery from her mother's hand and told her to sit down and relax. 'What has happened to you Rose, you never used to be frightened of thunderstorms?'

'Perhaps I am getting old.' she tried joking slightly.

'Perhaps as the table is in the window we should wait until the storm has passed overhead before we eat and then I thought mother as you have two spinning wheels and a fresh amount of raw sheeps' wool to be weaved then I would remain with you and in the attic you and I could weave together in readiness for your agent's arrival tomorrow morning.' Rosemary looked extremely kindly at her daughter.

'That would be simply wonderful.' Once more Elaine's suggestion only made her father scowl.

'Why can't you just remain here with us rather than going jaunting to London and starting a new life with that fiance of yours?' Elaine bent her neck forwards and kissed her father gently on one cheek.

'Father, Christopher wishes to begin a completely new life away from all these Midland villages and somewhere in which there is life and activity and a city where we can bring our child up with an exciting life ahead. Christopher and I believed when the Parish councils were each given a share of Parliament's money together they would develop all these small villages and by now there would be much more life and entertainment in them but sadly that just hasn't happened. That is why so many more young people are leaving the villages and making for the developing towns and cities.' Another loud rumble of thunder erupted directly over the house and all at once the heavy rain began to fall hammering the roof top and windowpanes. 'Farmer Blackwood will be a happy man. All of his harvest was gathered in and put away safely in his several barns.'

'Oh yes, and what about my two rows of crops which are still growing? I knew when I went out and had a look at them this morning they needed watering but not as much as this!'

'At least mother the wind is getting up strong and the storm now appears to be blowing over quickly.' Rosemary had a look through the window and deciding that the thunder and lightning at least had about passed over she went into the kitchen to bring in the plates and the pie. 'There is some fruit and cream to follow. Who knows dear this might end up being our final family meal together.' Carefully Rosemary began to serve the pie before going to bring in a pan of roasted potatoes and serving those equally too. 'I simply wanted to check if you had made all your arrangements for next Wednesday and if my wedding dress had been prepared for the event.'

'Of course every thing is done Elaine. Do you believe your mother and father are incompetent or uncaring about you?' Martin grumbled again.

'No father. Of course not.......maybe it is just me becoming increasingly nervous as my wedding day is coming closer. Christopher is exactly the same on his side of the family, he is going more and more to discuss things with his mother and father and two brothers and they tell him to stop worrying too.' The heavy rain continue hitting the ground and buildings hard a while longer before the sun began to shine brightly again and it was just like a fine summer day once more. 'That was rather nasty while it lasted.' Rosemary remarked. 'It will probably have uprooted every single one of my crops and flooded the small plots of land after all the hard work I put in to grow them this far.'

'You could always stand for election father the next time a general election is held or when there is a by-election at one of the Midland constituencies just like that young man did in Birmingham and now he is an MP. He has all kinds of ideas to develop the Houses of Parliament and have a new monarch sitting on the throne.' Martin could only scoff at his daughter's suggestion.

'Is that some kind of a joke Elaine, to regard your father as a future politician is simply ridiculous and as far as Birmingham's new MP Jack Parker to suggest he is going to reform the Houses of Parliament and get a new monarch established is completely insane.'

'As far as your big wedding day is concerned Elaine, there is nothing else your father and I can do.' Elaine screwed up her little face at her mother's remark and chuckled in a rather girly way. 'Of course mother, I knew you and father would not let me down. It was worth coming if for no other reason but to eat a slice of this marvellous meat pie. Mother this is something I will most definitely miss when I go away with Christopher to London.'

'Doesn't Christopher cook at all?' Martin asked laughing in his disparaging way as he knew what his daughter's reply would be; 'No father, Christopher has never been able to cook. As far as food is concerned in the future he shall be relying on me as the housewife to prepare all his meals for him.' Martin sighed as he finished his first course and waited for his daughter to take his plate away. 'Before I enjoy my fruit and cream I feel I should go outside and check what the heavy rain has done to my few crops although I can guess. I believe they will be completely ruined.' He almost had to pull himself up out of his chair and with his tired head drooping he went out through the kitchen and the back door to have a look at the strips of land. Very soon he was back inside and pouring himself a large mug of whisky. 'The few crops I had grown have been completely ruined. After I have eaten my fruit and cream I am going out for a drink again with my farming friends. I don't know if I can cope with this kind of life any more.' They finished their meal more sombrely than they had started it and the moment Martin had put down his spoon and finished his apples and cream he got a few coins and put on his worn shoes and doublet and angrily left the house. 'Never mind father mother, I shall help you with the washing up and weaving and then we can look ahead more cheerfully to the big day!'

The wedding of Elaine and Christopher was intended to be a big occasion to celebrate their marriage and give them a cheery send off to London and that was how the day turned out. Families from many small villages and hamlets all across the Midlands lined streets, lanes and footpaths and many fields up towards the village church at Tugby were filled with excited men, women and children all just wanting to have even a simple peek at the two celebrities of the event. The gold carriage that had been hired to take Christopher and Elaine to the village church and then after the church service on to London took the engaged couple through the bumpy, gavelly roads and lanes of Birstall, Whitwick, Little Dalby, Houghton-on-the-Hill, Syston and Swadincote before finally coming slowly to a stop outside Tugby church. In every village passed the streets were lined with families all cheering Elaine and Christopher onwards and wishing them all the very best for their future together. Elaine's wide pink wedding dress fitted with her dark brown hair tied back in a bow and her bright blue eyes sparkling were admired and approved of by Christopher and everybody who was standing around the church and watching their every move from the very moment they stepped out of the golden carriage smiling broadly and holding each other's hand with very deep affection before they walked the short distance into the church together which was completely full of family members from both sides. Sitting in the front row of the church Martin was pale both with nerves and with some anger, the thought of his lovely daughter travelling down to London to begin a new life with someone he hardly knew made him sick to the bone. The pretty little church not only was full of very supportive and excited people but had also been carefully decorated with flowers and blue boughs and many bunches of coloured ribbons to make the church seem particularly homely. The service was carried out perfectly and afterwards in front of the church's capacity crowd Christopher and Elaine held each other tightly and with great emotion and passionate feelings inside them they kissed each other long and hard and as their faces touched the bright twinkling light radiating from their eyes could be seen by everybody watching on. As they walked slowly out of the church there were several small boys in costume dancing in front of them until as they reached the carriage they stood still and waved to everybody watching on and their faces beaming with joy and now anticipation as to their new life ahead. 'I suppose this is it is it Rosemary, we will never see our beautiful daughter again?' As Rosemary and Martin stood outside the church door Rosemary could not prevent herself from feeling a slight sense of annoyance towards her husband and his pessimistic attitude. 'Will you stop this complete nonsense of our *never* seeing our beautiful daughter again. Elaine has told me time and again this is not the end of our relationship it is simply a new start in her life as a married woman and with a very handsome and educated young man.' After a lengthy period of time as Elaine and Christopher continued waving eventually Christopher signalled for his new wife to get in the carriage and very quickly he followed her inside. The two coachmen in corresponding blue costume with a large green hat checking that their passengers were safely inside made their final preparations to move away before eventually under a clear blue sky and scorching sunlight the fascinating journey as husband and wife to the distinguished capital city began.

Christopher and Elaine pushed their heads out of the carriage windows cheering and screaming their final loving remarks to such upright and obliging friends before eventually pulling their heads inside and falling silent as the cheering waving crowds disappeared from sight. 'Are you truly happy this afternoon my love?' Christopher asked taking one of Elaine's smooth soft hands and kissing her gently on the cheek. 'Of course I am truly happy my love. Today has been a most wonderful day……not for my father of course but for you and me. Now we can begin a new life together and I am very excited about it.' Christopher gave a deep purr of happiness before sitting back and for a time just watching the trees and open fields go by and then waving to the men and women who were standing outside their small wooden homes curiously watching the gold carriage go by and waving to the unknown passengers. 'The people in these villages and hamlets are all so very loving and kind but the fact that there is hardly any life in such villages was becoming too much for me to take any more.' Elaine listened to Christopher's emotionally put remark and kissed him gently.

'There are more and more young people in such small villages and hamlets who feel exactly the same way. That was why I was so surprised that there was such a large turnout for my twenty-first birthday party.'

'The land here is so dry and bare,' Christopher commented in no more than a whisper. 'Where are we now?' he asked looking through both sides of the carriage.

'It's difficult to tell, I would suggest now we are inside Worcestershire but that is just a slight guess I must say again.'

'At least the house when we arrive will be furnished and decorated, all we will have to do is unpack a few things and change and then I would suggest we go out and have a grand meal and bottle of wine to celebrate our new beginning.'

'And when are you intending to go and have your first day in your new job?' Elaine took a hand of Christopher's and squeezed it slightly with affection. 'I have said to my employees that my new business will be starting on the very first morning of September at nine o'clock.'

'All the fields around this part of England are increasingly busy with people gathering in crops and already preparing other fields for the sowing of fresh seeds.' Christopher looked out of his window at the many men and women who were working extremely hard in the many large and arable fields. 'At least the fields aren't full any more of young Jamaican slaves. They must be extremely hot in this blazing sunshine.' Christopher mused. 'We shall have more time for partying if we want to.' Elaine gave Christopher a slight selfless face.

'I believe already we must be coming into Buckinghamshire. Have you noticed the climate seems to be changing and I believe there is some cloud and possibly light rain on the horizon.' This time Elaine mumbled some gentle remark to Christopher which Christopher simply could not understand at all. Her head was lying back against the cushion which had been placed behind her and her eyes were almost fully closed. 'I believe things are beginning quickly to catch up with me.' she commented and gave a strange whining yawn which briefly filled Christopher with a little concern. 'Do you suppose your father's emotions will finally get the better of him and he will ride down to London to collect you and bring you home?' Elaine opened her tired eyes for a second or two and giggled. 'Is that meant to be a serious question Christopher?' Christopher looked rather offended by Elaine's question.

'Your father is a very good horse rider and you know just how upset he was when you were readying yourself to leave home.'

'That is a remark you can just put out of your mind.' As the coach approached Oxfordshire and then Hertfordshire there were slight sounds of thunder which were getting louder as they got closer to London and the air definitely began to feel increasingly muggy. 'That is strange Elaine,' Christopher said slowly and thoughtfully as he turned his head and lowering his window down looked outside behind the carriage. 'What is happening out there?' Elaine pulled her head up from the pillow and looked Christopher directly in his eyes. 'Now what are you talking about my wonderful husband?'

'Look behind us, there are a number of horses following and now the stagecoach is arriving in north London the two drivers are making the horses go even faster which makes no sense, in fact the way this coach is bouncing about of the pebbly ground I am beginning to feel a little unsafe.' Elaine wound down her window to have a look behind and see if she could make any sense of her husband's comment. 'That's most unusual.' she said after several minutes looking outside. 'Why on earth are they following us? Have we done anything wrong and they want to arrest us?'

'That group of horse riders has an armed sheriff leading them.' As the stagecoach was approaching Piccadilly and the cloud was getting thicker with the thunder booming through the air their stagecoach began to get slower and they could hear the two coachmen having a rather loud and at times impolite argument. 'I believe the coach is stopping right outside Piccadilly and the band of men following behind us is now beginning to catch up. Damn it this was not how I was expecting our arrival in London to start. I know one thing Elaine it would make your father laugh in our faces.' The two coachmen were being spoken to very clearly by one of the horse riders who had been following for some considerable distance before they were both pulled down with a slight scuffle before being led into an adjacent carriage and with two guards pointing muskets in their faces the carriage was driven away. 'I'm truly sorry about that unfortunate start for your marriage.' The tall muscular gentleman in a brown uniform was well armed with a musket, matchlock and two sharp daggers. 'If you would be kind enough to get out and one of my colleagues will drive this back to Leicestershire and return it to its original owner.'

'Excuse me;' Christopher replied with some anger as he and Elaine stepped out of the carriage. '…..but can you tell me please what on earth this has been all about?'

'My name is Richard Walsh and I am the Sheriff of Worcester. I and the rest of my posse have been given some signed information by Sir Edward Coke which has told us that your two coachmen were actually Ambrose Rookwood and Francis Tresham -' As the rolls of thunder were getting louder and the flashes of lightning were getting much brighter feeling frustrated and increasingly exhausted Christopher interrupted; 'So please will you just tell me, who on earth are Ambrose Rookwood and Francis Tresham, apart from two innocent stagecoach drivers?'

'They are the two remaining gunpowder conspirators who we have been searching for for many months. Now they have finally been found and caught they are being taken to the Tower for questioning and I suspect afterwards a straightforward execution. Now I must return to Worcestershire and get back to my work.' Richard in his loud commanding voice above the sound of thunder ordered his men to follow him back to the Midlands immediately and one member of the posse stayed behind to mount the stagecoach and drive the horses pulling the gold carriage away back to the Midlands. As the horses all disappeared and Christopher and Elaine were left alone standing in a derelict part of central London Christopher put a hand in the air to feel the first drops of rain falling. 'I believe at least here there is a regular horse and trap service running.' He and Elaine kissed and looked blank faced at each other in total disbelief. 'This was not exactly how

I had expected our wedding day to end up.' Christopher looked despairingly at Elaine and then gazed ahead on the bumpy broken road before putting a hand out to motion for the nearing trap to halt, pick them up and transport them finally to their new home and beginning.

John and Deborah had been living in their small and poky flat in Whitechapel for over six months and were already regarded as professional stall holders on Spitalfields Market. When they had slowly arrived on horseback in east London they had been teased about their loss of direction and uncertainty with which way they should go as they got increasingly close to the centre of the mighty capital. It seemed to both John and Deborah when it was suggested they left their horses behind and followed a young Londoner to a number of free flats they might as well simply do as they were told and it was in the grubby unsafe and insecure streets of Whitechapel where they had ended up living. Already they had made themselves popular with their pleasant and charming characteristics and every night when the market stalls closed a celebratory party was arranged on the green not far away shared with a number of sheep, cattle and hens which were roving free. For such insignificant people selling many simple and inexpensive goods on their stalls they seemed to live extremely well particularly with their fine clothes they always wore made of the finest and most costly materials. Deborah from the very moment she was given a spinning wheel and a large mound of wool and silk to weave had become a professional and highly respected weaver and with the large amount of silk that was being brought into England from overseas each day there was a fortune for Deborah to make. Another long and exhausting day on the market was drawing to a close and already John could see in the distance the large grassy field where the daily celebratory party was always held was being prepared for later that afternoon once more. 'It has been another successful day of trade.' John turned round to see a little dwarf like figure below him and pursing his lips opened his bag up with the day's money inside. 'I would say that you are about right there.' The little figure dressed in his regular sleeveless leather jerkin, leather breeches and knee length boots took his bag with all his unsold goods inside and his bag of savings and as fast as he possibly could hurried away to prepare for the night's party. For a time John stood alone dressed in his finest leather breeches and white silk shirt and looked from the top of a knoll across the wide market area at the many visitors who were still going around the great number of stalls feeling and poking at the goods and questioning the stall holders over their prices before returning to his own stall and finishing his work for the day. It was not a long distance to his little flat though always when arriving in the narrow lane at the back of Whitechapel John was extremely alert for the possibility of criminal activity of any kind where crime was almost a daily and very regular occurrence. He entered the flat safely and as he went inside the dark kitchen he locked the door tightly behind him. The flat was still and nearly silent but for the slight sound of the spinning machine working upstairs in the attic. John picked up one of the many cups which he and Deborah had collected since their first arriving in Whitechapel and poured himself a drink of ale. As he sat down on the smallest stool they had he picked up the black bag and tipped it open on the table to have a look at the day's profit. Although the sunlight was still extremely bright the flat had only one small front window which let in very little light of any kind, not even much light from the streetlight across the narrow road when it came on twinkling. He pulled himself heavily off his stool once more groaning and blowing as he got up and with a matchstick lit one of the candles which was used for light whenever it was at all necessary. 'Hello stranger.' Deborah remarked quietly when she came into the living room and saw John sitting inside and looking exhausted. John beckoned for Deborah to sit down as once again he began to count the day's profit. 'We have made a profit of over twenty sovereigns today.' he commented in his most thoughtful voice. 'That is excellent as long as we are careful how we spend it.' John looked at Deborah through the dullish light and his eyes were knit tightly together as he scowled at Deborah's remark. 'That is something we decided almost the very day we were led into Whitechapel.' He had another swig of ale and began to put the money back in the bag. 'Are we going to the usual party on the hill tonight?' Deborah poured herself a mug of milk and looked a little concerned. 'I will have to join the party a little bit later this evening, there is still a large amount of raw wool and silk in the attic that need to be dealt with this evening before my agent arrives tomorrow to pay me for all my work.' John nodded.

'Money comes before partying obviously. I will go out after I've changed and see you on the green later.' As they were sitting for a short time together there was a knocking on the front door which made both Deborah and John look through the darkness anxiously at each other. 'Normally an unexpected knocking at the door can only mean trouble.' John got up cautiously and went to find out who the unwelcome visitor may be. 'Alright Robert, tell me, what is it? What's happened?' Robert who lived with his female partner three flats away felt so exhausted himself he could not force himself to tell the whole of his story and was just able to say; 'I saw Julie when I came to my flat being led away by another market holder.......she left my flat over three hours ago and has not returned since and I'm absolutely worried sick about her safety.' John was unsure how to respond and shrugged. 'I'm sorry Robert but I know absolutely nothing about the disappearance of Julie. If I hear anything at all I will let you know immediately.' John watched Robert's small figure disappear and very quickly closed the door once more and locked it tightly behind. 'Sometimes this place gives me the creeps.' Deborah looked at John solemnly and poured herself some more milk.

'When we have enough money I think it would be a good idea for us to go and find somewhere in London which is a great deal more secure and safe than this part of the city. I wouldn't be at all surprised if Robert never sees Julie again after what seems to have been a most peculiar disappearance.' Falling down heavily again onto his little stool reflectively not for the first time John remarked; 'I never believed when I was arguing about future farm work with father on Harper Farm that one day I would be living in a little unrefined flat in Whitechapel, that is something I had never expected to happen in my life.'

'Whenever we do leave this part of London I definitely want to buy myself another horse.' Deborah remarked John thought with one of her most wistful voices. 'I know the horse I bought back where I used to live with father was not at all healthy and its trek to London seemed increasingly hard but I still miss it and I definitely want to buy another.' John got up slowly and lit a second of the six candles in the room and frowned very mildly at Deborah. 'I definitely do miss not having a horse, ever since I left Harper Farm I have missed not having a horse, buying two horses is something we will do the moment we leave Whitechapel.' Together they finished their drinks and little gossip before separating as Deborah went back up to the attic to complete her weaving and John went to the very small bedchamber to get changed for the evening.

The bedchamber was bathed in total darkness when John got inside and he had to start searching around almost on his hands and knees for the matchsticks. Eventually when the candles were burning he had a look at the sizeable collection of clothes he had bought himself since arriving in Whitechapel. For such a warm evening he chose nothing of any great extravagance to wear except for a simple white linen shirt, dark linen breeches and a pair of lightweight flat shoes. He washed himself quickly and left the house locking the door again tightly behind.

'You haven't changed at all John, you're still looking as well as ever.' John was sure he recognised the grating high toned voice yet he could not give it a name. He sat in front of a bramble bush on the top of bank and away from the centre of the party and the dancing and for now at least alone. Turning his head he recognised the figure and the young elegant lady by his side. 'Abram Croaker what are you doing here in east London and with your pretty little wife Carol too?'

'We're doing the same as you John, we've come to the big city to try and find a little work.' John got up and introduced himself again properly with a pleasant handshake and some more homely words of welcome. 'Is this the first time you and your lovely wife have been to the sellers' party?' John slowly took them to the little stall where Ian Pickering one of the regular stall holders at the market was selling drinks and refreshments. 'What can I get you both?' Abram and Carol had a look on the stall and selected two gin and tonics and a simple plate of cold meat sandwiches to be divided. 'Are you going to let your market buddy have them free this evening?' John was hoping his short tubby friend would say yes as he had forgotten to bring any money out with him. Ian looked at John's pleading face and muttered. 'For you then.'

'We have brought all the family with us.' Carol commented as they sat down together under the long branches of an apple tree. 'Our young ones Martin, Luke and Becky are all in the centre of the party dancing.' Abram laughed at his wife's description of the children.

'Except they're not as young as they used to be. Martin and Luke are both twenty-five and Becky is the youngest of the three, she is aged twenty-four.'

'So as your *young* ones aren't now so young as they used to be why did they come with you to London rather than going their separate ways?' John asked curiously. Abram scowled a little at Carol.

'They were brought up by my wife, not by me I must add there as being unable to look after themselves and needing always to rely on their mother to be looked after.' Carol was slightly insulted by the remark.

'That is not true and you know it Abram, the children have always looked up to both of us not just me.' Abram became red cheeked and bowed his head as he knew his wife was completely right in her comment. 'Yes dear I know, that's the way I've brought them up as well.' He had a drink and very quickly changed the subject. 'I was extremely sorry about Harper Farm and the way it just collapsed after Lord Montagu and his guards had taken it over. I was there the day when we arrived to find all the land had been enclosed and we were barred from entering to start our usual spring work. What a terrible day that was.'

'It didn't do mother and father any good, particularly father. Mother was already severely ill in hospital. Father came into the alehouse and told me the news of her death later and then left home and I have never seen him since.'

'I'm sorry t' hear such awful news John. 'What did your mother die of?'

'Father never really made that clear, not from the very morning he and the doctor helped mother out of the farmhouse and away to the nearby village hospital. I believe it was chicken pox and the severe fever it brings with it that killed her although on saying that she was extremely weak anyway.'

'And what has become of James?' Carol looked particularly upset by the news of Mary Harper's death.

'Unfortunately Carol the disappearance of father is something I shall probably never be able to understand or probably I will never see again. It was never the way I expected our family to break up, not at the time we were regarded as the fierce rivals of High Hill Farm.' Abram looked at John a little smug faced.

'The farm of Peter and George has collapsed as well and has been taken over by a group of individual farmers from Leicestershire who are acting as one.' John looked completely dumbfounded by the news of his rival's downfall. 'How on earth did that happen? When I was walking away from Wellingborough I could see the fields of High Hill Farm looking in perfect condition for farming and with their fields of sheep and cattle full of livestock. Was it a joint decision to sell the farm?' The conversation was briefly interrupted when Martin and Becky came running back up the bank looking a little uncertain of themselves. 'We were offered a glass of strong whisky each mama but we aren't sure if we would be sensible to drink it, something like that might not be good for us......would you agree with us?' John's twisted face and tutting suggested his disappointment at the question. 'Just this once you can drink it.' Carol replied and waved them both away from the conversation. 'Are they like that all the time?' John asked shaking his head with surprise. 'Not all the time John.' Abram responded quickly. 'They might still in some ways not yet have grown up fully but down there where all the dancing is taking place they will be dancing with every man and woman there is to dance with. They really are brilliant dancers.' John had a drink of whisky and pushing out his lips commented under his breath, 'It's amazing sometimes just how life changes.' He wiped a little perspiration from his forehead and looked to Abram. 'Have you found anywhere definite to live in London yet or are you still looking?'

'We are still looking around and trying to find somewhere that will fit a family of five, after that we can start and build a new life though other than farming we aren't quite sure just what we are going to do.' Carol looked at John and then at the other stall holders taking a more active part in the growing party. 'Maybe that is the thing to do do you suppose John, open up your own stall on a market?' John stuck his tongue between his teeth and slowly nodded. 'I must admit when I came to London with Deborah and was wondering what exactly I was going to do to begin my new life the simple idea of running my own market stall did appeal to me especially when my only other trade is farming and even then I was always under my father's influence and not making decisions myself.' Carol and Abram looked curiously at each other.

'Who is Deborah? That is a name neither Carol or myself recognise, certainly not a name we remember from Harper Farm.' John threw both Carol and Abram a warm face.

'Deborah is a lovely and supportive young woman I met when I had only just begun my walk to London. From the moment we set eyes on each other we recognised one another from our days when we were only very young. To begin a new life together is absolutely magnificent. Now what we have to do is make sure that our new life together is a success. She should be with us later, at the moment she is inside the flat finishing her day's weaving for what should tomorrow be a large profit from her agent.' Carol looked down from the bank to the centre stage where the next dance was progressing rapidly. Martin, Luke and Becky were all dancing with young partners and loving every second of it. 'Our young ones may not have grown up in some ways but they certainly are fit and active.' Carol remarked with a grin crossing her lips.

'What a magnificent sunset there is forming over London.' John immediately recognized Deborah's soft smooth voice from behind him. 'Meet Deborah my wonderful lady friend.' Deborah looked for a little more knowledge about the couple who were sitting beside John and he stood up and introduced her to the two visitors more precisely. 'The blue mist is still hanging over the river Thames.' Deborah remarked.

'The unpleasant smell of the mist is hanging all over London.'

'That was something we were never warned about when we made our way by stagecoach to London.' Abram remarked deliberately raising his head and smelling the unwholesome air. 'Let's hope then that the council's idea of having a new sewage system put under London shall do the trick and help make the river at least less filthy, brown and foul-smelling like it is at the moment.' When the latest piece of music for dancing finished to John's surprise before getting herself something to drink Deborah picked herself up off the ground and stretched out a hand for John to take. 'Come on John, before the next piece of music starts.' John was slightly taken aback by Deborah's comment. 'If you're sure you can cope. You look absolutely exhausted after doing so much weaving in the small confined attic for most of the day.' Deborah was unwilling to listen and took John's hand and pulled him down the hill to the centre stage where all the other young couples were getting into position and preparing to dance. 'It's possible we may start a new business together in another part of London.' John remarked loudly above the sound of the trumpeters and the single drummer. 'They sound very sensible, especially as they've brought their children with them to help with any heavy work they may have to do. Remember this morning we were saying this sort of life is not how we were intending to continue our lives for too much longer.'

'And when there is so much crime too.' Their dancing under a fading sunlight was as swift and professional as everyone else who was dancing with them and as the music finished they automatically hugged each other and kissed as though in celebration of their achievement. 'The sun is looking increasingly dull under the mist that seems to be rising off the river.' John commented as they returned to Abram and Carol at the top of the bank. 'I can feel the strong stink in my throat too.' Deborah went to get herself a drink and John fell heavily to the ground. 'You look more tired than Deborah.' Abram commented smiling and chuckling at John's red faced and exhausted figure. 'She is one year younger than me.' John retorted seeming by the red tears in his eyes and expression on his cheeks to be laughing and crying at the same time. 'I believe since Lord Montagu took over the fields of Harper Farm and the death of mother have aged me greatly. However my life changes with Deborah in future weeks and months are going to make me feel young again I'm sure!' John found himself gasping for breath and wheezing badly at the same time. As the hazy sunset became increasingly picturesque and colourful in a blurry sense directly over the heads of the people of east London John, Deborah, Abram and Carol sat together quietly just enjoying the cheerful occasion until as the dancing continued at the bottom of the bank Deborah and John got up slowly and prepared to walk back the short distance to their little flat. 'Please do keep in touch with us now that we've met up again and perhaps we will be able to start a new business together.' 'I advise you not to come and live in this part of London, the streets and the market place are not at all safe, especially at night.' Deborah made her comment in a loud clear voice above the sound of the music which had just begun playing once again. 'The blue dress you are wearing Deborah is absolutely divine.' Carol remarked as Deborah was standing up and preparing to leave. 'I weaved and stitched it myself with a little bit of the silk that I am given to weave. I shall weave one for you too.' Carol looked extremely flattered by Deborah's proposal. 'We shall see you at the market again and make further proposals.' With some additional warm words John and Deborah excused themselves and made their way with a large amount of caution back to their little flat in Whitechapel.

The following morning was just as hot as it had been for the last several and John dressing as usual in his plain and more grubby clothes had opened the back door to let some air into the stiflingly hot flat and was looking out across the market though not with any excitement of any kind but simple curiosity. 'The wool and silk have all been weaved and are ready to be collected by the agent who if he is his usual self will be arriving about ten thirty.' Deborah went into the kitchen and began to prepare the pottage for once feeling free from any work. 'At least with a flat so small there is very little housework to be done.' John went into the small kitchen as his lady friend was making the breakfast and gave her a small peck on one cheek. 'That was quite a coincidence last night to find one of my former farmhands here in east London.'

'It will be an even better coincidence if Abram and his wife do return and we can set up a new business somewhere safer and cleaner in London together.' Deborah lifted her eyebrows high suggesting her extreme hopes. She finished preparing the pottage as for once John laid the table and poured two cups of ale and sat down heavily as Deborah filled the bowls. 'It's going to be another scorching day by the look of that clear sky and bright dazzling sunshine.' Out of the door they looked straight across the market and already a number of John's closest allies in business were trading with visitors. 'I was told last night at the party that on Saturday Oscar, one of the market's most experienced sellers is to leave.' John was very taken aback by Deborah's comment. 'Who told you that piece of news?'

'Nobody told me, I picked it up last night at the bottom of the hill when I was buying myself another drink.'

'Well that is a sad surprise and extremely disappointing. If you remember it was Oscar who properly taught us both about becoming businessmen on the market.' John had a spoon of pottage and looked to the door. 'I must go and have a friendly talk with him before he leaves. I am hoping that one day Abram and Carol will come back here with an offer to start a new business together, more than anything else the amount of crime that is done around here I find terrifying. Another body was found last night as we were returning home from the dance night. Peter Regan who owned the fish stall was found dead in the narrow lane opposite us with his throat cut.' Deborah grimaced widely.

'I never spoke with Peter but I recognised his face from his stall.' As they were eating Deborah rolled her eyes to the door and looking out one corner made her smile, partly with some humour and a little with irritation. 'Look what has arrived.' John briefly put down his spoon and looked up at the door mat. There in a crouching position was the scrawny black and white cat that seemed to turn up in a number of different places around the market during every day as the market was at its very peak of business. 'I wonder how many people feed that poor half starved animal.' Deborah mused. Picking up his spoon again and finishing his meal John replied without any thought of his answer at all. 'Nobody!' The cat turned its little thin head to look at them with its empty eyes as if waiting for a response until eventually it looked outside the door again and leapt at something on the hard pathway. 'Either a mouse or rat I would guess.' Deborah commented and gave a yawn. As John emptied his bowl and put down his spoon Deborah motioned with a raised shoulder to the door. 'Aren't you going out to your stall to begin your day of trade?' John put his elbows on the table and his head in his hands and sighed. 'I will do very shortly, at the moment the rising crowds and all the hassling and arguing that is going on outside is putting me off slightly.' He refilled his cup with ale and swigged it down in one go before going to the kitchen and kissing Deborah on the cheek, finally having the gallantry to go outside and begin business on his stall.

Even so early in the morning all around so much of east London the many confined lanes, streets and side roads teemed with liveliness. Stalls displayed nearly every type of wares and many more were stored beside the doors of small buildings making confined lanes, avenues and streets even narrower and enticing crowds of loiterers who toyed with the goods and argued with the stall-holders about the cost. Particularly at the stalls of the fishmongers and butchers there were increasing amounts of blood and bones and entrails around which dogs of many kinds and the occasional familiar cat crept looking for an opportunity to dive in. The vegetable stalls were a prey to the occasional roaming goat and sheep which had escaped from the nearby field.

Some of the visitors automatically nudged their horses around the worst of the increasing rubbish and dirt. The sides of the lanes and pathways were dense with waste at which boar and hog rummaged and the mounds of animal and human manure which were meant to be swept into the channels often did not reach them. A dead cat had been lying outside one of the meat stalls for several days and by the look of its bloody corpse the large crows had been feeding on it considerably. There had been a growing row between Jim the butcher and Antony the jewellery seller who were trying to reach a compromise over who had the responsibility to remove the corpse and so far neither gentleman had intended to concede defeat. All day on the Thames there had been vessels of all sizes travelling towards east London full of goods and fresh food to be delivered to the relevant market stalls and as the day went on the Thames seemed to be getting increasingly busy. There were vessels stopping under London Bridge unloading their freight of a wide variety of fruits and vegetables not long brought in off the farming fields and completely fresh, meat, wines, fish only just caught in the Channel, spices and a few tapestries. John stood by his bookstall all morning and afternoon waiting for a little custom yet that morning more people appeared to be looking at the fruit, vegetable and plain food stalls than anything else. Increasingly the din and clamour of high pitched voices, loud crying customers, many arguing about the high prices and quality of goods that were for sale and those people who had simply stopped to gossip and had had to raise their voices more and more over the rising and abominable cacophony was simply getting ever more insufferable. Eventually John glanced at his watch and seeing it was almost midday he decided for a while to leave his work and go and have a cup of coffee and something to eat for lunch.

The small coffee house in Euston had been open for over two years now and was always doing very good trade. By the time John arrived there was a long queue at the counter and a large amount of money appeared to be changing hands. John peered at the food which was already on display and selected automatically. 'Hello John, how's business today?' Emily gave John her usual sweet understanding smile and waited with her usual caring expression for his reply. John felt almost too tired to reply and could hardly manage to keep his eyelids open yet he forced himself to reply simply, 'Unfortunately today Emily nobody seems to want to buy books.' He ordered his meal and took his plate and cup of coffee and sat alone at the furthest table simply for a little peace and quiet. It was not long after finding a quiet corner in the café that John's peace and desire for privacy was broken as a cup and a plate of beef and a few freshly cooked vegetables was placed opposite him and a familiar face sat down to talk. 'There's no profit by coming into a coffee house John.' John lifted his head and looked up to see Keith the more popular of the market's three butchers and most profitable. 'In which case why have you come in too?' Keith gave a smile over his chubby face.

'I have already made over fifty sovereigns this morning and my stall is empty, I'm just allowing my assistant to sweep up all the dirt and refuse on the ground and waiting for the fresh meat to be delivered and then I will be straight back at work.' Keith's loud and boastful voice made John's heart rate increase rapidly as it annoyed him very much. 'I'm hoping that one day very soon I shall be leaving this sometimes irritating business and going and doing trade in a more organised profession.' Keith was rather surprised by John's uncharacteristic remark and looked at him with his large blue eyes almost popping out of their sockets. 'All the time you have been working on this market I have never once heard you make a remark like that.' John simply lifted his head again briefly and replied in a yawn; 'For once Keith that is just the way I feel.' Looking at Keith's blooded butcher's apron increasingly made John feel sick and suddenly the thought of being able to eat any lunch vanished. 'I believe my only real job was on a farm, perhaps I made a mistake travelling to London.' John commented more to himself than Keith however Keith tried to comfort him a little. 'Why not open your mind just like you have and try to do something a little different just like you and your pretty lady friend have. Don't you feel coming to London has changed your life completely and given you a new start away from working land and tending cattle and sheep? That is how I would look at your new start in life.' Keith then shrugged with his tall broad shoulders and had some of his lunch. 'This food as usual is excellent.' John looked at his plate still full with untouched food and pushed it away.

'I am going back to my flat to have a word with Deborah.' As John got up slowly and wearily from the table he added slowly. 'I may see you at the dance tonight.'

At the flat there was no sound or signs of activity when John opened the door. He walked slowly through the living room and passageway before going up the small number of steps and into the attic where he discovered Deborah and Abram sitting and talking. 'What on earth are you doing up here?' John asked as he poked his head in. 'Abram has something private he wanted to tell us. As it's still only mid-afternoon he suggested we came up here and talked out of everyone's visibility.' John looked at both Deborah and Abram suspiciously however he asked Abram directly what the news was he wanted to speak of. 'Today I took the children and Carol to Soho and together we discovered the gentleman who owns and rents out all the arable land which he possesses.' Although John could barely see Abram's face in such murk he could tell by his shaky voice there was something else he had to add to his unfinished story. 'So Abram tell me, what did you and the landowner discuss?'

'I asked if he would let us rent some land to farm around the Soho district of London and we have after a long hard discussion come to a joint agreement about land and the amount of rent he will charge each month. We believe if we and the children work the land together we will be able to make it become a new and successful farm.' Deborah took one of John's hands as she could see he was unsure about the offer and sat him down next to her. 'Why don't we take Abram's offer and begin a quieter life with what you know and prefer more than anything else, working the land and not trying to trade on a market stall with such loud and trying conditions?' John was tempted by the offer and yet still suspicious of their move up into the attic to discuss a seemingly ordinary and non-troublesome subject. However as he sat quietly in the stifling attic air he said slowly and softly; 'Yes……..if you're sure this will work…….' Abram got up from his little stool and put out a large hand for John to shake in full agreement with the offer. 'I suggest now we go down to the living room and I'll pour us all a drink of ale. Today has been the most frustrating of days.' Although the sun was still beaming down brightly outside there was very little light in the flat and John to be able to see exactly where he was treading as he walked into the room had to light all of the candles to be able to see anything at all. 'I hope you also discussed where Deborah and I are going to live while we are working the same farm as you and your children.' Abram took his cup of ale and silhouetted by one of the candle's small flickering flames he commented more confidently this time. 'The places of dwelling are already organised and are right beside the farming land itself.' John could not sit for long before having to get up and slam the door furiously shut. 'The loud noise coming from that damn market is really driving me mad!' They finished their drinks together in a satisfied mood before John was already thinking about packing the belongings and preparing to leave. 'I think we should go to our final party on the green tonight before we begin another new adventure.' Deborah motioned out through the little window and the large mass of activity that was continuing. 'There will be some people working on the market who will miss us greatly.' Abram finished swigging his drink and prepared to leave. 'We still have the horse and carriage and will come tomorrow to pick you both up.'

'One of the first things I want to buy when I get to my new home is a horse for riding and a chance to relax away from the work and activity for a while.' Deborah for once looked extremely annoyed about things herself. 'That can be arranged almost straight away as there is are stables near Soho and there is a big selection of horses for sale to choose from.' Abram got up from his chair and excused himself from the discussions commenting; 'I shall see you early in the morning and with your luggage ready we shall leave all this noise and dirt behind.' As Abram left the little flat John looked at his red face still with a little suspicion. 'Why did you and Abram go up into the attic to discuss something so simple and harmless as that?' Deborah turned her face from John and with the assistance of one of the black stockings holding all their coins she put it on the table and began to take out a separate collection of coins placed in a different bag. 'I have something to show you John, for all the hard work that I did with the weaving of silk and sheep's wool. I was given 100 gold sovereigns by my agent, don't you think that is just absolutely amazing?!' John nodded his head in agreement before disappearing into the bedchamber to begin packing in readiness for tomorrow's early move.

The short walk to the open field to attend the day's celebratory party did not feel like a heartbreaking one to John and Deborah even though they knew it would be the last time they ever did it. It was more a matter of watching where they were walking and in their light footwear avoiding as hard as they could the large mounds of filth, litter, blood and skin beside what had been the stall of one of the butchers and some dead fish which had been accidentally dropped onto the ground and forgotten completely. 'Marketing was simply not in my nature.' John commented and looked a little shyly at Deborah. 'I have to admit, we Harpers can't do everything.' Already when they reached the open field there were several food and drink stalls set up and the little music band that had been organised by some of the more senior marketeers was playing with its usual gusto and verve. 'Should we go and dance as we are the first ones here and enjoy our final evening in a little style?' John and Deborah took each other's hand and on the large stage in the centre of the field they danced lively and excitedly as the music became increasingly louder. When they finished there was a loud round of applause from several other couples who had just arrived and John and Deborah for their small audience gave a round of applause. 'Let me buy you a drink.' John commented as he took Deborah's hand and led her to one of the little drink stalls. 'A gin and tonic would be absolutely adorable.' John smiled briefly at his half friend Adrian who was running the stall. He ordered two gin and tonics and he and Deborah returned to the tall bank overlooking the stage to enjoy the rest of the evening alone. 'I'm sure the blue mist off the river is thicker over the land than it has been for a long time.' John commented and turned up his nose as the strong unpleasant stench was seeming to fill the air. 'At least Soho is further from the river so hopefully the mist will never be as strong………' Deborah's voice faded and John laughed slightly at her remark. 'That is a comment made by someone who has never been to London before in her life!' He gave a sly grin on his face which made Deborah blush. They watched several dances which exhausted them simply as spectators before John began coughing badly as the sunlight disappeared shrouded by the thick blue foul-smelling mist. 'I think we should go back to the little flat now and get some sleep before our early start in the morning.' After coughing again for a time John finished his drink to try and help his parched throat and then remarked once again with some suspicion in his voice and the way he gazed at Deborah with his eyes narrowed; 'I'm still not sure if this farming set up will truly work across the Soho fields. It seems the most curious place to set up a farm.' John took a hand firmly of Deborah's and he almost picked her up off the hard dry ground. 'It still seems most peculiar that Abram took you upstairs into the attic to speak with you about such a plain harmless thing -'

'We aren't married John! The way you are talking at me now you'd damn well think we were husband and wife.' They stared angrily into each other's eyes before after several minutes of an uneasy silence they began their short walk back through the market stalls and through thickening foul blue smog back up into their poky and uncomfortable little flat for a short period of rest.

CHAPTER FIVE

Following Jack Parker's half-completed maiden speech in the House of Commons there had been a great deal of frustrated muttering and whispering between politicians which pervaded the Chamber air until Mister Speaker in his uncertain manner demanded silence and order. The short wispy haired man spoke with a very refined voice and to some politicians he appeared to look like a professor speaking down to his students which made them somewhat cantankerous. To the total disbelief of nearly every politician who had attended the day's sitting a debate on the future of Parish councils was announced and caused much more disorder and a further unwelcome delay in the day's proceedings. The outrage that streamed around the Chamber after Mister Speaker had made his brief announcement continued with a great cacophony of angry incomprehensible voices all trying desperately to make their displeasure known before after a long-lasting pause order eventually returned to the Chamber. What proved to many MPs to be a period of simple prattling during a meaningless debate was not at all long and the result was a comfortable margin of votes proposing the councils continue for the next three months. Afterwards by only the early evening the Chamber was breaking up and MPs were beginning to withdraw from the discontented scenes. For a time through the remainder of the evening politicians who had attended the Chamber could be observed in little clusters all over the Houses of Westminster mouthing to one another rapidly with fingers prodding in different directions and hands waving wildly upwards as many gentlemen could not control their anger and incredulity any longer. Jack went to the bar in the House of Commons for a drink of whisky before returning to the small inn that was keeping him. As he sat alone pondering over the several hours of discussion that had just occurred he was gradually approached by Oliver St John who had chaired the Cross Cabinet during the short time it had been given to operate. Somewhat uncannily the tall dark eyed figure was dressed totally in jet black attire which made Jack slightly wary of the unfamiliar gentleman. 'Excuse me for saying this Mr Parker but if you are intending to completely transform the workings of Parliament then you have got an extremely challenging responsibility on your hands.' Jack looked at the gentleman holding a glass of wine and smoking a cigarette and before saying anything else he asked pleasantly for a name. Oliver had an intake of his cigarette and somewhat apologetically introduced himself, 'The name's Oliver St John, I was in charge of the Cross Cabinet before the foolish politicians here decided to end it.' Coughing a little from inhaling thick blue smoke Jack sat back in his chair and could not help but agree with Oliver's discontented comment. 'I would suggest there is a slight feeling of anger still inside you as well regarding what you have told me about the Cross Cabinet which seemed to be working well while it lasted as perfectly fitting.' Oliver had a drink of wine and sat down opposite Jack at the table.

'There is definitely a feeling of anger still inside me I admit but I still can't help but suggest your task of reforming the Houses of Parliament will be near impossible.' After Oliver had had a draw on his cigarette and wafted smoke directly in Jack's face Jack's eyes began to water badly as he gasped; 'What is that you are blowing on?'

'It's a cigarette and it is marvellous, particularly as it helps you relax.' As much as he could in the circumstances Jack laughed; 'It hasn't helped you relax a great deal the anger there is inside your voice and the way your face is flushing as you talk politics.' He had a drink of whisky and putting his fingers together looked at Oliver biting his tongue before saying with some self-confidence, 'I really do believe that if I work on this hard enough then by Christmas Paliament will be a completely reformed and more efficient place.' Oliver decided he could take no more of the young man's confident chatter. He had the final blow on his cigarette and stubbing it out into a little tray he excused himself and went to join some more understanding colleagues at a far table. Jack finished his drink and going down the small flight of stairs made his way to Sovereigns Entrance where he paused for a while to look over the setting now the restorations following Guy Fawkes's gunpowder explosion had been completed. Standing outside still brought back terrible memories of November 5th 1605. He believed after the cheerless conversation he had left behind in the Lower House he had escaped from the sinister ambience which was filling the air.

As the majority of politicians had left Parliament that evening they had without any delay returned to their different constituencies and put politics completely out of their thoughts. Jack however remembering the two foremost guarantees he had made to the small number of politicians who had heard his short-lived maiden speech and the people he had addressed during his campaigning for the Birmingham by-election remained in London throughout the hot summer and dry autumn to discuss politics with more prominent officials. He travelled around London every day on his jet black horse and with his silver rapier by his side speaking long and hard with gentlemen of great standing including Lawrence Hyde, the attorney-general, James Villiers the Lord high-treasurer and Jeremy Howard the Lord Chamberlain proposing to everyone the time was right for Parliament to be completely transformed yet his intentions were overlooked and his desire for a new monarch to be elected was simply waved away. To the many significant people Jack had spoken to through the summer he had tried explaining how Parliament would function better and more efficiently with a captivating monarch to render politicians the honourable way forward and be respected by everyone in England and overseas yet his strong-minded and exasperated figure had his demands rejected entirely. Jack's original certainty that by Christmas Parliament would be completely reformed and sitting frequently with all its power returned now he knew would not happen and he felt extremely disappointed and overwhelmed by the summer's proceedings.

Now it was early December and surprisingly to many people all over England there were absolutely no indications that any cold winter weather was approaching. Dazzling warm sunlight streamed across London every day and trees, fields, flowers, bushes and undergrowth still flourished. Jack had quickly selected a small quiet inn between the Strand and Fleet Street in which to reside once he had left an uncertain Parliamentary building earlier in the year. His horse had immediately been taken care of when he had arrived and asked for accommodation by a stable boy from north London who had come to the centre of the city looking for work and a higher wage than he had received during his exertions in Finchley. The tall and occasionally hotheaded young man had taken Jack's sometimes excitable horse, jumping and kicking when the stranger took the reins to the local stables in Trafalgar Square and groomed, washed and fully nurtured him every day and as a farrier's assistant replaced all four of its shoes simply for his own satisfaction frequently. Jack had not wished to make himself at all garrulous when living at the inn only to keep himself to himself and do his work without any commotion or disruption made just as he had when living in the tavern as a skeletal figure in Birmingham.

On the first day of December Jack determined to have a final walk around the city before returning home and reflect on his seven years in London mostly as a security official which had been a magnificent and successful period for him. Strangely the night before he had not slept as once more any slight and trivial sounds had severely troubled him just as they had the moment Guy Fawkes's barrel of gunpowder had exploded. When he did wake up after a short sleep he deliberately dressed in some of the finest attire he had bought in the city during his seven blissful years. He put on his tasteful white silk shirt, black short-waisted doublet, his more elaborate knee length breeches and knee high black riding boots. He looked in the top drawer of his cupboard where he found a silk handkerchief he placed carefully in one of his pockets. The silver rapier lying by his bed he picked up delicately and positioned under his belt and finally before going downstairs to the small restaurant for breakfast he considered his reflection in the mirror. He eyed himself up and down tilting his head both ways before after a time hummed a little in thought. He picked up his key and departing his restful room locked the door tightly behind.

The restaurant was almost empty when he arrived and the young and agile waitress hurried across and served him. He wished her a very good morning and ordered himself a plate of fresh bacon, some bread and butter and a little ham, the choice surprised the waitress yet she smiled at him in her usual characteristic way and returned soon after with a pot of fresh coffee. When she returned a second time Jack for the first looked directly into the waitress's eyes and when their eyes did finally meet he felt a sudden jolt of emotion he had not expected to feel when having breakfast. 'Thank you very much.' he said deliberately slowly and in the most loving voice he could produce in such affectionate circumstances. The waitress became a little tongue-tied and red faced before very hurriedly and deliberately scuttling away. 'Do you always keep your sword beside you?' Jack was about to pour himself a cup of coffee but put the pot down and raised his head to find out who had made the comment. 'Yes, I do. The sword I regard as my own amulet. It's saved me a number of times in rather difficult circumstances.' The elderly gentleman with a craggy clichéd face and shrunken figure gazed at the rapier for several minutes before chuckling to himself and leaving

Jack alone and searching for a table. Jack had not long begun to enjoy his bacon alone and in peace when another hushed voice struck him from behind, 'You have put on weight now Jack haven't you.' With his mouth half full Jack put down his knife and fork and peered up to see a tall young man he recognized slightly from the day he had teetered slowly back to Birmingham. Jack eyed the well-dressed gentleman for several thoughtful minutes and finally recognised the traveller who had in difficult circumstances parleyed with him for a short time somewhere in Buckinghamshire. 'You have changed a great deal yourself too from what I remember of you as a simple ghostly traveller I believe.' The man toyed with both ends of his moustache and his brown eyeballs looked as they were going to burst out of their sockets as he was greatly upset by the word *traveller*. 'I USED! to be a traveller Jack but not any more. Now I've got myself employed as an oiler in south London.' Jack looked a little puzzled by the word *oiler*.

'What exactly do you do as an *oiler*?' he asked as he had a drink of coffee.

'It is my responsibility to walk around London's streets putting oil into the lamps which are empty.' The gentleman's quiet voice had risen quickly with pride showing on his face; 'Oh……..congratulations.' was all Jack could offer as anything of a reply. The young man again examined Jack's figure up and down. 'When I saw you walking the opposite way to me that November day you were looking extremely upset and very white just as though you had seen a ghost.' Jack bit his lip and his eyes narrowed;

'November 5th is a day I will never be able to forget.' he remarked directly and returned noiselessly to his breakfast. After he had finished his final cup of coffee and his meal had been fully completed Jack spoke a few personal pleasantries to the waitress that made her face blush a great deal and then went outside into the lovely bright sunshine and warm breeze that had just started to get up.

Although Jack had told himself his walk around London was intended simply to be a way of bringing back memories of his more happy and successful times in the city he knew inside himself and in his mind who he was going to try and find. He strode meaningfully through Fleet Street and though his original purpose was to make for Westminster Bridge he made firstly towards the Strand to see if Rose the flower girl he had stopped to chat with many times was still standing in her usual place. The little circle of steps in the centre of the Strand was where he hoped the flower girl would be standing and as he got closer eventually in one corner of his eye to his absolute delight he could see she was still standing there with one hand full of flowers of all different kinds and colours. 'D' y'u wan' t' buy a flower sir? Only a penny each.' she remarked in her broken and almost unintelligible English. 'Rose…….how wonderful to see you again, the true symbol of London's magnificence and history.' The flower girl was at first taken aback by the gentleman who was speaking with her yet after looking at him through her heavy tired eyes she said in her most agitated voice, 'Jack…….Jack how good t' see you 'gain……where've y' been all this time?' Jack smiled broadly. 'Oh Rose that's too long a story to go into now. All

I care about is your health, you're still wearing exactly the same black clothes I always saw you wearing when I passed you by almost every evening during my free time and you still stand on that cold hard ground with your feet bare and cut. Tell me Rose, how much longer can you go on living like this?' Rose wrinkled her grimy craggy face up and her heavy bloodshot eyes widened as much as they possibly could. 'I have n' choice Jack.......I can make money no other way......' her weak tired voice faded as another tall well-dressed gentleman stopped by and deliberately selected a red rose to buy with a penny in hand automatically to pay. 'Y' see Jack,' Rose commented when the gentleman had gone away. '....that's th' only way I c'n make any money.' Jack looked at her grubby rags and bare cut feet again and his face dropped as he gravely worried about the future of such a charming young London woman. 'Y' still have y'r silver sword beside y'u' Rose commented and smiled slightly as she pointed at Jack's side. 'I always carry my rapier Rose wherever I go, it's my lucky charm you could say I suppose.' For a brief time they merely looked lovingly into each other's eyes until their loving gaze was broken as another well-dressed gentleman stopped by and chose a blue flower that he paid the usual penny for. Looking at his watch and wanting to move on Jack took two pennies from his purse and selected the two finest red roses from the bunch that Rose was holding. As she handed them over and Jack paid her with the two coins he whispered in her grubby ear; 'Please Rose, do take care of yourself!' Although he felt reluctant to do so Jack turned round smelling the sweet scent from the roses he had bought and made his way towards the brown dirty waters of the Thames river and Westminster Bridge. As usual there was a thick blue mist which was hanging over the river water and with it came a sickly stench which got to people's throats making them feel as though they were burning. The closer to the river water Jack got the more his throat pained him severely and he began a coughing fit which made him pause by the bridge steps choking and breathless. After a considerable time the coughing fit had ended and he made his way up the steps slowly where the beggars, thieves and vagabonds which just as he had expected to seem were dressed only in torn, tatty clothes and were lined on either side holding out hands and beseeching desperately for a little money. As a young man followed Jack all the way along the bridge almost pulling him backwards until he handed over some money Jack got out his purse and handed over a gold sovereign which made the man's eyelids quickly rise and his eyes light up as the coin he was given was pushed into a pocket and he ran the opposite way out of Jack's total view. Yet even from the very moment his foot first touched the bridge, through the rising reeking haze and beyond all the uncanny young men who were filling the walkway Jack could see the young woman he had been originally seeking. Fanny Goodwin the artist he had missed so much since the fateful November day was once more standing at the far end staring out towards the skyline in the far distance absorbed with her crayons and chalks sketching in her large book. She was still wearing her dark green dress with her hair tied back by a ribbon which to Jack made her look younger than she actually was. Nervously getting ahead of several more beggars and thieves lurking in a threatening manner Jack approached Fanny and stopped behind her little plump figure suddenly unsure what to say. He watched over one of her broad shoulders as she was carefully sketching trying to understand how she was so brilliant at her profession until almost as her work was completed she lowered her head onto a raised hand and sighed as she began to carefully consider her own piece of work. 'What has made you such a fantastic painter?'

'Must you interrupt when I'm trying to work?' Fanny had angrily responded speaking with her refined and aristocratic voice. 'I'm sorry Fanny, would you like me to leave you alone?' Fanny as she thought about the voice became slowly aware of its deep confident tone and without looking at Jack she gasped and in such excitement her sketchbook and chalks fell out of her hands. 'I'm sorry Fanny, I didn't mean that to happen.' He knelt down on the bridge and began picking them up when he felt a hand in one of his pockets. 'It doesn't matter.' he commented when he stood up and put all her belongings in her large rucksack and finally they were able to embrace. 'Oh Jack.......I never thought I would see you again since you left London those years ago........when we stood together in Whitehall watching the State Opening of Parliament and the terrible explosion. I tried telling you it was not your fault but you just wouldn't listen.....oh Jack it is so wonderful to see your handsome figure back by my side!' Jack listened a while longer to Fanny's continuing emotional outpouring until the blue smog began to rise up from the dirty water and he started to cough badly. 'Fanny shall we leave the bridge and have a walk to the park where we can sit and enjoy the warm sunlight and the sweet sound of birdsong?' Fanny's round face lit up again and she automatically took one of Jack's hands as they made their way down the bridge steps and towards the palace. 'So Jack,' she began more calmly. '....tell me what has brought you back to London once again?'

'Would you believe it if I told you I have been elected to serve as MP for Birmingham?' To Jack's surprise Fanny did not this time show a great deal of excitement or elation. 'I am not at all surprised to hear that news Jack,' she replied quietly. '.....you are a well educated, honest and caring young man who keeps promises and I am sure whatever you have promised the constituents in Birmingham you will carry out.' Jack let out a groan which came from the very pit of his stomach and eventually when he was able to speak he replied in a wheeze; 'If only Fanny.......if only.....I'm doing my best Fanny but it's those damn politicians who are surrounding me in the Chamber who simply cannot see reason........they are the people who refuse to have the Houses of Parliament reformed into a place of respect and honour and who reject the idea of England having a monarch on the throne again.......I made promises Fanny, I really did make promises.....' Jack ended his brief moan and thought he was going to sob until he produced his handkerchief from a pocket and was able to wipe any tears out of his eyes. 'A new monarch is a good idea and having Parliament reformed and with all its true political powers back is what a lot of people want.' Jack nodded his full agreement. 'There is Fanny a period now where the people of England have no respect for their politicians but simply see them being uncaring towards the ordinary people they are supposed to represent. Ever since King James was killed and there has been no monarch to lead and organise the politicians Parliament has simply fallen. There is no proper system of government and nobody who can lead, not even Mister Speaker who is simply an inadequate and weak-willed figure.' Jack's feeling of elation when he and Fanny had hugged and kissed had been tempered by his feelings of deep irritation toward the politicians. They came to St James's Park where under a warm sunlight and dark blue sky they strolled a little before sitting under a cherry tree still fully in blossom and with the sweet sound of birdsong coming from the top of its branches. 'Who would have thought December could be like this after previous terrible winters that England has suffered in recent years?' Jack sighed in a thoughtful manner and pointed out a squirrel that was toying with a tree nearby. 'That's the sort of thing you could draw Fanny.' Jack suggested as he looked across the lush grass towards the many coloured flowers and far green hedge which were all still flourishing. Jack looked down at Fanny's large rucksack and remembered what he had put in with the sketchbook and all her drawing implements earlier on the bridge. 'Please Fanny, can you pass me your rucksack.' Fanny seemed a little surprised by the question however as requested she passed it to Jack who looked inside. 'These are for you.' he said and went red faced.

'Oh they are absolutely divine!' she squealed holding the two red roses. 'Oh Jack, how thoughtful you are.' She leaned across the bench and kissed him on one of his red hot cheeks. 'Where did you manage to find two wonderful sweet smelling roses like these?' Jack smiled slightly and his lips widened in pleasure.

'Would you believe I bought them from Rose the flower girl?' This time it was Fanny whose lips widened and she smiled broadly. 'Is she still a flower girl or a flower lady now?' Jack sniggered under his breath.

'Rose is no longer a flower girl sadly, more a flower lady. She has aged a great deal in the last few years and still appears a terrible scrawny figure.' Fanny nodded her head slowly.

'I believe ever since she was just a little girl selling flowers with her mother in the very same place on the Strand Fanny has been a lovely symbol of exactly what kind of a romantic city London is.' Fanny smelled the two deep red roses again and from then on held them carefully in one hand. 'You still look as beautiful as I remember you.' Jack commented as he stared warmly at Fanny between both eyes. Fanny took the remark as simply a piece of sweet talk. 'I think that's a slight exaggeration,' she replied and dropped her head. 'The last few months have aged me greatly.'

'What has happened to age you?' Jack remarked and he looked at Fanny seriously concerned by the distressing expression which covered her face. 'If you really would like me to tell you the awful news. About three months ago mother was taken into hospital suffering from a severe fever and not long after father too began to sweat and shiver uncontrollably until feeling so weak his legs just gave way beneath him. I got on my horse and galloped to Kensington to see Dr Fraser but by the time we got back home father was dead.'

'Oh Fanny….I'm so very sorry….' Jack took a hand of Fanny's and holding it tightly kissed it softly however tears began to stream down Fanny's face. 'That's not the end though Jack,' she sniffed. 'I went to visit mother in hospital that evening and was given the news that she had died that afternoon when she had stopped sweating and fallen into a deep sleep.'

'Oh Fanny……what can I say but that I am so very sorry…' He took his soft silk handkerchief from his pocket and handed it across to her. 'Here take this,' he whispered. Fanny took it and rubbed her eyes to try and stop the tears. 'Did anybody tell you what it was that had killed your mother and father?'

'Doctor Fraser has told me in recent weeks that at the time mother and father died there was a severe fever that was going round that part of London and a number of people had been taken seriously ill into hospital. Mother and father were weak anyway after suffering from fevers in the past few years. That made their large house in Vauxhall empty so in the last few weeks I have been transferring all my property from my small flat in East London and moving into the expensive and very luxurious house they owned.'

'I'm sorry…..' Jack commented again unsure what else he could say to be of any more comfort.

'It doesn't matter Jack……' she gasped wiping away the remaining few tears from her eyes, '…..there are plenty of things in the large house that I will never displace that remind me of them and their love and warmth they always had for me.' Jack moved closer to Fanny on the bench and they held each other tightly just listening to the birdsong and watching the three squirrels playing on the verdant deep green grass. 'I remember the green dress you are wearing today from when I saw you every day I was working in London.' Jack commented quietly in a thoughtful voice. 'I need another dress and a hat, that is something else that I have needed for a long time. The green dress is getting a little thin now all the years I have been wearing it.' Fanny lay back on the bench as she contemplated. 'Now we have met again I don't want to let you out of my sight.' she hesitated as Jack looked closely into her eyes.

'What exactly are you suggesting?'

'Now I am living alone in the large house it would be lovely if you would move in and live with me……..' The mere suggestion made by Fanny took Jack by total surprise. 'The thought sounds tempting but what about all my constituents in Birmingham if they wish to discuss their problems with me…….I'm afraid it wouldn't work………' Jack's voice trailed away as he considered Fanny's proposal. 'Yes, all right I will!' he quickly continued with an immediate change of mind, '………..if you are absolutely sure about your suggestion then I will do it.' He hesitated and thought a little more about the situation. 'I will have to return to Birmingham and collect some of my other belongings and there will be a lot of very upset people but I will move in with you and we will make our relationship work.' Fanny lifted her head up and she kissed Jack warmly on the cheek. 'You are absolutely wonderful Jack.'

They sat a little while longer watching the squirrels playing and pursuing each other around the trees and the flower beds until Jack suggested they had a little walk around the quiet streets of London and as they did so they had a look at some of the more well-liked and luxurious shops in Oxford Street. 'After your earlier generous offer I would like to treat you to something a little special.' They got up arm in arm, Jack carried the weighty rucksack and Fanny still held the two sweet roses carefully in one hand. They walked back towards the river and as they coughed in concert progressed along the bank towards Westminster and on further towards Bond Street, Regent Street and Oxford Street. As both Jack and Fanny knew there would be a large crowd was standing outside the hat shop not buying hats but chatting quietly and socialising in a pleasant manner. 'The hat shop has been an immediate success.' Fanny commented as she made her way through the large gathering of people and had a look through the hat shop window. 'The crafters has closed, after the promises I made to one of the assistants as a politician.' Again Jack's jaw dropped.

'What do you mean?' Fanny asked a little bemused by Jack's comment. Jack gave a sniff of contempt.

'I promised that as a newly elected MP I would use all my power and influence to save the shop from closing but my promises have as we can see come to nothing.' Jack's head dropped and he felt at that very moment totally inadequate. 'That is why I have told my fellow politicians

Parliament needs quickly to be reformed.' For a time he just stared through the window of the former crafter's shop looking at the empty shelves before returning his attention to Fanny and leading her into the hat shop. 'You choose yourself a nice hat that you really like and I shall treat you.'

'Oh but Jack - ' Jack passed Fanny for once an expression of decisiveness which she at that very moment remembered from Jack's earlier time in London. 'Now Fanny don't argue with my suggestion but have a look at all the magnificent hats that are available and choose your favourite.' Jack waited beside Arabella and they watched together as Fanny looked at the hats thoughtfully one by one until she returned to Jack holding a tall wide rimmed green hat which she passed to him and looked a little sheepish as she was passing it over. 'This one please.' Jack commented simply to Arabella. She carried out the transaction quickly and Jack and Fanny left both feeling extremely satisfied with the item they had purchased. 'The streets around this part of London are thriving all the time.' Fanny commented as they strolled down Oxford Street towards Bond Street and round into Regent Street. 'It's just unfortunate that people had stopped buying rapiers and other swords.' Jack felt tired as he made his hesitant remark.

'There is a new coffee house just opened in Piccadilly, should we stop and have a little lunch?' Fanny's suggestion made Jack's eyes light up. 'That I believe is an excellent suggestion.' They strolled through a pleasant little thoroughfare which took them into Piccadilly where they found the Coffee House already three quarters full. 'This place is extremely popular all ready.' They went inside and waited in the queue for some considerable time before finally being served, they ordered two plates of the roast beef and potatoes and two glasses of white wine to celebrate their new beginning.

'I shall return to the inn after we have eaten and pack my small number of possessions and then we can ride my fine black horse to your house in Vauxhall.' As they ate in a relaxed and happy ambience Jack once more thought restively about his future as a politician. 'I won't give up on my two promises Fanny never.' he whispered beneath his breath. At once they paused from their eating and raised their glasses of wine. Jack with a broad smile and self-assured voice called the simple toast; 'To us Fanny and our future together.' As their glasses were raised their eyes affectionately met and from that touching instant onwards they believed that in time all would be well once more with their lives.

All through England well into December people were enjoying the fine warm summer weather and the continuing sense of optimism which was filling the air yet such a widespread sense of optimism was becoming slowly and increasingly mitigated by a rise in food prices, high taxation and the average wage to lowest class workers remaining unchanged at only one shilling a day. Such unrest was increasingly resulting in minor demonstrations in streets and occasionally such demonstrations finished with wounded protestors. More people were believing that a new monarch was required sitting on the throne to lead the country with dignity and conviction something that clearly no politician or clergyman had the ability to do.

Totally unaware of people's complaints and frustrations throughout December Lord Egerton and Anne of Denmark were remaining happy and relaxed and very much taking pleasure in the fine warm weather. Midway through the month Princess Elizabeth Stuart packed her suitcase and left London once more to tour England with the young theatre company of which she had been made patron and now with her house completely free Anne regarded this as a perfect opportunity to entice Lord Egerton to move out of his small featureless flat and in with her and her house full of personal servants. For the first time since he had received such and offer Lord Egerton was too faint-hearted to reject the offer, he packed his small collection of belongings and moved in straight away. Since he had moved in Anne was teaching Lord Egerton how to play the piano after he had watched her playing with such grace and excellence. They woke up as usual at six o'clock in the morning and before having breakfast they went up to the private music-room and Anne sat by the piano and Lord Egerton sat beside her watching her hands and fingers and their every move. He watched her playing for over half an hour and then tried to copy her moves. 'This is not as easy as I believed it would be.' Lord Egerton commented almost every morning as he blew with tiredness and frustration. 'I think you may feel better when you've had a cup of freshly ground coffee and a piece of the fried bacon.' Anne made her teasing face as she watched Lord Egerton looking back at the piano with annoyance in his eyes. 'One day I shall learn to play that thing!' he muttered under his breath.

'These things take time, James never learnt fully to play the piano. Eventually he admitted that he would just have to listen to me instead.' Lord Egerton grimaced,

'I'm not going to give up.' They walked slowly downstairs and into the dining room which was all laid out and readied for their presence. 'The coffee smells wonderful.' Lord Egerton commented as he lifted his head and smelled the air. 'I suggest we go to the hat shop in Oxford Street as I need a hat for a good friend.' Lord Egerton was a little baffled by the comment. 'Is it a friend that I know?'

'No you don't, I don't believe you have met Marian before.'

'As it is such a wonderful warm morning we can leave the horses and walk the short distance.' Anne smiled and nodded in agreement. The three maids were at the table the very moment Anne and Lord Egerton had sat down bringing the plates and dishes and placing them carefully on the table. They were brought their cups and the coffee was poured and after several minutes of scurrying around them and waiting on them with such efficiency and a kind generous temperament Lord Egerton could not prevent himself looking across the table at Anne commenting; 'The service in here really is excellent!'

'I have asked some of my staff to prepare us a picnic we can have on the lawn when the hat is bought and we come back home.' Anne's comment again surprised Lord Egerton.

'What a very pleasant suggestion.' he replied with a little grin crossing his face. He had a drink of his coffee and let out a delighted breath. 'The rich coffee is absolutely marvellous he whispered contentedly. 'I wonder if we shall meet Sir Edward,' he remarked as an incidental thought. He paused for a moment wondering if Anne would reply before changing the subject and returning simply to the quality of the breakfast. 'This lovely bacon has been prepared perfectly.'

'Would you like another piano lesson before we go out?' Anne chuckled at her question and knew what Lord Egerton's reply would be; his face dropped and he muttered; 'Later on!' and sighed heavily in a short fit of annoyance. 'Do you have any idea when your daughter will be back from her jaunt around England with the theatre company?' Anne' face looked slightly blank.

'Just like last year when she went with the theatre group touring I had absolutely no knowledge of when she would be returning to London.' As they ate quietly with the bright sunlight streaming in through the large dining room window Anne looked out towards the lawn and the flowers and her thoughts became slightly wistful; 'If only James had still been with me to enjoy this wonderful summery weather.' She looked out of the window at the glorious blue sky and assortment of coloured flowers and sighed heavily again before returning to her fine breakfast. She had a mouth of bacon and looked thoughtfully towards Lord Egerton's eyes. 'Do you still miss Elizabeth?' Lord Egerton put his knife and fork down and had a drink of coffee and considered the question for several minutes before replying. 'I miss her occasionally;' He spoke slowly and thought about Anne's question a little longer. 'I wish I knew why she used to argue with me so much for no real obvious reason..........however.........' he said under his breath. 'I don't miss her now like I used to.' They looked uncertainly into each other's eyes before Anne returned the subject to more cheerful matters. 'I believe the butler is becoming more awkward as he gets older.' Lord Egerton was again taken by surprise at Anne's remark. 'What exactly do you mean by that?' Anne cleaned her plate and put her knife and fork down. After she had carefully wiped her face with her serviette she gave Lord Egerton a devious grin. 'I frequently ask the butler to go into the garden and amuse our little dog for a while yet every time I tell him to do so he rejects my instruction.' Lord Egerton had a drink of coffee and smiled;

'I have noticed before your butler is not particularly amused by your little dog.' For a moment they looked intently into each other's eyes before both maids quickly arrived at the table and took the empty plates away leaving Lord Egerton and Anne alone to finish their coffee and go and prepare for the quiet day ahead.

'London's growing now ever so quickly.' Lord Egerton remarked as they strolled through the Strand. 'I see the flower girl still remains in her regular spot.' Anne pointed a finger at the woman dressed in rags which were now severely torn. 'Have you noticed Anne how more people appear to be moaning to each other about the growing prices of food?' Anne shook her head slowly.

'Not at all although I don't have any reason to listen to other peoples' conversation.'

'Unfortunately there is a growing divide once more between the wealthier people in England and those who do not have as much money in their pockets to spend.' Lord Egerton's face expressed a slight sense of concern. 'I don't believe that is anything for us to get ourselves involved in.' Anne said simply and in a nonchalant manner. 'It is a subject our new MP Jack Parker is most concerned about.' They walked through the Strand, Fleet Street and back down towards the river with Anne remaining completely oblivious to Lord Egerton's sudden concerns. 'I do wish they would do something about this river.' Anne finally spoke as they walked down towards the river bank on their way to Oxford Street. 'That is something at the moment London's Parish council I believe are trying to sort out with the new underground sewage system that is being put in.'

'Well it can't come a moment too soon.' she retorted angrily as the blue haze made her start coughing a little badly. Lord Egerton smiled his best smile.

'We can just get to the bridge and across the other side and quickly we'll be away from this horrible smog.' Not surprisingly as Lord Egerton and Anne stepped up onto London Bridge the usual line of thieves, vagabonds and beggars with devious and threatening expressions covering their faces and dressed in shreds was there to welcome them holding their dirty rough hands out and mumbling inarticulate words as they pleaded desperately for a few pennies at least. 'Is this always how London Bridge is?' Anne questioned as they walked down the far steps and made their way back towards the city centre. 'This is the way all of London's bridges are almost all the time.' Anne's face became unusually distorted and unlikeable as she considered Lord Egerton's forthright reply. 'It just shows how out of touch with the world I must be.' she remarked and shook her narrow head as she considered Lord Egerton's comment a little more.

The large crowd as usual was standing outside Arabella and Nicholas's hat shop chatting pleasantly and enjoying the warm summer like weather. 'It's sad to see the sword crafter's shop has closed.' Lord Egerton stopped outside the empty shop and looked through the window at the empty shelves. 'I don't really believe that too many people like going around the shops looking for swords to buy!' Anne teased. '… … unless of course they were preparing to go into battle.' She had a look at the hat shop and glancing back over her shoulder commented in a more cheerful voice. 'There is no sign of Sir Edward Coke this morning.'

'You missed him by about fifteen minutes ma'm.' Arabella commented as Anne went inside. Anne smiled warmly at Arabella and thanked her for the information. 'This one is so pretty.' Anne remarked after she had been looking at the hats for a considerable period of time. 'I'll take this one.' Anne handed the wide rimmed brown hat to Arabella and paid the required two sovereigns before they slowly made their way back through Oxford Street and Bond Street and further towards Covent Garden.

The picnic on the lawn was a very pleasant and private affair for Lord Egerton and Anne. The sun shone like fluid gold from a deep sapphire paradise and the tree shade moved slowly over the grass keeping the sun's hottest rays from making them feel too hot and uncomfortable as it came towards them. The picnic had been prepared extremely well by several members of Anne's staff with cold food and drink arranged to go with the pleasant weather. There was a large selection of pies, cakes, salads, pickles, jellies and creams and tucked away inside the hamper bag a bottle of white wine and two small glasses. 'The maid has put in some champagne too kept cold by this ice box.'

'Are we supposed to be celebrating something with the champagne?' Lord Egerton thought as he rubbed his moustache and carefully considered his own question. 'I don't think so,' Anne smiled. 'It's just the cheerful and optimistic way my staff always seem to think at the moment.' The garden was full of life and activity with frequent birdsong and bees buzzing their way around all the thriving scented flowers and occasionally making their way towards the hamper to have a look at the selection of food inside. 'These insects can be rather irritating sometimes.' she complained to Lord Egerton as she tried with some difficulty waving a large bumble bee away.

They ate at their own leisureliness and conversed in a pleasant and gentle manner and as the sun became focussed entirely on them a pleasing indolence shrouded the complete atmosphere. 'When was the last December it was possible to sit outside like this having a picnic?' Anne questioned.

'Never during my long life.' Lord Egerton replied as he took the bunch of grapes and selected from it.

'There grapes are excellent, fresh as usual I presume.'

'Of course;' Anne seemed a little put out that Lord Egerton had even suggested the possibility of chosen food not being fresh. 'I have told you before Thomas, all the food my staff prepare is fresh.' Over the long warm afternoon and into the early evening as the sun was beginning to go down they finished eating every single item of food that had been carefully prepared. 'That really was a wonderful occasion.' Lord Egerton commented cheerfully as he had his final sip of champagne. 'Now the picnic is over do you feel up to a little more piano playing?' Lord Egerton frowned before in a heavy breath responding.

'Oh very well!'

On Christmas eve as Lord Egerton and Anne sat in the dining-room enjoying breakfast there was a dazzling warm sunshine lighting up the whole house and filling everyone inside with a sense of optimism and cheerfulness. 'I hope your friend Marian liked the hat that you bought her.' Lord Egerton remarked as Anne had handed it to the butler to take round earlier that same morning. 'I believe it is the kind of hat that she likes.' Still totally baffled by the talk of *Marian* Lord Egerton was going to inquire a little further but decided instead to change the subject. 'What are we going to do with our day today, should we have another walk into London?' Anne shook her head at the suggestion.

'A simple horse ride later this morning and some lunch at one of the pleasant little inns I believe would be just fine. I have arranged for a simple little gathering for this evening. It is meant to be a family re-union though I doubt anybody from the family will come. The death of King James has divided the family and I am being given much of the blame for the gunpowder explosion.' Lord Egerton had a drink of coffee and looked extremely surprised by Anne's remark. 'How could anybody put the blame on you? You have many advisors and officials working around you who are supposed to take care of all the security.' Anne took the coffee pot and refilled her cup looking stern faced at Lord Egerton. 'To us that is straight-forward common sense but nobody else in the family seem to look on the matter that way. It will be interesting this evening to see if anybody from my side of the family do arrive.' Anne motioned for the young maid who was quietly and unflinchingly watching on to take the dirty plates away and then sighed heavily in a most audible way.

'The horses have been prepared for you.' the butler commented slowly in his controlled one-tone voice.

Anne listened carefully as she could hear her puppy barking loudly from the far side of the house and jokingly commented to the butler, 'You can take the puppy out into the field while Thomas and I are away and amuse it.' As Anne expected the butler appeared far from delighted at Anne's remark.

'Excuse me ma'm but is that really my responsibility?' Anne ignoring the butler's question completely and directed Lord Egerton outside where the two stable boys were waiting with the two fine horses ready and waiting beside them.

The afternoon was another fine and enjoyable period of horse riding for Anne and Lord Egerton. They stopped for some light refreshment at the White Swan inn which was newly opened beside the Tower of London before riding back to Anne's large house and finding the butler was still outside on the lawn playing with the puppy. 'I didn't think you were very keen on amusing my little puppy.' Anne laughed as she watched the dog jumping up and down at the butler and running backwards and forwards in every direction as it barked excitedly with its eyes brightly lit up as it played. 'Oh it's not such a bad little thing as I thought is it?' Anne and Lord Egerton left the butler and the puppy to play as they went upstairs to prepare for the evening's socialising.

'You look beautiful particularly in that red dress and flat black shoes.'

'I don't believe all the face that I still use is helping to cover the breaks in my aging skin.' Anne commented as she looked in a wall mirror. The butler came into the house very soon after Lord Egerton and Anne had arrived and appeared extremely exhausted but very cheerful. 'Your joyful little puppy was obviously just as exhausted as I am, it's gone to sleep with the warm sunlight shining on it.' As he disappeared out the room Anne mocked; 'He's already looking ten years younger.'

'What are we going to suggest at the party if anybody from your family does attend this evening and they want to know a little more about the true attachment of our relationship?' Anne flicked her eyes fully open to see Lord Egerton's anxious expression. 'I don't think you need concern yourself Thomas……….' her tired voice faded and she sounded revolted. Lord Egerton felt a great sense of relief travel through him at Anne's sad and reflective comment. 'In other words it may be a very simple quiet evening with a few friends?' Anne nodded;

'I believe that is what it will turn out to be.' She got up and went to pour herself a glass of gin and tonic before the butler returned and commented on the preparations for the evening's small occasion. 'If anybody in my family do come Thomas I shall introduce you as I have introduced you to anyone, with great respect and stateliness.' Lord Egerton had a drink of whisky and looked at his watch.

'There is time for a piano lesson if you wish when the drinks are finished.' Anne closed her eyes and lay back in her armchair. 'I think a few hours resting will prove to be of more comfort the way I'm feeling at the moment.' She closed her eyes fully and fell into a gentle and most welcome sleep.

'Just as I thought;' Anne remarked mournfully as she and Lord Egerton sat together away from the rest of the guests who had arrived for the evening. 'Nobody from the family has made the slightest effort to prepare themselves and come and meet me again.' There was a small group of ladies and gentlemen dancing in the centre of the hall and many well-dressed guests were wining and dining at the far end where all the food and drink had been laid out. 'Who were you expecting to see?' a young fair-haired gentleman asked Anne as he was slowly walking past holding a glass of sherry and smiling broadly. 'I don't believe that is any of your business!' Anne's reply for once was curt and to the point.

'That's not like you.' Lord Egerton commented when the gentleman had gone.

'That's the way I'm feeling at the moment.' At Lord Egerton's remark Anne turned scarlet and she could feel her hands and feet grow increasingly numb. The dancing stopped to a slight ripple of applause and a large cluster of guests went over to the far table together to help themselves to some refreshments.

The quiet Christmas party continued until after four o'clock the next morning and could have continued a great deal longer as none of the guests were at all interested in leaving and almost had to be forced out of the house by the unfortunate butler who was still recovering from his hours of entertaining Anne's pet puppy. 'It was not the best or most successful party I have ever hosted;' Anne moaned at breakfast later that same morning. 'It was a pleasant Christmas occasion.' Lord Egerton responded in a more cheerful manner. As the butler came in to look at the state of the breakfast table Lord Egerton grinned a little at the butler's exhausted face. 'I think yesterday you tried doing a little too much.' Lord Egerton had a drink of coffee and put on a more grave face as he spoke to Anne. 'I wouldn't think it a very good idea if you were to try and get yourself mixed up with your side of the family any more.' Anne for once was not upset by Lord Egerton's advice on a most personal matter. 'I believe there Thomas you are absolutely right.' she responded nodding her head. 'I certainly don't want to host any more social evenings like last night's this Christmas.' Although leaving it until they were in the middle of breakfast they wished each other a happy Christmas and afterwards as it was another fine warm day they spent the morning quietly outside in the garden together enjoying the sunshine once more and relaxing to the sound of birdsong. 'The gardener got me a copy of the latest street pamphlet.' Anne remarked as she left Lord Egerton alone briefly to go inside and pick it up. As she passed it over she looked a little more concerned as she ran her eyes over a detailed article regarding England's communal state of affairs. Lord Egerton had a long thoughtful read of the main front page news story and his shoulders fell. 'There is no response by any official around the country to try in any possible way to deal with England's continuing unrest according to this. Food prices and taxes are continuing to rise and no employer is being persuaded to raise their wages at all as a fair-minded response. Apparently there are increasing angry demonstrations by the large majority of ordinary hard-working labourers.' He folded the pamphlet up in anger and mumbled under his breath; 'This is completely ridiculous!'

'What exactly is ridiculous?' Anne asked although she could not fully take in the more political side of Lord Egerton's commentary. 'More and more I think Jack Parker is right and his demands for a reformed Parliament and a sitting monarch to lead this country.........all this disorder is again starting to spiral out of control and nobody in any kind of authority seems to be able to understand that and respond.'

'I'm afraid this is completely beyond me.' Anne remarked in a tired voice. She was still severely feeling the effects of the previous night of partying. Lord Egerton unfolded the pamphlet once more and read the front page before opening it up and reading all of the stories inside. 'At least it says here there are more businesses opening up particularly in York, Birmingham, Leeds and Manchester. Unfortunately it gives no date here for the next sitting of the Lower Chamber.' They sat quietly in the garden together for a while longer before Anne alone got up and asked the stable boys to have the two horses prepared for riding in half an hour's time. 'I thought we could have a ride out for our lunch.' Lord Egerton pursed his lips and wearily nodded his head. 'We may as well......' As he still felt exhausted from the night's partying and was trying to take in all the grave news he had just read Lord Egerton could not take any time to disagree with Anne's suggestion. From the garden they simply watched the two young stable boys taking the fine tall horses out of the stables and brushing them down and carrying out their duties as they readied the horses for riding.

Anne and Lord Egerton rode across the flat dry land alongside the forests still flourishing in green leaves and vegetation and there was the charming sound of bird and animal life coming seemingly from every tree around them. 'Unfortunately Thomas there comes the haunting sound of gunfire and large hounds barking excitedly searching for the adorable animals that have so horribly been shot. Honestly Thomas.......it's all wrong don't you think?' They were riding side by side and Lord Egerton took his eyes off his horse and looked Anne directly in the face. 'Yes Anne.....it's all wrong,' he responded in a sigh, '......unfortunately there is absolutely nothing we can do about it.' They stopped once more at the White Swan where just outside there were incoherent sounds of a heated conversation down close by the river. They tied their horses up outside the front entrance and listened to the angry voices before deciding to leave the private conversation and go inside for a drink and something to eat. As Anne obtained the food and drink quietly Lord Egerton went over to speak with the landlord who also was reading a copy of the same pamphlet Lord Egerton looked at earlier. The landlord looked in his thirties or forties and seemed extremely concerned as he read the front page for a fourth time. 'What's going on outside your small inn?' Lord Egerton asked as he motioned towards the front door. 'I believe, from what I have been told by other visitors there is a small demonstration continuing near the river.' Lord Egerton was not at all surprised by the landlord's reply.

'Can't the Parish councils understand the protests that are going on and just why people are getting uptight about matters?' The landlord raised his hands.

'Search me.' he answered and shaking his head slightly he turned away from Lord Egerton and disappeared into a back room.

Anne and Lord Egerton enjoyed their pleasant meal of salad and wine quietly though still they could sense the shouting of angry words that were continuing outside.

The remainder of Christmas day and up until midnight on new year's eve was a very peaceful and private period of time for Anne and Lord Egerton spent alone in Anne's large house with the butler now enjoying his additional responsibility of amusing their growing dog and Anne continuing to give Lord Egerton piano lessons though still with no positive results. On new years eve once more as midnight was striking they sat together each holding a large glass of champagne and raising their glasses high as midnight struck called out happily together; 'Cheers to us!'

Doctor Peter Fraser regarded himself as a good, hard-working and reliable family man. He lived with his wife and four young sons in a large house in the more expensive area of Kensington and had hoped that Christmas would be a time when he could simply relax from work and enjoy life quietly with his family. At the same time however though he had hoped for a quiet festive season he knew as a respected doctor and JP the time was almost certainly going to be anything but private. His memories too of November 5th 1605 were extremely vivid and the complete day when he had arrived in Whitehall to watch and enjoy the State Opening of Parliament he could never put out of his mind. Wherever he went at any time of the day he always took with him his large case of equipment and medicines if ever his medical services were required and that morning, lasting late into the afternoon after the barrel of gunpowder had exploded and caused such mayhem and left so many people injured in need of immediate treatment he had immediately been commanded across the road by the authorities to tend the innocent victims. Outside Sovereign's Entrance he had knelt with his medical bag open tending the critically injured victims whose motionless figures were lying sprawled across the ground with many deep bleeding cuts in addition to a great number of severely mutilated body parts. He had knelt in the same place long into the afternoon doing his best to treat the more severely injured victims of the explosion yet with his bag of equipment so limited his hard work had been regarded by many people who had stayed in Whitehall to watch on as ineffective. Now often he would wake up in the middle of the night screaming as he suffered frequently from nightmares with vivid pictures in his mind of that very terrible and terrifying day. He and his wife Pat woke up in bed not until after ten o'clock on the morning when they had embraced and wished each other for the first time a happy new year. 'I didn't intend to leave you just before midnight last night, unfortunately it was another one of those times when my services as a doctor were called for.' Peter looked pleadingly into his wife's eyes as he hoped she would understand yet after being married over twenty years Pat understood her husband's strenuous life as a professional doctor perfectly well. They lay up in bed together and Pat fondled his complete face. 'You don't have to explain yourself dear, I understand your strenuous lifestyle perfectly well now.' Pat kissed him on his cheek and whispered in his ear. 'That is what happens when you are one of only three doctors who works in this enormous city……..I still love you no matter what happens to us on a normal day.' They looked affectionately into each others' eyes and kissed. 'I just hope today I'm not called out and for once this festive season we can have at least a little unbroken quiet and private time alone.'

'Do you include the children when you speak of quiet and private time?' Peter tutted and commented;

'Touche!' and again admired his wife's great intelligence and shrewdness. 'I will have to eat early this evening.' Again Peter looked apologetically towards his wife. If anything Pat seemed at a loss by Peter's remark. She again fondled him on one cheek. 'Why is that my love?' Peter tried as he always did no matter what the circumstances were to look cheerful and positive as he gazed into Pat's large blue eyes. 'I have the Parish council meeting to attend, I hope it will again accomplish something to help London continue to expand further.'

'The reduction of growing food prices would certainly help.' Pat quickly remarked. Peter screwed up his face and his eyelids fell again. 'That is a matter we have discussed during the last many meetings but we have decided there is nothing we can do. It is simply our responsibility to see how the money we have been given to spend each month can best be used.' Peter blushed and he became a little sheepish, 'It's not…… my responsibility…….it's a group matter……..' Pat stopped her fondling of him and began to dress herself. She opened the blinds and looked out at the blue sky and dazzling sunlight. 'Would you like to go for a horse ride this morning?' Peter welcomed the idea.

'Absolutely!' he answered very simply and in his most enthusiastic voice he could possibly manage. 'I think a horse ride by the little stream would be perfect and a chance to watch the fishermen trying to catch some fish for their evening meal.' Looking a little further ahead he got out of bed and looked at the tall cupboard on the far wall to check on the state of his musket. 'This afternoon I am going on a short hunt with several of my JP friends when we intend discussing a little business too.' Not for the first time since they had woken up that morning Pat looked a little put out by her husband's remark. 'Can't your discussing court matters wait until the festive season is completely over?' Peter again became slightly sheepish.

'That was not my decision dear.' Pat finished dressing in her finest white cotton dress and brushed her hair as carefully as she could before going downstairs where she expected to find the children waiting eagerly for their breakfast.

Michael, Andrew, James and William were already sitting around the living room table and waiting for their mother to arrive. 'I hope when you have been fed you can go to the stables and treat the horses before your father and I go out riding later this morning.' The children exchanged a series of nodding heads as Pat went into the kitchen to prepare the large bowl of pottage. Peter when he arrived made the coffee and taking a cigarette out of a kitchen drawer went into the large garden to have a smoke. 'It helps me relax.' he commented anxiously as he joined the others around the table. Pat screwed up her narrow girly face responding; 'I think cigarettes are absolutely horrible things.' She was intending to raise her voice and make her comments more angrily yet seeing the young children sitting around her she kept her annoyance quiet. Peter's immense wage compared with the wages of the majority of ordinary labourers caused much resentment and had led to a series of angry demonstrations taking place directly outside Peter's house. The house in which the large family lived was very well furnished and their life in the most expensive part of Kensington was extremely comfortable. Peter poured himself some coffee and filled Pat's cup before pouring himself the remainder of the pottage. 'I have told the children to go out after breakfast and tend the horses in readiness for our horse ride.' Peter looked at his children as usual with admiration. Their attractive slender figures, refined ways of speaking and great politeness towards others he respected enormously and praised his wife and himself for the hard work they had put in to bring them up so well and with such grandeur and dignity. As Peter was taking his first mouthful of pottage there came a loud knocking on the front door which Peter recognised as the knocking of someone in need of his help. 'I have a feeling my services are already required.' he commented to all members of the family sitting around the table eating quietly. Very shortly after answering the door Peter returned into the living room and picked up his case of medical equipment. 'It is only Anne next door, she is unwell again.' Pat sighed heavily as she watched her husband disappear out of the room closing the door firmly behind.

'The horses are ready,' Pat smiled slightly at her husband as he came in over one hour later. 'So tell me what is wrong with Anne this time?'

'It was another fever that has been travelling around London and spreading much sickness. My medication has been able to remove the fever and she is sleeping. This might not be the end though. Looking at her neck closely I believe there is a rash now growing. We shall have to wait and see.' Pat went to the kitchen and made her husband a pot of fresh coffee. 'After you've finished we'll go out for our ride before your brilliance is called for yet again.' Pat and Peter briefly exchanged sweet gentle glances.

'I wish I had some better equipment for treating the sick.' Peter said sadly. '……the infections that are going around London at more regular intervals are becoming increasingly severe and the equipment and medication I have to treat such severe fevers and illnesses simply is not improving to be able to cope.' His narrow pale face tautened and he lowered his head as he stared directly into his cup sniffing the fine aroma of fresh coffee. 'I do my best to treat people Pat but there are many whose conditions have been too severe for me to treat at all.' Peter's usual smiling face and voice of optimism momentarily dropped. 'There are people across London who simply regard me and my services as pitiable.' Pat thought her husband was going to burst into tears until she went over and sitting beside him fondled him across his face which made him give a tired wheeze but once more smile again. 'Where have the children gone?' he asked finally.

'I believe once they had finished preparing the horses they went down with their rods to the long winding stream to fish.'

'It's a fine day to be outside.' he remarked looking out of the window and admiring the garden full of roses, tulips and daffodils. 'Shall we go out too?' he questioned as he finished his last cup of coffee.

They took their fine steeds through the long garden full of intense vibrancy and life and with their horses moving in a gentle trot they headed straight on towards the twisting dark waters of the amusing stream and then on towards Belgrave Square.

'I believe horse riding was always in our blood.' Peter commented smiling as they rode gently alongside the stream and watched the line of young men sitting with their rods and the fishing lines dangling in the water as they hoped for a catch. 'I don't believe there will be much fish in that dirty water.' Pat remarked in a somewhat contemptuous voice. Pat as she sat on the horse riding in such a comfortable position often wondered how anyone could ever find horse riding at all difficult. 'You wouldn't think we were in winter with the blue sky and warmth of the sun.' Pat felt slightly regretful she had forgotten to bring her hat with her to protect he face from the heat of the sunlight. Peter looked across at his wife and the way she was lying forward as she rode and patting the horse's neck with such expression of love in her face; 'I believe sometimes when watching you riding that horse you appreciate horses a great deal more than you admire people.' As he chuckled Pat took him by surprise and replied with some force in her voice;

'The way that some people behave I really do!' She looked with some glumness at Peter which made him become red faced and he fell silent. A number of young men who were fishing broke off from their total hush as they sat about the waters when they saw Dr Fraser coming by and they called out and waved cheerfully at him wishing he and his wife a cheery *"Hello Dr Fraser, A happy new year to you and your wife!!"* Peter waved his hand as he went by them all as a gesture of thanks for such pleasantries.

'You have a great number of people who admire and appreciate you and all your hard work as a doctor so never reproach yourself.' Peter sighed a breath of thanks through his nose for his wife's thoughtful and kindly worded comment as she passed him one of her most telling expressions of love. As the horses continued their gentle trot across the fields Pat commented; 'At least horses are straight forward, more so than people ever were.' Peter raised his head to the sky and mouthed his complete agreement with Pat's remark. 'At least my heavy workload as a doctor over Christmas didn't prevent the children from enjoying themselves during the festive season.' Peter nodded over to the far side of the stream where their four boys were sitting together fishing, two of them had taken their shoes off and were dangling their bare feet in the water. 'I don't believe that is a very good idea.' Pat remarked pointing it out. Peter's green eyes glowed and his lips protruded in a personal manner suggesting the matter was nothing at all to do with him. 'That is another issue as chairman of the Parish council you should be managing, getting London's rivers and streams cleaned up.......tell me Peter, what exactly do you and your fellow council members achieve doing your time together?'

'It's a long story,' Peter began and hesitated as he thought more seriously about his wife's critical remark. 'We are making some progress with London's advancement, more houses are being built all around the city and there are further businesses opening and I believe a new almshouse has just been built outside north London. I promise Pat, as chairman of the Parish council I am concentrating hard on my responsibilities.' Pat pursed her lips tight and narrowed her wide brown eyes up as she regarded her husband's remark as complete nonsense.

They rode in a pleasant way as far as Grosvenor Square before Peter looked at his watched and suggested they turned back. 'I have the local hunt to attend a little later this afternoon before the council meeting begins at half past six.' Pat pulled on her horse's reins and glowered angrily at Peter.

'Why can't you ignore the hunt for once Peter?' Peter shuck his head gently.

'That's the way I make more contacts with influential people when we discuss business.' Annoyed with her husband Pat turned her horse round and galloped ahead of Peter all the way back to Kensington.

The local woods surrounding west London were extremely full of wildlife with foxes, badgers, hedgehogs and squirrels roaming boundless and disregarded. 'Have you enjoyed your Christmas doctor?' The tall heavily built gentleman from the army had been given a short period off work and was enjoying his afternoon of liberty. Although when working with the military Captain Sykes was always forceful, authoritative and often his deep heavy voice sounded extremely threatening this time as he asked Peter the question he sounded particularly cheerful and relaxed about his afternoon. As the captain was aiming his musket to fire at a red squirrel scurrying up a beech tree Peter sighed and looked up into the sky sadly; 'Being a doctor sometimes captain..........' there he had to break off as Captain Sykes took aim and fired. The explosion as the musket was fired made Peter jump with shock. 'Sorry doctor, carry on.'

'My work as a doctor can sometimes be extremely distressing mentally and physically. On Christmas day I was out tending many sick people around London. Christmas day was not a private day for myself and my family and the heavy workload has not helped my marriage. Neither have my obligations for the council.' Captain Sykes instructed his large black unruly hound leaping up and down in expectation at its master to go and bring him the dead animal before he lowered his gun and looked Peter sternly in the face. 'You have another meeting this evening I believe?' Peter nodded.

'Indeed, I have to be at Chelsea town hall for half past six.' He returned the captain's glare. 'Is there any particular reason why you mention it?'

'There are increasing protests in London and all around England against the rising food prices and low wages. As chairman of the Parish council can't you take any action to stop such demonstrations?' Peter was beginning to raise his musket and take aim at a passing fox but lowered it as the captain asked his question. 'My wife made exactly the same comment just a few hours earlier. I'm afraid captain taking action is not that simple.' The captain motioned his frustration by waving one of his large hands in the air and shaking his enormous round head directly in Peter's face. 'That doesn't say much for your authority as chairman of the Parish council.' All around them as members of the large group hunted in clusters there was the continuing sound of gunfire and the many excitable hounds darting backwards and forwards picking up the corpses of dead birds and animals and bringing the victims back to their owners with their mouths full of the nauseating remains. 'When do you return to the army captain?' Peter asked with his voice quickening in nerves. 'I only have the rest of this afternoon and evening to relax before returning to my base in Portsmouth. My fiancee is not at all happy.' The captain once more loaded some bullets into his musket and taking aim fired immediately. After the explosion had passed away he called out with more of the usual authority in his voice; 'Got it!' They spent the rest of the hunt striding through the trees and across the undergrowth shooting every animal that was seen running free until reaching the field where all their horses had been left untied. They were escorted by a large collection of excited and boisterous hounds barking their delight with their wide bright eyes glowing and tails wagging uncontrollably as once the hunters had mounted their horses the dogs ran hungrily by their sides as they returned home.

Peter mounted his chestnut horse and pulling hard on the reins began his short return journey to Kensington hoping that his wife might be feeling a little more understanding towards his difficult and exhausting life. He got off his horse outside the stable as it had begun to sweat badly and asked James to tend it before he had to go out again. 'I've made you a little tea.' Pat motioned to the kitchen.

"At least Pat is being a little more tolerant of me." he thought as he followed her signal to find a plate of roasted

chicken, potatoes and some bread and butter were waiting for him. 'Sit down and I'll pour you a glass of ale. Did you enjoy the hunt?' Peter was completely sincere about the afternoon.

'No, not at all dear! Going to that damn hunt was an absolute mistake.' He sat eating his meal quietly and thinking nervously about his evening ahead. 'I'm not even sure what we are supposed to be discussing this evening.' he muttered. He had a long drink of ale for his dry burning throat and gave a sigh of great relief. 'I have no idea how long the meeting will last or what time I shall be back unfortunately.' Pat who was reading a book quietly as Peter called to her put her book down and shrugged. 'It doesn't matter dear, I'm used to your uncertain times.' She looked towards him and smiled before raising her book once more and falling silent as she continued to read untroubled by her husband's concerns.

Peter was not feeling his usual self-confident and expectant character when he entered the hall and saw his eleven council colleagues already in attendance and staring back at him in an apprehensive atmosphere and stony silence. He got to the top chair and cleared his throat before explaining briefly what exactly the committee meeting was intended to discuss that evening. He looked at some notes jotted carefully down on a page in front of him and explained west London's financial budget for January. Pausing for a drink of water he hoped somebody on the council might interrupt but the stony silence continued. Nervously he read from the two papers on his desk and after hesitating again more confidently explained a number of ongoing jobs which still had not been completed including the more recent maintenance of local roads, bridges and houses. 'New wardens need to be elected by January 31st that is something we can do tonight.' As there was still no response from any of his colleagues again Peter asked if anyone sitting around the table would like to begin the conference. Martin Wilson, in his late fifties and with a protruding nose had been churchwarden for the Parish council for over six years. He decided to begin merely by complaining about the slowness of all the maintenance work that had been continuing around west London for the last eight months. As Mr Wilson spoke quietly noting the particular slowness of such maintenance he got a number of angry glares before David interrupted his slow and methodical grumbling. 'I am well aware of the slowness of much of the maintenance which has been progressing for many months and it is a matter I shall genuinely probe in the next couple of days.' David's simple interruption he believed had led to many raised eyebrows and much more displeasure. 'I believe what is most important during this evening's meeting is to set up the parish's poor relief scheme in the approved manner which since we first discussed it and tried to set it in motion caused a great deal of dissatisfaction from the more affluent families in the district and very simply didn't work. We must also work out how better to divide the monthly budget we are receiving from Parliament. In the month of December regrettably we overspent by £200.' Peter's news led to an awkward ripple of whispered comments and uncertain faces which went all round the table and resulted in several angry retorts; 'Doctor Fraser the person to blame for such an embarrassing mistake with the council's budget is Mr Scott the council's clerk who I notice is not even here for this evening's important meeting.'

Peter had not been aware until Andrew's dismayed comment that their usually punctual clerk was not present that evening. 'What we need to do more than anything else Doctor Fraser is persuade shopkeepers to reduce their food prices which it seems to me are rising for no particular reason and leading to angry demonstrations by people who have very little money to begin with.' Chris Watson was a short bespectacled young man who was a local professor and a politician and always gave an appearance of being overworked. 'Mr Watson, I don't want to sound at all ineffectual but I do not believe it is our responsibility to get involved in such a matter as food prices -'

'Or wages!' Peter looked at the far end of the table where Mr Berkiss a more authoritative figure was sitting. 'According to the leaflets which are being distributed it is low wages too which are leading to such angry demonstrations but we are unable to force employers to raise wages either isn't that so Doctor Fraser?' Peter looked extremely shamefaced by Mr Berkiss' statement which was a perfectly fair one.

'Yes Mr Berkiss, you are right.' Peter said in a tired voice. Again as a dissatisfied silence fell over the table Peter was sure he could see a number of hostile looks out of the corner of both eyes and several council members were shaking their heads with displeasure. 'From what we

have discussed since this evening's meeting began……..'
Mr Carter spoke with a hostile tongue, '………..it seems to
me doctor we are completely ineffective towards the angry
protestors and their complaints. More than anything else
it is the two items which have been mentioned not just in
this parish but all over England, food prices and wages
that need to be discussed and sorted out quickly. In this
parish is it because really doctor you are a gentleman who
does not care at all about the lower classes as you come
from such a high-ranking and condescending family?' Mr
Carter's narrow, hollow cheeked face expressed a sneer as
he made his absurd comment in his boyish voice. Peter
raised his head and his face became taut as he was unable
to believe what Mr Carter had suggested. For a time he was
rendered thunderstruck until calming his own emotions
he replied steadily; 'Mr Carter that is an absolutely foolish
and disgraceful comment you have made and before this
meeting progresses I would suggest you apologise to me
directly or leave the room.' Mr Carter suddenly at that
moment looked extremely embarrassed by the comment he
had made and lowering his head to keep his embarrassment
and dark red cheeks hidden he whispered his apologies. Just
as Peter was looking at some further papers carefully that
were on the table in front of him the large town hall door
was flung open by a broad shouldered man with a craggy
hollow cheeked face who had recently suffered a deep cut
down one arm from which much blood was still oozing.
'Doctor…..can you come quickly……..' the young man
gasped, puffing and panting in a deep heavy breath. '…….
my friend Robert is unconscious in the field……there's

something wrong doctor………' Peter was almost dragged by the powerful thick arms of the man who was heavily built and his black ringed eyes made him look to the doctor extremely intimidating. Peter picked up his bag of medical equipment and with the stranger's arm around him unable to control his movement out of the door followed the man outside to a large playing field where under a dark sky very little could be seen. 'What exactly happened before your friend collapsed?' Peter asked in a curious tone. 'He was in a demonstration that was taking place outside the town hall.'

'And what happened to the gentleman who is lying unconscious, did he simply collapse?' Peter was looking all around to simply try and get a glimpse of the unconscious gentleman until eventually at the very far end of the field the body could be made out with the bright rays of a full moon shining directly over it. Already standing over the still body Peter could see what had caused the injury with a deep cut to the man's forehead, he knelt down and nervously felt the man's pulse already looking at the white face and unmoving eyes he felt sure he knew what to expect. He got up off his haunches and looked at the group of men standing around him waiting with great concern and suspense for the doctor to speak. 'I'm sorry to say gentlemen…….' Peter paused as he had to catch his breath and decide how exactly to break the tragic news to everybody. Eventually he knew he could only break the news one way. '………..I'm afraid to tell you but this gentleman is dead.'

CHAPTER SIX

John Reynolds's desire to be loved by everyone had made him an obedient child. He was born in the little village of Buxton an only child to a working class family yet had remained with his parents in the same surrounds until he was merely fifteen then moved into a small plain house in Bretby alone. From the very moment he had started out he regarded himself as nothing other than a simple labourer. He began making a little money in time as a pedlar walking around England selling his wares and took ever increasing pleasure in his retiring times and the carefree life he led. Yet too John liked to make his feelings known whatever the topic of conversation may have been. As he travelled around England selling his wares he was willing and eager to speak out in public to anybody who was nearby him and though not knowing how he managed to do it he could attract anybody who was passing by to stop and watch and listen to him fascinated and manipulated by a peculiarity he simply could not appreciate. As a pedlar he listened to peoples' conversation and most of the time though not understanding the political or social implications of his own remarks he began to join the conversation. People always became spellbound by his peculiarity and would listen with extreme interest not interrupting his moralizing at all. Often as he ended his address he would receive applause and cheering with the crowd seriously deliberating over and believing everything they had heard. As time progressed John became increasingly self-confident with himself and his charismatic charm and he enjoyed being the centre of attention. As he walked the streets in towns, cities, hamlets and villages he would stop as he went through and loudly call out to people who would be passing by to listen to his personal sermons and such sermons always ended with the same response from the audience, great applause, appreciation and a cacophony of uplifting voices.

Increasingly regarding himself as a supporter and member of the large majority of labourers living difficult lives throughout England John also more and more regarded himself as their representative and any time their services were required during difficult times John Reynolds would stand up in public and through his rousing speeches fight for their cause. During the enclosure period when landowners had retaken their lands from plain tenant farmers and their hard-working farmhands leaving them without any finances of any kind and often living without any home John Reynolds had travelled through the lanes and over the fields of England pausing as he walked and speaking as usual with a strong and emotional voice, with verve and an unyielding character, vivacious and seemingly invincible. As the anger over enclosures had continued John had been able to rally mass protests outside the homes of such influential and wealthy figures as Sir William Harcourt, Lord Montagu, Lord Whitby and William Darby when they had come outside and listened themselves to John speaking with great gusto. They had invited him alone inside their large homes to discuss possible ways to end the ongoing protests outside. Eventually with some regret John knew when the issue of enclosures ended peacefully it had not been his own negotiations that had successfully won the day for the farmers and their hands but simply a debate in the House of Commons before its complete collapse.

For a time John had returned home to Bretby and begun work once more in his position as a pedlar remaining a little disappointed his many rallying cries supporting the mere underpaid labourers had not in itself defeated the landowners and their own personal desires for further wealth. Yet in more recent times as he had walked purposefully around England reading copies of the countrywide pamphlet handed out on every street corner and seen the news of growing unrest over low wages and rising food prices and taxes once more he had regarded this as his opportunity to begin his speech making in public places and his chance to rally the simple hard-working and under-paid labourers to fight for their needs. He had not long been away from Bretby when deciding to return home and begin his rallying calls almost outside his front door on the village green beside the small pond and cows and sheep grazing without any concerns. Returning on Christmas eve to everybody's surprise and puzzlement he arrived back in the village on a fine white horse, a tall stallion with a charming feathery mane and velvety tail. Although people wanted to ask him the moment he had dismounted his horse where he had purchased such a fine beast, over the festive season John had remained alone needing a little peace and privacy before his difficult campaign began.

After the warm pleasant Christmas and new year spell of weather with no indication of any snow or ice on its way much heavy rain began to fall which continued through three weeks of January and into early February when the spring like weather returned and throughout England people particularly those of the labouring class began to look ahead to their challenging year. On the morning of February 10th 1610 deliberately John Reynolds had left his house mounted on his fine white stallion and ridden across a simple lane to the village green where in his smooth, charming and sometimes slightly eccentric voice he cried out across the lane and towards the huts of the village for the gentlemen to come over and listen to his *battle cry*. Very soon after his loud inviting calls had begun hut doors were being flung open and the small green was completely hidden under foot as all around John Reynolds the gentlemen and labourers of the village had come to listen to him speak. John Reynolds very quickly before he began to speak with vehemence and verve decided to change his name; he called himself *Captain Pouch*. The motive for which he called himself *Captain Pouch* was the pouch that he kept by his side everywhere he went which had inside it an enchanted keepsake to keep every one of his followers safe during the mass protests. As the gatherers listened, hypnotised by his tall, handsome and spiritual figure they believed his every word demanding they rose up against the powerful and high-ranking gentlemen of England and fought strongly until their demands for better wages, lower food prices and later on another monarch to lead the people were met. At the end of his long and extremely vibrant rallying call he told the people; *"I have authority to lead you from the kingdom of heaven"* As the gatherers broke up excited and buoyant after hearing *Captain Pouch* speak *Captain Pouch* knew this was just the start of a long hard fight ahead of him. He had guided his stallion to cross the green and at the local inn he had dismounted and gone in for a drink; after giving such a long and very animated speech his throat was excessively dry and sore. 'A pint of your very finest ale would be very well received.' he had told the landlord who had been attracted automatically by the customer's white unblemished face and the mysterious dazzling light that appeared to sparkle from his wide green eyes. 'There you are sir.' the landlord had replied very quickly strangely overawed by the tall customer's charisma and smooth silky voice. 'My large utterance on the green is being acted upon without any delay!' *Captain Pouch* commented and gave the landlord a devious and persuasive grin. 'Pardon?' The small and plump landlord looked curiously back at the captain uncertain what he had meant precisely by his comment. 'I'm not going to repeat myself.' *Captain Pouch* gestured with his glass towards the door where many men were appearing still deep in discussion over the captain's recent speech. 'We hope Captain that a simple show of force will be enough to make those with all the power give in and accept our demands without a revolution as you suggest being necessary.' *Captain Pouch* lifted his face from his glass trying to recognize who exactly had made the remark but was unable to see who indeed was responsible. He reacted with a bright dazzling smile which once more made everyone stop in their actions and conversation ceased as the customers waited with fascination for the captain to speak. 'Listen to me gentlemen, we shall never be men under the command of authority!' To many simple and only poorly educated individuals such a comment was not immediately understandable yet it still received a great amount of cheering and applause which filled the lounge. *Captain Pouch* drank quietly for a while listening with one ear to the gentle ripple of conversation which was still going on around the lounge before with his drink finished leaving and moving on.

As *Captain Pouch* rode his horse through the small villages of Fritchley, Brimlington, Froggatt and Grindleford he gazed at local women working in their huts often weaving or sewing to make a little money or else if outside watching over their children and tending their cattle or sheep. Immediately they saw the white ghostly figure approaching they would stop what they were doing and watch him slowly riding through enchanted by his character and the magnificent horse he was riding before, as he approached the city of Nottingham he rode over to the large field opposite the row of newly built brick houses and when he was positioned properly he began his loud captivating rallying call and watched as doors were opened with excitement as the gentlemen of the growing city came out eagerly to listen.

On that same day in the growing city of York George and Elizabeth had set off early to attend a large fete being held inside the market square. They had left their baby son with the neighbour to watch over as Elizabeth was even before this day had arrived feeling the fatiguing consequences of lasting motherliness. 'What a wonderful spring like day.' she had commented simply as they had walked towards the city centre under a fine blue sky and brilliant sunlight. George looked closely under the bright light at her figure dressed in a newly bought blue silk dress. 'You are definitely looking well again.' George took a small hand of Elizabeth and kissed it with a strong feeling of gladness and much relief in his mind. From a distance they stopped and watched all the men, women and children looking around the many stalls full of different wares and cakes, jams and pickles produced in the homes of ordinary families in readiness for the sociable day out. 'What a wonderful and happy picture it makes.' George tilted his head back and for a time simply stood with his wife watching the events going on until gently in a soft voice Elizabeth suggested they moved on further towards the show. So early in the day there was already much excitement and a sense of anticipation hanging over the event and plenty of friends wandering around the stalls in a happy and contented mood. 'Already I can see Jack and Marina with a bag full of bought items.' Elizabeth and George slowly walked around the cake stall enjoying the warm sunlight shining on them and the sound of indistinct murmurs as people gossiped blissfully together. 'Do you realise Elizabeth,' George began thoughtfully, '........we haven't done this together ever since our very first day when I was introduced to you at Whitby all that time ago.....' Elizabeth held her husband's hand a little more tightly and smiled lovingly with her own particularly stunning expression covering her face. 'How our lives have changed since that very first wonderful day we had together.' George momentarily looked on the more negative side of their lives since their first meeting. 'Events have aged us since that wonderful day.........I'm certainly feeling older than I did when we were walking around Whitby fete laughing and introducing ourselves......I remember with a little curiosity and for my self some uncertainty.' Elizabeth again looked reflectively into her husband's face; 'Certain events perhaps have aged you just as father's shooting two of my friends shocked and aged me yet at the same time look what we have achieved, not least producing a wonderful baby boy.' Elizabeth briefly stopped the conversation as she went to the seller on one of the two largest food stalls and asked for a jar of the fresh honey. She paid the three shillings before returning to her husband. 'If you want before we leave later you can go to the far side tent and have your palm read.' She stopped and held George closely. 'Do you remember George, you had your palm read in Whitby and your reading came true, you were told that very soon you were going to get married........'

'Things could not have turned out better could they do you think?' Elizabeth fondled her husband's cheek which made him blush a little. 'Not at all.' she replied in a deep emotional voice. As they walked on again George cocked his head back and listened carefully to a particular sound that caught his attention. Looking at Elizabeth he pursed his lips as though a little concerned and slowly nodded his head. 'I recognise the childrens' voices dear.'

'I believe they are Jessica and Rosamund from two houses away.' They deliberately went into the tent where children were playing on the coconut shy and jumping up and down and laughing and screaming with delight as they enjoyed themselves with a feeling of freedom as they were away from the strict control of their mother and father for a short time. 'I'm glad to see your children are happy.' George called to Sandra the young and very authoritative mother. George had partly meant the remark to be sarcastic however Sandra did not look at it that way but as a simple remark commenting on the childrens' happiness. Sandra's face changed to a bullish expression; 'They might as well enjoy themselves when we allow them to.' She glared at George and Elizabeth rolling her large piercing eyes from one to the other as her husband Nicholas, a short and unusually wordless figure watched on with his arms folded tightly in an anxious manner. Elizabeth nervously wished them both good morning and leaning her head down made a cheerful comment to the children which made them chuckle and suggested to George they moved on. 'Sandra is a very religious person I believe,' George commented.

'She is, every time I am attending church services Sandra is there with the children by her side.' George chuckled, 'Is that really how church effects you, completely removing any sense of humour you may have ever had from your thoughts?' They strolled past the young men taking part in the archery competition and all looking extremely serious as they prepared themselves to fire the arrow, striving their very best to strike the centre of the board and win one of the outstanding prizes. 'I have never lost my sense of humour since I began attending church more have I George?' Elizabeth strangely looked a little sheepish when she had asked the question and dropped her head. 'Of course you haven't!' George said strongly and tenderly with one finger on Elizabeth's chin lifted her head and kissed her. 'Of course you haven't.' he repeated this time in a whisper. They stopped for a moment watching the young men taking part in the archery competition and George pointed out the silver salver on the prizes stand. 'That's something I would like to try and win later in the day.'

'Where would we put something that size when we only have a very small house and why would you and I need a serving tray when we never have any visitors?' George looked at Elizabeth a little upset by her short critical remark. 'I thought perhaps one day we might have a party and a few visitors from roundabout us.' Elizabeth shook her head; 'In such a tiny house?' She sighed heavily. 'One day perhaps.' she mumbled under her breath. 'I was concerned when we first moved in to our new home our horses may become restless when they were kept in a field rather than in proper stables but they have settled down perfectly well.' Elizabeth licked her dry lips and returned a *"good morning"* remark to a young couple who had smiled affectionately as they passed the other way. 'Perhaps during the summer I will build us two stables in the field and pay for two young men to come over and act as our part-time stable boys.' George's suggestion made Elizabeth nod her head vigorously in agreement. As they walked back outside into the dazzling sunlight and growing crowds the sound of lively traditional music had begun playing and on the stage the morris dancers were performing with great gusto and grinning broadly as they danced. 'That was something I shall never be able to do.' George cried above the sound of the musicians who were playing just in front of them. 'Oh my darling……' Elizabeth began, '…….perhaps one day our child will be able to dance on your behalf.' They watched the energetic and jolly dancing for some considerable time before deciding it was time to go to the refreshments tent and have a little lunch. 'That child is learning to be a siren.' George commented as they heard the sound of a young boy screeching piercingly at his mother for several minutes in a very un-likeable tone. 'What would you like to eat dear?' George asked casually as they were about to be served. Elizabeth selected a simple coffee and chicken sandwich and George ordered the same. 'At least the food here is not expensive.' Elizabeth remarked as George paid the small charge. 'I have been reading in the pamphlet a gentleman calling himself *Captain Pouch* is beginning to ride round England asking labourers to rise up and demonstrate against the employers who are paying their workers the mere one shilling a day.'

'At least the captain hasn't arrived in York yet.'

'His desire to raise the labourers only just began today.'

'Well let's hope that *Captain Pouch* with his rallying cries is not successful.' George made his remark and chuckled taking the news without any concern or seriousness at all. He had a drink of coffee sitting back in his comfortable chair and looking around at all the colour and smiling faces and the many children clothed in fancy dress and vibrant cloaks with make-up and ointment completely disguising their faces. 'I believe that is John and Sara coming towards us. They are both looking well again after their slight fever.' Elizabeth looked towards the area set aside for the tug of war competition later in the day. 'That is good to see.' She and George had been introduced to most people of York totally by Sara alone when very first arriving in the city and swiftly they had made many acquaintances who had made themselves loyal and understanding towards the city's newest arrivals. 'We had better not be too late returning home. Our young carer is extremely kind and helpful towards us but I don't believe Jenny really understands children all that well.' George laughed. 'Good point.' he remarked simply. To George's utmost surprise as Elizabeth watched a young mother walking past her and amusing her young child by singing in an animated manner as they disappeared from view her eyes immediately looked tired; 'I believe in time I'm going to need some assistance in looking after our little boy.' George had a drink of coffee and paused for a little while before replying. 'That's the first time you have mentioned such news to me dearest.' Elizabeth replied a little more faintly as she looked at George. 'It might have something to do with the fact we're living in uncertain times right now. It effects different people in different ways.' She turned her head around from George's puzzled gaze and watched out towards the far-away stage as the morris dancers continued their performance still with great gusto. 'How is your own business doing at the moment?' It was a question Elizabeth deliberately asked merely to change the subject and take her husband's mind off other matters which appeared suddenly to be disturbing him slightly. He carefully placed his elbows on the table and rested his chin on his hands and thought about Elizabeth's question. 'At the moment things are a little subdued…….' Again he paused and thought about the rest of his reply. 'More people I believe are starting to feel the effects of the food increases and all businesses are experiencing the aggression of simple underpaid labourers towards their employers.' George's face at that moment looked extremely white and it seemed to Elizabeth that he was going to take ill. 'Would you like me to call a doctor?' she asked with great concern in her voice.

'Just give me a moment or two dearest.........I shall be all right thanks.' He sat back and closed his eyes a while before opening them and beginning to show a little pink returning to his cheeks. 'I am sorry to be suddenly looking on the more pessimistic side of things when we are enjoying such a pleasant afternoon but unfortunately I do believe if wages of the simple labourers aren't quickly improved then the growing frustration of ordinary hard-working men is going to simply spiral out of control.' Elizabeth looked around the large gathering of men and women chatting merrily and laughing as they conversed or watched their young children playing with each other and everybody simply having such a wonderful time. 'Looking at the cheerful scenes in front of us you wouldn't think there was anything wrong in England today.' They finished their light lunch and got up arm in arm returning to the archery tent where George had earlier determined he was going to try and win the silver salver. 'You've never tried your hand at archery before.' Elizabeth commented smiling slightly as she watched George pay his money. 'Just watch me try now.' A few minutes later he was being passed over the prize and returned to Elizabeth beaming with joy and satisfaction. 'I believe we can go home now and regard our visit here as a great success.'

John Granger had lived all his life working hard as a simple glover in the small village of Syston near Leicester. He had not been particularly well educated and as he had found out when he was just a child he was not at all self-confident and for much of his life he had been easily led whatever decisions nearly of any kind he had had to make. He was now in his early forties and had been living a quiet life with his wife Mary and working as a glover in Leicester, it was a job that he quietly enjoyed. As a simple employee of Mr Davis who was the manager of the business he had for over twenty years been paid the simple labourers' wage and until recent months he had lived without any concerns of any kind, especially when he was looked after by his wife who was powerfully built, authoritative and protective of her husband. Mary as a woman curiously had been given a much greater education than her husband and was much more well-spoken and decisive in her mind than John ever was. They lived with their two small children Peter and Susan in a simple wooden hut in the quiet village and like many other people in the village owned two cows and one sheep which they looked after in the wooded garden they owned also. As John had a considerable distance to travel to work each morning, as a glover working sometimes till eight or nine o'clock at night it meant that until a Sunday arrived he and his wife would see very little of each other and John saw very little of his children yet it was a gruelling lifestyle which they had both become used to and until recently when food prices had started to escalate their life had been almost completely untroubled. Now however, John as a labourer with a meagre labourer's wage was struggling to pay for ordinary food for the family to eat in addition to paying the rising taxes. John like all his fellow workers at Mr Davis's glove making factory had left work several times to go and watch *Captain Pouch* speak all over the Midlands when he had been travelling around on his fine white stallion and was completely overcome with enthralment and incredulity as the captain had spoken in great animated fashion. After the captain had taken some considerable time travelling the country throughout the summer to try and organise demonstrations though curiously without much success he had eventually returned to the Midlands and spoken again on the large green in Leicester city centre and chaired a meeting of people from the many surrounding villages afterwards in the local King's Head tavern when a large demonstration had been arranged for the first day of August. The demonstrators had been commanded to meet outside *Captain Pouch's* home in Bretby and from there together with the captain leading the way they would march towards the large mansion of Sir William Harcourt where the long angry demonstrators were to remain until some form of compromise was reached between Sir William and the captain to end the protest. As usual without his wife to look after him John had been easily taken in by what the captain had told him and much to his wife's anger now the morning of the demonstration had come John was going to attend without too much uncertainty in his mind. As they were sitting in the small kitchen having breakfast Mary was still trying desperately to persuade him not to take part. She served the whole family gruel as John filled two cups with a very cheap ale and gave the two children half a cup of milk each. As they ate their breakfast John appeared somewhat confused by the whole situation as he was trying to understand exactly what *Captain Pouch* had been talking about when he spoke of the demonstrations continuing all over England until wages were raised, food prices were lowered and a new monarch was elected to sit back on the throne. 'There's an awful lot you don't understand about ordinary life isn't there John, if you are absolutely candid with both of us?' John's face became increasingly ashen. 'I believe dear that is a fact we have always known.' He smiled slightly but his wife did not show any of her normal characteristics John recognised when she was in a cheery mood. 'Is *Captain Pouch* the man's real name?' Mary asked in her loudest and most authoritative voice and stretched her body to its maximum height as she completely looked over John's small thin body in an intimidating way. 'I believe the gentleman's name is *Captain Pouch* dear. What makes you ask such an unusual question?' Mary drew in her breath deeply and as she did her eyebrows lifted high which always made John feel even more intimidated than usual. 'If you believe that John then unfortunately it does not say very much for your *great* intelligence does it.' Mary had a drink of ale and watched the two young children eating as usual quietly and with wide smiles covering their faces, completely unaware of the annoyance going on between their mother and father. '*Captain Pouch -*'

'*Captain Pouch* indeed' Mary interrupted and sniggered in her mannish way. John tried to begin his own unsafe actions again. '*Captain Pouch* told the many men who were outside on the field listening to him and in the King's Head that everybody who supported and followed him would be made safe by some spiritual object he has inside his pouch that he always keeps beside him.'

'And do you really believe that nonsense?' Mary asked again with a particularly annoyed tone as she gnashed her damaged teeth together. 'Absolutely.' Mary's strong tone made John recoil and his nervous reactions made him drop his spoon onto the table, the loud noise made the children cry out fleetingly with concern. 'His pouch was beside him in the tavern, he stood up and showed it to everybody who was there filling the room.'

'And did he open it and show you just what is inside that pouch?'

'No, nobody asked him to show us.'

'I believe all your friends have as little authority or understanding as yourself!' Mary was going to shout her anger at John but as she watched the two children sitting not too far away she kept her deep authoritative voice down. 'Mary.....dear.......look at things this way.......we are struggling with money.......just buying ordinary plain food is difficult.......' John had to stop and have another drink of ale for his dry throat. Briefly he was opening his mouth and trying to speak but no words would come. He had a long drink and licked his dry sore lips as his wife's angry face watched him and waited agitatedly for her little husband to continue. '....*Captain Pouch* says that to get ourselves a higher wage we need to begin a revolution -'

'Hah!' Mary interrupted this time with venom in her reaction that made both their little children cry. She and John took hold of a child each and began hugging and kissing them and asking them very kindly and softly to stop crying and calm themselves down. 'I need higher wage my darling to look after the children properly and keep this roof over our heads……..' Mary and John paused in their rather heated discussion until quietness had fully been restored in their small hut. 'Can't you understand the dangers you and your fellow protestors are causing yourselves?' This time as Mary asked John the question there was genuine tenderness and caring in her unusually melodious tone and in her more loving face she expressed to him. 'Demonstrations are not permitted in England at the moment, they are illegal and if necessary will be broken up with force which could mean by the army being brought in and muskets being fired at yourself and other protestors!' John returned to one of his earlier points which again made Mary's blood heat.

'*Captain Pouch* told everybody when he was speaking to us, we are all going to be protected by the pouch he keeps beside him……he also told us he has the power and authority of God who has given him the right to lead us all.' Mary looked at the childrens' red faces and with a small piece of tissue wiped away the remaining tears from their eyes. John opened the wooden door and went over to the little field to have a look at their small supply of livestock. 'What a wonderful day it is again today.' he said, having a yawn and stretching his arms high. As Mary took a moment away from the children to come outside and join her husband in their grassy garden John commented on the family's present supply of clothes and pulled on one sleeve of his cotton shirt. 'Look at this dear,' he said quietly. 'This shirt has needed replacing for many months yet with such a small amount of money that we have we simply can't afford to buy any new clothes……' John looked at Mary hoping to see a little more understanding in her eyes, Mary however was biting her bottom lip tightly with stress and worry and was shaking her head as her husband once more tried to explain the difficult situation in financial terms. '……..we need to buy some new clothes for ourselves and for the two children yet we simply can't afford it.'

'Protesting like this John simply is not going to make any difference.' They stood on the lawn watching the cows and sheep feeding on the grass until John from the corner of one eye watched some of the other hut doors opening and men he recognised beginning to come out together and making their way towards the dusty track leading into Derbyshire. 'They look a little threatening don't they John, armed with bats, swords and flintlocks……..doesn't that suggest you keep away and just go and do an ordinary day's work at the glove factory?'

'I haven't got any weapons at all.' John commented completely unaware of his wife anxious remark. 'I must go.' He kissed Mary on one of her large cheeks and almost fled out of the garden and away from his large wife before she could make any further protests and ran over to join his many friends and allies who were already fully prepared for the long and challenging day they had ahead of them.

Captain Pouch being a man of precise punctuality did not have any time to wait for foot-draggers. He was already looking a man of dominance and power sitting high on his exceptional white stallion looking over the hundreds of men who had come to take part in the mass demonstration. To some men powerfully armed with dog locks, matchlocks, rapiers, left hand daggers and wheel locks *Captain Pouch* appeared particularly intimidating dressed in complete white and sitting on top of his white horse with no arms of any kind to defend himself. 'Will *Captain Pouch* be safe without any arms during a demonstration?' was a question many people waiting for the march to begin were asking each other in a controlled whisper. John joined the long line of demonstrators looking and sounding extremely threatening and fierce with their clubs, sticks, spears and spare rounds of ammunition in readiness for their challenge. Strangely using his loud piercing and magical voice *Captain Pouch* was able to cry out excessively loudly over the heads of every one of the several hundred men already chanting, whistling and cheering with passion in their hearts and tell them to quieten down which immediately brought silence. At eight o'clock precisely with his sparkling wide eyes looking far behind him he cried out;

"MEN; BEFORE THIS TIME TOMORROW
WE SHALL HAVE GAINED OUR

OBJECTIVES AS GOD MY LEADER HAS
TOLD ME! FOLLOW ME MEN
AND MAKE YOURSELVES MY
HEROES!"

He pulled on his horse's reins and with loud celebratory screaming and shouting beginning to ring out once more *Captain Pouch* made his way meaningfully westward towards Leicester. John who was armless and feeling somewhat intimidated by the local villagers surrounding him just as he had felt at the breakfast table when he was sitting beside his large wife commented to the gargantuan and very heavily built man who was striding forward beside him and with having such long legs making John run to keep up with him, 'Mary is not at all happy about me coming on this demonstration.'

'What does it matter what Mary thinks? This is a man's thing, it's to do with food prices and wages and it is up to the men to sort this problem out and put the class difference right. That is what *Captain Pouch* has been telling us during his many speeches.' John was increasingly becoming breathless as he followed at the very back of the long line of demonstrators. Nervously as he was gasping for breath he remarked. 'My wife believes……..th….e man's n….ame is not *Captain Pouch* and he has no……..' For a moment John had to pause and catch his breath before, needing to raise his voice to try and pierce the chanting and angry calling all around him he began again. '……no magical object in his pouch that will keep us safe………' The gargantuan figure slowed down deliberately so he could speak more broodingly with John. 'Don't you believe what *Captain Pouch* has been telling us?' John tried with difficulty to think logically about his friend's simple question. 'I believe the captain, it's just at the same time I don't like to argue with my wife and upset her.' The gargantuan ally peered down at John's little figure and decided there was no more point in continuing the conversation and once more began to stride ahead leaving John a long way behind him.

As they marched through Derbyshire and into Nottinghamshire they passed many farming fields with crops and rape seed growing well with the fine warm weather and with much livestock standing almost motionless and yet for this one day it seemed strange that no farm hands were to be seen in the fields as every individual had vowed to take up arms and follow *Captain Pouch's* commands. Most of the marchers had taken to the large and momentous event believing this demonstration was going to be a single event when Sir William Harcourt would speak inside his large mansion with the captain and take his demands to London where gentlemen of influence and authority would have *Captain Pouch's* demands met. Men increasingly poured out of their huts wielding weapons of power as the protestors were marching through the Midlands villages. The nearer the march came towards Glenfield just north of Leicestershire where Sir William Harcourt's large expensive mansion was situated curiously the quieter and more uncertain the protestors suddenly became. They arrived at a large playing field only a mile from Glenfield where *Captain Pouch* stopped on his stallion and turning his round head to face the long line of men who had now fallen silent he commanded them all to sit down and rest until sunset when they would march to the boundary of Sir William's mansion and set up base until Sir William appeared outside to negotiate with he alone. As the men dropped to the lush grass field, some looking almost battle weary, there was a whispered rumour going round that the captain may be misleading them with his curious comments and yet such a rumour was in itself dividing the protestors between the captain's sceptics and his supporters. The high spirits there had been much earlier in the day when the protestors had just started to arrive in Bretby suddenly had disappeared. For a time *Captain Pouch* simply vanished, as the protestors sat waiting for his return to lead them on the final part of their lengthy march there were many men who had collapsed onto the field and immediately fallen into a very deep sleep which was unbroken until the captain simply reappeared out of nowhere. Under a vibrant and very picturesque sunset in his emotional voice and animated bodily movements the captain called for his followers to pick up their weapons and travel behind him onto the land of Sir William Harcourt where there they would remain until he appeared in person to listen to their demands.

To the demonstrators' immense and unwelcome surprise when they got further inside Glenfield they were greeted by armed soldiers and some of Sir William's own band of heavily equipped guards eying them vigilantly as they advanced with an increasing feeling of disinclination inside them. The moment Sir William Harcourt's mansion came into view the protestors stopped in their tracks and watched *Captain Pouch* advance alone to begin his negotiations with the two most senior looking military men. As the protestors continued to pause with jumpiness and disquiet awaiting the captain's further commands from nowhere there began to be uncontrolled and furious scuffles involving simply members of *Captain Pouch's* own followers which brought a cessation to the captain's negotiations. All the attention was taken off *Captain Pouch* as armed soldiers began trying to stop fierce outbreaks of fighting between the demonstrators which continued to break out all around the mansion's boundary and lanes and pathways nearby. *Captain Pouch* when left unaccompanied mysteriously disappeared from the complete ferocious situation and was not recognized by any of the day's protestors again.

After several hours of ferocious fighting when some shots had been fired in a sense of ill will and a number of violent arrests had been made the protestors broke up and many fled back to their villages from where they had originally emerged leaving the armed soldiers and Sir William Glenfield's large brigade of equipped guards alone to look over the surroundings where the fighting had taken place and clean up any human remains lying untouched. In the very early hours of the following morning the news of such unwholesome actions first emerged to Sir William Harcourt. Surprisingly at such an hour in the morning he was not in his splendid bedchamber resting but instead he sat alone drinking wine in the drawing room of his magnificent mansion when such peace and tranquillity was broken by his personal butler's arrival to inform him of the news. The butler was a little hesitant as he opened the door and saw Sir William's large intimidating figure reading peacefully in his armchair yet advanced further into the room and received the gentleman's attention after giving a deliberate mannerly cough. Explaining that there had been a planned demonstration outside the mansion which had ended with seven protestors being shot dead and six men being arrested and taken to the local jail in Leicester Sir William merely raised his large eyebrows and nodded his big round head still totally unmindful of his butler's news. He very quickly told his butler to leave him alone and not disturb him again unless the news was of more meaning. Only the following morning Mary Granger was told by a local man who lived in a small hut opposite in Syston that tragically her husband John was one of the innocent victims who had been shot dead by accident during the mass riots.

John Reynolds sat alone in his small private and hidden office in Derby already putting the failed protests in Glenfield out of his mind and preparing his speech for the next part of his ride around England trying to raise further mass support for the hard-working and under-paid labourers. On returning from Glenfield John had picked up a copy of the latest pamphlet to be handed out and read the details of the events that had taken place not too far outside Sir William Harcourt's mansion. There were two lists of names, one a list of those who had been taken alive by armed troops and driven by horse and cart to Leicester jail and another list of men who had during such violent scuffles been shot dead. A little to his personal dissatisfaction he read in a separate article that demonstrations were already beginning to take place around England without having any authority from himself. Immediately he had read the two stories he folded the pamphlet up and put it away in a cupboard drawer. As he was having a drink of whisky and putting the finishing touches to his long rallying speech there was a subdued knocking on his office door and somewhat unhappily and with a little reluctance he told his caller to come in. Even before the door was opened John knew who it would be. His personal messenger would be outside his office with further news about the protests around England and minor incidents of unrest. As the door was opened he readied himself to listen to his messenger's mournful tone. 'Yes Jeremy, can I help?'

'*Captain,* I have a message for you - ' Tired and conflict weary John interrupted angrily.

'That is what I pay you for, to bring messages!' Jeremy looked a little offended by the abrupt and hostile interruption. 'Yes captain…….if I can please finish…..' John gave a tired wheeze and dropped his head.

'My apologies of course.' He felt a little sympathetic to the young man who came from a broken home and had just lost his wife and baby boy in an appalling crash when riding on their horse and trap. 'Please do continue.'

'I have a message for you which comes from St James's Palace. Anne of Denmark and Lord Egerton would like to speak with you about the continuing protests and disturbances taking place across England and try and negotiate some kind of truce to stop the devastation.'

'Are the negotiations demanded as soon as I can make my way to London?'

'Yes captain, as soon as you are in London.'

'Very well. I shall go and have a drink at the local tavern and then ride directly to London. If you can take my message back down to London for me then I would be very grateful.' The young messenger's face gave a nervous smile before he pulled on the rim of his large black hat and for the first time since his arrival enthusiastically turned around and left the darkened room. John knew the Flying Swan would be quiet at that time of the day. Dressed in his white suit he changed his flat black shoes for his extremely elegant and expensive riding boots and looking in his small mirror put on his tall white hat before going outside and mounting his white stallion which he rode across to the nearby duck pond and quickly dismounting went inside. 'Hello Charles, a large glass of your very best ale.' Charles the tall fair haired landlord always greeted John Reynolds with a wide smile and referred to him only as *Captain Pouch*. 'I still don't know *Captain Pouch* if you were leading the failed march that ended in chaos near Leicester only a few days ago.' As he passed John his glass John looked angrily at him;

'I demand I am authorized to keep such news sacred.' Charles smiled broadly at him, he was used to the captain making his feelings known in a statement which most of the time was not made in plain English. 'Just as you say *Captain Pouch*.' John stood at the bar and drank peacefully before afterwards wiping his lips dry and in a pleasant manner wishing Charles a good day. He looked up into the blue sky and mumbled a few sacred words then mounted his horse to begin his lengthy journey to London.

John left Derby mid-morning determining not to stop during his journey to the capital at all. He followed a lengthy dry track out of the city and deliberately made his way west towards Stafford before turning south en route for London. As he rode through the county he was tempted to stop on village greens and give his rallying call to all the local gentlemen yet for once he did not feel up to such a task. To his surprise after all the news there had been in many pamphlets speaking of the ongoing unrest which was spreading right through England there were no signs of such disturbances in any of the villages and towns he rode through and everywhere appeared calm as women went about their work looking after their children, staying in the house doing family duties or else weaving for some extra pay. In the fields farmers were working hard on the land, harvesting fresh wheat, sowing fresh seeds and tending the sheep and cattle. There was the sweet sound of birdsong coming from hedgerows and undergrowth which were flourishing in the warm weather and the occasional sign of foxes, rabbits and squirrels in the fields or scurrying up and down tree trunks and across branches looking for food and frolicking around together. The peace and tranquillity appealed to him suddenly a great deal more than the idea of sitting on his stallion demanding his followers continue to rise up and demonstrate wildly against all the senior powers that be. He passed travellers, beggars and pedlars who were mostly making their way towards the nearest burgeoning town or city to try and make a little money. Feeling suddenly a little bit more relaxed he cheerfully wished people a very good day as he passed them by. On his fine mount he rode into Hereford and through Wiltshire where he decided with some reluctance to stop at a small tavern and have another large glass of ale for his dry throat.

When he went inside he got many strange looks from the large gathering of people who though it was only late afternoon were filling the lounge deep in conversation. As he was buying himself a glass of ale and paying the pleasant young lady who had served him, his exchange of loving glances with the charming lady was broken by a call from behind which took him completely by surprise and made him jump with shock. 'Is your name *Captain Pouch*?' The question which was called out in a deep manly voice by a woman John guessed by her rather scrawny and hollow cheeked appearance would be in her mid-40s was one he wished to avoid answering after the dreadful events in Leicester had been made so public all through England. At first John tried to find a seat at the back of the lounge where he could drink his ale alone however more and more local customers became curious at the question and in turn demanded to know the answer. 'Have you a magic pouch which will make all your followers safe and well?' Again the question received a great many laughs and a great amount of jolly applause and some whistles. 'What do you keep in this pouch of yours? Is it a magic potion maybe……..?' John lowered his head and allowed the curious and inquisitive questions to continue however when he had had only half of his glass of fine ale he angrily got up and left without uttering a single word in reply.

The remainder of his ride into London was quiet and to his great relief he was not approached again by anyone. Just as the fine sunlight was beginning to set and a pleasant picturesque sunset was making a stunning backdrop over the brown waters of the Thames and the magnificent Palace of Westminster John entered north London feeling increasingly weary. Once more with some reluctance he decided for the night to rest at the next inn or public house he came to. John came to a small inn just inside the small hamlet of Barnet. He rode up to the arid and mildewed stables where a young and extremely tall boy calling himself *Bertie* offered to take the visitor's horse and look after it as he said in his boyish voice yet with a forceful tongue, *"for a price!"* Looking a little bemused by the boy's remark John took two sovereign coins from his silk purse and handed them over which made the boy seem incredibly proud of his achievements with his *"negotiating skills"* The boy commented on John's fine horse before taking it into the stables and feeding it a little straw as it began to play up slightly. On entering the inn which was bustling with customers drinking and happily enjoying their evening there was an immediate pause in all the conversation when they saw the white *"ghostly"* figure appear. There was an uncomfortable period of whispering and finger-pointing as some of the regular customers believed they recognised the peculiar and in some ways aberrant figure. 'Isn't that the gentleman who calls himself *Captain Pouch*?' After a spell of being alone under the pleasant sunlight and listening to the relaxing sound of birdsong John suddenly felt a little more like replying to the questions which were asked of him. He stood in the doorway and lifted his head high with the dullish sunlight shadowing his tall thin figure, saying in his more hypnotic and compelling voice; 'There is a divinity that shapes our opinions. I with all my pride have hope and a feeling of Godliness for us very soon to be able to live in peace and harmony once more!' John paused and waited for some replies from the ordinary customers who were watching on with some intrigue. After several minutes of near silence when John and the drinkers exchanged long hard faces one local man standing at the back of the bar asked in a common one tone voice. ''cuse me sir but might you explain yourself to us?' A furtive expression crossed John's lips and he could feel his eyes begin twinkling once more. He went through the crowd of enthralled and mostly tongue-tied customers and asked the young landlord for a large glass of ale and a room for the night. As his drink was passed over the landlord rolled his eyes up and down John's strange white outline several times before nodding his head with approval of the man's character and arranging him a room. John had just taken his first sip of ale to which he had let out a drone of delight when the lady standing beside him he guessed must be in her late twenties going by her pleasant youngish outline asked in a curious voice. 'What exactly do you mean by your talk of causing an uprising?' she asked.

'Trying to raise the ordinary labourers to stand up and protest with violence against the establishment.' Listening to the lady's refined voice and looking at the pretty blue dress and the pearl earrings she was wearing John guessed she herself did not come from a family which was in any way struggling financially. With his eyes once more sparkling he looked down on the small figure and replied quietly. 'However lady I do not believe you live in a family which is having problems buying food and keeping a little money to pay taxes.' He had a drink hoping the lady would make no further comment to his remark. She raised her head as much as she possibly could to see into his eyes and was so overcome by their brightness she decided not to converse with the stranger any more but took her drink and walked across the floor to join a tête-à-tête continuing in a more relaxed and homely manner. John was allowed to finish his ale alone for the remainder of the evening before he left the contented drinkers and was willingly given his room key and wished a very good night. Before preparing himself for bed and a good night's sleep before his long day ahead he went across to the window and peered out at the dazzling lights of London city and feeling hypnotized for a time he just stood looking out towards the river where even in the darkness with the faint light of the moon shining on it the dirty thick smog overhanging the river was clear to see. Eventually once more he felt completely overcome by exhaustion and decided after a wash to prepare himself for bed.

Lord Egerton and Elizabeth were once more entangled in rivalry on the chess board and listening to Anne nimbly playing the piano up in her private music-room. Elizabeth had not returned with the theatre group until mid-July much to the surprise of her mother yet she had enjoyed the tour enormously. Lord Egerton had discussed returning to his flat before Elizabeth came home just in case she was not happy with the new and possibly awkward circumstances she was facing however when Anne had sensitively and in her motherly fashion explained the present position with Elizabeth her young daughter had seemed very contented with her new surroundings. A game of chess after tea had very quickly become a daily affair after Elizabeth's return home and this time Lord Egerton found himself in a most difficult position on the board. His frustrations were beginning to get to him and in his frustration he called out angrily for the little dog to stop its yapping which he had been able to hear for much of the evening. 'I'm sorry.' he said slowly as Elizabeth gave him one of her telling expressions of annoyance. 'It's still your move.' she murmured after she had been waiting over twenty minutes for Lord Egerton to play. He folded his arms and placed them on the table before with a sigh moving his King to the far corner and waiting for Elizabeth's reply. 'Check mate!' she called with delight almost immediately. Lord Egerton stood up and emptied his glass of whisky. As he finished drinking he walked over to the window and looked out over the large fields and woodland and gazing up at the hazy moon he decided before bed and a little sleep in preparation for the big meeting next morning to go out and have a walk to get a little *fresh* air. Passing his decision to Elizabeth she gave a pretty expression on her cute round face as she chuckled pleasantly at him. 'I don't believe the air of London at the moment is particularly fresh.' However once she had finished chuckling at her own amusing comment she suggested she accompanied him on his jaunt. Lord Egerton could not hide his elation as she made the suggestion. 'That would be absolutely marvellous…..absolutely wonderful…..it would be just…….' Elizabeth came over directly and told him to keep such elation quiet. She called for the butler to get her her best shoe roses and favourite blue jacket to wear while they were out before she and Lord Egerton very quickly left the house. 'I just want to go to the stables and check on the horses for mama.' Elizabeth commented as they departed the house. Inside the stables the darkness was lit up slightly by a small lantern which had a slight glow coming from it. Elizabeth picked it up and went further inside to see the stable boys lying sound asleep beside the two horses which were lying flat out on a large pile of dry pale hay. Holding the lantern still over the stable boys and horses to check on their health she eventually gave a little smile and put the lantern back on its hook and went back out to join Lord Egerton. 'Are the horses well?' Lord Egerton asked in a slightly cautious voice. Elizabeth looked up at Lord Egerton and gave him a telling face. 'No problem at all! The two stable boys we have here really are excellent. Now, shall we walk?' Together they began their night time stroll.

'I believe that little dog of yours has come as well.' Lord Egerton commented as the sound of it heavy fast breathing could be heard in the still air. 'It was your idea to buy the dog for mama I believe, at least that was what she told me when you brought me back from Spain.'

'Touche!' Lord Egerton grumbled to himself.

'Are we going to walk towards the city?' Elizabeth remarked as they walked across the long flat open land in the direction of Soho. 'We may as well although London is becoming an increasingly dangerous place to live in with the protests of angry labourers.' Elizabeth with her short but growing figure turned and lifted her head to look up to Lord Egerton. 'Do you believe Mr Reynolds will come tomorrow or is he merely deluding you? According to the pamphlets that is the kind of man he is.'

'He is that kind of a man who also will not admit to his own mistakes.' Elizabeth stretched hey little neck to look up at Lord Egerton and appeared a little confused by his comment. 'Whatever do you mean by such a remark Thomas?'

'Mr Reynolds admits he is a man who likes to raise and lead demonstrations yet although he was seen leading the recently failed Midland's protest he says he played no part in the event. Your mother decided we should have this meeting with Mr Reynolds but I should not be at all surprised if he fails to appear.' As they walked towards the new brighter streetlights that had recently been erected across the centre of London they could hear the sound of gunfire going off sporadically. 'People will hunt at any time of the day or night, your mother would not be at all happy now if she was out walking with us.' Elizabeth pursed her small lips and nodded in full agreement with Lord Egerton's remark. 'Mama was never keen on the killing of innocent wildlife, she was never very keen on the killing of wildlife when papa was alive come to think of it.'

'And what about your father? Was James at all keen on hunting?'

'Papa was always keen on hunting with his many hounds. That was the way papa was brought up, I remember my grand papa was always excited about hunting and sometimes they would take me when I used to ride on my beautiful little brown pony. I was rather like mama, I never did like hunting.' As they walked towards Whitehall and closer to the river the unpleasant smell of the hanging blue mist began to get stronger. 'I wonder how long it will take the council to get this sewage system fitted.' Elizabeth said in a reflective voice as she scratched her brow and grimaced slightly. 'I think that unfortunately is a task which is going to take many years to complete. I don't like to criticise your father Elizabeth but I wish James could have done something about the pollution even before he became King, he complained to me a number of times about the horrible smell from the river water when I worked under his influential figure.' Elizabeth nodded her full agreement much to Lord Egerton's surprise. 'Papa spoke to me a number of times about the horrible odour of the river...........' For a young and thin lady Elizabeth was able to give a very loud sad sigh which came from the very depth of her chest. 'However Thomas, I'm not going to criticise my late papa now he is dead......' She mumbled her comment with her head lowered and looking mournfully down at the newly erected white paving stones.

They walked deeper into London than they had intended and got as far as Oxford Street before deciding to turn back. 'I think this is far enough for our little stroll we spoke about.'

'What happened to the dog?' Lord Egerton momentarily looked horrified when he realised the irritating yappy sound of the growing little dog had stopped some considerable time ago. 'Don't start and worry yourself about the dog,' Elizabeth stood on her tiptoes looking into Lord Egerton's eyes and smiled. 'That annoying thing will probably be back in the house or outside in the garden being amused by the butler.' Her bright tantalising grin put Lord Egerton's mind at rest quickly enough. As they were returning towards the grassy patch of the Soho fields there was the sudden explosion of gunfire that sounded extremely close by. 'Where the hell did that come from?' Lord Egerton cried out unable to control his sudden sense of total shock as the thunderous blast of gunfire rang out reverberating around several London streets. Not thinking about his own safety Lord Egerton ran over towards a small lane nearby where under a newly erected street light he could see a dead man lying with blood running from his chest and as he looked up he caught the momentary sight of a slight figure of a man peering back across the lane at Lord Egerton holding a flintlock in front of him before running off into the distance. Elizabeth came up to the lane to join him and was almost sick as she looked at the dead blooded corpse. 'I'll have to try and find somebody who can do something about the removal of this body.'

'Why would anybody kill an innocent gentleman like this?' Elizabeth asked. Not surprisingly her voice had become a little shaky and distorted. 'I believe this is a simple angry attack carried out for no reason, one terrible incident of the many spreading throughout England…….' Lord Egerton paused to think a little more about what he had said. He felt in the pockets the obviously wealthy gentleman who was dressed in a fine red jacket and expensive blue velvet breeches. 'He has absolutely no money or purse in any of his pockets at all which is extremely unusual. I believe this shooting has been just a simple robbery which has ended in this man losing his life.' Lord Egerton stood up and exchanged nervous glances with Elizabeth before returning to the motionless body and trying to decide what next to do.

'This afternoon's *"little gathering"* as you put it Thomas is bigger and more important than you seem to be suggesting.' Lord Egerton and Anne were sitting in the music-room as Anne again was trying to get Lord Egerton to understand a little more about piano playing. He began once more slowly playing a few notes in rhythm and creating a slight melody but without any real success. Anne gasped with disbelief as she watched Lord Egerton play and listened to the tuneless sound. Lord Egerton inquired with some curiosity about the arranged meeting's organisation but Anne was unwilling to answer. 'All I ask for Thomas is you to come to the conference and give me your full support.' Lord Egerton nodded.

'I shall be there at the palace as long as you really believe the devious Mr Reynolds will arrive.' Anne for once shared Lord Egerton's mood of uncertainty. 'According to what I have been informed by other officials who shall be present at the palace this afternoon Mr Reynolds is regarded by many as a trouble-maker but at the same time as a good negotiator and he is the only man who may be able to help bring all the demonstrations taking place throughout England to an end.' Lord Egerton tried for a final time to play a few notes tunefully before going down for breakfast with Anne but after a moment folded his arms in frustration. Anne, shaking her head equally frustrated brought the piano lid down and suggested they conceded defeat for the time-being and left the room. 'Where is Elizabeth this morning?' Lord Egerton asked with his furrowed brow expressing some concern. 'Elizabeth didn't get to her room last night until about two or three o'clock, I would guess this morning she will just want to sleep.' Lord Egerton's furrowed brow for a time did not change its expression. 'That was my fault, it was simply a spur of the moment decision when I looked out of the window at the moonlight over the woods. It looked such a fine night. The thought we might find a man's dead body later during our walk had never even entered my head.' Anne shrugged; 'It's not the sort of thing that crosses a person's mind before they go out for an evening stroll. 'Had anyone identified the man by the time you and Elizabeth decided to leave the gruesome scene and return home?'

'No, the man was not identified but it was obvious that he was a gentleman of substance and prosperity. To hear the gunfire so close came as a horrible shock to your daughter and myself but to find the bloody body was extremely terrible.' The butler was waiting for Lord Egerton and Anne at the bottom of the staircase to inform them breakfast was ready. 'Thank you butler.' Anne retorted in a more irritated voice.

'A gentle ride out later this morning I would suggest shall be enough for us before the meeting at the palace later on this afternoon.' Anne remarked as she entered the dining room. Lord Egerton could not find the energy to disagree with Anne's observation and simply nodded his head which was feeling extremely heavy. Immediately they were seated at the table Anne's two most regular house maids arrived to serve them plates of fried bacon and tomato. 'What a magnificent morning it is once more.' Anne commented looking outside onto the lawn. After an almost sleepless night Lord Egerton for once had not dressed as elegantly as he liked to each morning after rising. He fidgeted with his wired collar for several minutes and frowned to himself. 'Before I go out I must tidy myself.' Immediately the coffee pot and two large cups were placed on the table Lord Egerton himself poured the coffee and quietly asked the maid just to leave them alone for the moment. Anne sat thoughtfully for a time looking outside at the pleasant garden before commenting happily to Lord Egerton, 'It's strange Thomas but the way I feel now living in this house I'd been living here all of my life.' Lord Egerton looked a little blank faced at Anne.

'I suppose so.' he responded in a most casual and seemingly uninterested voice. 'I believe Elizabeth is coming to join us.' Elizabeth's small elegant figure came quietly through the dining room door and placed herself at the far end of the table looking still extremely tired. 'Good morning mama……..good morning Thomas.' she remarked in her smooth elegant voice. The maid quickly arrived following Elizabeth's attendance and put a plate of bacon in front of her and a glass of apple juice. Elizabeth had a drink and looked a little uncertain of herself. 'Did you sleep all right my dearest child?' Anne asked with a little shrewdness in her kindly expression. Elizabeth's face for once appeared tired and drawn however as always she replied to her mother's question cheerfully and sounding particularly positive; 'Yes thank you mama but for a slight headache.' She had a piece of the bacon and commented to Lord Egerton, 'The dog came back safely last night.' She gave him a slight grin that made Anne a little curious.

'Was there any particular reason for my daughter's remark Thomas?' Lord Egerton straightened himself blushing. 'It was just me worrying about that irritating little dog of yours that decided to come and join us during our walk.' He emptied his coffee cup and a little angrily pointed for the maid to come and refill it for him. They had the rest of their breakfast quietly before Lord Egerton excused himself and went back up to his bedchamber to dress himself again.

As Anne was sitting comfortably in the living room and Lord Egerton and Elizabeth had just started a further game of chess the butler arrived to inform Anne and Lord Egerton their horses had been readied by the efficient stable boys and were outside the front door waiting to be mounted. Elizabeth still looking weary headed was trying to decide her next move when her thoughts were interrupted as the puppy entered the room yapping in its most irritating manner. 'I believe we should adjourn the game for now and complete it later when you come back from the official gathering.' Before Lord Egerton could respond Elizabeth had got up and throwing the puppy the most fearsome expression she could manage in the circumstances left the room and disappeared upstairs. Lord Egerton asked the butler to bring him his light cloak hanging up in the hallway and after he was fully dressed he and Anne left the house preparing for their own challenging day.

They rode across the long wide open ground towards the Soho fields and upwards in the direction of Piccadilly and Westminster. The sound of gunfire was coming over from the wooded area of Westminster district and the loud deep barking of the hounds as they searched for the hunters' victims could be heard filling the air. 'Hunting is wrong is it not Thomas?' Lord Egerton's eyes rolled in Anne's direction and he sighed at her remark. 'Yes......... hunting is definitely wrong.' To his relief Anne did not take their conversation any further. They rode the considerable distance alongside the grimy waters of the Thames towards the Tower of London and stopped at the newly opened inn for a light lunch. 'A glass of wine and a salad will be enough for me thank you Thomas.' Anne remarked the very instant they had gone inside. She sat at the far table and waited for Lord Egerton to return with the plates.

'I suggest we ride straight on to the palace after we have finished eating as we don't have any idea when Mr Reynolds shall be arriving.' Lord Egerton pulled a distorted face. 'Or even if he shall be arriving at all.' Anne with her narrow shoulders shrugged. 'There is nothing we can do about

Mr Reynolds, all we can do is wait at the palace with the officials who have been invited to attend also and merely hope Mr Reynolds does come.' They ate without speaking for a short time before Anne smiled a little as she reflected; 'It will seem a little strange being back inside St James's Palace after all this time away.........it will certainly bring back some memories.'

'Both good memories and bad I should think.' Lord Egerton remarked in a thoughtful voice too.

'Yes, of course the memories shall be divided.....' Appearing a little sad Anne closed her eyes and looked as if she was suddenly having a slight snooze until the sound of the inn door being pushed forcefully open and several raised voices all talking rapidly at each other in the middle of an animated conversation woke her. 'How are you feeling now Thomas?' Anne asked almost as though it was instinctive when she had opened her eyes. Lord Egerton, unlike Elizabeth decided to be more honest towards Anne's question. 'I have felt better!' As they were simply looking at each other neither one knowing what to say their awkward silence was broken rapidly as the door was opened and the very tall young landlord came in and recognised Lord Egerton as one of his most regular customers. Knowing too Lord Egerton came from an upper class and refined background he hurried over to give him some news. 'If you are still unsure who the dead gentleman you found last night is it is Lord Percy who lived in Bloomsbury.' Lord Egerton was startled by the news of his seeing the body to begin with. 'I was given some information first thing this morning by one of the officials you were talking to last night who came and collected the body as you asked.'

'You mean Mr Leaming I presume?'

'It was Mr Leaming I was speaking to earlier in the day. He told me nobody else knew whose the corpse was.' Lord Egerton and Anne looked at each other astounded by such niceties. Eventually Lord Egerton reflecting on the dead man's name said slowly, 'Lord Percy was certainly not a man I was familiar with. Has anybody found his murderer yet?'

'Unfortunately not yet.' Lord Egerton and Anne looked at each other and thanked the landlord for his information. As he hurried away and left them in private again Lord Egerton asked Anne thoughtfully. 'Does that name mean anything to you?'

'Not at all.'

'How strange Lord Percy was a gentleman with refinement and riches yet his is a name neither of us recognise.'

'Perhaps Lord Percy had only just moved to London,' Anne mused. 'After all it is a city that is growing all the time and increasing numbers of businessmen and political figures are coming to London to live.'

'Maybe.' Lord Egerton agreed as he cleaned his plate and had another drink of wine. 'That salad was absolutely divine.' he remarked emptying his glass and wiping his face clean.

'I thought we might go to a masque tonight after the stressful meeting is over.' Lord Egerton considered Anne's remark. The thought of an early night's sleep appealed to Lord Egerton more but the mere act of agreeing was straight-forward. 'As long as I don't have to do any more dancing, I am definitely not up to that any longer!' The force that he put into his voice when making his remark took Anne by surprise.

'Just as you wish Thomas!'

'London is extremely quiet today.' Lord Egerton ruminated as he turned his head and peered out the window at the river bank and the deserted streets further up. 'Perhaps the shooting last night has something to do with it……people might be in shock after such a horrible event.' Lord Egerton considered Anne's remark though he did not take it particularly seriously. 'I suppose that's one possibility for the quietness.' He made as a simple cursory remark. 'If you are absolutely sure there is any point in us being in St James's Palace early this afternoon then I think it may be a good idea for us to go now don't you think?' Anne peered at her watch and herself was rather reluctant to leave. 'Yes, I suppose that is a good idea.' she remarked and finished her glass of wine as they readied themselves to depart.

Their horses were tied up in a small field not far from the inn and were motionless but for the occasional swishing of their tails. Before joining Anne inside the field Lord Egerton went into the nearest lane where a young man was handing out pamphlets though the lane itself was completely deserted. Lord Egerton opened it fully running his eyes up and down the latest stories to make its few pages. 'It gives all the information about Lord Percy in here -'

'Of course it would!' Anne a little angrily cut in. 'I don't know how their reporters get the news so quickly but they obviously pick details up from somewhere.'

'That's what all the politicians in Westminster have been wondering for a long time and still nobody knows.'

'Does it say anything else about Lord Percy's background and where exactly he's from?' Lord Egerton untied his horse and mounted before reading any more information to Anne. 'It says here that originally Lord Percy comes from Edinburgh and had moved to London only four months ago.'

'That explains how we didn't recognise the name.' Anne screwed her face up and mulled a little over her own simple remark. They pulled on the reins and their two fine horses left the small green and they began their ride alongside the river westwards towards St James's Park and the palace.

On arriving at the outstanding edifice there appeared a stable boy outside the front entrance and as he took the horses now sweating and neighing wildly Anne and Lord Egerton could sense that all ready there was a large gathering of officials waiting patiently for the stragglers to arrive. They went under the high arch and paused half way. Looking at each other they remained silent until Anne commented simply in her most nervous tongue that certainly Lord Egerton had yet heard her speak with; 'Very well Thomas; let's go inside and find out what is to come?'

John Reynolds had risen that morning reflecting on his failed mission to rally England's hard-working labourers.

After months of journeying through England on his magnificent white stallion he had only managed to lead one organised rally which had merely ended in chaos and bloodshed. At least today he would have an opportunity to bring peace to England and have the labourers' demands met. After dressing and grooming himself as best he could in such a small and confined room he went downstairs for a little breakfast and a drink of coffee hoping he would find the bar quiet with no-one present and ready to irritate. Peering from a distance towards the bar on seeing there was nobody at all inside he went across the floor feeling a little more self-confident. He walked over to the counter and was greeted cheerfully by a middle-aged gentleman who instinctively offered him a glass of ale. 'I would like one of your lightest breakfasts and a cup of coffee please.' he commented in a laid-back manner. He went to the nearest table and waited for his food to be brought looking out of the window towards the many narrow lanes and pathways leading onwards into London. The thought of a casual ride into central London before continuing into St James's Palace he found appealing. The young waitress who came over with enthusiasm to his table to serve him his breakfast paused as she got closer to him somewhat amused by the outline the sunlight shining on one half of his white figure made. His tall thin character dressed fully in white made her start. 'Your breakfast sir....' she said slowly and with anxiety etched over her small pale face. 'Thank you young lady how very kind.' he replied in his most polished English possible to calm her at least a little. 'Your horse has been tended carefully overnight for you Mr Reynolds and is ready for you the very moment you wish to leave.' John turned his head to see who had made the unexpected approach to his table and was greeted by the very tall and well-built man, Mr Cameron the manager. 'I think I'm beginning to feel my age.' John remarked without looking back at him. Mr Cameron looked at John's back and was not at all sure what kind of a reply to make. 'What makes you say that Mr Reynolds?' Mr Cameron decided to play safe and ask John a further question rather than making any self-opinionated remark of his own. John rubbed the palms of both hands down his face. 'My face is feeling weathered and rough.....' For the very first time he had remarked candidly to anyone about the failed demonstation just outside Leicester he said as he wheezed with tiredness. 'My organized demonstration in Leicestershire failed badly and the majority of the protestors afterwards put the blame on me for the scuffles and fighting that ended in some of my men being shot dead.........overall my rallying calls have gone wrong and the only protests against high food prices and low wages for the labourers have been organised badly by the demonstrators themselves.' Mr Cameron was astonished by John's revelation said with great melancholy. He came and sat down a little sympathetically beside John. 'So my drinkers who regarded you as *Captain Pouch* were absolutely correct in their observation?'

'Yes they were. There have been plenty of details given in all the street pamphlets about my name John Reynolds and how when I am crying out for my speeches I like to be called *Captain Pouch*.'

'And according to the pamphlet you call yourself *Captain Pouch* because of the pouch that is always beside you when you are sitting on top of your fine stallion my stable boy has been tending all night?'

'I do call myself *Captain Pouch* for that reason.' John felt a silly expression cross his face as he considered just how so many of his following protestors had been taken in by his remark. 'Tell me Mr Reynolds if you are wanting to be so open about yourself, is there a magic formula that keeps you safe when you are demonstrating with your followers or is that just one more of your misleading statements?' John this time could not stop his dry pale face from breaking into a grin and he laughed out very loud which made the young waitress sitting behind the counter shiver. When he finally calmed down he answered with his cheeks having turned from white to dark red in embarrassment; 'There is no magic potion inside my small pouch but a piece of green cheese!' John once more began laughing out loud. Mr Cameron could not completely prevent himself smiling on his large head and chuckling slightly. 'What is it about you that attracts so many people to almost believing every single falsehood you tell them?'

'Search me!' he answered shrugging his shoulders and with his dry throat he began to cough steadily that lasted for several minutes. Bemused by John's outpouring of honesty without wanting to Mr Cameron had to pull himself up from his chair as he was so interested in what John was saying and return to work in his small office. 'I must get back to my work Mr Reynolds. Just tell me when you are ready to pay your bill and I shall attend to you.' Mr

Cameron unintentionally gave John a pat of understanding and some sympathy on a shoulder which fell as it was touched by Mr Cameron's heavy large hand.

John had been intending to have a reflective ride around London before going on into St James's Palace to begin his official conference with Lord Egerton, Anne of Denmark and their official invited guests to help debate and solve certain ongoing troubles yet after sitting alone in the quiet lounge just enjoying the relaxing and restful atmosphere by the time he felt able to go out and face the busy and exciting city of London he looked at his watch to discover it was already after midday. As he got up he put his hand over his mouth and gave a refined and gentlemanly yawn before going into Mr Cameron's office and paying the bill. In addition he thanked the manager for sitting down beside him earlier and listening to his sudden outpouring of openness which he had not expected to happen. Their short and official meeting to conclude financial matters ended with a relaxed and friendly handshake before John went outside to find his tall white stallion directly at the door. Sitting on such a tall horse John as he looked towards London could see far into the distance and was able to spot an English flag flying high on top of St James's Palace. He lowered his head and thought fleetingly about his enormous task awaiting him whispering to himself, *"This is my opportunity to make myself a hero."* With that thought in mind he pulled gently on the reins and began his ride into London.

CHAPTER SEVEN

By August 1st 1610 as John Reynolds was approaching St James's Palace he and everyone else who would be involved in trying to negotiate a peaceful settlement to England's continuing upheaval knew exactly how significant these talks were going to be. For a number of months there had been intermittent outbreaks of disorder throughout the country which were being generated by the slow rise in the cost of food and the daily wage of a meagre one shilling a day for the ordinary hard-working labourers remaining unchanged by each and every employer. For a number of weeks these minor scuffles in the main occurring in streets and lanes had never escalated into anything worse than merely one lone individual expressing his frustrations in an unruly manner and they had very quickly been brought to an end and peace had returned. Yet as food prices continued to escalate these minor scuffles had become not just the violent actions of one lone individual expressing his frustrations in a moment of madness but involved small groups of men often armed with daggers, dog locks and sticks protesting in disorganised mobs. These growing demonstrations more often than not took place in town or city centres and would not end until soldiers well armed with muskets arrived on the scene when peace was eventually restored. Frequently following the soldiers' arrival there would be a period of fierce confrontation and sometimes the use of gunfire was required to bring reconciliation when arrests were made and occasionally there was bloodshed. Though for a lengthy time the countrywide anger and protests by the mass majority of plain hard-working labourers did not escalate and people in authority did not take the ongoing scuffles and disorganised demonstrations particularly seriously. Parish councils continued to raise land taxes and paid no attention to the two issues of food prices and labourer's wages that were causing the escalating anger and unrest. A single incident which was reported in the increasingly prevalent street pamphlet created more raised eyebrows by the more influential figures in England and made councillors slowly pay more attention to the underlying causes of the unrest. In Liverpool on January 1st 1610 six Parish council members were shot dead by a group of exasperated low-paid labourers just as the council meeting broke up and the members were coming out of the town hall believing their frank and honest discussions had been extremely successful and the people of the city were living happy and contented lives. The shocking and hostile occurrence after it was published appeared to give rise to further incidents of bloodshed when labourers seized matchlocks, doglocks and wheel locks and approached their employers in their offices while at work demanding their wages were immediately increased, if their employers rejected their demand they would be shot dead on the spot. This further aggressive and direct form of protest also escalated to nearly every part of England and sometimes ended with businesses closing and their employees losing their jobs altogether. Disorganized rallies escalated particularly in the bigger cities and on two occasions protests that had begun in Oxford and Hampshire ended with large crowds of irate protestors armed and ready to fight for justice waiting outside the Houses of Parliament for a negotiator to arrive and listen to their simple everyday needs. Both rallies had after long standoffs between the protestors and armed soldiers only been ended by several hours of fierce fighting and both times with several protestors being shot dead and dozens of people being arrested and taken to the Tower where they had been kept without being officially charged.

As the more intimidating and fanatical forms of protest and confrontation continued to swell through England lesser scuffles involving troubled individuals simply were unceasing throughout towns, cities, villages and hamlets. Sporadic violent criminal acts ranged from simple street robberies to the sinister acts of wooden huts particularly in villages and hamlets being burned to the ground often without warning the family inside at the time. Increasingly grimy disease ridden jails across England became filled with protestors caught during the burgeoning violence and often they would be put in a jail cell and left without any Justice of the Peace sitting in court and officially charging the offenders. As unrest continued larger businesses and simple shops were increasingly devastated as their labourers took ever more time away from work to instead demonstrate in the country's streets, lanes and the city's thoroughfares. As time continued without any official action being taken to try and bring peace and stability back to the nation the expanding protests spiralled steadily out of control and people were living in fear of their own safety as well as in uncertain and treacherous times.

Eventually it was Anne of Denmark alone who had taken the first decisive step to try and end the labourers' unruly and devastating actions. Surprisingly to Lord Egerton Anne had made arrangements for an official conference to take place in the grand-hall of St James's Palace secretly without informing him of the conference's details until they had sat down for breakfast that morning in the dining-room. Anne's confidential meetings when he was finally told about them shocked Lord Egerton and on the morning the conference was to take place he was somewhat critical and gently poked fun at Anne believing after all he had read about John Reynolds and his untrustworthy and devious character that he would not appear.

To most peoples' great disbelief Mr Reynolds arrived through the palace door not long after Lord Egerton and Anne. A seat had been left vacant for him at the far end of the table opposite Anne and Lord Egerton and as they sat waiting for the conference to get underway they had glanced at each other with inquisitiveness and a little distrust. Anne had asked Lord Egerton as the more authoritative of them to launch the whole affair. 'The most beneficial way to begin our conference I would suggest is to ask Mr Reynolds as a representative of the largest class of labourers simply to tell the rest of us what the labourers are demanding.' John Reynolds looked at some papers he had brought with him and put them down on the table carefully to glance at and his eyes opened widely as he looked up at all the expectant faces and began to speak. Regarded as a simple labourer who had come to represent the largest social order of residents in England it was a surprise to everyone sitting around the table that first of all John spoke of a demand that had been made more than anyone else by the middle class men and women who lived in large and well furnished houses and owned a significant amount of land surrounding their home. 'First of all it is an essential condition that land taxes across England are reduced to reasonable limits. Secondly all those hundreds of men and boys who were taking part for months in the labourers' protests and were arrested for their criminal acts and are still being held in jail must be released immediately. Thirdly labourers in England who are receiving the labourers' derisory daily wage of one shilling must have their daily wage increased by three pennies a day. Fourthly food prices must from this moment be frozen. Finally the majority of ordinary labourers wish to see a new monarch enthroned to lead the country with both conviction and stateliness which is something England has been calling for ever since King James I was murdered.' There was a period of hush as every invited official considered carefully all that Mr Reynolds had said. It was obvious after the demands of Mr Reynolds had clearly been set out, by the expressions of uncertainty being exchanged between invited officials that if an agreement was to be reached that satisfied all sides then the meeting was going to be long and negotiations were going to be difficult. Lord Egerton looked around the table wondering just who wished to reply to Mr Reynolds first. As the uncomfortable silence around the table simply continued and no one official looked at all enthusiastic in replying Lord Egerton looked towards Sir Frederick Glass in the centre of the table and gestured for him to stand up and speak first in response to these demands. Sir Frederick got up onto his feet and merely said what most people were thinking in the hall at the time, that Mr Reynolds's demands would have to be carefully discussed before there could be a conclusion to the meeting that satisfied everyone sitting around the table. John Reynolds sat watching Sir Frederick speaking in a refined manner without showing any signs of frustration or annoyance and did not show any indications of standing up and heckling but simply remained silent and calm as the speaker continued. At least to Anne it suggested much to her relief that even if the conference was going to be a long one it would be held in a pleasant and dignified manner. Though Sir Frederick at first stated something that everybody already knew his speech proved to be more lengthy than anyone in the hall had been expecting it to be. When he eventually sat back down Anne this time got up automatically and asked John Reynolds if he would wish to stand up and in turn respond to Sir Frederick's remarks yet at that moment Mr Reynolds made it extremely obvious he was not going to back down on any of the demands he had made. As John sat down quickly there was a lot of frowning and head scratching by the officials and Lord Egerton this time stood up and having watched Lord Williams writing a great many notes with his quill since the conference had very first started asked him to speak and give the gentlemen in the hall his own opinions on the present situation. Strangely after making so many notes and showing much animation Lord Williams stood up and spoke with a subdued voice and his speech was short and simple. 'I believe Mr Reynolds' demands can be met exactly as they have been set out today and if they are to become law then can be brought in prudently in a way that will satisfy everyone and as we all hope bring peace and stability back to England.' John Reynolds's eyes immediately sparkled and widened as he heard Lord Williams speak and he jumped up out of his chair responding excitedly; 'Is that it gentlemen? Are we going to have a vote on Lord Williams' statement and then the meeting can come to a close!' Lord Egerton however stood up automatically waving a hand in the air and gesturing across the table for Mr Reynolds to sit back down. 'Mr Reynolds Lord Williams' comments are only his own and need to be discussed by others. The conference is not as simple as you would indeed be hoping.' There were a number of folded arms and tired faces as Lord Egerton sat back down and some words were quietly spoken with Anne beside him before the next speaker was selected.

By the late afternoon the meeting was continuing with almost every invited guest giving his own separate and different opinion on the present state of affairs. The slowness at which everyone was speaking and almost always contradicting their colleagues particularly irritated Lord Egerton watching on in total silence. It progressed well into the evening and only by the early hours of the following morning did any signs of a conclusion to the conference emerge. Mr Reynolds had said very little during the long hours of discussions. Every time he had been asked to give his opinions on the remarks of other parties he had merely said he was not backing down on his demands and it was up to everyone else at the table to find a solution to the meeting to satisfy everyone. Otherwise after making such a plain remark several times he had just sat at the far end of the table watching and listening as the men of power and influence had discussed the position in a more business-like tone before at about two o'clock the next morning there were indications that an agreement had finally been reached and Lord Egerton stood up and explained briefly to John Reynolds that the three demands he had made would have to be passed by the House of Commons and become official laws which would then over time be brought into process. John Reynolds not surprisingly looked totally delighted with the whole affair. He stood up as everyone else was in turn shaking hands with Anne and Lord Egerton the two hosts and made one of his more unusual remarks which he was known for.

> *"Man propounds negotiations,*
> *Man accepts compromise!"*

Nobody in the hall felt like discussing a remark so philosophical at that time in a morning. There was a little bit more time when quiet remarks were whispered by the guests before the hall door was opened and everyone slowly made their way outside and towards the stable yard to find their horses which had been carefully tended during the afternoon and evening and readied for their riders' return. John Reynolds remained in the hall a little longer when only Anne and Lord Egerton were left and went over to them to comment on the discussions. 'I do believe the meeting has been extremely successful, I hope you both do too.' Without asking for Anne's response Lord Egerton retorted the moment John Reynolds's voice had tailed away. 'Just go Mr Reynolds, we have no desire to speak with you any more.' John was going to respond to Lord Egerton's unpleasant comment spoken in a hostile tongue but not wishing to end the meeting in angry terms after what had been an extremely satisfying day he left the hall with all the items he had brought and went outside to the stables to find his fine white stallion.

As Lord Egerton and Anne rode back towards Covent Garden reflecting on the extremely long and exhausting meeting they were both reflecting the same way on the character and appearance of the pale outline of Mr Reynolds dressed completely in white. 'What a simply horrible man Mr Reynolds is don't you think Thomas?' Lord Egerton gave a gentle yawn and let out an exasperated call.

'I told you how I felt towards that man the very day when you told me you had arranged a conference to take place with Mr Reynolds present. I was merely surprised that he appeared to be absolutely honest with you.'

'At least the meeting was a success and now once parliament has passed these demands then they can be put into practice and hopefully then peace can be restored to England at long last.' Anne looked up at the clear star filled sky. 'What a magnificent night for riding.' Lord Egerton chuckled.

'I believe it is almost time for daybreak Anne rather than night time any longer.' Under the reflection of a dull moon he looked at his watch and turned his head back to chuckle into Anne's eyes. 'It is now almost three o'clock.' They came closer to the river Thames which again had a thick blue haze hanging over it and as always it smelled extremely unpleasant. 'When is anything going to be done to put an end to this horrible odour?' Anne asked as it began once more to get into her throat and lungs and make her cough badly.

'I was telling Elizabeth when we were out walking and she asked exactly that same question. It is going to be a number of years before the new sewage system is completed and the horrible fog that hangs over it shall be gone forever. That is something everybody living in London wishes to see, an end to this hateful cloud.' After Anne had finished her lengthy spell of coughing she returned her thoughts to Mr Reynolds.

'I believe once England has had peace and stability restored and everyone is happy again then Mr Reynolds shall be arrested at his home and left in the Tower until it is decided how he should be punished for all those weeks he was riding around England trying to get labourers to rise up and demonstrate. Mr Reynolds shall be regarded as having been responsible for a great deal of the continuing violence and demonstrations.' Lord Egerton this time had begun coughing badly and Anne had to wait for some considerable time before he was able to respond to her personal thoughts. Eventually when his prolonged coughing fit ended and he had cleared his throat his response was simple enough. 'I absolutely agree with you there Anne.' They rode up en route for Soho fields and towards Covent Garden where they finished their ride and as they were dismounting their horses they watched the two stable boys waking up from their deep slumber and taking the two fine horses feeling somewhat uncomfortable with their untidy appearance and still feeling three quarters asleep. Lord Egerton and Anne stopped outside the house and watched as the stable boys took the reins and led the horses into the stables where two dull lanterns were hanging over the large piles of pale brown hay. 'We might as well go inside and ask the butler to get us a drink before we go upstairs and get a little sleep before breakfast.'

To their surprise Elizabeth was still downstairs in the living room and wide awake reading and having a drink of apple juice. 'My darling child, I never believed you would still be awake at this time in the morning.' Elizabeth smiled with her own bright warm expression.

'Mama, I could not sleep while you were both at that meeting in the palace, especially not after reading about so many meetings having been ended by shootings. Anyway, I have been playing chess for much of the evening and the early hours of the morning with the butler.'

'Where is the butler?' Lord Egerton asked a little bit with frustration as he was waiting for him to arrive and pour him a drink. 'I told the butler he could go up to his room and get some sleep. He spent a great deal of time amusing your little dog in the garden and then after he came back inside already looking considerably tired I asked him if he would like to play chess with me.'

'I never knew the butler played chess.' Anne replied curiously with a slightly wrinkled face.

'He has told me before that he plays chess………but not very well I have to add.' Elizabeth gave one of her wily grins. 'I hope your little meeting all proved to be meaningful mama.' Anne poured both herself and Lord Egerton a drink of gin and tonic and fell heavily onto the large armchair opposite the log fire. 'I believe the meeting has proved to be successful, now it is the politicians who must make the next move and pass them all in the House of Commons.' Elizabeth gave her mother a very warm grin.

'That really is excellent news mama.' Elizabeth finished her glass of apple juice and got up from her chair with a little hesitation in her thoughts. 'I must go to bed now mama;' she commented slowly giving a gentle ladylike yawn. 'I shall see you at breakfast. Goodnight mama……goodnight Thomas.' Both Lord Egerton and Anne wished Elizabeth a very good night before returning quietly to their drinks. 'I must call on one of my official friends in the next few days and find out when the special sitting is going to be held in the Houses of Parliament. For such an important occasion I would believe the Lower Chamber will be full on that day.'

'I hope on the day when Mr Reynolds's demands are debated in the House the debates do not last very long and they are merely voted on and passed without any protests.' Lord Egerton showed no signs of arguing with Anne's remark but only gave a half smile and looked casually in her direction. 'I do believe all three demands Mr Reynolds made will only be discussed for a very short time in the Chamber and even then the discussions shall all be agreeing with each other saying why the demands have to be passed and made law for the sake of having peace restored throughout England.' Lord Egerton then made a remark that took Anne a little by surprise as he referred to Nicholas and Arabella's hat shop in Oxford Street. 'Did you know Anne that the hat shop has been closed for three weeks now as the employees have been away from work every day and taking part in the outbreaks of violence that have been occurring increasingly throughout London.' Anne looked extremely surprised by Lord Egerton's comment.

'I had absolutely no idea of the news you have just given me.'

'An awful lot of people have been extremely upset and worried about the safety of both Nicholas and Arabella. I hope amongst the many businesses that have been struggling to continue successfully during this hard time their's will be back to normal very soon.' Lord Egerton finished his drink and had a struggle to pull himself up from his chair before looking down at Anne's small figure. 'I think I shall retire for a few hours of well earned sleep before seeing you at the breakfast table a little later in the morning.' He turned round and Anne watched as he made his way towards the staircase and slowly and carefully up towards his large and splendid bedchamber.

It was only two complete days after the important conference at St James's Palace had ended that all the details of the conference and its final agreed outcome had been made clear to the pamphleteers and it had been prepared as an article which was long enough to fill all four pages of the pamphlet. Again the pamphlet was very quickly available on every street in England and throughout the country as increasing numbers of people read the news there was an immediate sense of excitement and expectation hanging in the air and spread right through the country. Particularly in every town and city throughout England everyone knew just how important the next sitting in the House of Commons was going to be as most people had been seriously affected by the ongoing attacks and random unorganised street demonstrations. A date was given in that same edition of the pamphlet, 19 August when the sitting was to take place, the day of Princess Elizabeth Stuart's fourteenth birthday. As the day became slowly closer people were getting increasingly anxious and excited about the day and already many people were planning to travel down to London from all parts of England to wait outside the Houses of Parliament for the results of the day's sitting to be announced.

The night before the sitting was going to take place many people from across England were already beginning their journey down to London travelling either on horseback or simply the longer and harder way on foot. Unlike their journey from West Yorkshire when they had gone to see King James I and the State Opening of Parliament this time to prepare themselves to stand outside the Houses of Parliament on August 19 for most of that day Nicholas and Arabella were able to ready themselves on that very same morning. They dressed in casual clothes and had breakfast at six o'clock waiting for their daily nursery maid to arrive. Sitting in the large breakfast room eating and watching over their two little children they at least felt happy with their lives and the way their hat shop had flourished ever since it had first opened yet still concerned by the threats that had been made on Nicholas's life by two of his angry underpaid labourers. Nicholas filled their two coffee cups for once not feeling his more authoritative self. 'Let's just hope the day ends on a brighter note than it did when we went to Whitehall to see the State Opening of Parliament.' he remarked for once sounding a little subdued. 'Those cigarettes aren't helping you at all are they.' Arabella suggested as she pointed to the ash tray full of cigarette ash and remains. Nicholas could not help but agree with his wife's remark. 'Plenty of people have told me ever since our little hat shop opened just how good cigarettes are for your nerves particularly Sir Edward Coke who told me he started smoking cigarettes on the very same day they were brought into England.' Arabella looked at her husband with her expression dropping to show disappointment. 'I would not trust anything Sir Edward tells me, he is very good in courts but about ordinary life I don't believe he is as wise as you are my dearest.' Nicholas looked surprised by his wife's extraordinary comment yet decided not to take the matter further. 'We must hope that the House of Commons understands just how everyone in England wants to see the labourers satisfied and their anger calmed and we can all just get back to work and live an honest life again.'

'I assume we are losing money are we every day our hat shop is remaining closed. Am I right with my assumption?' Nicholas scratched his head and bit his lip as he considered his wife's question.

'I believe that shall be so though I do not know whether the figure is a large or a small one.' Arabella looked at the two children who were both sleeping soundly. 'They have not once been any trouble for us to look after have they.' she remarked chuckling a little. Nicholas gave Arabella a slightly sarcastic look.

'That is not what you have been saying each night they have woken us up between two and three o'clock when we have both been sleeping soundly!' Arabella buttered herself a piece of bread and nodded her sudden agreement. 'I was forgetting wasn't I.' she remarked with a little reluctance as she glanced again at the two restful children. She peered thoughtfully at her husband as she changed the subject and looked ahead to the day. 'You may end up seeing some of your very good friends from West Yorkshire later on today if they decide to come and wait outside the Houses of Parliament as they know exactly where we are residing.' Nicholas had a drink of coffee and looked at Arabella giving one of his hopeful expressions with his lips very tightly pursed. 'I would like to think so.' he replied thinking of the many close friends he had missed ever since leaving for London with his wife and begun his new business. He had been longing to return to Bradford one day later at the end of the summer yet his business commitments had always prevented him from spending any time at all away. 'If we don't meet them here in London during this big occasion then I shall ride up to Yorkshire sooner or later to see my friends again, there is much for us to discuss.' Despite what they had agreed not long ago about cigarettes Nicholas got up from the table and went to the cupboard opposite where he kept his packet full of cigarettes all ready to be smoked. 'I must have a cigarette before we go out, it will calm me.' Nicholas spoke nervously as he spoke knowing she would not be at all impressed by his remark. 'Is it really necessary?' she responded angrily. Nicholas found a match and went outside into their pleasant little garden now full of vibrancy and colour and began to smoke his cigarette listening to the sound of birds singing sweetly all around. 'It's another fine warm summer day again.' he commented cheerfully as he came back into the house. Ignoring his remark Arabella got up from the table and leaving all the remains of the dirty kitchen for the nursery maid to deal with when she arrived shortly, ruminating on particular matters she went to finish getting herself ready for her day out in Whitehall.

It was not far to walk into Whitehall and already the streets, roads and thoroughfares felt as though even so early in the day they were fully alive with activity. All the shops around Regent Street, Bond Street and Oxford Street were closed and showed absolutely no signs of opening that day. 'People must be desperate for the politicians to accept the demands Mr Reynolds made for all the poorly paid labourers.'

'Absolutely.' Nicholas agreed; 'At least every hard-working individual in England will be able to stop worrying about all these unnecessary demonstrations and simply get back to work and a normal life.' As they strolled on towards Westminster already there was much activity and many hundreds of gossiping tongues stretching across Westminster and in all directions throughout the city. 'I never believed London would be so busy so early in the morning when we were having our breakfast earlier.'

'Remember what London was like when we rode down to the city for the State Opening and the horrible shock we were to get later?' Nicholas asked as they began to look ahead again through Whitehall at the exact spot they had been standing in when the King had put his foot inside Sovereign's Entrance and the explosion had occurred. 'I suppose so.' Arabella at last agreed. 'What an amazing atmosphere,' she commented softly. 'I can tell already listening to some of the accents around us there are people here from other parts of England, not just London.' Nicholas glanced at his wife and her simply observation.

'For a day like this I believe people would come from overseas to stand outside the Houses of Parliament and wait to find out the outcome of the sitting no matter how long it takes.' As the crowds very quickly began to surround them and picked their positions to wait opposite the Houses of Parliament Nicholas and Arabella almost immediately they had arrived stood where they were and decided not to move until the day's news in the House of Commons had been announced to all of the large masses surrounding Westminster. As with everyone arriving so quickly to London to remain there for the day, Nicholas and Arabella had absolutely no idea when they stood in their position and waited for the outcome just how long they were going to stay on for that was simply an incomplete uncertainty.

The large gathering of excitable crowds which had already arrived by early-morning as the politicians began to assemble inside the Houses of Parliament gave them a nervous feeling as they prepared themselves for the day's sitting to begin. Though a little reluctant to leave his leisurely breakfast with Anne and Elizabeth Lord Egerton went out early and decided to walk over to the Houses of Parliament rather than riding his horse round. He had gone straight to the Lower House and after buying himself a coffee he had then gone across to the library where he was hoping for a little peace and quiet before the ten minute bell rang out and the large gathering of politicians that was already there was summoned to the Lower Chamber for the lengthy session ahead. 'It is not as though we must pass all these demands made by *Captain Pouch* is it Lord Egerton?' Lord Egerton was a little surprised by the boyish voice that came from behind him. He had been doing a little bit of private reading and looked extremely upset by the disturbance yet as he usually did in such circumstances he turned around to look at the gentleman who had made the remark and asked him to come and sit down at the table. 'Every MP who shall be sitting in the Chamber later on today knows it's just that for the sake of peace and security for everybody in England today it will be best if all these demands of John Reynolds are accepted officially and they become law which can then be enforced. Is there any particular reason why you should object having these demands enforced?' The short young politician threw Lord Egerton a boyish face and produced an earlier edition of the countrywide street pamphlet. In as angry a voice he could possibly produce the young MP pointed to the pamphlet as he scanned his little blueish eyes up and down the front page article. 'All the things it says here about *Captain Pouch* sir, the man simply is not to be trusted all the deviousness he has used trying to bring a mini-revolution to England.' Lord Egerton had a sip of coffee quietly thinking exactly what his political counterpart had just suggested to him. 'That is exactly the way that I feel about Mr Reynolds, yet at the same time it is also obvious that peace is required to allow the people of the country to settle down in their stressful but quiet lives again don't you think?' For once Lord Egerton's face expressed more of a professor look as he explained his thoughts carefully to the young man. 'Don't you think it is better to look at an argument from both sides?' The young MP looked a little sheepish and red faced as Lord Egerton explained himself slowly and clearly until the ten minute bell rang and together they got up from the table and with the large crowds of politicians all looking stony faced and preparing for the serious business ahead began steadily to make their way towards the Lower Chamber.

The buzz of excitement and anticipation there was outside, in Pall Mall, Whitehall and blossoming right across London was inside the Lower Chamber also and in the air there was a great feeling of heightened expectation. The Chamber was completely full of MPs all arriving with something to say on each motion that was to be debated. To Lord Egerton it was immediately clear the day was going to be a very long and hot one. For once the Speaker of the House appeared more of an authoritative and decisive man when he entered the Chamber despite his short and delicate figure. There was much cheering and crying of self-opinionated comments when he arrived yet he was able to sit down in his large formal chair and with the help of his masculine professor voice he was able to bring quite a quick end to all the unrest which had until that moment been continuing without any signs of ending soon. Mr Speaker looked all around the Chamber to make sure every attending MP was paying great heed and began to explain the day ahead. 'Gentlemen I am sure I do not need to explain to you precisely why we are here in the House today. We have been summoned here today to debate three motions which have been proposed after an official meeting that was held in St James's Palace on the first day of August. These motions are, firstly that all full-time labourers who are being paid the minimum wage throughout England of one shilling a day should have it raised by three pennies every day. Secondly food prices must be put on hold immediately and finally land rents are to be reduced to reasonable levels. I hope my good colleagues that you will not block any of these motions from being passed later in the day and becoming law and finally we can debate and vote on our new monarch to replace the late King James.' There was a slight eruption of sound from some parts of the Chamber yet the majority of politicians who had arrived that day remained quiet and many were simply waiting for their opportunity to speak agreeably about each of the three motions and explain to every other MP sitting around him just why he believed it was necessary to vote in favour of them. The Speaker announced that the first motion, the raising of labourers' minimum one shilling a day by three pennies would begin with a speech to be made by Jack Rodwell MP explaining why precisely it was so important to have the motion passed. When the Speaker made the announcement there was a lot of sighing and grumbling that swelled rapidly right around the Chamber. Jack was known to be an extremely long speaker who whenever he gave speeches no matter what the subject he would repeat himself a number of times stating so many facts people already knew extremely well and sometimes would stand for over thirty or forty minutes speaking before finally with a fair amount of grumbling around him he would sit down looking extremely satisfied with his own performance. To everybody's disappointment Jack had brought a large collection of papers which he had placed carefully in front of himself and as he stood up he gathered everyone of the papers of details ready to slowly read and explain his position on the matter.

Just as every MP in the Chamber had expected Jack Rodwell stood up for over thirty minutes explaining just why it was so important to give labourers a higher wage after living for so many years on just the mere one shilling a day wage. When he did finally sit down there were such a great many groans billowing around the Chamber that at first nobody else felt like standing up and speaking in response to such a long speech. However Mr Speaker's short figure stood up from his seat and asked the name next on his list, William Harris MP to stand up and speak.

The debate was extremely one sided in opinions as most politicians were in favour of passing all three motions and making them official law however it was the fact that so many wanted to stand up and have their own say on the issue that made it continue until the early evening before the gathered politicians were asked to go to the lobby and vote. It was obvious as every MP made his way out of the Chamber and towards the central lobby the way that the politicians were talking there would be a large majority voting in favour of the motion. As the politicians divided at the central lobby there was a very small minority of gentlemen who were obviously not at all happy with giving in to somebody who was regarded by a number of people as *unruly* and *untrustworthy.* Yet about twenty minutes after MPs had made their way back into the Chamber the result of the vote was announced by one of the clerks and only ten had voted to reject the motion.

At nine o'clock when the second motion was anounced to put the present food prices on hold many MPs looked extremely weary. 'Hopefully this time not so many will wish to speak but merely go after the debate and vote.' one of Lord Egerton's colleagues sitting nearby him stated to him much to his agreement. This time Mr Speaker asked Peter Roach MP to begin the debate. He was known to be a fast thinker and any speeches he did make were never long. As the very tall gentleman stood up he had few papers in front of him and to the relief of many in the House his speech was extremely short. The second debate lasted only half the time of the first and by midnight once more MPs were lining up in the central lobby in preparation to have their vote on the issue. Once more as the majority of politicians who were in attendance that day had expected, the motion was passed by an extremely large majority of votes.

As Mr Speaker was announcing the third motion involving the reduction of land taxes Lord Egerton and a number of other exhausted MPs decided to go to the lobby bar and have a drink. 'At least today's sitting will keep all the agitated crowds happy anyway.' Peter Roach who hard started the second debate had followed Lord Egerton into the bar for a drink and bought himself a large glass of scotch. 'I don't believe the third debate will last long either to keep the middle class people of England satisfied.' Lord Egerton's remark was slightly vague yet at that time in the morning he could not think of anything more meaningful to say. A young MP who had just bought himself a drink and sat down opposite Lord Egerton and Peter raised protesting eyebrows at Lord Egerton's remark. 'Perhaps that is so but all the same you still have to think of the disadvantages of keeping a scheming and devious man like John Reynolds happy.' Lord Egerton could not force himself to debate the issue now, already he was thinking about his lengthy walk back to be with Anne and Elizabeth again in great need of a little bit of peace and quiet.

Although they had not intended to Lord Egerton and his two friends who were drinking with him remained in the bar drinking until the debate had come to an end and MPs were making their way for the third and final time of the specially arranged sitting to vote. Lord Egerton finished his drink last and remained in the bar until he could see the end of the long line of politicians, again most of whom were making their way into the *Ayes* lobby. Back in the Chamber after the result of the MPs' vote had been given and there had again been a favourable response to the motion though this time with a majority of only five votes it felt as if there was a massive sigh of great relief when all three motions had been successfully passed. There was a great release of deep sustained cheering and a lot of contented whistling and wide smiling faces as everybody knew the majority of people living in an uncertain England would automatically also feel a great sense of relief and a feeling that there was now the chance to end all the violence and outbreaks of rioting and deadly assaults that was making England a most unsafe place in which to live. Eventually after giving the politicians a long chance to celebrate their achievements that afternoon and into the morning Mr Speaker announced at two o'clock that it was finally up to the politicians to decide on who the next monarch of England had to be and take the place of King James I now the throne had been left empty for almost eight years. This time as discussions began the atmosphere in the Chamber felt a great deal more joyous and politicians were still continuing with their earlier celebrations. There were a great number of politicians on all sides of the House who wanted to have a short say on why they believed it was only right that Princess Elizabeth Stuart should become Queen Elizabeth II. Some politicians said that more than anything else it was her charm that should make her the next reigning monarch, others suggested it was her beautiful sweet and charming smile and others said it was her complete elegance and pleasant sweet voice. Overall however the large showing of hands made perfectly plain that Princess Elizabeth Stuart at the age of fourteen was to become the new monarch of England.

When the Chamber broke up at later than three o'clock the majority of English people except for a small minority of powerful businessmen who had not wanted to see the *"wicked" Captain Pouch* get everything that he had demanded simply given to him were going to be completely delighted on hearing the news when it was later announced outside the Parliament building to the masses of people who had been standing outside for a great length of time and had not shown any signs of moving at all. Rather than walking all the way back to Covent Garden immediately after the Lower House had broken up and emptied Lord Egerton decided instead to do the same as many of his political friends had done and go to the Lower House bar for a drink to refresh himself before leaving for home. 'Well Thomas, are you pleased with the day's outcome?' Lord Egerton's good friend James Blateby had come out of the Lower Chamber and followed him directly into the bar to buy himself a glass of whisky. Lord Egerton lifted his own glass high saying; 'Absolutely! Things have worked out perfectly……..and you?' he added just before he had a drink.

'I feel the same way as you Thomas of course, I am highly delighted at the day's outcome. I hope when these laws are enforced then nobody ignores them and everybody for once at least even if only for a short time is happy and can live together in peace.'

'I'll definitely drink to that!' Lord Egerton quickly added and had another mouth.

'At least today shows Parliament does still stand for something.' Peter Stallingforth MP announced as he was sitting down at the same table. 'That true is a good point to make.' Lord Egerton once more agreed and had a further drink before wiping his mouth dry and preparing to go home. 'Maybe when she is made Queen then Elizabeth will think about taking action to reform the House of Commons and bring other powers it has lost back.'

'That will depend on Elizabeth's advisors all around her. At the age of just fourteen she can't make the decisions herself.' Lord Egerton then reflecting on his morning's breakfast with Elizabeth and Anne gave himself a rueful smile. 'I forgot to give Elizabeth her birthday card with yesterday's breakfast.' As he pulled himself up from the table and prepared to leave he looked at his watched as he could not control a wide yawn. 'Nearly three o'clock I can give Elizabeth her birthday card at the breakfast table in a few hours time as well as breaking the news with her and Anne that Elizabeth is going to be made Queen very soon. Now, having said all that I must leave.' Lord Egerton had to force himself through the crowds of MPs all having a celebratory drink together and going outside and making his way home.

The waiting and excited mass crowds outside the Houses of Parliament had gone wild with joy at the new which had come out of the House of Commons. All of the roads, lanes and thoroughfares of the capital were filled with massive crowds of tense people awaiting desperately for news from the House of Commons and very quickly such news had been spread around through many whispers which had swelled in every direction. Even roads and lanes outside London leading to all surrounding counties had been full of expectant people and the news they had been hoping for had reached them in absolutely no time at all. For many hours, through the remainder of the night and into the following hours of sunrise the swelling crowds remained where they were with not one person leaving their position still acknowledging everything that had happened since they first arrived some considerable time ago. When eventually the crowds did slowly begin to separate and everybody made their own discrete ways home Arabella and Nicholas began to make their way slowly back to Bond Street passing through Oxford Street first and their own closed hat shop as they did so. 'We could go to work now if you wish.' Nicholas commented. Arabella frowned a little bit although she knew really her husband was not being particularly serious; 'I think you're being a little bit over enthusiastic Nicholas.' she replied in a quiet and lighter tone. 'We must enforce the new law on ourselves when we find out just when exactly it has to be put into practice.' Nicholas looked untroubled by his wife's comment. 'That will be no trouble as long as we are informed when exactly the law on the raising of the lowest paid labourers' wages by three pennies has to be completed.'

'I hope we can afford it.' Arabella remarked suddenly her smiling jovial face came over rather grave and her cheeks and forehead furrowed momentarily. 'We can afford to pay our small workforce the additional three pennies, that should be no trouble at all as we have already been making a handsome profit ever since our hat business first began.'

'It will feel good for everybody when England has a monarch sitting on the throne again after the terrible death of King James.' Nicholas nodded his head in full agreement with his wife's comment. 'Elizabeth shall make a wonderful Queen with all her sweet charm, beauty and her warm and cheerful personality.' Arabella looked at her watch. 'Our professional nursery maid for the children will have been wondering what on earth has happened to us.' Nicholas simply chuckled slightly.

'We can explain and say we shall pay her a little extra.' Arabella shook her head slightly.

'Our childrens' maid will be demanding a great deal more than *a little extra* as you suggest, especially when we have kept her in our home looking after the children throughout the night.' As they were turning into Bond Street Nicholas pointed a long finger towards their large house and suggested Arabella went in first. 'You can explain our position with the nursery maid while I go outside and have a cigarette.'

The day's events in the House of Commons had an almost immediate effect on the whole of the English people and brought a new air of optimism and hope that at last after months of violence and uncertainty peace could be restored. Soon after the special Parliamentary sitting had ended it was announced by further officials in London that a number of horse riders in London would be selected with a list of the new laws which had been passed by the House of Commons. Such horsemen would announce their messages to bell ringers in every single town, village and city throughout the country. This news would then be announced further by bell ringers and from August 31 these new laws would have to be put into practice by every business, food shop and Parish council concerned or else harsh consequences would be felt. On that same day it was announced that Princess Elizabeth Stuart would have her Coronation on December 15th. All such news was further announced in the newest copies of the countrywide street pamphlet and all of the news made very happy reading for most people. The only news that appeared to create any more anger and unrest was the announcement that all those men who had been arrested for minor crimes committed during all the unrest and the ongoing disturbances which had now been brought to an end were to be released from all jails in which they had been imprisoned without any delay at all. A number of people throughout England were particularly angry about this immediate release after the serious crime they had had committed to them. All businesses and shops that had been closed for long periods of time as the unrest and severe disturbances had continued suddenly began to feel safe again and started once more to open their doors and commence trading and the economy began slowly to prosper. Throughout England as the warm dry summer became early autumn the English people began to look optimistically once more to the future. Strangely Elizabeth did not take the news of her forthcoming Coronation particularly seriously and her daily games of chess with Lord Egerton continued with seemingly nothing else on her mind.

Only one week before the Coronation was going to take place and London's inns, alehouses and taverns were becoming fully booked with people who wanted to be able to say later to their friends they had been in London on the day of Elizabeth's Coronation. Elizabeth and Lord Egerton were still playing chess every evening before they retired to bed and Elizabeth was just as irritated by the growing puppy as she had been for a very long time. 'That damn dog of yours.' she commented angrily to Lord Egerton when a game of chess was coming to its climax and she had found herself in a difficult position. As she continued with her move trying to find a way out of her difficult position Lord Egerton looked at the little dog as it came in the living room and found its yapping equally as distracting as Elizabeth. 'It's not my dog Elizabeth, it's your mothers don't forget.' Elizabeth raised an eyebrow at Lord Egerton and moaned some comment of irritation in his direction before returning to the board. 'I have a feeling I can't get myself out of this position.' Elizabeth said suddenly chewing one of her fingers. After several more minutes as Lord Egerton continued waiting patiently for Elizabeth to play she eventually played one of her pieces only for Lord Egerton almost immediately to play a piece in response commenting with satisfaction. 'Check mate!' As Elizabeth began to clear the board Lord Egerton was still enjoying the sound of the piano playing coming from Anne's private music-room. 'I wish I could learn to play the piano like your mother can.'

'These things take time.' Elizabeth mused and having cleared the board she went to get herself a drink. Lord

Egerton was a little surprised when Elizabeth sat back down to discover she had filled her glass with whisky. 'It's not like you to drink whisky.'

'I just felt I needed something a little stronger this evening than simple fruit-juice.'

'You're not nervous about your Coronation in just seven days time are you?'

'Just a little.' Elizabeth replied to Lord Egerton's question candidly. 'It's not something I had been expecting at all after father's wicked murder.'

'A lot of people right across England believe you will make a magnificent Queen.' Elizabeth looked rather taken aback by Lord Egerton's remark. 'Is that just meant to be a little bit of excessive adulation Thomas?' Lord Egerton shook his head. 'Not at all, just you wait and see what the reception is when your special day comes and you are made Queen of England.' Anne suddenly appeared from upstairs feeling greatly relaxed after what had earlier been a difficult day after having played the piano for over four hours. 'I wish I could play the piano just like you can Anne.' Lord Egerton once more commented rather sorrowfully. As Anne poured herself a glass of lemon and lime she pulled a slight grimace at Lord Egerton and sat down. 'I've tried my hardest Thomas but unfortunately I accept I can't make a music student out of you.'

'We will have to make sure that well before Coronation day comes we have made every part of London safe unlike we did when it was the State Opening of Parliament. That day will go down in English history as a day none of us shall ever be able to forget.' Lord Egerton sighed the heaviest of the three.

'I never believed my colleague and very good friend Lord Howard would give away inside information to Sir Robert Catesby the way that he did........I never even knew he was in any way Catholic.' Lord Egerton got up and poured himself another glass of whisky looking suddenly very ashen after reflecting on what he had just uttered. 'There's no point in reflecting back on the incident so badly now Thomas.' Anne commented gently to Lord Egerton as she came over and sat down softly beside him. 'I suggest when these drinks are finished we go to our rooms and get a little sleep. Today has been a particularly tiring day.' Lord Egerton looked at Anne and Elizabeth's quiet face and nodded his definite agreement to Anne's simple suggestion.

Once more it had been another failed piano lesson for Lord Egerton as he and Anne came downstairs for breakfast. 'Did it take you as long as this to learn to play the piano Anne?' Lord Egerton asked almost sounding as though he was going to burst into tears. 'Not at all!' Anne remarked simply to make Lord Egerton feel even worse. 'My music teacher told me I was a brilliant musician when I learned to play the piano so soon.' Lord Egerton folded his arms in frustration as he entered the dining room. Elizabeth was already in the dining room having a plate of bacon and tomato and two slices of bread and butter. 'You're early my dearest child are you not for breakfast.' Elizabeth looked towards her mother and smiled.

'Perhaps mama it is a feeling of my future grandness as the Queen of England, I shall be able to do whatever I wish no matter what mama tells me!' As usual Anne's two favourite maids came into the kitchen almost the moment Lord Egerton and Anne had arrived and served them a large breakfast and put the coffee pot in the centre of the table. Picking it up and filling his and Anne's cups Lord Egerton commented on the delightful fragrance of the fresh coffee. 'That is just divine.' he remarked quietly.

'I would suggest a ride out into London this morning and a little lunch at our favourite inn beside the Tower.' Elizabeth nodded her agreement though remarked about her commitments later in the evening.

'I am going to the Strand this evening to see another peformance by the London Stage Company. I suppose as I am to be made Queen soon I will have more formal commitments in front of me.'

'I should think so my dear.' Anne looked at her daughter a little sadly. 'I remember following your father round during his own official visits he would take me on expecting me to enjoy them.'

'And didn't you?' Lord Egerton asked smiling slightly as he thought about the many official exciting trips and voyages she must have been on when she and James were happily married. 'Most of the time not really!' Elizabeth stopped eating a moment and looked up at her mother with her jaw hanging down.

'That was not what you used to tell me when I was little mama. You always told me you loved travelling everywhere with papa.'

'Elizabeth, in front of your father I could not very well say I absolutely despised travelling everywhere I went with James. I was a great deal happier staying at my lovely little home in Scotland if I am absolutely honest with you now.'

'At least the weather isn't showing any indications that winter is on its way yet.' Lord Egerton remarked quickly to change the subject. The sound of a yapping dog nearby came increasingly closer until the butler appeared for once quite cheerful as he arrived in the kitchen. 'I am going into the garden your ladyship to exercise your puppy if you would so wish.' Without waiting for her mother to reply Elizabeth lifted her head to look at the butler and nodded one or two times before waving the butler away. 'It will be a little awkward Elizabeth if you are going on another tour of England with the theatre company this winter.' Elizabeth looked untroubled by Lord Egerton's remark. 'That is something I can sort out with my advisors when the time comes.' Elizabeth finished her breakfast first and went upstairs to change and prepare herself for her new morning arrangements.

'At least my daughter doesn't ride sidesaddle anymore.' Anne remarked smiling profoundly as the three riders approached Soho fields. 'I never rode sidesaddle mama.' Elizabeth responded sounding somewhat irritated by her mother's comment. 'It looks to me as though your daughter has loved riding horses all her life.' Lord Egerton looked over from his fine chestnut mount to Elizabeth and the smooth way she was sitting on her smaller mare, holding the reins and controlling her horse. 'Elizabeth is now a fine rider but it took her a long time to learn!' Elizabeth turned to her mother looking particularly unhappy about her mother's critical remarks. 'Is there any way why you must be so hostile towards me mama?' Anne looked troubled although she was unwilling to explain just why. On the wide open Soho fields, without giving any indication to Lord Egerton or Elizabeth Anne pulled on the reins and kicked her heels and galloped alone towards the river and very soon had disappeared out of sight. 'It will be something to do with the Coronation Thomas that is on her mind. Maybe she will tell me about her concerns later in the day.' Elizabeth and Lord Egerton looked untroubled as they glanced at each other before very quickly galloping on towards the Tower to join Anne.

'Here is the future Queen of England! Do we bow to you now Elizabeth?' The landlord of the small inn appeared overawed when Princess Elizabeth arrived with her mother for a little lunch. Lord Egerton told Elizabeth and Anne to sit down as he got the order. 'I hope you shall be all ready for the event shortly.'

Lord Egerton remarked as he ordered the glasses of wine and three simple plates of salad and chicken. 'Everybody who owns pubs and taverns alongside the river Thames is ready for the grand spectacle. Already bookings have been made for rooms and people from every part of England will be coming to watch the crowning of our young princess.' As Lord Egerton was paying the landlord the money the landlord for the first time showed a face suggesting relief more than anything else. 'At least ever since the sitting at the House of Commons took place everywhere seems to have quietened down and all the hostility that was continuing across England appears finally to have stopped.' Lord Egerton put his purse away and nodded. 'At least parliament does still have its functions. I hope when Elizabeth is made the new monarch with the advice of her men around she will begin to make some reforms to that place just as a number of politicians have been suggesting for an extremely long time.' Lord Egerton returned to the table while he, Elizabeth and Anne waited for their meal to be delivered. 'Apparently Elizabeth London is going to be absolutely full of excited crowds coming to watch you being crowned next Friday.' Elizabeth began to blush a very deep shade of red. 'Mama that is not what I was wanting, just a quiet and private event.' Anne shook her head slowly; 'During Coronations in England privacy is something that simply does not happen my child.' The young waitress arrived in her usual enthusiastic manner and looked particularly excited as she served Elizabeth with her plate and glass of wine. Lord Egerton got his purse and gave the young woman a sovereign piece for her eagerness and efficiency when she had served. 'Mama, are you going to tell me what was making you so short-tempered with me when we were horse-riding earlier.' Anne looked anxiously first at her daughter and then at Lord Egerton. 'I am simply hoping that after what happened to my husband during the State Opening of Parliament is not going to happen again, only this time my dearest to yourself.' Lord Egerton turned his head just after he had begun eating and tried his best to put Anne's mind at rest. 'The men who were responsible for the gunpowder plot have all been arrested and executed and now throughout England there is not one single individual who wants the same thing to happen again. Sir Robert Catesby was responsible for the complete affair concerning the gunpowder plot and it was he who organised the group of eleven men who were responsible altogether for the deadly event.' Lord Egerton had a drink of wine and gave Anne one of his most reassuring smiles he possibly could. 'That deadly and I suppose to all three of us here what will always remain an unforgettable occasion outside the Houses of Parliament is over and the people responsible are dead and gone. Now all the people of England want just a quiet and unruffled life without any violence or wickedness ever emerging again.' Anne had a drink of wine and looked at Lord Egerton with a great expression of relief covering her face. 'Mama did you not notice on our ride into London just how peaceful the city was as we approached the river. The Thames seemed to be extremely busy this morning did you not think Thomas?' Lord Egerton turned his head peering through the front window towards the brown dirty river. He nodded his head quietly watching the many cruisers and other light vessels that were journeying past. 'Perhaps people around are simply preparing for the big day ahead.' They suddenly all began to enjoy their casual lunch in a much more relaxed and peaceable manner than there had been from the very moment they had set out that morning.

'I need to return to the house immediately now lunch is finished mama.' Elizabeth's emotional statement given with some force as she finished her glass of wine took both Anne and Lord Egerton by surprise. 'Is there any particular reason why you speak like that just after lunch is finished dear?' Anne questioned yet Elizabeth was already outside and tending her horse which had been left with those of Anne and Lord Egerton, simply standing in the field grazing nearby. The ride back to the house was swift and very direct.

Elizabeth looked absolutely magnificent after she had bathed and changed into her favourite red satin dress with much jewellery around her slender figure. Yet it was only just after four o'clock when she was prepared to leave and her horse and carriage were already waiting outside. When the butler called that her carriage was waiting Lord Egerton casually nodded at the chess board. 'Haven't you even time for a game of chess Elizabeth?' Elizabeth looked a little uncomfortable as she shook her head and explained why she wanted to go out so early. 'Rehearsals begin tomorrow morning for the Coronation and I want to enjoy myself with friends my own age before business becomes extremely serious!' Elizabeth looked very grave and pale faced when she had made the statement to Lord Egerton. She followed the butler to the front door and waited as he held the door open for her. When she went outside to the carriage she began to feel increasingly nervous and very ill at ease.

So far through December the weather had continued more like a glorious fine summer rather than the beginning of the winter season. There were still leaves on the trees and gardens and parks were continuing to flourish from the magnificent conditions. Not only had all the inns and public houses right along the Thames' riverbanks been fully booked for three days including the day of Elizabeth's Coronation but inns, public houses and taverns had been fully booked right through the capital and outside the city in all directions also. People across England who had booked for the occasion were hoping that both the weather would remain just like summer and this time unlike when the State Opening of Parliament had occurred the security during the grand occasion would be a great deal better organised. Even from the day before the Coronation was to take place all the streets and thoroughfares of London were swarming with large excited and jubilant crowds of men, women and children mostly lingering cheerfully for the time being in the centre of the city. That same morning many of the individuals now standing in the centre of the city and simply waiting for the amazing official event to begin had been waking up in the boarding house they were lodging in and had filled every lounge as they had been breakfasting together before making themselves a little food to take into the city as they went. The public travel service, now having been operating in London successfully for a great many months, the horse and trap had become extremely useful taking many people into the centre of London who had never been to London before and did not know their way around. People were dressed in all kinds of clothes ranging from black formal clothing to casual wear of every possible colour that could be imagined. Once more Nicholas and Arabella had closed their hat shop which had started to thrive again after the many months of unrest and came into the centre of London the day before the

Coronation was to take place simply to stand in their chosen position to watch the future Queen and all the welcome officials ride by smiling and enjoying the grand occasion. Elizabeth and her husband George and young boy had come from York to watch the event having stayed at an inn to the west of the city. Though it was only the day before the crowning of Elizabeth London was already becoming an utter crush with the crowds having almost forced their way into the centre of the city to try and make sure of a good position. To everyones' relief also as nobody had prepared themselves for any possible rainfall the weather was absolutely magnificent with total blue skies and not the slightest wind to bring any possible change either. Yet still crossing the Thames' bridges as some people had discovered to their horror and disappointment was London's most perilous part of the city where many of the capital's thieves, vagabonds, travellers and beggars had made their way to and remained to try and catch any strangers unaware of their presence and rid them of a little money. Their shrewdness in heckling the strangers to London had paid off several times when people had come down the far bridge steps and found themselves short of a few coins. By the time sunset arrived London was already abound with large gatherings of people who had come to see Elizabeth's crowning and during the night trying to get a little sleep proved almost impossible.

By dusk next morning strangely the crowds which had been arriving in London the previous day full of verve and sounding particularly joyful and animated suddenly had become extremely tired and almost silent by eleven o'clock, the time the Coronation service was officially to begin at Westminster Abbey. The crowds were sweating a lot with the crush that had been mounting against them ever since their first arrival in the city and feeling somewhat uncomfortable. For such a long and exhausting delay they were hoping they would be rewarded twice to see the little and young Princess Elizabeth travelling to Westminster Abbey for the ceremony and coming back as Queen Elizabeth II wearing the royal crown and returning to St James's Palace for the formal banquet later in the evening. The crowds seemed to wait almost the full morning before there were any sounds of activity eventually when to everyones' great relief and delight there were the sounds of many horses' hooves coming into Whitehall and turning towards the Abbey. The black State Coach pulled by four magnificent black horses on which Princess Elizabeth Stuart, Anne of Denmark and Lord Egerton travelled was led by a hundred strong Guard of Honour from the Foot Guards and was accompanied by vibrant military bands. This time it was obvious to see security had been tightened greatly as the entire route the procession travelled was being vigilantly watched over by armed guards. People as they observed the coach hurriedly pass them by only caught a slight glimpse of Princess Elizabeth Stuart waving back out of the coach window at the excited crowds of onlookers but at least were able to enjoy the long procession of royals, clerics, peers and other invited guests all riding horseback to the grand occasion.

When every member of the mass procession had finally gone by to a measureless crescendo of cheering and applause which reverberated right across the city as the final carriage disappeared out of sight there was an increased buzz of eagerness and expectation throughout the crowds. People became impulsive to see Princess Elizabeth Stuart returning safely in her new position as Queen Elizabeth II wearing the splendid royal crown and looking even more regal as she went by. Elizabeth and George were standing almost stock still in the second row of the restless throng of spectators holding their child cheering and waving wildly with everyone else. When the long procession had gone by Elizabeth as best she could turned to George commenting; 'I do hope you think it was worth coming all the way from York to see this rather short occasion.' George squeezed a smile from his taut face;

'Of course it was worth coming to catch a slight glimpse of our new Queen……..of course.' They waited for the long convoy to return with the new monarch at the front for over two hours and some people who were feeling particularly hot and tired were beginning to get a little impatient about the complete situation until further towards Westminster great applause began breaking out from all sides and all of a sudden the area was full of cheering and jubilant crowds of expectant spectators as the coach carrying the new Queen of England came towards them. This time it was going much more slowly giving everybody there the chance to see the new monarch wearing her magnificent white dress and large crown. As the coach travelled slowly en route for St James's Palace beside the long colourful crowds slowly Elizabeth looked particularly nervous and pale as she went along trying to wave to every individual spectator with her white silk gloved hand. 'It's about over with now my beautiful child, now we can look forward to the quiet banquet away from all the mass crowds and ear-splitting noise.' Anne leaned her head back in the carriage to catch a fuller picture of her daughter wearing all the magnificent formal robes and jewels. 'Who is invited to the banquet tonight?' Lord Egerton looked rather surprised by the new Queen's question.

'What makes you ask such a curious question about the banquet Elizabeth?'

'I just hope nobody will ask me to dance, dancing is something I have never liked and I shall never be very good at it I'm afraid.' Elizabeth looked rather red faced and sounded somewhat hangdog as she looked up from under her crown into her mother's eyes. 'Don't worry dear, nobody shall force you to dance if you do not wish to.'

'Did you enjoy the crowning ceremony?' Lord Egerton asked quietly as Elizabeth continued to wave her aching hand. 'The ceremony was a magnificent occasion Thomas.' Very soon the coach arrived outside the arch of St James's Palace. 'All you have to do now Elizabeth is remain where you are and wait for your two pages to arrive and carry the royal train.' Immediately the coach doors were opened the loud resounding from the noise of church bells could be heard unmistakably ringing out in abundance over every part of London. As the other coaches and horse riders quickly began to follow behind Lord Egerton suggested to Anne they went inside and waited for Elizabeth's arrival a little later. As they went back into the front entrance of the palace they stopped a moment and looked back at the royal coach where several royal attendants were now helping the new Queen of England out. As they stood watching while other invited dinner guests went in past them Lord Egerton looked at Anne's reddening eyes and put an arm gently around her waist as a kind of comfort. 'This is a brand new beginning for all three of us;' he whispered in one ear. 'Who knows after Christmas just what next year will bring us?' Anne watched her daughter having some trouble striving hard to depart the royal coach before eventually she stepped onto the ground and was escorted inside the building to play host to the splendid occasion. 'We had better go in;' Lord Egerton chuckled gently; '...... otherwise we are going to be late for your own daughter's own banquet.' Anne smiled a little at Lord Egerton's slightly jovial comment before kissing him softly on one cheek then taking a hand and leading him inside.

AFTERWORD

On Christmas morning to almost everyones' surprise after the earlier part of December had been so warm and dry snow flakes were beginning to fall and there was a definite feeling in the air that suddenly there was more of a usual sense that a proper and bitter winter was now at last on its way. Although Elizabeth had been crowned the new Queen of England with more royal responsibilities, still on Christmas morning after a quiet breakfast with Lord Egerton and Anne of Denmark she and Lord Egerton were having an uninterrupted game of chess and were perfectly happy and contented with the way the year was finishing as were most people of England after so many long dangerous months when violence had been everywhere. At his quiet home in Bretby John Reynolds, better known to many people as *Captain Pouch* was spending all the festive season alone. He was still feeling proud of his achievements at the conference back in August in St James's Palace when he had successfully represented not only the large majority of labourers but also the middle classes who had complained most of all about the high land tax. Already the land tax had been reduced, labourers' wages had been raised by three pennies and food prices had been put on hold just as he had demanded in addition to now at last having a new monarch on the throne. On Christmas morning John had risen at eight o'clock and dressed in some of his more worn casual dress. The thought of going out for one of his quiet walks alone around his home village appealed to him. Calling himself a simple labourer he made himself a plain labourer's breakfast and prepared himself a dish of gruel and poured himself a cup of ale. As he ate at his small table in the living room he simply could not stop himself from thinking about his successful negotiations inside the magnificent St James's Palace. *"That's somewhere I shall probably never visit again."* he commented to himself. As he ate he looked out of his window at the narrow deserted lanes of the village and watched as the snowflakes began to fall more steadily. The thought suddenly of putting his stallion away somewhere where it would be better protected appealed to him and he decided while he was out on his walk he would take his horse with him and try and find someone who would be able to look after it over what may be now an extremely bitter winter. While he was finishing his gruel he set his eyes on a short horse and trap that had just pulled up directly outside his small house. Before he was able to get out of his seat there was a loud and forceful knocking on his door. As he struggled to get up from the table and the firm knocking did not relent John called out angrily; 'ALL RIGHT CAN YOU JUST GIVE ME A MOMENT!!' When he finally answered his small door there was a tall well built man waiting directly in front of him and not showing any signs of giving way. John could also see behind the formal gentleman who was well armed with a dagger and flintlock there were several other tall and well armed men waiting. 'Yes, who are you and what do you want here?' The tall visitor was dressed mostly in black and had with him a piece of paper with a signature at the bottom. 'Is your name sir Mr John Reynolds, better known to the majority of people as *Captain Pouch*?' John looked somewhat disturbed by the question.

'It is…….what is your name? Is this anything to do with a special visit for Christmas?'

'No Mr Reynolds it isn't. My name is Richard Walsh, I am the sheriff of Worcester. I have a warrant for your arrest which has been signed by Sir Edward Coke. Will you come with me and the rest of my posse we wish to take you to London where you shall be kept in the Tower until further instructions are given to officials in London for your future.' John looked completely horrified.

'What have I done to have Sir Edward Coke sign a warrant for my arrest Mr Walsh?'

'It is alleged by many people, many of the officials you spoke with in St James's Palace that you rode around parts of England trying to start a massive revolution and were responsible for organising a march which ended in Leicester with several men being killed.' John looked at the sheriff long and hard.

'But at the same time I was responsible for negotiating today's peace.'

'Perhaps Mr Reynolds but that does not change the fact that you tried your very best to travel around England and start a mass-revolution and there are a great many people who are extremely angry and offended about that. Now sir, I would be grateful if you could please come with us and we shall transport you to London.' Seeing there was absolutely no point in trying to argue about this any more John got his long cloak as the snow was becoming steadily heavier and followed two of the guards to the horse and trap where one sat on either side of him holding a well loaded musket. Very quickly the trap was pulled away in a southerly direction and he began his lengthy journey to the capital.

When John Reynolds was taken up into the Tower he was not tortured for information yet at the same time he was not given any food to eat. It was obvious not just what the majority of officials wanted to happen to him but many ordinary people also after he had spent so much time riding his fine white stallion asking people to rise up and fight against authority. Sir Edward Coke discussed the future of Mr Reynolds with a number of senior officials and they all demanded his execution. On January 1st 1611 as Queen Elizabeth II began her formal duties with all her advisors around her Sir Edward Coke gave the officials inside the Tower the right to go onwards and execute John Reynolds by having him beheaded without giving him any chance to appeal. On that very afternoon, in the Tower with nobody from outside being allowed to come and watch the proceedings a very weak emaciated John Reynolds was brought out from his cell and put on Tower Green inside the Tower where he was blindfolded as his head was put onto the block. Very quickly the executioner carried out his duty and beheaded Mr Reynolds whose head was put on Tower Bridge and whose body was buried quietly inside the Tower's surrounds.